ST. LOUIS
13 through JUNE 25
out these acts on the Johnny Carson Show
them at the Saint Louis Playboy Club now!
IONIST
ELL
MIRTHQUAKERS SUPREME
CURTISS & TRACY
ERVE EARLY, Call OL 2-4700
COMING June 27—July 9
Allen, baritone Johnny Janis, songstress Jean Trevor
BRIGHTEST SHOW IN TOWN!
T0290248
J.C. Curtiss
OPENING JUNE 30TH IN THE
-MIAMI-
TWO ALL-NEW SWINGING T
PEGGY LORD
Steam-heated Singer-Comedienne
ARNOLD DOVEN
Show-Stopping Comedy-Imp
WANDERERS THREE
bulous Folksingers
PATTI LEEDS
Beautiful Blues-Belter
JERRY VAN DYKE
Comedy and Pantomime with a Ban
US
JULIAN GOULD TRIO
TEDDY NAPOLEON
and swinging pianist
HERBIE BROCK
NTRELL
TING VO
TONIGHT
through
Sunday, November 9
THE MANY SIDES OF
GEORGE KIRBY
at the
playboy club-hotel
LAKE GENEVA · WISCONSIN
site of the Midwest's greatest golf course
Reservations: 1-248-8811
MING ATTRACTIONS
JULY 22nd
MARTINE DALTON
PENIE PRYOR
MICKEY ONATE
MARK RUSSELL
JIMMY AMES
OPENING AUGUST 12th
MARK RUSSELL
THREE YOUNG MEN
FRED BARBER
VAN DORN SISTERS
LURLEAN HUNTER
CLUB OPEN 7 NIGHTS A WEEK
EARLIEST SHOW IN TOWN—PLAYBOY'S PENTHOUSE 8 P.M. DINNER SHO
LATEST SHOW IN TOWN—2 A.M. IN THE PLAYBOY LIBRA
STEREO
The Keith Greko Trio at the Phoenix Playboy Club

PLAYBOY
LAUGHS

OTHER BOOKS BY AUTHOR

PATTY FARMER

The Persian Room Presents

Playboy Swings

Starring the Plaza

PLAYBOY LAUGHS

THE COMEDY, COMEDIANS, AND CARTOONS OF *PLAYBOY*

PATTY FARMER

BEAUFORT BOOKS

PLAYBOY LAUGHS

FIRST EDITION

Library of Congress Data On File

Hardcover ISBN:9780825308437

For inquiries about volume orders, please contact:
Beaufort Books
27 West 20th Street, Suite 1102
New York, NY 10011
sales@beaufortbooks.com

Published in the United States by Beaufort Books
www.beaufortbooks.com

Distributed by Midpoint Trade Books
www.midpointtrade.com

Printed in Canada

Book designed by Mark Karis
Author photo by Bill Westmoreland
Cover photo: Comedy team of Bill Tracy and Jackie Curtiss. The Curtiss Family Collection

TO HUGH HEFNER,

who refused to live anyone else's dream

IN FOND MEMORY OF VICTOR LOWNES

Playboy Extraordinaire

April 17, 1928 to January 11, 2017

Contents

Author's Note

In my book *Playboy Swings,* I chronicled the rise, history, and cultural impact of the Playboy empire, including the magazine, clubs, music festivals, and television shows. The story of Playboy is at the heart of our popular culture; it's not an exaggeration to say that the world is a different place because Hugh Hefner had a bright idea... and then another and another and another.

While it isn't necessary to have read that book to enjoy this one, I urge any readers interested in the details of Playboy's history—and particularly Playboy's influence on popular music—to take a look at it. For the sake of clarity and completeness, however, I have included some of the key anecdotes from that book in *Playboy Laughs.* A great story is worth repeating, so I know my loyal readers won't mind.

On with the party!

Preface

BY BILL MARX

I read and savored Patty Farmer's previous book, *Playboy Swings*, but it is this one that deeply touches my heart and resonates with me. Not only is comedy in my blood; I worked and hung around with many of the people whose stories and reminiscences are shared here. Turning these pages sent me back in time....

I was ten years old, sitting with my dad in our den. (The world knew him as Harpo, the zaniest Marx Brother, but he was "Dad" to me.) We were watching a comedian do his standup routine on a small black-and-white TV. Dad was well-known for his silence, and as we watched, he turned to me and said, "I could never do what he's doing. I couldn't do what I've been doing for all these years without my brothers. A monologist is completely vulnerable and naked out there—it's the toughest job in the world."

"Dad, what's a *mon-o-log-uist*?" I asked. What did I know? He dutifully informed me that it was a person who stood in front of a live audience and tried to make them laugh by telling them jokes. "Can you imagine having the courage to come out on stage, tell your first joke and, after the punch line...silence? No laughter at all?" he asked me. "And then you look at your watch and realize you still have six-and-a-half minutes to go? You'd probably break out into what we call 'flop sweat.'" It was the beginning of my lifelong education and love affair with comedy.

According to Dad, stretching all the way back to the great vaudeville era with its live audiences and diversified acts, wise comedians employed a "starter": somebody planted in the audience whose job it was to laugh like hell and inspire others to do the same. A good starter could whip an audience into a frenzy of hilarity. My grandfather Sam—known to one and all as Frenchie—was always there for his boys in the early years, making sure that Groucho's, Chico's, Gummo's or Zeppo's opening quip landed perfectly and started the festivities off on the right foot.

What I learned at Dad's knee was that comedy—good comedy—may look easy, but it's far from it. And every single one of the entertainers who spoke with Patty for this book confirmed that. So...if it's so hard, why does anybody do it? That question is answered over and over in these pages, if you know how to read between the lines. They do it because it is the only thing they've ever wanted to do. It's the only thing they *can* do. It's what gets them up in the morning. And, apparently, it's a great way to meet girls! But, seriously—if you learn nothing else from this book, you'll come away with the knowledge that comedy isn't just a profession—it's a calling.

For a number of years, I played piano at a very popular restaurant/nitery called Dino's Lodge. Somehow, the owners had procured the use of Dean Martin's famous nickname, and a large neon caricature of him out front helped pack the place. It happened to be just steps away from the very hot, Los Angeles Playboy Club, so lots of the guys working at Playboy would come over to hang out before, between, or after their shows. Some—including Jackie Gayle, Jackie Curtiss, and others you'll hear from in these pages—even tried out their new material at Dino's. In turn, I would wander over to the Playboy just to schmooze with the great musicians and see some of those top-notch comedians slay the crowds.

Reading *Playboy Laughs*, which is full of backstage stories about those days, took me back there like it was yesterday. And it all made me think about the mirthful, musical, and medicinal purpose that the Playboy Clubs served for both its audiences and performers. Propelled by their love of what they were doing, a lot of great singers, musicians, and comedians polished up their acts, supported their families, and had a ton of fun in the process. If I can put it a little more poetically: They carved their initials in the history of live performance.

And, before I forget, I want to mention artists of another stripe—the legion of brilliant illustrators and cartoonists who lent their particular genius to the pages of *Playboy* magazine. These "scribblers," as Patty calls them, are as responsible for the laughs of this book's title as any of the "schmoozers" I've been talking about. Clearly, Patty understood that a book about the Playboy brand of humor would be incomplete without including them. You might or might not know their names, but you certainly know the work of Shel Silverstein, Leroy Neiman, Dean Yeagle, Mort Gerberg, Arnold Roth, Harvey Kurtzman, and many others Patty spoke with about their experiences at *Playboy*.

I think I'm correct in pointing out that every single person quoted in this book has given thanks to one man—a person who, in his own unique way, changed the culture of this country, and gave us new perceptions and insights. You know I'm talking about Hugh Hefner. I'm not sure how many people understand the full range of contributions he's made, but this book should certainly move the needle on that particular statistic.

I want to add my own deep thanks to him, for providing me with not only new thoughts and viewpoints, but new friends—including such stellar talents as Shecky Greene, Redd Foxx, Al Jarreau, and many, many others. I also want to thank Patty Farmer for understanding the importance of gathering all of this material together and making it fun to read and think about. Playboy and its valuable legacy will never disappear, thanks in part to her efforts to capture the heart and soul of the Playboy era in the words and stories of those who lived it.

I have to end with an image: Can you picture my dad, that energetic scoundrel with the pop eyes and overactive libido, running around the Playboy Mansion? With all those blondes to chase—and brunettes—and redheads. I'm sure he would have been in paradise. And now, just by turning the pages, you can join him. Enjoy!

—BILL MARX, JANUARY 2017

Part One

THE SCHMOOZERS

1

A FUNNY BUSINESS

To contextualize Playboy's contribution to the evolution of comedy, let's travel back to the state of things prior to its emergence. With few exceptions, comedians of the early twentieth century didn't shoot to the top of the entertainment hierarchy overnight. They worked their way up, typically scraping and scrapping through hard years in either vaudeville or burlesque, the two variety circuits that prospered side by side during the twenties, thirties, and early forties.

In the beginning of what we now call standup, there was the brick wall. *But seriously, folks,* that's all there was, and it was always there. The brick wall signified the lack of everything else: plot, sets, costumes, dialogue, supporting cast...and, in the very beginning, even microphone. Comedy was just a guy standing up and telling jokes.

It may seem as if standup comedy has always existed but, like jazz and musical comedy, it is a relatively new invention with very deep roots. Standup evolved out of three interrelated theatrical forms: The oldest was minstrelsy, the longest lasting was vaudeville, and the most directly linked to modern standup was burlesque. And all three art forms are distinctly American.

Minstrelsy combined music and humor in a highly stylized, outrageous caricature of "African-American life." Performers, both black and white, donned blackface and painted on exaggerated features to portray an array of stock comic characters in stock comic situations. In this regard, the form was not unlike the European *commedia dell'arte* of the sixteenth-eighteenth centuries. Minstrel shows included music, mainly of the choral variety, though soloists occasionally stepped out to perform as well.

Vaudeville was much looser. Not unlike the TV variety shows that would come much later, it featured a string of unrelated, independently produced acts. A musical group might be followed by a comedian, then a dog act, and finally an acrobatic troupe or juggler. The comedy segments in vaudeville, like those in burlesque, tended to rely on sight gags and pantomime rather than wordplay or storytelling—which makes sense when you consider the lack of amplification. Today's standup comedians would have had a hard time landing their punch lines in vaudeville's cavernous theaters, which tended to be full of rowdy patrons. Jokes had to be seen rather than heard, so clowning and slapstick were the norm: a guy in baggy pants doing a pratfall or one goofy character hitting another with a rubber chicken or oversized mallet. All the audience needed to hear was the loud *thwack* that punctuated the joke; verbal punch lines would come later. In fact, the term *punch line* originally referred to the moment when somebody got punched!

Vaudeville gave rise to many of the great silent film comedians, the first superstars of the movie industry. The Marx Brothers, for example, first stepped on stage in the early 1900s and slayed live audiences for twenty-five years before exiting the footlights for the movies. (For more on the early work of these comedic pioneers, take a look at Robert Beder's fascinating *Four of the Three Musketeers: The Marx Brothers on Stage.*) It may seem hard to believe, but in this formative era, even Douglas Fairbanks Sr.—every inch a romantic leading man on screen—was a comic actor.

Vaudeville could be anything. It appealed to everybody and prided itself on being family entertainment, sidestepping anything lewd, suggestive, or politically charged. Burlesque, on the other hand, was a walk on the wild side. It was aimed specifically at adult males, who occasionally brought their women along but never their children. While burlesque shows included music and comedy, their main attraction was the display of women in various stages of undress. Burlesque theaters tended to be smaller than their vaudeville counterparts because, what good is looking at a semi-naked woman from across a football field? A side benefit of this relative intimacy was that the acoustics were better as well. Comedians could tell jokes and have a prayer of landing them.

Most burlesque comedy, like minstrelsy, revolved around stock types: the tough guy, the henpecked husband, and the "nance" (an exaggeratedly effeminate man), to name a few. Many modern comics, from Bud Abbott and Lou Costello to Phil Silvers, got their start there.

Since naked and scantily clad women were the main attraction—appearing before, after, and sometimes even during a comedian's set—the crowds could be tough on the poor funnymen. Shecky Greene, who emerged from this era to become one of the most successful and highly paid comedians of the sixties, tells of stepping over women engaging in back-alley "dates" in order to reach the stage entrance. As for material, everything was fair game to get a laugh, including racist or vulgarly sexual gags that would be met with groans or boos today.

Vaudeville theaters, by contrast, posted lists backstage of unacceptable topics, including all profanity and anything sexually suggestive. It was in vaudeville that the term "blue" came to signify objectionable material. Apparently, when management had a complaint about an offensive act, they delivered it to the performer in a blue envelope. Bill Marx—son of Harpo—recalls traveling with his father to perform at the London Palladium when he was just twelve.

This was long after the eclipse of vaudeville, but the routines Harpo had honed on the circuit with his brothers remained in his repertoire.

"Dad anointed me his chief prop man," Bill says, "and insisted I take part in the show. I didn't know what the hell was going on. One of his famous skits involved a magical coat that he pulled things out of all the time. My job was knowing that the rubber carrot went in the upper left pocket, the rubber chicken in the lower right, the scissors down the left-hand sleeve, and so on.

"One of Dad's most memorable bits was the 'dropping of knives' gag. In the routine, a police officer accused him of stealing silverware. 'I'm no thief,' he'd say, and look all indignant. 'Really?' said the policeman. 'Well, okay, I might have made a mistake.' At that point, the policeman would shake Dad's hand and out of his sleeve would drop a few knives, then a few more, and a few more. He had more than 350 knives up his sleeve! It was my job to load up those knives, and I had to get it right. I always put the handles in first so he didn't poke himself. His act was completely visual.

"Groucho and my dad were impulsive behaviorists. They believed in their characters, they became those characters, and consequently their audience believed in them, too. 'Excuse me buddy, but I'm kind of down and out.' So my dad would take a cup of steaming coffee from his coat and for that split second the audience would be right there with them. They wouldn't see anything wrong with him pulling steaming coffee out from a coat. It's the way you do it and the way you believe it. That's what worked for the Marx Brothers. We had our Jackie Gayles and our Joe E. Lewises and a bunch of guys in the good old Playboy days. It's a different comedic world now.

"There were standup acts in vaudeville, but the Brothers were not that. I really didn't realize what an important man Dad was until the audience applauded. Most of the time, he was just Dad, but when he was on stage I used to sweat 'flop sweat' for him. That's what old-timers call it when you're afraid you're going to hit clunkers. You get the *schpilkes* because you want it to be so right, but you're afraid it's going the other way. It's funny, nothing ever did go terribly wrong but I still worried.

"I have the ominous, dubious distinction of being the last person who worked with the Marx Brothers professionally. People still crave hearing my perception of them and the times. I always tell them, he was just my dad and they were just my uncles. It's just that they had a different kind of gig."

Besides having been one of the youngest prop men of all time, Bill was a musical prodigy and worked as Harpo's arranger and conductor starting at age sixteen. All of those scenes in the films where Harpo is playing piano, he's executing Bill's arrangements.

Vaudeville was a breeding ground for people with natural talent, as well for those who had some honing to do. Bill recalled, "George Burns, who was my dad's close friend, used to say in his later years, 'There's no place to be lousy anymore.'"

We've mentioned that vaudeville was more wholesome and family-oriented than burlesque, but it had its dark side, too, exploiting children for the purpose of entertainment and propagating racial caricatures just as burlesque did. Child safety groups mounted protests but they had little effect. Vaudeville eventually ran out of steam for other reasons—but blackface acts didn't disappear altogether until well after that.

Many of the comedians who eventually made their way to Playboy's stages started out as children in acts with their parents. Some, including Jackie Curtiss, even got their starts in the circus.

"My first job," recalled Jackie, "was as a baby clown. I pretended to be a little chick in an egg that another clown, a midget, sat on. When the rooster came by, I 'hatched,' kicked him in the shins, and ran. That was funny back then."

Jackie's father was a carnival man and his mother a full blooded Mohawk Indian. After Jackie's first appearance in the show, his father was approached by the circus bosses, who'd seen him (literally) hanging around the trapeze tent. They said, 'This little kid's got great balance and some talent, we'd like to train him and we'll pay you. "That's all my father, who was an alcoholic, needed to hear," said Jackie.

So Jackie began his circus training at age six. Ultimately, he learned to work the trapeze, the tightrope, and do all kinds of high-wire acrobatics and stunts. He was quick to point out that nets were only for rehearsal. He walked the wire thirty or forty feet in the air, sometimes right over the lion cage while the big cats were doing their act.

"As a kid, that was the thrill of a lifetime and I caught the infection of applause. You catch that and you're hooked for the rest of your life."

Sadly, child welfare would not become a top priority in this country until decades later, so Jackie saw little of his hard-earned money. His next assignment was behind the scenes, as "Wonderboy," a profane, supposedly thirty-two-year-old midget. This was during the early thirties, when there was a semblance of Child Labor laws, albeit vague and loosely enforced. When Labor Department representatives would come around to check out the treatment of young circus performers, Wonderboy would go out to greet them, smoking a cigar and spewing curse words. "I'd say, 'You goddamn son-of-a-bitch bastards get out of my tent!'" recalled Jackie. "They thought I was a midget so we didn't get hassled." All this before he hit puberty!

At nine, Jackie, was living on his own. "Circus life was seasonal, and during the winter we had what were called 'Winter Quarters.' These were usually in Sarasota, Florida, or Newark, N.J. One day, right after my ninth birthday—I was nine years and four days, to be exact—I was in Newark with my parents. I returned home from Miller Street Elementary School and called out for my mother, who I adored more than anything. I disliked my father to the same extent. There was no answer."

Jackie never saw his parents again; they'd moved while he was in school and left no note or forwarding address. Sadly, this was not uncommon during the Depression, when many families believed that leaving their children to find their way to an orphanage might result in a better life for them.

Jackie managed on his own for five days before it sunk in that his parents weren't returning for him. At that point, he knew he had to find another family. He headed off to the freight yard in New London, Connecticut, where the World of Mirth Carnival was in residence. As you can imagine, the trip wasn't easy for a boy of nine without funds. He was forced to "ride the rails," and that didn't mean hiding out inside a cozy boxcar. Jackie had to summon all his strength, position himself under one of the train cars, and literally hold on to the rods while the train whizzed down the track.

It would be an amazing feat for anyone, but Jackie said "It was worth it. As soon as I arrived and reminded the carnival boss, Max Linderman, that my father had worked for him in the past, I felt like, for the first time, I was home and with a father who cared. He walked me over to the food tent and fed me. I stayed with him for five years, working my way through the carny ranks."

We'll catch up with Jackie again later in the book, when, after a stint in the Navy, he hooked up with two different comedy partners and performed around the country as a standup comedian.

* * *

Another comic who got his start in those bad old days made his mark as Professor Irwin Corey, an irascible political commentator and "world's foremost authority" on everything. Irwin started out performing with the Lionel Stander Vaudeville Tour, though that didn't last long; he was fired after a few weeks because Stander wanted to save the fifty dollars he owed him.

John Regis, who would eventually make his way to the Playboy circuit, grew up in Forsyth, Missouri—population: 292. His stepfather was a vaudevillian who taught him a standup routine, and he credits that with setting him on the road to show biz.

"In the act, Dad was Mr. Henderlockenender and I was Sambo," John explained. "I had to put on blackface and do this terrible accent—which was expected in vaudeville back then—and he made up this bit where I'd say to him, 'I'd like to be a comedian.' And he'd say, 'Well, what do you do that's funny?' 'I don't know,' I'd say. And then he'd explain, 'Well, first you have to learn to be a straight man. I'll ask you some riddles, and you say, "I give up. What is it?" And I'll give the answer.' And he'd start, 'What's the difference between . . . a turnip and a pig?' But instead of saying, 'I give up,' I'd give the correct answer!

"That got a big laugh from the audience. It was like I was taking over the act. So he'd say, 'No—you were supposed to say, "I give up. What is it?"' And I'd shoot back, 'But it got a laugh.' He'd insist that we try it again, but each time we did, I gave the answer and the audience screamed with laughter! I liked the feeling I got when I made them laugh."

Larry Storch traveled a remarkable path to the Playboy Clubs. He grew up during the Depression, in a brownstone on Manhattan's 77th Street, where his mother took in boarders to help make ends meet. She was partial to actors, although most of her lodgers were of the starving and struggling variety. Some were immigrants, and when one of the foreign-born boarders would use the phone, ten-year-old Larry would listen in and learn to imitate his accent. It hadn't yet occurred to him that he was building the foundation for a long, adventurous show-business career. He was just being a little wise guy.

A few years later, Larry was becoming known among his neighbors and friends for his wonderful grasp of dialects and deft impersonations. He was fifteen when he went to visit three of his friends backstage at the Winter Garden Theater, where they were appearing in the variety show *Hellzapoppin*. As usual, they started asking him to do impersonations. That day, he entertained them with a dead-on Marlon Brando followed by a pretty good James Mason.

A short time later, the same three boys were performing with

Benny Goodman at the Paramount Theater when one of them got sick. You guessed it: they asked Larry to fill in.

"I didn't show up to high school for three days," Larry told us. "I was sixteen and performing at the Paramount! I couldn't get over it. I was in a state of shock to be on that stage."

"I told my mother, 'I'm not going to conjugate verbs in school anymore, Momma. I ain't going back.'

"'Oh yes you are,' she said, and she took me right to the principal to get him to talk some sense into me. The principal had my records in front of him and he said, 'You know, his grades aren't that good. I advise you to let him get started in show business. Let him go.'"

Larry's friend Sid soon recovered and took back his role, leaving Larry to look for work as an actor-comedian. He cobbled together an act that inspired his mother to dub him "the Rembrandt of Impressions."

"My first job," he said, "was at a striptease joint in Albany. I went on between two dancers who would come out wearing outfits no bigger than a Band-Aid. Then I'd come on doing impressions of James Mason and whatever English actor was popular at the time, and nobody could figure out what the hell I was doing.

"The boss came over and said, 'Hey, Larry, you see what you're in here with, right? I gotta let you go, 'cause—who's Rembrandt?' I was disappointed because my salary was twenty-five dollars a week, which was a lot of money in those days, and I could send home fifteen of it. My rent was only three dollars a week and the rest was mine to spend."

With World War II raging in Europe, Larry joined the Navy. It was on board the USS Proteus in 1942 that he met Tony Curtis. The two became fast buddies and remained lifelong friends. Knowing that Larry had been an entertainer prior to enlisting, Tony confessed to him that he, too, wanted to go into show business.

"Tony said to me, 'I'm going to be a movie star. That's what I want to be, a movie star.' Now, here I was, a veteran at that stage in the game, and I'd worked in nightclubs and dives and all manner of places, and I said to him, "Are you crazy? Do you want to starve? It's a tough market, kiddo. You're a good-looking kid. Why don't you become a model instead?'

"'No, no, no, I'm a movie star,' said Tony.

"'Alright,' I said to him, 'when the war is over, if you need any help, there's a theatrical paper called *Variety*, and they print a list of all the nightclubs in the country and who's working where. If you're in trouble, look in the paper, find out where I am, call me, and I'll help you. Okay, kiddo?'

"As it worked out, Tony didn't need my help. In fact, it was me who did the calling. Forty-five years later, I called him up and said, 'Hey, Tony, I need some help!' And he was there for me. He and I were absolutely the best of friends, right from the beginning up until he passed away. I was in his last show, the stage version of *Some Like It Hot*. We toured it all over the country."

* * *

Nightclubs and Las Vegas casinos came into their own in the 1940s and '50s, as elegant alternatives to the seedy burlesque and vaudeville circuits. These glamorous venues offered a cornucopia of entertainment that included comedians, singers, and other variety acts. It was during this time that the idea of "opening acts" took hold, and comedians were often called upon to "warm up" audiences for the headliner. At such prestigious clubs as the Persian Room in New York City's Plaza Hotel and Ciro's in Hollywood, superstar singers such as Frank Sinatra, Vic Damone, and Doris Day typically followed a comedian, whose job it was to elevate the mood of the crowd and build anticipation for the star. Comedians who made their names this way eventually turned the tables, engaging lesser-known but attractive female singers to warm up *their* audiences.

Before Prohibition in 1920, there were cabarets. As described by F. Scott Fitzgerald and other writers of the era, these were essentially huge restaurants with bandstands and ballroom-like floors. Resident orchestras would play and the focus was on eating, drinking, and social dancing—not listening to singers or comedians.

After the Volstead Act prohibited the sale of alcohol, people were forced to do their drinking and dancing in much smaller, illicit spaces: speakeasies. These varied widely, ranging from well-known, highly publicized joints such as Helen Morgan's and the Cotton Club down to holes in the wall where you had to use a special knock and a secret password to gain entry.

As soon as Owney Madded was released from Sing Sing, the maximum-security prison in New York, he began looking for an outlet to sell his homebrewed and illegal beer. He found what he considered the perfect set-up at the Club Deluxe in Harlem. Owney rechristened the club the Cotton Club and found no shortage of patrons for his hooch. His control of the establishment lasted only a scant few years until the police shuttered the place for selling liquor. It reopened under new management that shifted the focus and classification from illegal drinking to viewing a show, with the introduction of *The Cotton Club Revue*—but that didn't make the place "respectable" by any means. Even more frowned upon than offering liquor during Prohibition was providing black entertainment for a white audience—even if the roster included such greats as Duke Ellington and Cab Calloway.

The so-called speakeasies were the direct progenitors of modern supper clubs; the dance floors were smaller than those at the cabarets, and so were the bands, which tended to be combos rather than full orchestras. That meant you could actually hear an individual performer sing or talk. The main act was often someone who would sing, tell jokes, and emcee the evening—and the greatest of these was the legendary Joe E. Lewis.

Lewis continued to reign in the nightclubs that sprang up after the repeal of Prohibition in 1933. He cracked wise, quipped, and sang funny songs, as well as funny versions of serious songs. He made faces. Even his body was funny, in spite of the tuxedo he wore. Lewis set the standard for what a comedian-entertainer would be for decades to come.

If Lewis is less celebrated today than he should be (you'll read more about him later), it's because he only rarely left the "speaks" and clubs for greener pastures. He was only occasionally seen on Broadway, in movies, or on television, and never seemed to make much headway in those media. In this, he was a direct contrast to Bob Hope, the man who perfected standup comedy for electronic reproduction and dissemination—who did for comedy what his longtime collaborator Bing Crosby did for popular song.

Like Lewis, Hope turned the comedy monologue into a high art. He employed timing, pauses, tempo, and dynamics as a great musician does. He knew when to shout out a punch line and when to make it funnier by whispering or burying it. He created and played a consistent character that proved funny in every medium that existed at the time, and today his comedy translates well to the Internet.

In any case, the bootleg hooch may have been the initial attraction, but entertainers began to take center stage and the "night club" was born. As Prohibition ended, the small dives, as well as the swanky uptown clubs, began including entertainment to entice patrons in and to keep them there, consuming pricey drinks and food. Comedians proved the biggest draw.

* * *

During the Second World War, Larry Storch joined the Navy, and it wasn't long before the brass got wind of his comedic talents. They weren't running a nightclub, of course, but they did have a band, whose function was to tour the country raising funds for war bonds. They asked Larry to join the band in a special capacity.

"When the Navy band showed up, money would pour in," Larry recalled. "We put on a great show wherever we went. They put me on cymbals: 'Ladies and gentlemen, we've got a cymbal player and he's a funny guy, too. Hey, come on down here, Larry.' Then I'd do some bits and the audience would crack up—and open their wallets. For that they put a 'musician' patch on my sleeve!"

Once discharged from the service, Larry wanted to see the country before settling down, so, still dressed in his Navy uniform, he stuck out his thumb. In short order, a driver pulled up and said, "Anywhere you want to go, sailor," to which Larry replied, "I'm heading east, sir."

Larry got as far as a bar in Palm Springs, where he met Phil Harris, famous at the time for playing "Hiya Jackson" on the *Jack Benny Show.*

"Phil was sitting on a stool right next to me, and we got talking," Larry recalls. "He saw my patch and said, "'In the band, huh? Whaddya play?' I told him I didn't exactly play anything—and I started doing my impressions of Cary Grant and all those guys. After a few minutes, he said, "'Listen, I'm taking you back to Hollywood.' I tried to say no but he pushed me into a car and we drove right up to Ciro's, a nightclub on the strip.'

"As we walked in—me, still in my uniform—I saw Lucille Ball sitting by the stage watching her husband, Desi Arnaz, rehearsing his band. Phil said to Lucy, "'Don't ask questions.' To me, he said, 'Do some of your voices.' I did the English things and the Frenchmen, I did the Germans and the Russians, and finally, Lucy said to me, "'Desi opens tomorrow night. I want you out of your sailor suit—buy a dark black suit—you're in the show with him.'

"All this happened so fast! I mean, it was too much! I opened up for Desi for two weeks. My salary was 150 dollars a week—a lot of money. It was amazing!"

"There were only a few nightclubs in Los Angeles," Larry went on, "and Ciro's was it. After I played there, I had an agent from William Morris, Benny Holtzman, who booked me into the Copacabana in New York.

"'How close to a thousand can you come?' I heard him saying.

Mind you, it wasn't that long before that I'd been making twenty-one dollars a month! Benny got off the phone and said, 'You got $750!' I'm thinking, *I must be dreaming*. That was the beginning of it."

* * *

Not all nightclubs during that time were the caliber of Ciro's and the Copacabana—not by a mile. Howard Storm and Lou Alexander worked in a few at the other end of the spectrum. Both second-generation comics, Howard and Lou became lifelong friends because of their fathers. Lou's father JoJo was working as a nightclub comic in Miami at the Fifteenth Bowery when Howard's father, Jack Sobel, contacted him for help. Jack was recovering from a debilitating surgery that had put him out of commission for a while, and JoJo helped get him a job at the Miami club.

"It was a horrible, low-class nightclub," Howard explained. "There was an air hose in the vestibule and when a woman walked in they blew her skirt up. All the performers had to wait tables, and people threw money into a big wash basin on the stage. The performers would split the take at the end of the night."

Lou's family and Howard's ended up living in seedy apartments across the hall from each other, above the club.

"It was humiliating to my father," Howard told us, "but watching him work...being a comic was all I ever wanted to do from the age of four or five."

Lou's father, Jojo Gostel, was a burlesque comedian who put Lou on stage at the age of eight, in one of his Catskill Mountain gigs.

As Lou explained, "All the comedians came out of the Catskills—Jerry Lewis, Danny Kaye, Sid Caesar—that was the backdrop where they all learned the craft. So my father put me in little sketches and I said, 'Hey, I'd like to do this someday.' I looked up to my dad like he was Jackie Gleason or Sid Caesar or any of the other greats. He was just a guy scuffling to make a living but he was a superstar in my eyes. So I never had that big career decision to make—I wanted to do what my dad did.

"Funny enough, I ended up working in the Catskills myself, as a social director, when I was starting out. Nobody wanted that job because the social director had to get up at nine o'clock in the morning and teach water polo and swimming, play games, coach softball, and, on rainy days, call bingo. All I really wanted to do was perform at night, but the other stuff was part of the job. From there, the natural progression was to play the small clubs in New York, where you'd get fifty dollars for Friday and Saturday nights. That paid your rent and your phone and you could live halfway decently. We all fought for those weekend jobs.

"For some reason, comedians always tended to hang out together. The singers didn't, the novelty acts didn't, the dancers didn't, but—in New York anyway—the comics would always get together. We used to gather at Hanson's Restaurant. We'd support each other and share how we were doing in our careers. Basically, we lied, because none of us were moving along as fast as we wanted to. Don Rickles, Norm Crosby, Corbett Monica...we all hung out together then; we were all just beginning to find our niche.

"Another favorite hangout was the Stage Delicatessen. Hanson's was our place during the day and the Stage was for after work. We'd finish our Catskill jobs or our club jobs and meet up at the Stage, and some pretty funny stuff happened.

"I remember one comic who hardly worked—and we all knew it—would put on makeup and come to the Stage and tell us where he'd worked that night. But he didn't. He just put on the makeup. One day, he said, 'I just worked at Grossinger's.' This is sad and funny, but *I* had just come from working Grossinger's and I said to him, 'Well then, you must be me, because that's where I was!'

"I was a pretty wild kid at the time and always trying to meet girls. Once, I saw a gorgeous woman walk into the Stage. I was sitting with my friends, this pack of crazy comedians, and I said, 'I have to find a way to meet this woman.' I did something a little weird. Most guys would send over a drink, but I sent over a bowl of chicken soup. So the waiter brings the chicken soup to her table and she says, 'Excuse me, but I didn't order any chicken soup.' He says, 'That guy over there sitting with the comedians sent it over.' I figured it was fifty-fifty she'd either get insulted or think it was the funniest thing in the world and come over and say hello to me. It worked like a charm, and it wasn't long before I told my bozo friends I'd see them later. So fifty-fifty wasn't a bad bet. We were young and we were comedians. We were always doing something different."

You'll hear more from both Lou Alexander and Howard Storm separately as we progress through both their evolution and Playboy's.

* * *

Numerous experts have expressed theories on the precise origin of the standup comic, but most seem to agree that it is rooted in the *crossovers* of burlesque. It's unlikely that you've heard of these, as they have long since passed into memory, but here's the rundown: During breaks between the numerous disparate acts that made up a burlesque show, an emcee would come out and address the audience in an effort to keep patrons in their seats and excited about the next group of performers. It was a tricky job because the nearly all-male crowd wasn't the least bit interested in the emcee or what he had to say. These guys wanted to see the girls! Enter "crossovers"—fast-paced comedy routines performed while the emcee was on stage. A classic example might be the sudden appearance of a guy from behind the curtain, carrying a case—perhaps a Coca-Cola case. The emcee would look him over and ask:

"What're you doing with that?"

The fellow would reply, "Oh, I'm taking my case to court."

Pause. Laughter. Exit.

The emcee would then go back to his spiel and, two minutes later, the funnyman would re-emerge from the opposite direction, this time with a ladder.

The flustered host would ask, "Now what are you doing?"

"I'm taking my case to a higher court," the wise guy would respond, and then head off stage.

By the time the comedian returned again, this time with a hanger, the audience was intrigued.

"Now what?" the exasperated emcee would demand.

"I lost my suit!"

These brief interludes, usually based on silly puns, broke up the tedium that threatened to settle over the audience while the next routine was being set up backstage. From burlesque, the concept slowly crept over to vaudeville, which (as we discussed earlier) had always been more inclined toward visual humor and slapstick.

It would take time for this silliness to evolve into standup as we know it today—but its roots had taken hold.

Scholars of comedy have offered different, sometimes conflicting theories as to who the first actual standup comedian might have been. There's a case to be made for Charley Case, a black vaudevillian who seems to have performed something akin to modern standup as early as the 1880s. Along with funny stories, Case performed parodies of the overly sentimental ballads of the late nineteenth century. His song, "There Was Once a Poor Young Man Who Left His Country Home," was immortalized by W.C. Fields in an early sound film as "The Fatal Glass of Beer." Case died in 1916 as the result of a gun accident.

The case has also been made for Frank Fay (1891-1961), who came along around the time that Case died and is said to have performed a standup act as we think of it today as early as 1918. Fay was the opposite of the "baggy-pants comics" who had preceded him. He emerged from the wings impeccably attired in a proper tailcoat with a flower in his lapel, and the humor of his act came from what he had to say rather than how he looked or moved. In fact, it was enhanced by the disjunction between the two.

Within a generation, the first standup comedians of the modern era—giants such as Milton Berle, Bob Hope, and especially Jack Benny—were proudly admitting that they had been influenced by Fay. Benny went so far as to say that he'd based much of his act on the bespoke funnyman.

With a deep bow to the pioneers and precursors, we'd posit that standup as we know it today really emerged in the 1950s. After decades of Depression and war, the Eisenhower era was characterized by a sense of well-deserved complacency. Perhaps it was this "everything's fine" atmosphere that spurred on the funnymen—and women—to get out their needles and burst a few metaphorical balloons.

Standing on bare stages in the countercultural clubs of San Francisco and New York—such venues as the Hungry I and the Bitter End—comedians began to address audiences directly about real-world stuff, and no topic was off limits—from the vagaries of marriage to the hypocrisy of politicians. Prior to this time, the great comedians—including Hope, Berle, and Joe E. Lewis—could be classified as "joke delivery systems." They had style and personality, but what they really had was surefire material that knocked audiences out every time. They weren't out to make people *think*, for heaven's sake—quite the contrary. The new, socially conscience comedians, on the other hand, believed it was no longer enough to make people laugh; they were on a mission to provoke and persuade as well as entertain.

As random as the comparison may seem, there's a classic episode of *The Simpsons* that perfectly expresses the difference between the two schools of comedy in a way that is, in itself, extremely funny. Titled "The Last Temptation of Krust," the story centers on Krusty the Clown, who represents the old, laughter-at-any-cost school of comedy. When he appears at a contemporary comedy festival, his jokes about mothers-in-law and TV dinners fall flat and his demeaning caricature of an Asian (undoubtedly inspired by Buddy Hackett's famous "Chinese Waiter" routine) fares even worse. Krusty is booed and hissed to the point where he decides to quit show business altogether. When a reporter asks him why he's retiring, he offers this rant in response:

> "Because comedy ain't funny anymore. Instead of time-tested jokes about women drivers and doctor bills, you got some big-chin schlub reading typos from "The Palookaville Post." [This is a specific zinger at Jay Leno.] Well, here's a headline for you: 'Nobody cares!' These comics today... [in a mocking voice] 'Oh, look at me. I can't set my VCR, I can't open a bag of airline peanuts... I'm a freakin' moron!' Then you got these lady comics talkin' about stuff that would embarrass Redd Foxx, God rest his smutty soul. Who they slept with, what time they sit on the can... This is supposed to get you a husband?..."

But, as he unloads on the crowd of reporters, an odd thing happens. They start laughing hysterically.

"What the hell are you laughing at? I'm just tellin' the truth!" says Krusty.

"And it's funny," the crowd roars back. Krusty immediately announces his triumphant return to comedy.

In the next shot, we see him in jeans, sneakers, and a turtleneck sweater, sporting a ponytail and looking for the entire world like George Carlin. He's standing in front of a brick wall. Krusty's "transformation" is a testament to the inevitable rise of a new era of comedy that has been around ever since.

By the end of the fifties, comedians such as Mort Sahl had established themselves as more than joke artists; these creative writer-performers were the new social commentators of our time. Sahl, Lenny Bruce, and Dick Gregory were the antecedents of Bill Maher, Jon Stewart, and Samantha Bee. Call them comedians if you must, but many of their fans consider them a primary source of news and opinion. Can you imagine a serious news show in 1950 with

Bob Hope and Milton Berle on the panel? Of course not; yet Bill Maher includes comedians and actors on his HBO political panel show *Real Time* just about every week.

* * *

"The rebel forces were heavily backed by Hugh Hefner, whose Playboy magazine and nightclub circuit made him a major comedy power broker of the time. Playboy's panels and interviews showcased all the rising, new socially relevant wits, with Hefner functioning as a kind of Medici during the Renaissance—especially of the Chicago school—Bill Cosby, Dick Gregory, Bob Newhart, Shelley Berman, Nichols & May, the Second City. Hefner provided a major monthly forum in which they could strut and expound." –GERALD NACHMAN, SERIOUSLY FUNNY: THE REBEL COMEDIANS OF THE 1950S AND 1960S

Hugh Hefner, whose empire was founded in the fifties and on the rise at the same time as this new vein of socially conscious comedy, was an equal-opportunity employer when it came to comedians. He supported the upstarts right alongside the old school, and was just as close to Sahl and Gregory as he was to Newhart and Bill Cosby. He was particularly devoted to Lenny Bruce, whose legal battles he helped support. Hef was key in introducing his particular demographic—the young men who read his magazine, went to his clubs, watched his TV shows, and aspired to the lifestyle he epitomized—to the rebel comedians that were shaping the countercultural discourse of the day.

In fact, the modern comics were very much like the modern jazz musicians in that they required audiences to listen and think rather than simply follow along. You could say that Lenny Bruce was a kind of comedic equivalent of Charlie Parker, whose artistry helped move jazz from smoky clubs to concert halls. Similarly, Bruce flushed the last whiffs of vaudeville from contemporary comedy and elevated it to an art befitting the aspiring intellectuals of the Playboy cosmos.

America was evolving from a nation of "we's" to a nation of "me's," and both comedy and jazz played their part in the process. In the age of Bing Crosby and Elvis Presley, singers were simply "song delivery systems," while songwriters were artists. Virtually no one, other than a few special cases such as Hoagy Carmichael and Johnny Mercer, did both. This was as much true in country music and rhythm-and-blues as it was in mainstream pop. Then, along came Bob Dylan and the Beatles and the whole equation went sideways. Suddenly, when pop singers performed songs by professional composers—or even from Broadway shows—it seemed somehow dishonest and inauthentic. "Real" artists expressed their ideas and feelings in their own words and music, and by the 1970s, nearly all the leading figures in pop were singer-songwriters. Think Joni Mitchell and James Taylor in folk; Johnny Cash and Willie Nelson in country; and Luther Vandross and Michael Jackson in soul. Singers were now expected to tell true stories—preferably from their own experience—on stage. They were expected to have a point of view. Anything less was just a little bit vacuous. And as the musicians went, so went the comedians.

In 2016, the essayist and provocateur Malcolm Gladwell offered some theories on the purpose of comedy in his incredibly popular podcast, *Revisionist History*. Discussing what he describes as "The Paradox of Satire," he argues that comedy has become the place in contemporary culture "where truth is spoken to power." The most potent form of political commentary cannot now be found in any of the serious media, he points out, but in the realm of satire.

It isn't surprising, says Gladwell, that *Saturday Night Live* gets better ratings than anything on Fox News—but it is significant that the so-called "rebel comedians" are encouraged to skewer politicians that they disagree with and challenge modes of thinking that don't sit well with them. So how is that working out? Not so well, in his opinion.

The problem with it is exemplified by Tina Fey's admittedly

hysterical portrayal of Sarah Palin, which Gladwell calls "toothless" because the comedy derives mainly from mimicking Palin's outer accouterments: her looks, her clothes, and her mannerisms. It seems to Gladwell that Fey is less interested in making a mockery of Palin's politics, or the notion that someone profoundly unqualified would be running for high office, than of skewering her accent. The nadir for Gladwell comes when *SNL* invites Palin herself to share the stage with Fey-as-Palin, allowing her to show the world that she has a sense of humor about herself and is a good sport. This, to Gladwell, is diametrical to the real purpose of satire.

Such a viewpoint is itself highly extreme, and we beg to disagree. In our opinion, the purpose of all comedy—or the main purpose, anyway—is to make us laugh, and this Tina does consistently and brilliantly. Perhaps Gladwell is asking too much of comedy when he insists that it must exert influence on our political views.

Whatever your own feelings about the meaning and purpose of comedy, you have to agree that its evolution over the past century is nothing short of astonishing. Seventy years ago, comedy was expected to be entirely free of ideology and, for the most part, it was. Today, it is almost expected that comedy is a bit empty and pointless—sophomoric, even—unless it is challenging the status quo.

As the conservative fifties rounded the corner to the swinging sixties, comedy had come a long way from its crude and slapstick beginnings in vaudeville and burlesque—but greater changes yet were on the way.

Vaudeville, burlesque, and to a lesser extent, the "Borscht Belt" theaters of the Catskills constituted performance "circuits," but it wasn't until the early 1960s that a circuit of venues was put in place by a single organization—Playboy. With forty venues worldwide at its peak, the Playboy Clubs smashed barriers in numerous and untraditional ways, perhaps the most notable being the fact that it could provide the most industrious performers a full forty weeks of employment per year. This ensured a continuity of atmosphere and attitudes across the clubs as well as a steady salary for the artists, many of whom went on to become household names.

Hugh Hefner's support of comedy in all its permutations helped form the rich landscape of comedy today. Playboy, it turns out, not only changed the way we behave in the bedroom; it also had a huge impact on the culture surrounding it. Read on and you'll see what we mean.

2

ALONG COMES PLAYBOY

The peak years of the Playboy Clubs—from roughly 1960 to about 1975—were transitional years for American standup. The period would be the last in the history of the art form when comedians were part of the ecumenical nightclub experience. After that, music and comedy would diverge and begin to inhabit their own venues and positions on the entertainment spectrum. At Playboy, comedians and musicians consistently shared stages and even shows, making for a full and well-rounded evening of entertainment.

The opening of the first Playboy Club came about as a quirk of fate. Victor Lownes—Hefner's second-in-charge and good friend—remembers it well.

"Here's what happened," he says. "*Playboy* ran an article about Burton Brown's Gaslight Club in Chicago, which had opened in 1953 and was inspired by nostalgia for the 1920s. The waitresses were pretty girls in skimpy outfits, and you had to buy a membership to join. Right after the piece came out, we received over a thousand letters inquiring how to get in touch with them to join. I thought, 'Hmm...' and took the stack of letters to Hef.

"'Look at this!' I said. 'Maybe we should open up our own club.' Right away, Hef agreed that it was a good idea. I admitted that I didn't know anything about the business, but I said, 'I have a friend who runs restaurants. He's got a little place called Walton's Walk on the North Side. Let's go over and talk to him about coming in and managing the restaurant side of the place.'"

The friend turned out to be Arnold "Arnie" Morton, a savvy young restaurateur who later launched the eponymous and wildly successful Morton's Steakhouse chain. "We had this meeting," said Victor, "Hef, Arnie, and I, and before you knew it, we were partners. We divided the new venture four ways: Hef personally had one share, the Playboy corporation had one, and Arnie and I each had one. We each put in ten thousand dollars—it was very inexpensive. We took over the Colony Club site, which was owned by Arthur Wirtz.

"We'd just worked with Arthur on the jazz festival," Victor continued, "and he liked us. The building had been turned over four times before we took it; people were having a tough time making it work. So Arthur let us have it for no rent—just a percentage of the gross. Of course, this ended up being an amazing deal for him! He became a very good friend of ours."

For the sake of variety, they decided to include a comedian in the grand opening line-up. Of course, Playboy didn't hire just any comedian, but the controversial, politically left-wing funnyman "Professor" Irwin Corey.

Irwin told us how he first met Hefner. "Hef used to hang out and play gin at the Cloister, a nightclub in the Maryland Hotel that was co-owned by Shelly Kasten and Skip Krask. He was so bad at the game that he never got to put his initials down, which was something you did when you had a good score—he must have lost thousands of dollars through the years. But we became acquainted and he liked my brand of comedy. Victor Lownes and I were good friends, too. We got into a lot of trouble together."

Keith Hefner, Hef's younger brother, worked in the organization supervising the Bunnies' training, behavior, and protocol. He remembered that Irwin was quite a handful. "Corey was always going into the Bunny room, which was not allowed," he told us. "He chased them everywhere and did all kinds of ridiculous things. He had to be spanked often and didn't get away with as much as he likes folks to think."

Here's a little sample of the Corey wit, circa 1960:

A man was praying at the Wailing Wall for twenty years and was being interviewed. The reporter says, "You've been praying at the Wailing Wall for twenty years?"

"Yep, morning, noon, and night I'm praying. Twenty years I'm praying! In the morning, I pray there should be peace in the world, and in the afternoon, I pray that misery and hunger should be eliminated, and finally, at night I pray that the Palestine's and the Zionists should get together. Make peace!"

"That's a nice thought,' the reporter said. 'Tell me, what's it like, waiting for twenty years?"

"To tell the truth, it's like talking to a %&% wall!"*

In his memoir, *Playboy Extraordinary,* Victor Lownes wrote about Corey and others whom he termed *genuine funnymen.* "These men all created one or more comic characters and then established the characters in the public mind to the point that it is impossible for them to be unfunny. Corey's deranged professor is as much a part of the funnyman school of humor as Chaplin's magnificent little tramp. Corey's outlandish pedant, who rants and raves and confuses all, derives his comedy value from the same source as the caricature of 'teacher' that the class prize delinquent scribbled on the blackboard a few minutes before the bell rang."

From the Chicago club, the professor's sublimely entertaining blend of chaos and confusion soon spread across the country via the Playboy circuit. Looking back on his start, Irwin recalled, "Not only did they like my comedy routine, but Hefner and Vic Lownes decided I had a lot to say and ran me for President in 1960, on the Playboy ticket, with Lownes as my campaign manager."

The shenanigans were documented on a comedy album entitled *Win with Irwin.* Lownes himself penned the liner notes, which read in part, "What we were doing, in effect, was channeling the famed Corey bombast from its main purpose, of being 'The World's Foremost Authority,' onto a very logical sidetrack, by suggesting that Corey would make an excellent 'World's Foremost Executive.' We carried the campaign to its logical extreme, including campaign buttons ['Irwin will run for any party, and he'll bring his own bottle'] and posters ['Corey is the only candidate named Irwin'], and we even hired a sound truck to prowl the North Side of Chicago blaring martial music and booming out the good message to the voting public ['Relief is just a ballot away—elect Corey—then go on relief'].

"But our candidate let us down," Victor continued. "He simply wouldn't stick with the issues and insisted instead on delighting his audience with the famed Corey zaniness—and only occasionally did he touch on the Corey-Plan-for-Saving-the-Nation. I can't help thinking that we lost a great chief executive when Corey insisted that he'd rather be funny than President."

He may have bungled his bid for the Oval Office, but Irwin did contribute a number of aphorisms to the American lexicon—according to Irwin, anyway. He insists that he was the first to say, "Wherever you go, there you are." And he is adamant that Al Capone stole his line, "You can get further with a kind word and a gun than you can with just a kind word."

"I'm going to sue," he confided—which might be a little tricky, since Al departed this world in 1947.

Another taste of Corey:

Did you ever hear the story about the guy who had just gotten married, and on the night of his honeymoon, said to his wife, "Tell me darling, am I the first one?" She looked at him and said, "Why does everyone ask that same question?"

The Professor filled us in on his unusual arrangement with Playboy: They picked up his entire tab when he entertained at the various clubs around the country. "I had carte blanche," he said. "Anything I wanted at the clubs or resorts, Hefner picked up the bill. Almost everyone was fine with this except for the manager in the Florida club. He didn't like me at all. If I was in the kitchen and asked a Bunny for a Coke, he'd say, 'Put that down, he's going to pay for everything.' Well, I had to annoy him some more, and I'd buy the Bunnies gifts from the shops, you know, whatever—maybe a tennis racquet, golf balls, candy—whatever, and at the end of my gig, I'd have a big bill that said, 'Your bill has been picked up by Hugh Hefner.' The manager used to get so mad!"

As you might imagine, a 102-year-old who has worked continuously and enjoyed success after success has too many stories to convey in one telling. No problem—we went back for more, and were rewarded with a few more recollections.

"One day I called up Hefner," Corey said. "I wanted to borrow some money and he said, 'I never lend money to friends.' I said, 'You dirty-son-of-a bitch-bastard! Now, how about lending me some money?'"

Believe it or not, in 1943 Irwin was screen-tested with Elizabeth Taylor. She was up for the lead in *National Velvet* (the rest is history) and Irwin was there for comic relief. The test went well but the producers didn't know what to do with this oddball. Much later, in 1969, Irwin appeared in *How to Commit Marriage* with Jackie Gleason, Bob Hope, Jane Wyman, and Leslie Nielsen. Comic turns in *Car*

Wash (1976), *I'm Not Rappaport* (1996), and other films followed. His Broadway credits include *New Faces of 1943, Heaven on Earth* (1948), *Flahooley* (1951), and *Thieves* (1974), and he was a staple on TV variety shows as well, including those helmed by Steve Allen, Jack Paar, Johnny Carson, and Ed Sullivan. Irwin's mock "thesis," titled, "Sex, Its Origin and Application," was excerpted in *Playboy* in 1961. But all these achievements pale in comparison to the mark he made on standup—thanks to his start at the Playboy Clubs.

Irwin was instrumental in the careers of some fellow comedians, as well. For starters, he helped get George Carlin in the door at Playboy. "I was a regular at the Clubs and when I was working the New York Club, George asked if he could come up and try a bit or two on my audience. I said, 'Sure,' and gave him my time. I gave him a real upbeat introduction and told the audience they were going to be guinea pigs. George was going to try out some new material before he went on *The Ed Sullivan Show*. 'A bit or two' turned into an hour, but he thanked me and he was a hit on *Sullivan*. George ended up working at Playboy whenever he didn't have a bigger job after that."

Then there was the case of Dick Gregory.

"Dick got a job at Playboy because I wouldn't work on Sunday," Irwin told us.

"Were you a religious man?" we asked.

"No," he shot back, "but even God got a day off. Dick sent a pot of flowers to me at every job I had for the longest time, thanking me for not working on Sundays. We became friends and did a lot of shows together through the years."

* * *

Not to downplay the role of the Professor, but we suspect that Dick Gregory would have ended up on a Playboy stage in any case. Hef had made his progressive views on racial equality clear at the Jazz Festival in 1959, and the decisions he made about the magazine and clubs were consistent with these beliefs. The outspoken Gregory credits him with helping to break down the gates that separated blacks and whites on stage and in audiences. In the early sixties—in Chicago and nearly everywhere else—the races didn't mingle much in entertainment venues. Yet, as early as 1965—shockingly to many—Hef hired the first black Bunny. Nineteen-year-old Jennifer Jackson worked her way through Chicago Teachers College as a Bunny, posing occasionally for the magazine as well and cementing her place in pop-culture history in March 1965 as the first centerfold of color.

"It's undeniable," says Dick, "that Hugh Hefner—aside from what everyone knows or think they know about the girls and all that stuff—believes in humanity. He waged a lifelong battle for racial equality."

In 1938, an amazingly far-sighted entrepreneur named Barney Josephson opened Café Society in New York's West Village, the first truly integrated nightclub. But Josephson was too far ahead of his time and was pilloried during the Red Scare a decade later. When Hefner and Lownes opened the Playboy Club as an integrated operation, the move was permanent, and there was no going back.

Victor adds, "With the hiring of Dick Gregory, Playboy was the first organization to introduce black cabaret performers into essentially white clubs. We didn't discriminate in our clientele either, but there weren't many blacks applying for membership in those early years."

Dick had begun honing his comedic chops in the Army when, because of his affinity for kidding around, his commanding officer suggested he enter one of the service's many talent shows. He won handily and continued to participate in them—and to triumph—until his discharge.

"The way we ended up hiring Dick is one for the books," Victor told us. "He was working in a garage where I parked my car and had it washed. After work one day, I looked at my car and said, 'If you call this car washed, you must be some kind of comedian.'

"He said, 'I am.'

"'Well,' I replied, 'if you're a comedian, come and audition for me at the Playboy Club. If I like your act I'll book you.'"

Dick picked up the story from there, corroborating Irwin's version of things. "About a month later, Irwin Corey, the "Professor," refused to work seven days a week, and my agent called and said, 'You've got a job at the Playboy Club next Sunday for fifty dollars.' Shit, wow! I didn't know there was that much money in the world! I had been making ten dollars a night at the Negro nightclub, the Robert Shaw Club.

"I didn't know much about downtown, but I paid my quarter and got on the bus with my little suit in a plastic bag. Because I wasn't sure where I was going, I got off at the wrong stop and I didn't have a nickel to get back on. I was counting on the money I made that night to get me home! I didn't even know that clubs like that pay your agent. I thought I'd get fifty dollars cash!

"So I ask somebody, 'Do you know where the Playboy Club is?' The guy says, 'No, but it's that way.' It's snowing, and I'm running—because there's this myth that Negroes can't be on time—and I'm slipping and falling, holding my suit up in the bag, and I round a corner, and about eight blocks away I see this huge Playboy sign. Thank God!

"I get to the door, and there's a black doorman, and I ask, 'Where's the Caramel Room?' Maybe it was called something else, but he knew what I wanted.

"'Second floor to the right,' he said. Aretha was on the first floor. No one had heard of her and no one knew me—but that's the kind of club it was. So many big people had starts there and worked there.

"So I get where I need to be, put on my suit jacket in a second, and what I don't know is that Playboy has accidentally booked me to perform for a group of southern white men in the frozen-food business. Playboy was all for integration, but they didn't want to stir up trouble, so someone was waiting to tell me I didn't have to work the show, but they'd still pay me the fifty dollars. But I never talked to the guy, because I was running late! If I had, I would have been happy to get that fifty dollars without working—but my life would have been a lot different.

"At eight o'clock sharp, I jumped out on stage. And they laughed. One of them actually said, 'You know we're from Alabama?'

"'I said, 'Ain't nothing wrong with that. I spent thirty years in Alabama one night.'

"Two hours later, Victor Lownes went over to the mansion and woke up Hefner. I had gone on stage at eight. At a quarter to eleven, Hefner came into the room and at one thirty, I finished the show. They had never seen anything like it in their lives! I'd only been hired for the one show, but they kept me two weeks. And this is where you really see the importance of Hefner.

"To understand how dramatically things have changed, you have to understand how they were for Negroes at that time in history. After the Playboy Club engagement, I worked at Mr. Kelly's in Chicago and the *New York Times* sent a reporter to interview me. It happened to be a white woman and after the show, I'm sitting at a table doing the interview and a white man walks by and says,

"'Nigger, what you doing with that white woman?'

"This is Chicago! The South was much worse. To protect myself, I hired a white PR man, so that if a white woman wanted an autograph or whatever, I could give it to my PR guy and he'd pass it on. He was always with me because, if a white person was there, it would be assumed that the fans were talking to *him*, and we wouldn't have any trouble.

"While I was performing at the Playboy Club, my PR guy went over to *Time* magazine to ask them to send somebody to cover this young black comic—because there were no Negro comics that anyone was talking about. They didn't say whether they'd come, or when. Now here's how the universe—or God—works. The man who covered the space program for *Time* came to town from Cape Canaveral. He and his wife had heard about the Playboy Club and wanted to go—not to work, but just to see a show—but when they tried to make reservations, they were told the show was sold out.

"Then someone in the *Time* office remembered the invitation and handed it to the the space guy. So he came to see me and when he walked out of there he was so wiped out that he wrote a big review that really changed my life—and changed the world.

"I have to tell you one more thing to help you understand the entertainment culture back then. I loved watching Jack Paar and dreamed of being on his show one day. Right after the *Time* article hit, I'm hanging at the Negro nightclub and talking with Billy Eckstine, probably the biggest Negro singer then. He tells me that a Negro can't sit on Jack Paar's couch. He says, 'All you can do is come, do your act, and leave. Pick your cotton, boy.' I was crushed; so mad and sad at the same time.

"Well, Jack Paar reads the magazine article and calls me. My wife answers the phone and she's screaming and hollering, 'It's the Jack Paar show!' I hadn't told her what I found out from Billy, but I take the phone, and some guy says:

"'Is Dick Gregory there? This is Mr. Silvers, Jack Paar's producer. My God, did you see the article in *Time* magazine? Mr. Paar read it and thinks it's great, and he wants to know if you want to be on the show tonight!'

"I say, 'No sir, I don't want to work the show,' and I hang up. I start crying, and then the phone rings again.

"This time, I hear, 'It's Jack Paar. Hey, Dick, I know things are probably happening so fast, you think this isn't me.' I say, 'No, I believe it's you.'

"'Well, how come you don't want to come on my show?'

"I tell him, 'Because Negroes never get to sit on your couch.'

"He says, 'Well, come on in, I'll let you sit down.'

"That was the first time a Negro sat down on Jack Paar's couch.

What I didn't know was that if you sat on the couch, you became part of Jack Paar's family. When I took that seat, my salary went from eighteen hundred dollars a year to 3.5 million in a year and a half. And all because Hugh Hefner didn't care if you were black or white or purple, only if you were funny or could sing."

Irwin Corey and Dick Gregory: Michael Dobo/Dobophoto.com

Fellow comedian Tom Dreesen recounts a story Gregory once told him, about a ritual that he and his wife performed on the nights he worked in various nightclubs. While she was ironing or doing household chores, she'd shout the most humiliating, discriminatory slurs she could think of at him.

"Nigger, get off the stage," she'd say. "We don't want no niggers in here!" He'd practice keeping his cool and zinging lines right back:

"Well, I'm getting paid whether I work or not, and you're paying for those drinks whether you see a show or not! So maybe we should both do what we came here for." It was a rehearsal, her yelling the vilest racial insults she could think of so that he'd be prepared when it actually occurred during a show, and he wouldn't be thrown.

* * *

Comedy wasn't a completely funny business. On stage the standup gagsters may have seemed the most carefree, jovial people on the planet, but once the spotlight went off it was another situation—one that even a young performer could recognize.

Julie Budd, "the mini-girl with the maxi-voice," opened for and worked alongside of some of the most illustrious celebrities in entertainment history, many of them comedians. Julie began her professional career as a twelve-year-old prodigy, when she entered—and won—a talent contest at the Tamarack camp in the Catskill Mountain Resorts. In the process, she attracted the attention of the renowned producer and songwriter Herb Bernstein. He quickly became not only her manager, but her mentor and lifelong friend. Right off the bat, he got her a recording contract at MGM, where she launched her first record at age thirteen. Appearances on *The Merv Griffin Show* followed, where she was greeted with a standing ovation, and this catapulted her into service as a supporting act for such luminaries as Bob Hope, Milton Berle, George Burns, Liberace, Frank Sinatra, and many other household names.

By the age of sixteen, Julie was a recurring, opening act at the swankiest casinos on the Strip in Las Vegas, and the youngest-ever opening act for Frank Sinatra—who introduced her as his "guest artist" when she appeared with him at Caesars Palace. By the time Julie was a legal eighteen and able to perform in nightclubs, she had a roster of regular gigs with Liberace, Bob Hope, Joan Rivers, Bill Cosby, and George Burns.

After Julie's first appearance at a Playboy Club, she had definite ideas about the guys she opened for, and it might surprise you to hear her impressions of the comics on the circuit at the time.

"They were and are *peculiar*," she told us. "The good ones are always observing and they can be very moody. I've worked with *everybody,* starting as an opening act and then as the headliner, and they're just odd. But don't forget, what they do is very difficult. As a singer, I go out on stage, and if they like me they like me and if they don't they don't, and I just keep singing. But when you're a comic and the audience isn't laughing, you're toast. So consequently, as a whole, they're a nervous group and always edgy.

"These guys were not so funny off stage. Very, very rarely did I sit around with any of them and just laugh. We'd be on the road together, in strange cities, and yes, we'd go to lunch and dinner and everything, because there wasn't anyone else to hang with. But they were *peculiar*! Always wondering where their next gig was... A lot of them, like David Steinberg, were really, really brilliant guys and they did interesting work. David was *so* bright that I conjectured that being a performer was not going to be enough for him—and of course I was right. He became one of the most sought-after directors in television, as well as a gifted writer and actor.

"I worked with Charlie Callas at the Playboy Clubs, and he was *nuts*! But you have to acknowledge that he was a funny guy. He had a rubber face. If you asked him, 'Charlie, do you like the eggs?' he would give you this face that would actually scare the waitress.

"Some of the comedians I worked with were genuinely unhappy for any number of reasons. Jack Carter was a very brilliant artist. I always wondered why he didn't do more Broadway, because he was a fantastic dancer, a good actor, and a great comic, but he wasn't a barrel of laughs off stage. I think his career was winding down when I met him and he was bitter and resentful and angry. He was a little disappointed in his life, I guess, especially when he saw all these young guys coming up, It made him a little difficult to be around.

"Jerry Van Dyke was one of 'Hef's guys,' when I was a kid working there. I'd see him all the time, hosting a lot of the functions—because the Playboy Clubs and Resorts were sought-after venues for corporate events and conventions. Jerry was one of the good guys."

The talent coordinators at the Playboy Clubs liked the juxtaposition of having a young kid like Julie appear with an established older comic—but as her career blossomed, Julie started headlining. That meant she was no longer working with superstars such as Milton Berle, Jackie Mason, Myron Cohen, and Shecky Greene, but with younger up-and-comers such as Arsenio Hall, Steve Bluestein, David Brenner, Gabe Kaplan, and others. As she put it, she cherished them all.

"Arsenio was just starting out and such a nice guy. He and Patti LaBelle were the only two who gave me a company bow. He was just a sweet, smart, gifted man—he was a treasure.

"As I told you, the really, really talented comics are not a riot off stage. The only one I ever worked with that cracked me up off stage was Mel Brooks. He's the same on stage as he is off stage—insanely funny—and he's nice and smart. He can write stories and music, direct and produce, and be hilarious—he's the original complete package.

"Hugh Hefner was a bright guy; he knew how to balance the sensual with the brain. He was the first person I ever met in this business with real power who was extremely nice to people. And, let me tell you, nobody knew the business like Hef. I interacted with studio heads, club owners, and Las Vegas mob bosses, and he just had a core understanding of how things should work. Everybody loved working for him.

"Having said that, he didn't abide anyone bringing trouble into the clubs. It was a funny time for our country, a very liberal time. There was a big drug culture, race relations were strained, anti-war sentiment was in the air, and the women's lib movement was taking hold. Hef was very liberal; he understood what was going on, but he realized that his key revenue source wasn't the swingers but the average Joe. I worked all his clubs and most of the people who went to them were everyday married guys who wanted to pretend they were hipsters for a few hours. Hef wanted them to enjoy that daydream and he didn't want disruptions of any kind in his place. He wanted his members to have that Walter Mitty moment.

"When Playboy hired you, if you showed up on time, did a good show, and didn't give the band leader any grief, you were usually invited to work the circuit. If Hef saw you hit your mark and behave like a pro, you could work with the man forever. He booked a lot of conventions and the people who came in had money. If he could rely on you and you weren't a flighty airhead, he was going to give you work."

Julie told us that Myron Cohen was one of her favorite comedians to work with at Playboy. Myron, who launched his career in comedy after working as a textile salesman in New York's garment industry, had an innate comic sensibility that he'd honed on his customers. To put textile buyers—and himself—at ease, he'd tell jokes before presenting his fabric samples. His clients were so entertained that more than one of them suggested he try his luck as a professional entertainer.

Good idea. Myron soon became a nightclub headliner and recording star, while maintaining his affable and easygoing persona. No wonder he was one of Julie's favorites Playboy Club partners. This is but one illustration of the Playboy organization's good judgment when it came to creating perfectly balanced bills. Not only that, but they'd book a veteran Borscht Belt comedian to pack in the crowds on Friday night, followed by a youthful newcomer such as David Brenner on Saturday. (You'll read some of David's recollections of those days later in this book.)

Okay, we heard about the guys Julie thought were the sweetest—but what about the flipside? Jackie Vernon, she told us, was a "maniac!"

She went on, "I remember as if it were yesterday. We were coming back from working the Toronto Club and were approaching Customs when Jackie reached down and put something in my purse. It seems he bought these Ivory trinkets and didn't want to risk having them confiscated.

"'Nobody's going to bother you,' he said, 'you're just a kid.'

"I said, 'Are you out of your mind? I'm not going to get arrested.

Mr. Hefner will never hire me again if I get arrested!

"Even at my young age, I understood that although everyone had this impression of Hefner as a swinger—which he was—he was also a very straight businessman. He sure didn't want his entertainers getting in trouble with the law. So I told Jackie,

"'Put those things back where they came from or put them in your bag. Just get them out of my purse and never, ever do that to me again!' He was one funny guy, though, and we were paired up in Toronto, New York, New Jersey, then on to Wisconsin and Chicago. It was like a triangle circuit.

"I used to work a lot with Milton Berle, Bob Hope, and George Burns, too, and they loved Hef because, as they got older, he kept them on the road. We didn't have the Internet back then, didn't have blogs or Twitter or *Schmitter*. But Playboy had a wonderful PR department that made sure the older guys—and everyone else—had newspaper, radio, and TV exposure when they were on the road, and it kept their names out there. They had to go from one town to the next to keep their following, and they loved Hef because he was pleased to do it, because they packed the rooms. The audiences I saw *loved* the older performers—the legends.

"Lake Geneva was a sprawling property. Even after you landed, you had a two-and-a-half-to-three-hour drive to get to where you were staying. And gorgeous doesn't begin to describe it; each room had a big gas fireplace and anything you could want. Because I was so young, I always had an escort, and security would have to come get me almost a half hour before I was due to go on because the place was so spread out. I wouldn't be surprised to learn that Steve Wynn modeled his properties and philosophy on Hef's. They both generously cater to their guests and believe that the experience they provide is worth more than the money you leave behind, because if you're happy, you're coming back.

"I've played hotels, resorts, and casinos around the world, some of them very lavish, but I never saw anything as sexy and sumptuous as Hef's place in Lake Geneva. He put a lot of money into it and I guess that's why he lost a bundle."

In closing, Julie reiterated her initial thoughts: "Comics are odd people—and I really don't mean that in a nasty way. They're quiet and moody because they're always creating. You can almost watch them taking in everyday situations and mentally figuring how to make them sound funny. *They're peculiar!*"

For more about Julie's Playboy experiences—and they're uproariously funny— I direct you to read *Playboy Swings.*

* * *

By the end of 1960, the Playboy Clubs were off and running, but even Hef couldn't have envisioned what was to come, and the history he would make. That first club, located on Chicago's Magnificent Mile, served more than 17,000 guests during its first month. In just a few months more, it was considered the Second City's most popular venue—and it would hold that record for a decade. At this juncture, Hef could have easily been content. He'd added a groundbreaking and successful enterprise to what was already an empire. But "content" wasn't in Hef's DNA. Within the next few years, he'd open Playboy Clubs around the world to showcase both emerging and celebrated talent. Chicago was just the barest beginning.

Jim Brown enjoying the comedy at the Playboy Club: The Curtiss Family Archives

3

COMEDY MARCHES ON

Barbi Benton and Hef visit Great Gorge Playboy Resort: The Margie Barron Collection

Riding the crest of the unprecedented success of the Chicago Playboy Club, plans for expansion into new markets were rapidly put into place—but how to finance the grand scheme? Not wanting to deplete Playboy capital to fund the swift growth, Hef decided to set up the new clubs as franchises, each one with its own owner-partners. This relatively new business concept seemed like a good idea at the time, but was not without its complications for someone like Hef, who had a very clear idea about what the Playboy brand stood for and would settle for nothing less.

By agreement, Hef's franchise partners controlled the hiring and membership policies in their own clubs, and—remember, this was 1961—they didn't all agree with his progressive views about race. When he visited the new clubs and saw nothing but white faces in the audience, on stage, and among the staff, he simply would not stand for it. Never mind that in some cases, segregation was still being upheld by state law—it was a policy he found abhorrent.

Hef's push for desegregation of the Miami and New Orleans Clubs was waged at an overwhelming cost to the company. He very quickly paid—through the nose—to buy back both franchises, at an unprecedented profit to their owners, so he could direct the venues as he and Playboy had always advocated: with equal opportunity for men and women of all races and creeds.

As the corporate footprint grew, Victor Lownes jumped into the breach as usual. He took over the operations of the repurchased clubs, and then set his sights on New York and London. As more clubs were added to the chain—or *circuit,* as it was coming to be known—talented musicians, singers, and comedians were needed to fill the many new showrooms.

Enter Arlyne Rothberg, who would go on to play a pivotal role in the development of talent at the clubs for years to come. Arlyne began her career in the publicity department at several supper clubs in Chicago, namely Mr. Kelly's, and the London House. The Marienthal brothers, Oscar and George, owned both clubs.

"For a nightclub, Mr. Kelly's had great food," Arlyne remembered, "and that was due to George. Oscar was the tastemaker. He liked jazz, and ran the nightclub and eventually the theater. I received my education from him. People would come to the club not even knowing who was headlining, but they knew it would be wonderful. Then Oscar died suddenly. I stepped in, made myself indispensable, and took over booking the acts. I'm sure if I had given George time he would have hired someone older and with more experience than I had."

That would have been a mistake. Arlyne traveled the country procuring the freshest acts on the scene.

"The first acts I got from New York were Woody Allen, the Smothers Brothers, and Barbra Streisand, all secured for $1,500 a week. I knew nothing about jazz but the musicians and Oscar taught me, and they couldn't have been nicer about it. Luckily, I knew what was funny. Shortly after Oscar died, I hired Richard Pryor, who, at the time I engaged him, was doing a variation of Bill Cosby's family theme. When he returned the next time, he was starting to get more controversial—he *was* Richard Pryor—irreverent and fantastic."

That particular act didn't go over well with George Marienthal, and he instructed Arlyne to fire him.

"I held my ground," she told us. "I told George I couldn't do that because Pryor was great and our audiences loved him. 'Well, if you don't fire him, *you're* fired!' he said, so I said, 'so be it.' I was out of a job that night!"

Victor Lownes, whose official title was Promotions Director, found out about the upset and called Arlyne the next day.

"Victor is wonderful, amazing in so many ways," gushed Arlyne. "The next day I was at Playboy and booking Richard Pryor into the Playboy Club. Within a short time there were twenty-two Playboy Clubs, each of which had at least two rooms—most had more—and I had to have forty-four entertainers a week, at the minimum. At the beginning, I'd have each performer audition, but with the need to have a steady stream of quality entertainment, that became impossible. I abandoned that process and started stalking other clubs and pilfering their talent, which is what everyone did.

"Actually it was just another form of the audition process. I'd go to the shows and if the acts were good, I'd hire them. And hire them again and again, I'd put the artists I found into slots on the circuit, which was wonderful for the performers. Some of the guys were good but just beginning their careers. They needed the experience and the steady paycheck to move up. Others were more established but liked augmenting their other tour dates. So it really worked out well.

"I kept tabs on all our clubs, all over the country. They all had the same characters in the audience, no matter where they were. It really was the 'Mad Men' era. Those 1960s executive types really existed. They could be young guys or old men with bald heads, but they all had to have that famous 'three-martini lunch.' That was the Playboy stock-in-trade! It's funny, but Playboy was known at the time for being daring and risqué—pushing the envelope, so to speak. But when I look back to the early 1960s, it all seems so innocent. Wholesome, even."

Arlyne has especially fond memories of the comedians she booked. "Apart from Richard, George Carlin and Shecky Greene were probably my favorites. George was brilliant, a total package as an entertainer. I would love to watch Shecky, especially when he was in front of a tough audience. That meant he would really have to work to get the crowd in his corner, and that was something to see. He never failed."

Arlyne eventually left the clubs to go into television. "I could tell the age of nightclubs was reaching its climax, whereas TV was getting bigger and bigger," she explained. Her good friend Dick Cavett landed a morning show on ABC and Arlyne was asked to coordinate the talent and guests. "I had never lived in New York, but I moved there, and I had never worked on television either, but I made the most of it," she said.

When Arlyne told Hef about her decision to move into television, he suggested that, instead of leaving Playboy, she pursue both careers.

"'Well, you know we have an office in New York, and Dick's show is a *morning* show, so you can take care of both of us,' Hef told me. This shows you how dumb I was—I said yes—and did both the Playboy gig and the Dick Cavett Show!! Who thinks about sleeping when you're young?

"To this day I have fond memories of the whole Playboy experience. Playboy represented a time and place unique in history. It will never come back again. It was an amazing moment and I was thrilled to be a part of it."

Ultimately, Arlyne handed off her duties to legendary agent and manager Irvin Arthur, so she could concentrate on managing Dick Cavett, Woody Allen, David Steinberg, and eventually Carly Simon, among a distinguished group of other performers she helped leverage to stardom. But she remains an integral part of the clubs' early history.

* * *

Larry Storch, whom you've already met, happily reminisced for us about his early years in show business:

"I performed everywhere, including all of the Playboy Clubs. It was at a Playboy Club that I first told a story that was the least bit—*whoops!* The story was about two ladies of the evening and it got a big laugh, and I remember thinking, *whoops* is the way to go. Not dirty, but with a little bang.

"Once, I opened at the Great Gorge Club in New Jersey, and the next morning, I got a call from the manager, who said, 'Larry, if you look out your door, you'll see two police officers.'

"I said, 'The jokes were that bad?'

"He said, 'No, we have a woman who works here as a telephone operator, and she's also a psychic. She had a dream where she saw you being shot by a bald man wearing a green suit.'

"'But she's only a telephone operator,' I said.

"Then the chief of police, who was also on the line, said, 'Yes, but her record of being psychic and calling future shots is alarmingly accurate.'

"So the cops followed me around for the next two weeks—two in uniform and two in plain clothes. They even came to my shows.

"'Don't worry, and don't ask questions,' they told me.

"I hadn't told anyone about the psychic or the cops, so the bass player couldn't figure out why I was doing a lot of jokes from behind his bass fiddle. As soon as I finished the gig and left the grounds, it was, 'That's it kid, you're on your own.' My patrol detail disappeared.

"My wife traveled with me most of the time, but especially when I had a Playboy gig. I'm not complaining, but every evening before I went down to do my show, she wanted to make love. Finally, one night, I asked her, 'Why do you always want to make love before I go to work?'

"She said, 'Because that way, all those half-naked Bunnies will look like John Wayne to you.' I told that story to my buddies one night, and the manager overheard it and said,

"'You have to tell that story from the stage,' so I did.

"I loved playing the Playboy Clubs, and every once in a while, a friend of mine, another comedian, would be in the audience and I'd bring him up. Shecky Greene came up once and tore the place apart. They loved him. One time, I made a bad mistake and invited Brother Dave Gardner up on stage. He was a Southerner and had all these—excuse me—'N' jokes. Well, I crawled out of the room because I was so embarrassed."

Larry worked steadily in nightclubs, in movies, in theaters, and ultimately on television—which proved the fulfillment of one of his wildest dreams.

"Jackie Gleason was an idol," he told us, "and why not? He was a giant. I had done an impersonation of him in one of my shows, and one day, I received a call asking me to go see him at the Sheridan Hotel where he was staying. He came out of the bedroom in a bathrobe at twelve noon—just like Hugh Hefner—and said to me,

'Larry, I've got to take a ten-week vacation from the TV show. I'm giving the gig, the show, to you. Remember, we run live. Hundreds of people will be watching'—really it was millions—'so just don't say *fuck* and you'll be fine. Can you remember that?' He was my idol.

"At one point, I was in a Broadway play called *Who's That Lady?* playing a Russian spy.

"Tony Curtis called me and said, 'I hear you're on Broadway doing a show, but I'm making a movie, so pack your bags and get on a plane. We start in a week.' He put me in *Some Like It Hot*, *Forty Pounds of Trouble*, *The Persuaders*, and others."

Today, Larry lives just blocks from the turn-of-the-century brownstone in which he was raised, where he was inspired by his mother's multicultural tenants. Smart money management has provided him with a double penthouse on Central Park West, where he can point out his childhood home from his luxurious wrap-around balcony.

"It's all from telling jokes! I can't believe how fortunate I am," he told us. "Now, I get my kicks from going down to the park and blowing my saxophone. There is one last story I have to tell you. One day recently, I was playing my saxophone in the park. I had my eyes closed, searching for the notes, you know, and feeling my sax pull, when a little boy came up and put a dollar into my horn.

"His mother was standing with him and said, 'I told him we had to help you out.'

"I said, 'Thanks lady, but I really don't need it.' Jesus, I thought to myself, if another Depression ever comes around, I'll take my saxophone over to West End Avenue and play on the corner."

"Why West End Avenue?" We asked.

"So I can keep an eye on my penthouse."

* * *

Howard Storm was one of the early and consistent Playboy entertainers until he found his fundamental aptitude for directing and producing. His agent, Jack Rollins, who was also Woody Allen's manager, got him a job on one of Woody's films—*Take the Money and Run*—where he learned the craft and got hooked on working behind the camera. Howard went on to direct for television, including such cultural touchstones as *Mork and Mindy, Too Close for Comfort, Laverne and Shirley, Everybody Loves Raymond, Taxi, Full House* and many other series of the seventies and eighties. But, like most comedians, Howard didn't enter show business at the top. His father was a vaudevillian and once vaudeville ran its course, he worked in burlesque and nightclubs. "It was a natural thing for me and, from the age of three or four, all I ever wanted to do," Howard said. "I knew I was going to be a standup comic." Howard met Lou Alexander when they were both very young, because they were neighbors and their fathers worked together. To say the least, the boys didn't fit into the deep-Southern neighborhood where they lived. They were registered at a high school named Edison High, the last stop on the bus out of Miami.

"It was like being in Biloxi, Mississippi," Howard told us. We were two New York Jews and the *only* two New York Jews in school. We had fights every day. We hated it and decided not to go to school anymore."

Since neither boy had the nerve to tell his parents about their decision, they enlisted the cooperation of Pat O'Brian, an Irish alcoholic who cleaned up the club over which they lived, and where their fathers entertained. They gave Pat a dollar a week to be on the lookout for notices from the school, and when they predictably arrived, to tear them up.

This went on for a while. The boys would get on the bus to school, slide down in their seats, and simply not get off. The bus driver would turn around after his run and head back to town, presuming that the bus was empty. When the coast was clear, the two scoundrels would get off, head over to a diner where they'd gorge on Boston Cream Pies and the like, and then head to the magic shop.

"'How do you do this trick? How is that one done? Where are the strings?' we'd ask. And the guy would show us the entire trick and entertain us. After that, we'd go to a movie, and all the theaters had a vaudeville show, so we'd see all the comics. It was like the best candy in the world to watch those guys. But it was also an education in entertainment."

When the two pals reached the ripe old age of fourteen, they decided to put an act together. (Well, actually, Lou was fourteen-and-a-half. Howard likes to point out that he's the "baby" of the two.) Their plans were put on hold for a little while, though, because Howard's parents were making plans to leave Florida to go back home to New York. Their plan was to take Lou with them.

"After living over the seedy nightclub strip joint our fathers were working, my mother said to JoJo, Lou's father, 'That's it. We're going back to New York and taking Lou with us. This is not a place for a young man.' So we moved back to New York and Lou came along."

Lou lived with an aunt for a while, but headed back south to Florida as soon as he was able. Howard followed him the minute he finished high school—and the friends could finally polish up their act.

JoJo got them their first job, as assistants to an old burlesque comic named Matt Dennison and his partner, George Tuttle.

"Twenty dollars each and room and board," Howard told us. This was the start of lifelong careers on the road for both comedians. "My father got a call to work a week in Boston—at a club called the French Village, which was a dump—and he wasn't interested. But he talked them into taking us. We put together a bunch of burlesque skits, and the audience loved it! We were just nineteen—well, I was eighteen-and-a-half. We went in for a week and stayed eight."

After that, the agent found them work at a sister club, also in Boston, called the Shamrock Village. Initially, guaranteed a week's work there, they were quickly offered a year-long contract—but

Lou had had enough of winter weather and they headed back to Florida. "He just refused to work in the cold anymore. We went back to Miami and couldn't get a job there for the longest time."

Down to their last few dollars, they finally got work at the Patter Club in Key West, where something interesting happened. All the top comics in the area started to come in to watch their act because they had heard that two kids were doing burlesque routines.

"We did three shows a day, including a 'morning show' at two a.m. Just a bunch of strippers and us. Joey Bishop would come in, Phil Foster, Red Buttons, Jan Murray. They would all come in to watch us, and ask, 'How do you kids know this material?'"

This was the early fifties, and burlesque-type stuff was brand new to many in the audience, but not to the boys who had learned and polished the slightly dated material they'd learned from their fathers.

The act broke up when Lou was drafted into the Marines. "At this point, I started working on my own," said Howard, "and in time I wound up being managed by the legendary Jack Rollins, who managed people like Woody Allen, Dick Cavett, Mike Nichols, Tom Poston, and a ton of other wonderful people. He was *the* guy."

Jack eventually invited Arlyne Rothberg—who was working for both Mr. Kelly's and Playboy at the time—to come and take a look at Howard. She liked what she saw and Howard found himself opening for singers such as Jack Jones and Mel Torme on the ever-expanding Playboy circuit.

By this time, Howard had abandoned the vaudeville and burlesque skits he'd learned from his father and was trying to find his voice.

"I was in therapy and telling the therapist stories about working this club or that, and he encouraged me to build an act around my own life—my experiences on the road and other things. So, basically, I told the Playboy crowds about growing up on the Lower East Side of New York and dealing with the tough guys. Starting out, I'd worked clubs that were run by gangsters and I worked that into my routine. I didn't have to make anything up; it was all true. I told them about the time I worked a club in Youngstown, Ohio, and a guy came running through the club with fear in his eyes. There were doors on either side of the stage, leading to the kitchen. Beyond the kitchen was the parking lot, and this guy came running in to get away from this other guy, who was after him. I was on stage, and he came in running to my left, terrified, and this other guy just walked after him as calmly as could be. I said in my act, 'He was very well dressed. He was wearing a black suit, a black hat, and a matching black gun.' And he shot at the guy! He literally shot at him. I dove off the stage to the right. The guy was on the left so I went right, and I rolled into the kitchen through the swinging door. And there was the owner. His name by the way—and this is not made up—was Shaky Maples. His real name was Santino, but they called him Shaky. I said, 'Shaky, there's a guy out there with a gun and he's shooting!'

"And his response was, 'Eyyyy, is he shootin' at you?' I said no, and he said, 'Then get back on stage and finish your act!' So I did. Since I didn't die, it was a great story to share."

Another bit from Howard's act involved a job he had in Florida. There were six striptease dancers in the show and Lou's job was to introduce each new dancer, then do a few jokes. At the end, he would do his act. It seemed his audience was exclusively sailors, which made sense since it was a port town.

"The sailors would scream, 'Get off the stage!' but I hadn't said a word yet, you know?" recalled Howard.

Obviously, they just wanted to see the girls and they soon started to shake their beer bottles and spritz the comedian. Howard had to figure out how to win these sailors over so, quite cleverly, the next day he found out what ships were in town and when he walked out on stage that night, he started by saying, "I want to welcome the battleship *Maine.*" Naturally, they screamed and cheered. "And welcome to the carrier *Michigan,*" he continued. More cheering. The club owner had a speaker in his office to monitor the show and he heard the crowd cheering and applauding—so he held Howard over for a second week. "I spent two weeks just announcing ships!" he recalled with a laugh.

Howard remains very upbeat—and nostalgic—about his experiences at the Playboy Clubs. But he does harbor a few not-so-happy memories of his time there. One of those involves the inimitable Irwin Corey. As you know by now, Irwin wasn't one to hold back on expressing his opinions. One night, he was railing against Woody Allen, who happened to be a good friend of Howard's.

"Corey was so obnoxious," Howard told us, "and we got into an argument about whether or not Woody was funny. He thought Lenny Bruce was funny, which was a safe answer, considering Bruce was dead by that time, but said he didn't 'get' Woody. At some of the Playboy Clubs, they introduce you from off stage. So, one time after our little disagreement, all the audience heard was this disembodied voice saying, 'Here he is, Woody Allen's best friend trying to be funny.' Corey was a very mean guy and that was a rotten thing to do. After the show, I went up to him and said, 'Irwin, stay away from the microphone. Don't do that again, I'm tellin' ya, or you're going to have a problem.' Then I told the club manager not to ever let him introduce me again. After that incident, the introductions were made by the Bunnies."

Another unpalatable incident Howard recalled for us involved the wholesale theft of an entire seven-minute set. "Billy Falbo—who supposedly had mob connections—started using material word for word from my TV appearance, but I didn't know about it. Unfortunately, I was scheduled to follow him at the L.A. Playboy Club. After I finished my act the first night, the club manager came up to me as I was leaving the stage, and told me to stop doing that routine.

"'You're doing the material Billy Falbo just did,' he told me.

"'He stole it from me—it's mine!' I told him. It was crazy."

Howard got some satisfaction when fellow comics who knew about the pilfering made a point of letting Billy know:

"Jackie Gayle went to see him," Howard recalled, "and when he walked off the stage, he sat with Jackie and asked him how he liked the show.

"Jackie said, 'I liked it fine when Howard Storm did it!'

"Jeremy Vernon, another friend of mine, was in the audience at one of Billy's shows, and when he got to the point where he asked the audience to name an actor and he'd do an impression of him, Jeremy hollered back, 'Do Howard Storm!' But there was nothing I could really do to stop him. I wasn't willing to get beat up over it. For all I knew, if I picked a fight with him, the next thing might be a couple of goons showing up to break my legs."

Howard told his audience stories about his relationships with the owners of different clubs, and a wide variety of everyday occurrences. Keep in mind, though, that *everyday* means something a little different for Howard than for other people. He was constantly walking the line, trying to keep the wise guys happy. But that's what made for a fascinating show.

"I always ran into tough guys in the club. There was this one guy who insisted I have a drink with him.

"I told him, 'I don't drink.'

"And he said, 'You're not going to have a drink with me? What? Are you trying to insult me in front of my friends? I'm with people ova here.'

"Finally, I sat down and he asked what I wanted. 'I guess I'll have what you're having,' I said. He called the waiter over and ordered Johnnie Walker Black doubles! He made me drink mine down and then another round came, and through it all, he's telling me how much he loved my act and how funny he thought I was. When the third round came, he said to me,

"'You're very talented and you have a chance to make it big-time...' Then he picked up his glass and said to me, '...but this stuff is gonna ruin you. Haha!'"

Howard also had the good fortune to travel and entertain at the offshore Playboy Clubs. He mentioned that two of them—for very different reasons—stood out.

"I landed in London and another comic I knew, Marty Freedman, from New York, had been hired to play in a different room. We were the only two Americans there so we hung out and explored the city a lot. One day we went to Apple, a haberdashery that the Beatles had opened. I bought a black suit—one of those suits with the wide Benjamin Franklin collars and a long jacket, hitting just above my knees. The pants had bell bottoms and I topped it off with a ruffled shirt that had an attached sash that you tied in a huge bow. My hair was down to my shoulders then and I flipped it out—it was all quite a sight. Believe it or not, everyone was wearing the same look over there. I did the Dick Cavett show later and wore that outfit and he didn't know what to make of it. He just said,

"'What is that you're wearing?'

"'Just something I picked up in London,' I said."

Ocho Rios, in Jamaica, also holds fond memories for Howard, but not for the clothing. "It was just sensational! Every room faced the ocean. Working the club, you got room and board and got paid. It was magical, like you were getting paid to be on vacation. On top of that, you could get sensational weed. Dick Capri had worked there before me and clued me in on that.

"'Look for a bellhop named Trevor. He's the guy, and don't buy more than five dollars' worth,' he told me. So I found Trevor, bought five dollars' worth, and he delivered it rolled in a ball and wrapped in newspaper. I took two tokes and, because I was heading home the next day, decided to throw the rest of the stuff away—just flush it. The girl I was dating came over and saw what I was about to do. She insisted on taking it back home with her.

"I told her, 'This is crazy. Don't do it.' She did, though—by putting it in her hair. She rolled up a big bun and tucked it in there. She carried a little more than an ounce back and we enjoyed it in New York."

One of Howard's prized memories is of the time he visited the Playboy Mansion in Chicago. He had finished doing his act, where the lounge featured Barry Manilow playing piano for singer Jeanne Lucas.

"He sure went far from there," Howard pointed out, unnecessarily.

"Allen Kent was also a comic, a great friend of mine, and also very close to Hef. One night, we visited the Mansion fairly late, about two in the morning, and Hef came down. It was just the three of us. Hef showed us a mockup of the DC-9 that he had just purchased. At this point, not many people knew about the plane. It was amazing to all of us, even Hef—and he's the one who designed it. It was crazy for us to imagine back then: a plane with a bedroom, a shower, and luxury seating. The main section was like someone's living room! We sat around and talked about it for a long time."

Howard eventually gave up the footlights to direct his talents toward writing and directing. The day we visited him at his home in Beverly Hills, he was busy with a memorial show honoring the late Robin Williams, whom he had directed in *Mork and Mindy*.

* * *

Fred Willard entertained at the Playboy Clubs many times, with different partners.

"One of the first times was at the Phoenix Club and I was part of a comedy duo called Greco and Willard," he recalled. "Then we moved on to Boston, Cincinnati, and New Orleans. New Orleans was a tough job because we worked a *lot* of shows. If there were enough customers, we'd work six shows a night! We'd start with our A show upstairs, then the manager would lead us downstairs for the B show and then back up for another A show. It got to be a little confusing. The Boston Club was one of my favorites. We only had to perform two shows a night and it had a great atmosphere.

"The unique thing about the clubs was that the room manager

would always submit a written report on each entertainer. It would go to headquarters in Chicago as well as to your agent. This didn't happen in regular clubs!

"People came to Playboy for the Bunnies and because it was a key club. They also expected a certain level of entertainment. It wasn't like playing at coffee houses, where you'd follow a folk-singing duo in front of a bunch of hippies. You really had to have your act down well."

In between career revolutions, Fred spent a year at Chicago's famous Second City improv club. Based on his work there, he was asked to join a newly forming comedy group.

"We became popular pretty quickly," Fred told us. "Before we even had a name for the group, we were recruited to appear on *The Tonight Show* and *The Ed Sullivan Show*. We did some sketches and some improvisational routines, and one of them involved a man-on-the-street interview. In the skit, one of our characters said he worked for the Ace Trucking Company in New Jersey, and we thought that was the funniest thing because every place has companies with the name Ace—Ace Typewriter, Ace Plumbing, etc. So we called ourselves the Ace Trucking Company!"

This was all before Fred hit the resorts. "Lake Geneva was kind of the gem of the whole Playboy Club rotation," he said, echoing what we heard from many others. "You got to stay right on the property, which was a beautiful resort, and when you weren't swimming or whatever, you'd spend time with the other performers and celebrities. I remember hanging with Lorna Luft—who was terrific—and even Jesse Jackson. My wife had a long conversation with him while he held our daughter, who was just a toddler at the time, on his lap.

"It was such a well-run organization. I don't know if they have any place like it today. Those days are pretty much over—it's tough to go out and have an evening with dinner and a show. I hope they come back!"

We doubt Fred would have time to appear at any new club these days, as he has segued very successfully into movie and TV roles.

* * *

Tom Dreesen opened for Frank Sinatra at nightclubs around the world for the last fourteen years of the great singer's career. He was also a close friend who spoke at his funeral in 1998. In his own right, Tom made more than 60 appearances on *The Tonight Show* and did 500 guest shots on national variety and episodic TV programs from *Columbo* and *WKRP in Cincinnati* to *Murder She Wrote.*

But Tom's success wasn't handed to him on a platter. He grew up in extremely meager circumstances, one of eight children in a cold-water flat by the railroad tracks in Harvey, Illinois. "We were raggedy-ass poor!" is how he describes it.

As soon as Tom finished school and was eligible, he enlisted in the Navy. In 1968, after serving his term, he joined and was active in the Jaycees (the United States Junior Chamber), a civic group that helps train young adults to be leaders and good citizens. It was there that Tom met Tim Reid. Based on their shared commitment to helping teenagers avoid the pitfalls of crime and drugs, they collaborated on and produced a humor-based drug education program that was a hit at local schools.

"We had the kids laughing and playing music, anything to get their attention," Tom told us. "Ultimately, our program became Number One in all fifty states and twenty-two foreign countries."

It was a precocious eight grader who floated the idea that the two men were so funny that they should become a comedy team. Eureka! Tom and Tim soon became America's first black-and-white standup duo.

"There were no comedy clubs in the 1960s," recalled Tom, "so Tim and I worked what was called the Chitlin Circuit. These were black-owned and operated nightclubs where most times I was the only white guy for miles."

Instead of ignoring the white elephant in the room, Tom and Tim addressed race issues straight-on: In fact, the majority of their act was a jab at racism. They spared no one, poking fun at both white and black injustices and offering up their own unique, first-hand experiences of the issues. While this material elicited much laughter, it didn't come without a heavy price.

"Once, a guy put out a cigarette on Tim's face—while we were on stage," Tom said. "I was pretty nervous in Atlanta, when two or three guys cornered me in the men's room and I thought it was all over. They sure did a number on me."

Interestingly enough, a lot of the hostility they encountered wasn't across racial lines but along them. When the duo worked a black club, the haters tended to attack Tim as an "Uncle Tom." In white clubs, when patrons had trouble with the idea of a mixed act, they took it out on Tom.

Tom's wife at the time hated the idea of him going into show business. As he put it, "She wanted a man who worked at a factory like her dad, and brought a check home every Friday, went bowling on Tuesday, and stayed in the community." In fact, show business was a foreign concept to everyone in their Harvey neighborhood. "They thought I was nuts for even attempting to pursue it, and a white guy with a black guy? Totally nuts."

In spite of the fact that Tim was getting the same kind of flak from his own family and friends, the team wrote and practiced at his house, writing new material daily and driving Tim's wife Rita crazy.

"Poor Rita," said Tom. "'Rita, do you think this is funny? Should we try it like this? Or should I say it instead of Tim?' When she'd had quite enough of all this, she just said, 'Go out and do it. Get an audience and try it in front of them!'"

This was more easily said than done. Tom found a small jazz club and talked the owner into letting them try out their material during a break.

"We bombed," he said simply. "We were afraid of forgetting our lines, so we went way too fast: 'Goodeveningladiesandgentlemenwe'rethecomedyteamintownhe'sTimandI'mTom…' We just rambled." They ran from the stage after finishing, and when they asked the manager how they did, he said, 'I don't know how you did. You never gave me time to laugh.'

So it began. The Chitlin Circuit put them in the heart of America's discontent. The year was 1969 and the Vietnam War was raging, students were protesting, and black communities in every major city were going up in flames. In the middle of all of it, Tom and Tim were trying desperately to make people laugh.

"If we worked an all-black club, there would be some guy who hated white people—*hated* them with a passion. He wasn't mad at me, though; he was made at Tim for being *with* me. If we worked an all-white club and there was someone who hated blacks, he was mad at me because I was a 'nigger lover.' Keep in mind, that in those times you didn't see a black man and a white man walking down the street together unless they were police, and even then, they were usually paired up with their own. So seeing a black and white guy on stage together, well, for better or worse, that got their attention."

Tom especially loved entertaining at schools and colleges, which was, after all, where the duo started. "We'd do a little comedy but then we'd talk to them. And seeing us together, just a few years older than they were, opened their minds a little to alternative thoughts. It gave some of the students the courage to stand up:

"'You know, Mr. Dreesen, I have a black friend that I like but I can't be friendly with him because of the peer pressure.'

"Or, a black kid would say, 'You know, there's a white guy I'd like to be friends with but the brothers would wear me out if I had a white friend. But seeing you and Tim up there together, I think I'll be able to talk to him.' I'll tell you…that meant more to me than any Academy Award."

All of that said, Tom emphasized that the point of the act wasn't to deliver a message or be overtly political. "It was *never* about skin color," he said. "It had to do with laughter and friendship."

It would be years before Tom and Tim could get a talent scout like Billy Rizzo from Playboy to watch their act—much less hire them. The two decided they'd better school themselves a bit if they wanted to get in the door, so they'd go to the Chicago club and watch other comedy teams.

"It was fascinating watching Tracy and Vader, for example," Tom told us. We'd seen a lot of old-time comics on TV, but you rarely got to see the new ones working live, and to watch how they played off one another helped us a great deal."

Eventually, they did get a foot in the door at Playboy, and began working the circuit regularly. Tom, like many others, enjoyed the New Orleans Playboy Club most of all.

"It was the most wonderful place in the world. I was a young guy and thought, *God, this is heaven; Bourbon Street, and the prettiest girls....* The very first time there, we asked the entertainment director, Al Belletto, 'Where do the Bunnies hang out?'

"As you probably know by now, it was Playboy policy that the Bunnies couldn't date the customers or the entertainers. To work around this, the girls found a nightspot in each city that became their after-work hangout—a bar or restaurant where they could unwind and meet up with friends old and new. So, the first question each arriving performer would ask was, 'Where do the Bunnies hang out?'

"Al informed Tom and Tim that the local Bunny hotspot had just burned down; they didn't have a specific place.

"So, Tim and I set off down Bourbon Street and found a comfortable bar. The owner was a wacky, crazy guy who asked us,

"'You new in town? Are you tourists?'

"'No, we're working at the Playboy Club,' we said.

"'Oh, well in that case let me buy you your first drink.' We really got to like this guy and the next night we brought in a couple of guys from the band, along with a few Bunnies. And word got around. The next night, the Bunnies brought more girls, and by the end of the week the place was packed. The guy that owned the bar was a deep-sea diver who must have been oxygen-deprived at some point, because he was really off-the-wall nuts—but he was so grateful for all the business we brought in that he came to the club to see our show. We couldn't do anything wrong in his eyes. One night, two of his diving buddies were arguing back and forth, 'I'm going to kick your ass,'

"'No, I'm going to kick your ass....'

"And he's yelling at them, 'Don't start any fights in my place! Don't start nothing, you understand? I'm warning you guys.' Well, we're encouraging everyone to stay out of it and the Bunnies are backing up, and Mac, the owner, says, 'I'm telling you for the last time, *no fighting*!' At which point he reaches down under the bar and pulls out a forty-five-caliber pistol and fires a shot into the ceiling. *Boom!! Loud*!! It got real quiet, and a few minutes later, in one of the funniest scenes ever, a guy stumbles into the bar in his pajamas, all disheveled. We all got it at the same time and erupted into laughter: Mac had fired right into this guy's upstairs apartment while he was sleeping on the couch! It ended well but he was lucky.

"Another incident happened at the same bar. The place was packed and we heard a *roar.* A minute later, a guy drove right into the bar on his motorcycle. It was one of Mac's crazy diver friends and he rode it right into the back room. I could hear Mac saying, 'You son of a bitch,' and then we heard, 'What the hell?' There were fumes everywhere and all of a sudden, the bike reappeared with Mac on the back. The two took off, leaving no one to tend the place. So Tim and I got behind the bar and started waiting on customers. I'd been a bartender in Chicago so I knew what was what. Some of the Bunnies helped out. About two hours later, Mac reappeared and took back over. He was just one of those wacky, wacky guys."

It was while Tom and Tim were working at the New Orleans club that former Alabama governor (and notorious segregationist) George Wallace was shot. Tim's first response was, "I hope a white guy shot him and not a black man!" It was a sober reminder that underlying all the fun times down there, New Orleans was very much a part of the Deep South, right down to the confederate flag that flew over the hotel where the performers were staying. Bigotry and racism presented a constant minefield.

To illustrate the point, Tom told us a story about one of the New Orleans Bunnies. "Pat was one of those white Southern girls who didn't realize she was prejudiced.

"Once, she said to me, 'There are some niggers that are mean as hell, but we have some nice ones in my neighborhood.' It never occurred to her how wrong that was. One night, Pat came to our dressing room before the show and said to us, 'Y'all, there's a redneck out there and he's a racist. He's out there saying some nasty things.'

"Tim looked at her and said, 'Pat, if *you* think he's a racist, he's a *racist.*' We went to Al Belletto and told him about the guy, so he could head off any potential problems. The girl singer was on, and Al said, 'He seems to be having a good time; I don't think he'll start any trouble—but I'll keep my eye on him and if he starts anything I'll get him out of here.'

"We hit the stage and went into our typical routine: 'Hi, we're the comedy team, Tim and Tom, I'm Tom and he's Tim…' And Tim would say, 'Yeah, he has to be Tom because you'd never call a black man 'Tom.'

"And this guy started, 'We don't give a damn what your name is. Make me laugh, *boy.* I didn't come here to learn your names …' I realized we had a problem, and Tim was disappearing on me upstage! So I tried to deal with the guy.

"'Sir,' I said, 'let's make a deal. If you don't interfere with my work, I won't come to your job on Monday and take your shovel and interfere with *your* work.'

"The rest of the audience was nervously laughing as I was trying to put this guy down.

"'Hey, what did you say?' he shouted, and the woman with him said to him,

"'He's saying you work with a shovel.'

"He said, 'You're damn right I work with a shovel, boy! I have a construction company in Calhoun, Alabama.' Well, there was an *Amos and Andy* show years ago with a character named Calhoun, the shyster lawyer.

"So I said, 'Calhoun? Wasn't he the lawyer on *Amos and Andy*?'

"And the girl said, 'He said they named your town after someone from *Amos and Andy*!' Uh-oh. I'd insulted Alabama. You don't insult Alabama.

"Before you know it a real donnybrook had broken out. The bouncers were trying to get the guy out; he was throwing punches and turning tables and chairs over, and *boom, bang*, the fight worked its way up the stairs and soon everyone was involved. Finally, the brawlers moved toward the door and the bouncers threw the guy and his girlfriend out and slammed the door—but it didn't latch properly! The guy managed to get his big hairy arm back through and grab a handful of one of the bouncers' hair. And the fight was back on!

"Eventually, we managed to get back on stage and resume our act. We did some impromptu routines about the troublemaker and the audience gobbled it up. As long as I live I'll never forget some guy coming up to me after that show and saying,

"'Ya boys are funny. Y'all made us laugh harder than most of us have in a long time. Tell the truth now, that guy was part of the act, right?'

"We said, 'Oh, yeah, we have him travel the country with us, trying to beat the shit out of us five shows a night, seven days a week!' That was the Deep South during those years."

Tom told us he got a kick out of hanging around the front door of the Detroit Playboy Club. Because of a Michigan state law, you couldn't designate a club as *private* there, so customers were not required to have a key to enter. But, as Tom tells it, "The guys would come and *want* to show their cards. They were told they didn't have to but they wanted to. It was really important to them to flash that Playboy card."

While on the circuit, Tom wasn't above sidestepping the rules a bit—primarily the one that said not to date the Bunnies. It was when he was booked to perform at the luxurious Great Gorge club that he had his closest call.

"We'd met up at the local Bunny hangout and made out in my car for awhile. Then I dropped her at her car and since we were heading in the same direction, I followed her back to the resort. The Bunnies had a 'hutch' and I had a suite provided by Playboy. I made sure she got home safely and I was driving to my room, when I saw flashing lights—property security. I parked my car and started running and the security guy was running after me, but back pretty far. I made it to my room with time to take off my clothes and put on a robe. Soon, the guy was pounding on my door and I answered it as if I had just woken up.

"'You just ran in here,' he said.

"I'm sweating, but I calmly said, 'I don't know what you're talking about.' 'You're not allowed to go out with the Bunnies!' he shouted, and I said again, 'I don't know what the hell you're talking about! Quit bothering me.'

"Two weeks later, Sam DiStefano—who took over booking the clubs from Irvin Arthur—said to me, 'I got a letter here that says you went out with one of the Bunnies.'

"I said, 'Now, who would tell that lie?'

"He said, 'I don't know,' and he ripped up the letter. He was my buddy...but he knew."

Turning his attention back to the bigger picture, Tom grew thoughtful. "The Playboy circuit really bonded Tim and me, because prior to Playboy we'd worked only sporadically. Along came the circuit and we were doing five, six shows a night, sometimes seven nights a week. We went around the country! We weren't practicing in front of the mirror any more.

"I was married with three kids and Tim was married with two, so we tried to save money wherever we could. We were paid $750 a week—$375 for each of us. We wanted to send money home, so instead of taking them up on the discount at a local hotel we bunked together. That opened the door to a lot of other speculation, but… you know. I spent four years in the service, and I always make the analogy that the Playboy circuit bonded Tim and me as if we'd been in combat together.

"The Playboy Clubs were ahead of their time and had a reputation for being socially liberal, and that's why we were able to survive. I will be eternally grateful for what they did for Tim and me, and later me personally. Even after Tim and I went our separate ways, I still worked Playboy. In fact, the first time I appeared on *The Tonight Show,* Johnny Carson plugged my upcoming gig at the San Francisco Playboy Club."

Tom and Tim ceased performing together in the mid 1970s but neither disappeared from view. Tim went on to win hearts as the super-cool Venus Flytrap on *WKRP in Cincinnati*, while Tom continued performing live—most notably with Sinatra—and became a regular on *The Tonight Show*.

* * *

Julio Martinez entertained at the Playboy Clubs with Al Jarreau, as the duo Al and Julio.

"My memories are that Playboy generally headlined a comedian and had a musical act as an opener. That was because the musical acts were more expensive than an unknown—or even well known—comedian. Singers usually had a trio backing them up and everyone had to be paid. They were happy to have Al and me because we were starting out and willing to split a single salary between us. If we did have a backup trio, I usually did the arrangement for them—but they were more than willing to sit it out and let me and Al play alone.

"The Playboy Clubs were wonderful for entertainers of all ilk, but especially for the comedians. The circuit served as one of the best bridges to popularity for comedians of the fifties, and were great for the established guys, too—Mort Sahl and even the self-destructive Lenny Bruce. As the sixties unfolded, other clubs began to fade—places like Mr. Kelly's in Chicago and the Hungry I, and Blue Unicorn in San Francisco. Mort Sahl used to work the Hungry I at almost no cost, just room and board, to help keep Enrico Banducci's club going. Mort ran into his own political problems when he couldn't get off the subject of the Kennedy assassination and many clubs didn't want to hire him, but Enrico always booked him.

"Meanwhile, while these other places were going down, Playboy established a circuit where comedians could keep working. If you were any good at all, you could work your way across the country, on to London, then back through again. The circuit was the bridge from the sixties to the late seventies and early eighties, when the comedy clubs began to dominate the scene.

"Al and I opened for Jackie Curtiss in Chicago. He had to change his name to J.C. Curtiss because he did some acting on the TV show *Dragnet* and was forced to join the union—but there was already a member named Jackie Curtiss. He was much kinder than Jackie Gayle, though he had a similar rapid-fire delivery. The poor trio backing him would go crazy because he always wanted an underscore: a drum beat here, a break there. Fortunately, he was on the circuit for a long time and all the trios became familiar with his style. Our part of the set, the first twenty minutes, was a relief for them. They could relax—but then they'd have to take a deep breath and go nonstop for the next forty.

"The king of them all was Jackie Gayle. We started with Jackie in LA., at Dino's Lodge, right next door to the L.A. Playboy Club. Bill Marx was the leader of the trio at Dino's, and really good at spreading the word for us. One night, we got a standing ovation and this chunky fellow jumps on stage and grabs the mic. That was Jackie Gayle. He wanted to ride the crest of the applause. He stood up there for twenty minutes. "Afterwards, Al and I were back in our tiny dressing room at Dino's, and Jackie and his cohort, including Howard Storm, came in and said,

"'What are you doing here? You should be at the Playboy Club, and I'm gonna make it happen.' Sally Marr—Lenny Bruce's mother—was booking some acts then, and Jackie said, 'I'm going to introduce you to her.' By this time, Al and I were used to all kinds of people spouting off, so we didn't pay much attention to it. But about five days later, we were hanging out and decided to go to Schwab's. As we were walking, we noticed a group in front of the restaurant, all talking at the same time. Jackie was holding court with a bunch of other comedians—just riffing on anything in sight, including the cars going by. The crowd was made up of his disciples. Anyway, true to his word, Jackie soon had us as his opening act at Playboy. Which is a good—and bad story.

"We were supposed to open for Jackie for two weeks, and then we would have a week off to get up to Sausalito, where we were scheduled to work a club called Gatsby. By this time, we had appeared on *The Steve Allen Show*, so the club put out a big campaign for us, really pushing and promoting us. Well, the day before the last day of our gig with Jackie, our manager came and said,

"'Jackie signed on for an additional two weeks and that means you stay, too.'

"'No,' I said. 'We have an obligation to Gatsby's.' He said not to worry, that he'd work it out with them. Well, he got us fired from Gatsby's—a club we'd always return to in between other jobs. They were really unhappy with us. We went back a year and a half later, but it wasn't the same.

"Our manager just said, 'That's show business,' but I don't operate that way. Al just wants to sing and tries very hard not to get caught up in the minutia of the business of it all, but it still bothers me, just remembering it.

"So we're on tour with Jackie, this time in Chicago, and Jackie says, 'There's a kind of ritual for newbies on the tour. The first time you play Chicago, you go see the Mansion—let's go see the master. So, Al, Jackie, and I all go to the Mansion. I had heard all about it, how Hef only wore pajamas and there were naked girls running around, so I was pretty excited to go. But it wasn't exactly like that. We walked into the Mansion and there was Hef and his girlfriend at the time, Barbi Benton, both in their PJ's. Hef had on a smoking jacket. But there wasn't a crazy party going on; they were playing backgammon! Hef was drinking a Pepsi and looked like he just stepped out of an ad. We shook hands and I chatted with Barbi a little. It was just not what I expected."

It was while finishing a run at the New York Playboy Club that Johnny Carson slotted Al and Julio into a coveted spot on the his show. The boys had a few weeks off between the end of their Playboy run and their scheduled appearance, and Julio's wife was threatening to divorce him if she didn't get some time with him. So he decided to fly to California. As luck (the bad kind) would have it, their appearance was suddenly moved up and Julio couldn't make it back to New York in time to do the show with Al! He helped with the arrangements by phone and had no choice but to watch his partner on TV, being introduced to America as Al Jarreau and receiving a standing ovation.

* * *

Stan Musick, the musical director and bandleader of the Miami club, smiles remembering the nightlife of Miami in its heyday. "During the middle of one of Milton Berle's shows, I was in front of my orchestra with my bass guitar, ready to conduct any musical cue I got from Milton. In the middle of a story, he happened to glance over at me and something caught his attention, because he dropped his microphone to his side, strolled over to me, and said,

"'Stan, do you know that you have a tear in your pants?' I looked down and there was the smallest tear in the seam of my tux pants. It was, at most, an inch long—in the seam! Now, I had to struggle to even see it, so how he spotted it from across the stage is still beyond my comprehension. Nobody in the audience would ever notice it. He was a micro-perfectionist. I still find that funny.

"Alan King was very interested in politics. I enjoyed talking to him because he was very astute in his grasp of world affairs. There wasn't much humor when he was off stage; instead, I got to see that introspective, intelligent side of him that few others were witness to. Alan had a very talented singer working with him, Donna Theodore. I remember seeing her many times on *The Johnny Carson Show*, and when I heard that she and Alan were coming to my club, I was looking forward to playing her excellent musical arrangements. I got a surprise at rehearsal when she said that her conductor couldn't make it and that I would be conducting her show. I understood that the most important thing was to know the correct tempos of her songs, and we didn't have a lot of time to rehearse before hitting the stage. But everything turned out well and we both enjoyed the results.

Miami Musical Director Stan Musick and Alan King: Courtesy of Stan Musick

"I remember conversing with George Carlin at the Playboy Club in Miami—before it was the Playboy Plaza Hotel—and back then, he looked like a college graduate. He had short hair and a preppy suit. He was very cordial and nothing like the George Carlin that he was when he finally emerged from his cocoon. Gabe Kaplan was another great guy I liked working with, both at the club and later, during the 1972 Democratic Convention, at the Playboy Plaza Hotel. He was always on top of his game and a lot of fun to be with. I was glad to see how big he made it."

Decades later, memories of the clubs' special magic are still vivid. Stan told us about a recent conversation he had while at the gym.

"I was working out at LA Fitness in Miami," he said, "and I struck up a conversation with another guy about this and that. I mentioned that I had once worked at the Playboy Club and he said,

"'I remember the Playboy Plaza Hotel. On my first date with my wife, I took her to see Stan Musick and his orchestra.'

"'That was my band!' I told him—and he freaked out. He couldn't wait to go home and tell his wife about it.

As the Playboy Club concept spread across the country, and ultimately the world, Hef found himself stretched thin; he couldn't adequately oversee each Playboy enterprise personally. Yet, the ideas kept springing forth: the Playboy Jazz Festival, the TV shows, Playboy Records, Playboy Models, Playboy Limousine, Playboy Publishing, and more. *Playboy* magazine, his first passion and the cornerstone of the company, remained his top priority and consumed so much time that Hef took to working from home—the Mansion—often toiling straight through the night. Foregoing typical daytime attire for pajamas and a smoking jacket may have seemed like an affectation (and we're not saying it wasn't), but it made a kind of sense for a man who worked night and day.

Hef's most trusted lieutenant, Victor Lownes, took on more and more responsibility for running the clubs—and diligently scouted locations for new ones— although every detail of each venture had to be approved by the top playboy himself. Victor's discerning taste was evident as each building was turned into a new jewel in the corporation's crown. Victor also took on the weighty responsibility of personally selecting the perfect young women to become Bunnies in each club. Rough work, but someone had to do it!

Entertainment directors were hired for each club (you've met a few of them already): Al Belletto in New Orleans, Kai Winding in New York, and Stan Musick in Miami are but a few of the people who made the clubs top talent showcases. Sam DiStefano, who started at the Chicago Club fronting a trio, eventually became the organization's overall entertainment director.

The sixties and seventies were a fabulous time for emerging comedians, thanks in no small part to Playboy. The reputation and caliber of the comedians performing on its stages made the clubs a hunting ground for talent scouts and TV producers, resulting in many "I was discovered at the Playboy Club" stories. You've already heard about Dick Gregory's discovery at the Chicago club; a few years later, Flip Wilson would barely be able to control his nerves knowing that a rep from *The Johnny Carson Show* was in the house.

George Kirby and Jerry Pawlak: Courtesy of Jerry Pawlak

Of course it wasn't just emerging talent that benefited from the Playboy circuit. Already established funny guys who made it their home included Shecky Greene, Jerry Lewis, Don Rickles, Henny Youngman, and Rodney Dangerfield. Some did it because they loved the atmosphere (i.e. the girls); some used it to fill in blank

Gene Barry: The Curtiss Family Collection

spots in their busy schedules; and some saw it as an opportunity to try out new material in front of lively audiences, while watching the next generation of comedians emerge. Whatever their reasons—and whatever it was that drew audiences to the clubs in droves—everybody went home happy.

Sidney Poitier and friends: The Curtiss Family Archives

4

FIRST AND LAST RESORTS

Arthur Platt Jr. looks pretty darn happy as twins Glenda and Brenda help him celebrate his 14th birthday: The Margie Barron Collection

At the pinnacle of their golden era, from 1963 through 1984, the Playboy Clubs and Resorts numbered forty, including those in the Philippines, Canada, Japan, and England. In the States, clubs dotted the map from Los Angeles to New York, San Francisco to Dallas, Boston to Atlanta—but there's no doubt that the jewels in the crown were the Playboy Resorts. These pleasure palaces were located in Lake Geneva, Wisconsin; MacAfee, New Jersey; Ocho Rios, Jamaica; and Miami, Florida.

Nothing if not ambitious, Hef conceived of the 1,350-acre Lake Geneva property—his first resort—as the ultimate family destination. You read that correctly: *family*. Still elegantly naughty by night, Lake Geneva's daytime offerings included skiing, fishing, golfing, horseback riding, swimming, and boating. There was even an airfield large enough to accommodate private jets—his own, as well as those of his most privileged guests.

But the most family-friendly resort in the chain—and the most expensive to build—was New Jersey's Great Gorge. Playboy funneled more than $33 million (in 1971) into the development of that lush property, in hopes of attracting weekend guests from nearby New York City as well as the adjacent New Jersey communities.

With the addition of Great Gorge, Playboy took its definition of *entertainment* up a notch. For years, the clubs had been hiring impressive musical and comedy acts, but they weren't what you'd call superstars—at least not yet. (Many went on to achieve that distinction.) When occupancy at Great Gorge lagged behind expectations, headquarters decided to bring in genuine A-list headliners, including Mimi Hines, Phil Ford, Shecky Greene, Rich Little, Trini Lopez, and Sonny and Cher. Sadly, the strategy didn't provide the hoped-for bounce—and these artists didn't work cheap—but it was great while it lasted. Guests swam with the Bunnies while the sun was out and enjoyed the work of their favorite comedians, singers, and musicians after dark.

Playboy's strategy was to prepare Great Gorge as a prime destination for gaming, having gotten wind of impending legislation that would make it legal throughout the state. Toward that end, no expense was spared to book top headliners.

"Great Gorge was supposed to be a big deal—a really big deal," comedian Shecky Greene told us. "They paid me a lot of money to play there, which I feel a little bad about, because they weren't making any money at that time. But they were setting the stage for the legalization of gambling, and I always drew the gambling crowd."

Margie Barron worked at the resort during its heyday, and was happy to share her experiences with us. She was raised at the Jersey Shore, in the small town of Beach Haven.

"I heard about this great resort, up in North Jersey that had just opened," she told us. Fresh from high school, Margie went to work in Las Vegas for a couple of months, as a "gofer" for Liberace. After that heady start, there was no way she was going back to Beach Haven and a job at Bell Telephone or the local Chevy dealer. "Right after Christmas," she continued, "I drove up the Garden State Parkway to check out Great Gorge." Duly impressed, Margie realized the compound wasn't the den of iniquity she'd imagined. "You know, *Playboy*, wink, wink, nudge, nudge. There were families walking around and kids playing at the pool. And the Bunnies couldn't have been nicer. I actually shared lunch with a few and chatted. 'What a neat place,' I thought. 'I wonder if they're hiring.'"

Serendipitously, she passed a woman leaving the personnel office who had just given her notice. Margie had written for the local paper and knew how to type, so she seized the opportunity and was quickly asked when she could start.

"So the job fell into my lap and it couldn't have been a better experience. Plus, I didn't have the expense or challenge of finding a place to live. MacAfee was a lovely, sleepy little community, but the only place to stay there was at the Playboy resort. There weren't any apartments or other hotels. When the personnel director found out I didn't live in town, she said I could bunk at the Bunny dorm, which was similar to a little motel right off the main resort hotel. You entered the dorm from the outside, and every two suites shared a bathroom. I shared with Bunny Christine. It was wonderful because I really got to know the girls better in their off hours.

"Bunny Christine was saving her money to get married and buy a house. Others were going to college or saving for school or their own place. It wasn't the lure of the Bunny outfit for most of the girls—it was a good way of earning a nice paycheck. Of course, some of them were chasing the limelight. Bunny Allison was our Great Gorge Bunny of the Year, and she wanted to be a centerfold and a star. She was ambitious and also very beautiful—she looked like Jaclyn Smith in *Charlie's Angels*.

Brothers Tom and Dick Smothers are both holding on tight to Margie Platt: The Margie Barron Collection

"The Bunny Mother was Bunny Sandy and she took her job very earnestly, looking after the Bunnies as if they were her own girls. She not only made sure they looked exactly perfect, but was also like their guidance counselor. Great Gorge hosted lots of conventions, and the conventioneers were always trying to date the girls by enticing them with promises they probably had no intention of keeping.

"'Hey, I can help you, baby,' you know. The girls would talk to Sandy about it and she offered good counsel. All of them were young and many very naïve, and they were taught how to handle any situation with humor and subtlety. And if that didn't work, the room director was always on the lookout for troublemakers."

By the mid seventies, the Playboy Clubs as a whole were in precarious financial shape. By contrast, the London Playboy Club and Casino was generating more profits than any other casino in the world (some $32 million in 1981), and was the beacon of hope for the organization. For a while, London kept things afloat, offsetting year after year of losses elsewhere. But if they wanted to stay in business, Hef and Playboy knew they'd have to replicate the success of London in the States. To help lobby for the legalization of gambling that they were counting on, Playboy deployed the Bunnies, sending them out into the community for a wide variety of events.

"All the local organizations, like the 4H Club, the Sussex County Fair, any ribbon-cutting ceremony for a new bank or whatever, would invite the Bunnies to participate," Margie explained. "That way, they were assured they were going to get their event in the newspaper, because everyone liked running pictures of the Bunnies. You could have the head of the Chamber of Commerce attend, but it was a Bunny helping to cut the ribbon that would assure it hit the news the next day. So there was a lot of community involvement and, even though I looked like I was only twelve years old, Bunny Mother Sandy had a lot of trust and respect for me, and picked me to chaperone the girls when they were sent on these jobs. They were always looked after. Mr. Hefner never wanted them placed in uncomfortable or awkward positions. Plus, they had to represent the company in a certain prescribed manner."

The Bunny traveling uniform consisted of a modest, long-sleeved black turtleneck, black mini skirt, black stockings, high heels, and Bunny ears—but no tail. This was quite a departure from the traditional Bunny outfit, which had evolved to include a wild array of prints, pastels, and solids along with the regulation ears, perky tail, collar, and cuffs. But the most requested and coveted outfit was still the sophisticated black Bunny suit.

"All the girls wanted to wear that black outfit," Margie recalled, "but Sandy knew we had to have a variety of colors and patterns on the floor. To make it easier for the girls, she'd tell them, 'Oh, those are reserved for the girls who need to lose a little weight, because black is so slimming.' Well, of course, that encouraged the girls to opt for the Peter Max prints!" In the summertime, poolside patrons had the pleasure of being served drinks and snacks, by bikini-clad Bunnies.

Margie's official title was Assistant PR Director, and she has fond memories of her encounters with the many brilliant comedians who entertained at the resort. "Henny Youngman *loved* seeing the girls, and they just flocked around him. He never got tired of posing for pictures with them and was quite a character. During his show, the Bunnies could barely do their job they were laughing so hard. Rodney Dangerfield had a fondness for pushing the envelope and we'd all just laugh and giggle—and the girls would pose for the Camera Bunny with Rodney and any customers who requested it. We had twin Bunnies—Glenda and Brenda—cute as could be, and they caught the eyes of both Smothers Brothers when they performed. After the show was over, I took them back to the suite to meet the brothers and pose for pictures. They wanted to try on the girls' ears, and we have a picture of it—it's very cute. Tom and Dick couldn't have been sweeter and—of course—asked the girls out, which they declined. Even though dating customers or performers was strictly forbidden, girls would have hook-ups. In every work place where girls and guys mix, you have that going on, but it definitely wasn't sanctioned."

In addition to the comedians, headliners at the New Jersey Club included prominent singers and even fighters. "Vic Damone, Jack Jones, Peggy Lee, and Johnny Mathis worked there, and we were one of the first to present Natalie Cole. Jerry Quarry trained on the property and we hosted one of his fights. He brought a lot of the sports people into the compound."

Margie eventually migrated to the West Coast, and in 1979, Frank Barron—then editor of the *Hollywood Reporter*—asked her for a date and took her to the Los Angeles Playboy Club. I guess she didn't mind the trip down memory lane, because they married the following year and just celebrated their thirty-sixth year wedding anniversary.

Dick Smothers makes quick work of getting twin Bunnies Glenda and Brenda's tails off: The Margie Barron Collection

Alas, the legalization of gaming didn't come to pass—but the scaling up of entertainment filtered throughout the chain and there was no going back to the minor leagues.

* * *

John Byner, the comedian, singer, actor, and impressionist, got his big break while performing standup at New York's Vanguard Theater. A talent coordinator for Ed Sullivan saw his show and asked John if he'd be interested in doing a few minutes of his act during a dress rehearsal. If Mr. Sullivan liked him, they would book him sometime in the future. As it turned out, Sullivan loved him so much that he invited him on his show that very night! John wound up doing *The Ed Sullivan Show* a total of eighteen times.

When we asked John how he got started in the business, he answered the same way many comedians have.

"I was funny," he told us, "always funny—funny at home, funny in school, and even funny in the Navy. In high school, I could make the kids laugh and I loved it, but if they laughed too long, I was dead.

If they laughed just a little bit and then stopped, it was great, but if they laughed too long, I knew I was going to the principal's office.

"I liked making people laugh, and even though I could sing, there were a thousand and one singers. At the time that I was starting in show business, I remember Red Skelton saying that there were only about a hundred comedians in the world. Now there are a hundred on each block!

"I was in the Navy and had duty one night, which meant sweeping down the rec room where the guys played pool and that kind of stuff. Well, I hadn't gotten any mail for a few days, and I was in a lousy mood. I was only eighteen or nineteen, and I was sweeping, and there was one guy—I really didn't realize how big he was—but he got in my way and I said,

"'Get the heck out of here!'

"And he said, 'Hey, what are you going to do about it?' I dropped my broom and I was ready to go at it with him. Next thing I know, I'm over his head—he's got me over his head by my legs and arms—so I said,

Soup Sales celebrating his birthday at the Great Gorge Playboy Resort: The Margie Barron Collection

"'And don't come back!' He laughed so hard both of us collapsed to the ground. So, making people laugh sometimes got me out of jams."

"The Playboy Clubs took great care of the people that worked there. I was even able to bring my kids to Great Gorge and most of the other clubs. Having said that, I'll tell you that once, I had the worst experience

I ever had working a nightclub there.

"I was working with the King Cousins, and I love them. They are really great girls, but—oh, God—this one night was awful. I wasn't long in the business and I didn't have my 'heckler chops' yet. The place was packed, and there was a trio on stage with me because I do a lot of impersonations of singers. Well, the stage had a two-foot lip off the main floor, and there was a fellow with his foot up on the stage because it was only a few feet up from where he was sitting, which was at the end of a sixteen-person table. I walked out to do my act, got big applause, and I started into it, and he went,

"'Naw, you don't want to do that. No, don't do that.' Every time I would start into something, 'No, no, don't do that. No, no, no.' He went on and on, and I kept waiting for the maître d' to come and get him the heck out of there, but he just continued going on and on, and now people from the audience were starting to shush him: 'Hey, cut it out. Hey, shut up.' And the band was even starting to say things to him, and it just started to get ugly, just ugly, *ugly*! I felt like the only girl in San Diego when the ships come in.

"It was finally the end of my act, and after going through all of this pain, I said to him, 'What do you want me to talk about?'

"He said, '*Sex*.' I don't want to tell you what I said to him, but after I did, I dropped the microphone, walked off stage, and went back to my suite, where my thirteen-year-old son could see how upset I was. He tried to cajole me out of it by asking me to help with a model plane we had been working on that afternoon. But I just couldn't shake that terrible feeling from a bad show. I wanted to crawl in a hole and die—but the King Cousins called me late that night and said, 'Hey, John, we're having a picnic tomorrow.' I said, 'Gee, I don't know . . .'—word must have gotten back to them about what I had to deal with—and they said, '*C'mon, c'mon, c'mon*.'

"So my son and I went out in the morning, even though I was still feeling lousy. Right by the golf course, they'd laid out this amazing spread that the hotel had boxed up picnic-style, and it was lovely—but I still couldn't bounce back. It wasn't until two guys walked over with their golf clubs in their hands and said, 'Hey, John, we traveled from Detroit just to see you, and if it makes you feel any better, we followed that guy into the men's room and gave him a stomach ache.' Aah...there is a God. He was punished for his sins.

"The next night, there was a knock on my door and it was the maître d', and he said,

"'Mr. Byner, I'm so sorry about last night. I could have come over and removed him, but it was such a large crowd, and he was with sixteen people, and they would have been upset.' He was fired the next day. The Playboy organization likes things running smoothly! After that, everything was great."

John was on a roll, and who were we to stop him? "Another wonderful story is that one night after the show, the Playboy folks said to me, 'John, we'd like you to fly to Chicago tomorrow to do a morning show and publicize your appearance here. You'll fly in a four-seater, land at the Chicago airport, do the show, and then we'll bring you back.' So I woke up early, about five-thirty, and I looked outside, and it was raining and hailing, but we still headed out. The weather was so bad that, I'm telling you, the flight was like a nightmare. At one point, the plane dropped forty feet. It got so bad that the pilot could hardly reach the controls on the dash because he was holding on to the steering wheel so tight, and the plane was bouncing, bouncing, bouncing! Finally, we landed, and I did the show, and it was actually the only show I've ever done where I wished it could have gone on longer—because I didn't want to get back on the plane! Turns out, though, that during the time I was on, the weather had totally cleared up and the flight back was nice. That whole experience was really something: exciting and scary at the same time. I've been on some pretty bad flights, flying back and forth both in this country and internationally, but that was the most horrendous!

"One time, I was working another club in Chicago—The Palmer

House—and about halfway through my show, I saw a woman in a beautiful white fur coat get up and leave . . . and she never came back. It bothered me, and after the show, my friend and I went over to the Playboy Club around the corner, and I remember saying to him, 'I have a feeling that I'll find out what happened to the woman from my show.' Now, it's about three or four in the morning, and we straggle out of the Playboy bar and get in the elevator to go down, when another guy gets on and says,

"'Hey, great show last night.'

"I don't know what made me ask him, but I said, 'You wouldn't happen to know why the woman in the beautiful fur coat walked out in the middle, do you?'

"He said, 'Yeah! That was my wife. She had a terrible ear infection and had to leave to go to the doctor.'

"Isn't that crazy? That this is the last guy in the whole club awake with us—and I ask him—and it was his wife! Can you believe it?

Liberace cruising the Playboy golf course with a Bunny to help navigate: The Margie Barron Collection

I was worrying, 'Did I offend someone?' Sometimes I used some weird material, and I was concerned."

John would go on to become a cast member of the new *Gary Moore Show*, as well as a regular on *The Steve Allen Show* and a perennial favorite on variety shows and sitcoms. He was offered the role of Mork from Ork when the character was first introduced on *Happy Days*, but turned it down. I think you probably know the name of the guy who took the part.

* * *

We talked to comic legend David Brenner shortly before his death in 2014, and we feel so fortunate to have captured some of his precious memories of Playboy and the effect it had on his career. David had a reputation for having a special sense, an intuitive ability to just *know* what would get the laughs.

"I've always known what was funny and what wasn't," he confirmed. "Sometimes it's a tiny thing, like figuring out that a number you used in a bit was the wrong number—it was too high or too low. It might sound strange, but I'd change the number and the joke would work.

"I lived with the funniest man in the world," David said, "my father. I learned from him. You could put him up against Benny and Burns and he was the best."

David's father performed in vaudeville from the time he was nine, as a juggler, a song-and-dance man, and a comedian. On a visit home to see his own father—who was a leading Orthodox Rabbi in Philadelphia—David's father agreed to give up performing so that he wouldn't have to work on the Sabbath, which is forbidden under Jewish law.

David told us, "Dad never appeared again on stage but was the funniest guy in the neighborhood, the funniest in the supermarket, and the funniest in the elevator. He was just the funniest guy around. And he lived vicariously through me."

The apple clearly didn't fall far from the tree. In addition to his comedic genes, the years of honing his skills on the treacherous streets of Philly played a part in shaping David's comedy. He was both a gang leader and class president because he could grab anyone's attention and relate to that person on their own level.

"If a man walked by with a funny hat," he said, "I got five minutes of comedy out of it.

"There's no instruction book on growing up in a bad neighborhood and how to escape from it. The surest ways are to get married or become a criminal. So I joined the Army."

David was sent to Germany to work as a cryptographer, and discharged after serving two years with the Signal Corps. Upon returning home to Pennsylvania, he enrolled at Temple University, where he majored in mass communications.

After graduating first in his class at Temple, he was completely lost. "I didn't know what I wanted to do," he said, "but I knew I wanted to do something creative. I knew I'd like to work with people and that I couldn't have a boss over my head. I knew all the things I couldn't do, wouldn't do, didn't want to do. I didn't know the opposite side of that coin, though—what I *wanted* to do.

"For the first time in my life, I couldn't get a job. I had started working at eight-and-a-half years old. All of a sudden, I've got a degree and can't get a job."

Soon enough, David received a call from a former professor of his, who told him NBC was looking for a documentary film writer in their Philadelphia offices.

"'That's great,' I told him, 'except I don't know anything about documentaries—I majored in drama.' I asked my professor what I should do, and he said,

"'Write a documentary; you have the weekend.'

"'About what?' I asked, and he said, 'Pick something you know about.'

"What I knew about was growing up in a neighborhood in transition. We were one block away from the black ghetto and then the ghetto moved even closer, and everyone ran from the black people, until I was the only white kid left. That lasted about twelve years, so I knew a lot about that, and that's what I wrote about. I think I even called it 'Neighborhood in Transition.' To prepare for the interview that Monday, I wrote an outline, made my points, and then added a summary. It was a short little report—maybe six pages long.

"When I went in for the interview, the man asked, 'What do you know about writing for documentaries?'

"And I said, 'Absolutely nothing.'

"He said, 'What do you know about directing film for a documentary?'

"Again, I said, 'Absolutely nothing.'

"And then he asked, 'What do you know about editing film for a documentary?'

"I said, 'You know . . . what's happening here is that this is embarrassing for me and a waste of your time, because if you're looking for someone with experience, you'd do better to pull someone out of New York City. But if you're looking for someone who's going to work hard and learn fast, you're not going to find anyone in this building who's going to beat me.' I thanked him for his time, gave him the documentary I wrote, and left. I told my professor I messed up!"

At the time, David was living with someone, and though he didn't yet know it, she'd just lost her job. She'd put off telling him about it until she could either work up the courage or it couldn't be avoided. She came home that day and asked David how much money he had.

"I said, 'Whatever I have is on the dresser, which isn't much, because I bought a paperback and took the subway.'

"'Okay,' she said, 'well, what's in the cookie jar?'

"'We don't have a cookie jar,' I told her. We went through everything: the jeans going in the wash, the little spaces in the sofa, the purse.

"Finally, she said, 'The worth of this organization is eighty cents! What are we going to do about it?'

"'I don't know about you,' I told her, 'but we live above a laundromat and it's 120 degrees in here. I'm going to lay down and sleep on it.'

"A call woke me up," David continued, "and it was Mr. Riley, the man who had interviewed me. I got all excited, figuring, 'Oh my God! He's going to give me a second interview. I've got a shot, and boy, do I need it!'

"He said, 'I'm calling to let you know that I'll see you at nine o'clock tomorrow morning.' I was never a morning person—always nocturnal.

"So I said, 'Well, I've got some things to do in the morning, I wonder if we could make it at like two in the afternoon?'

"He said, 'Well, you know the studio opens at nine.'

"I said, 'Yeah, I figured that, but two or three would really work better for me.'

"He said, 'I don't think you understand. You got the job.'

"Eight weeks turned into eleven, and then into thirteen. I learned fast and worked hard and ended up with my own documentary series. I thought I was going to change the world, but it didn't happen. Nothing changed. I did 115 documentaries, and if you dust them off and ignore the style of hair and fashion, you'd think they were just done. I dealt with issues such as federal government overspending, misunderstanding of gay issues, the immigrant situation, and so forth and so on. Ultimately, I quit. I took a vacation down on one of the islands, where it rained, and I came to understand that I liked getting laughs. It was there and then that I made the decision to give myself a year as a comedian."

During that period—the late sixties and early seventies—there was only a handful of up-and-coming comics, including Steve Martin, Steve Landesberg, Jimmie Walker, Albert Brooks, George Carlin, Richard Lewis, Freddie Prinze, Ray Romano, and Bette

Midler (before she turned her focus to singing). They all knew one another and most were friends.

"I met Jimmie Walker," said David, "at the African Room on Forty-fourth Street. He was a skinny kid doing a pitching penny routine that was very funny. Afterwards, I introduced myself and asked his name. When he told me 'Jimmie Walker,' I said,

"'I'm not good with names, but he was the mayor of New York, so I'll remember. What do you want to do with this?' I asked him. 'Where do you see comedy going for you? Do you want to be a star?'

"'Yeah,' Jimmie said, 'I'd like to do that.'

"So I said, 'Well, you're not going to be a star if you keep playing to this crowd. I like to make people laugh; why don't you hang out with me?' And we started hanging out and became best friends. There were only about twelve of us starting out then, and we all hit it pretty big. And the Playboy Clubs were instrumental, I'll tell ya that.

"The image I had in my mind of Playboy was *glamour*. Almost like Hollywood in the 1940s. Everything was beautiful. The way the women dipped to give you your drink and the way you were served. The décor and the wonderful entertainment—everything had that pull toward elegance. Even the jerks in the Midwest with the brown shoes and white socks who came on to the women and had to be taken out added to the allure.

"I don't care how small the club was. They all had that special *oomph*—there was nothing else like it. And we were treated great. I mean, *they treated you like gold*. We all were just starting out and working places like the Improv, where, if you wanted a Coca-Cola, you had to pay a quarter for it. And if you took the glass into another showroom to watch your friend perform, you had to pay another quarter! That's the way we were treated elsewhere—and we didn't get paid, either, except for tips. At the Playboy Clubs, you had a little dressing room and they'd actually ask if you'd like a soda or water in there. They'd introduce you nicely and keep the place quiet and respectful.

"At the larger clubs, it was like playing a club in heaven! And then Chicago—if you worked in Chicago…please! They were some of the happiest performing days I ever had. The Playboy Mansion was there, and I would walk barefoot to get to it! It was fabulous—seeing naked women swimming—even now, I can't fully describe it. I was young and there weren't the terrible diseases that came later. I mean, c'mon, you couldn't ask for anything better.

"Steve Martin and I were friends—I met him at the Troubadour and he got my funny bone. I thought he was the *funniest* guy. I introduced myself and we became friends. You have to picture what he looked like then—he had long, straggly white hair and a big beard like the Smith Brothers, and he wore one-strap bib overalls with suspenders that crossed catty corner. One day, I was working at the Playboy Club in Chicago and we got together for lunch. He always asked me for tips, and I told him,

"'You're getting popular, and I don't want to offend you, but when you walk out on stage dressed like you're dressed and looking like you look—you look like you should have an arrow sticking through your head. My suggestion is to get rid of *all* the long hair. Put on a business suit with a nice shirt and tie. Polish your shoes and look like a gentleman—then go out there with an arrow through your head—that's a juxtaposition that would be hysterical. What's this clean-cut businessman doing with an arrow through his head?'

"Now, the next week Steve is working the Playboy in San Francisco, another fabulous club, and he calls me up and says,

"'David, I did what you said, except I made one change. I got an all-white suit.'

"I said, 'Brilliant! Brilliant!' And that was the staple of his career."

Maybe it wasn't magic, but David did have an abundance of comedic insight.

"I have to tell you a story about Great Gorge, which was a wonderful Playboy resort. I had befriended another comedian—Freddie Prinze. I had a gig there, and he was opening for me. As you know,

I had a reputation for this 'magical' comedic talent of reading an audience and knowing what would be funny or what wouldn't. It wasn't anything magical, really, just intuition. Anyway, I told Freddie that I could tell how well I was going to do just by looking at the audience—how they were dressed, the expressions on their faces, that kind of thing.

"He said, 'Would you do that for me?'

"I said, "Yeah, sure, I'll take a look right before you go on.'

"So I looked through the curtain, turned around, put my hand to my cheek, and said, 'Oh man, you're in trouble!' He could tell I was kidding and, of course, he wasn't in trouble. He was brilliant.

"I started moving up the career ladder when I was working at the Bitter End, one of the hippest clubs in New York. Unbeknownst to me, my agent, David Yeager, brought the booker for *The Tonight Show* in to see me. I was doing all my hip stuff and he was *not* a fan. He said to my agent, 'David Brenner does *vomit material.* Not only will he never do *The Tonight Show*, we won't even let him into 30 Rockefeller Plaza!

"I got angry and decided that I was going to get on the show one way or another. What I did was make believe that I was a manager and went to the Victor Jay Theater, where they held auditions every Wednesday. I watched what made these people laugh and I wrote a monologue tailored to their taste. I auditioned in December 1970, and after a while, I got a call asking if I was ready to go on the show the next night. I went on, the magic happened, and Johnny invited me back the next week. Soon after that, Ed Sullivan put me on as the last live *Ed Sullivan* comedian. That's when Buddy Hackett put me in the main showroom in Vegas and I started working for all the superstars. It was the first year I made six figures.

"I was lucky—I was the young kid with a new face, new beat, and new approach, and all these great guys took me under their wings. Shecky Greene was so kind to me in Vegas—we're best friends. Redd Foxx and Johnny Carson introduced me and did what they could to help me. After Buddy Hackett got me that gig in Vegas, I spent my career making money there. You don't see that today.

"The Playboy Clubs were wonderful. I keep using that word, but it was the way you were treated. They treated the entertainment as well as the mob did, and the mob was *grand*! As far as work—working for the two of them was absolutely the best."

After David's untimely death, his family honored his request that he be buried with one hundred dollars in small bills tucked into his left sock, just in case tipping was required where he was going. We know he has the angels laughing.

* * *

Dyn-o-mite! This was the unforgettable refrain of Jimmie Walker during his six-year run as the wisecracking J. J. Evans on Norman Lear's *Good Times*. It also describes Jimmy as a comedian. When we spoke to him, he confirmed what David Brenner had told me: He and the other emerging comedic talents of the time—including Robert Klein, Jay Leno, Bette Midler, and Steve Landesberg—formed a little posse. They worked together and encouraged one another until each found his or her career path to the big time. They established many of these early friendships when they performed at the African Room and continued as David moved the gang to the Improv.

"We were all very close in those days," Jimmie reminisced. "What I remember happening was that the Playboy talent scouts were always looking for people to play at the clubs, and they liked what they saw at the Improv. So they raided the talent there and a lot of people found a lot of work making the rounds of the Playboy Clubs. They had *volumes* of work, because they had clubs all over the country and, actually, off shore, too. So I started working the circuit. I was at the Playboy Clubs in New York, Baltimore, Cincinnati, San Francisco—pretty much all of them—and as I became better known, I got booked at the resorts. Playboy provided *work*—good, pretty steady, paid work! It gave us that opportunity to get in front of different crowds and try different stuff or perfect the material we had.

"Irvin Arthur was my agent and a good friend, and he booked most of the clubs. He didn't mince words—he would call you and say, 'Hi, Jim? Irvin Arthur. Got a Playboy for you. Cincinnati. Four hundred for the week. Get there the best you can.'"

Jimmie laughed at the memory. "That was his deal. That's exactly what he would say, and then he'd hang up—end of conversation! One day, he called and said, in that abbreviated way he had, 'Cincinnati Playboy Club—Wolfgang didn't like ya.'"

"Were they grading you?" we asked, because we'd heard all about that from a few other artists.

"Definitely," said Jimmie. "Wolfgang—at whichever club it was—was not a fan, but I went back and he liked me the next time. So I guess I was on the cusp. I wasn't *that* bad.

"If you were a regular act, not a headliner, you did your own little show. You didn't work with anyone. The club had a small billboard type of thing with your name on it—something that glowed—and the Bunnies who introduced you would slip it in the slot. And when you moved to another room, you took it with you. You ended up passing other performers in the halls and stairways, all carrying their name plaques under their arms—this was a funny sight in itself. They'd make a little announcement: 'Jimmie Walker in the Playroom in fifteen minutes—Jimmie Walker, comedian.' No one knew you, starting out, but you built a following.

"One of the big problems we had was that, because the clubs were so big, so popular, and so incredible, people from all over the world would come. So you'd have fifty Japanese guys with a tour group or whatever—and for comedy, that's a bad thing! They have to be able to understand the language to understand the joke. That would happen a lot—we'd get Germans, Spanish people—a lot of foreigners, who just sat there.

"You'd start at the top of the club, do a show, then go down to another room to do another show, and eventually, you ended up at the bottom of the club and you'd start working your way up floor by floor again. After so many shows, you'd think, 'Was I here before?' 'Did I do this already?' It was always that kind of thing. You never really knew where you were by the fourth or fifth show. We did a lot of shows! They weren't long, but still, it was a lot of work."

We had to ask Jimmie about dating the Bunnies because, well, we knew that most of the comedians and musicians had broken that particular rule at some point.

"No, I never really even got to *meet* the Bunnies. At that stage of my career, they were way out of my class! I was just happy to be there because it was a lot of work, and I just wanted to stay in the rotation. You know, there was a guy who was always on you about this and that. You had to put on a suit jacket—which was not what anyone wanted to do. We were not dress-up guys. That's not to say we were that funky-funky, but this was very straitlaced. You also had to be clean, and to mingle if they told you to mingle. So most of the clubs were just work—except the one in New York. Working there...that was an ego thing. You got to say, 'I was at the New York Playboy Club.'"

While Jimmie and the rest of the gang were working hard at the Playboy Clubs, they continued to perform at the Improv, waiting, working, and hoping for their big breaks. David Brenner broke out first, with his appearance on *The Tonight Show*, and he helped the others. Eventually, they all landed on shows—all but Jimmy.

"Jack Paar was a dream for me," he said, "because everyone I knew was doing TV. In those days, Carson was in New York, we had Merv Griffin and David Frost out here, and Mike Douglas was in Philly. But I couldn't get on any of them."

In 1972, Jimmie still hadn't reached mainstream America. Meanwhile, his friends David Brenner, Steve Landesberg, and Bette Midler were scheduled to appear on the star-making *Jack Paar Show*. According to Jimmie, they asked,

"What about Jimmie Walker being on the show?"

The talent coordinator replied, "Absolutely not. We don't think he's funny."

And they said, "If he doesn't do the show, we don't do the show." So Jimmie was included in the lineup.

Boy, was the talent spotter wrong! The audience ate him up—they couldn't get enough of him. Dan Rowan, of *Laugh-In* fame, saw the show and immediately flew Jimmie to Hollywood to be a guest on the show. That was followed by other TV appearances and the job of warming up the audience for the sitcom *Carlucci's Department.*

Jimmie continued to perform at the Playboy Clubs, and because of his growing following, he was finally invited to work at the resorts (where we're betting he finally got some Bunnies to talk to him). In 1974, he scored the iconic role of J. J. Evans on *Good Times,* which led to movie roles in such films as *Airplane!* and *Let's Do It Again,* with Sidney Poitier and Bill Cosby. Jimmie remained a TV fixture for years, making regular appearances on *Love Boat* and *Fantasy Island.*

Shelley Berman autographing a Bunnies cuff: Courtesy Shelley Berman

Today, his main love is still his first love—standup. After nearly five decades, he continues to work an average of forty weeks a year, keeping audiences in stitches in Vegas and around the country in between writing books and movie scripts.

You might say he's still dyn-o-mite.

* * *

At this point, you might be under the misapprehension that Playboy's comedy offerings were all fairly traditional. Not exactly true. There was at least one ventro-impressionist: Gary Willner. What is a ventro-impressionist, you ask? As Gary explained it, it's a cross between a ventriloquist and an impersonator. He was about five when he saw the great Paul Winchell on TV and became obsessed with ventriloquism.

"Later on, Paul became my friend," he told us, "and really helped me. He was brilliant! Did you know that he invented the Jarvik-7 artificial heart and the disposable lighter? And he loved show business."

Turning to the development of his own skills, Gary went on, "At the start, when I was about five or six, I had the little Jerry Mahoney dummies, and as I got older I taught myself how to do it, because there were no teachers at the time. There weren't even mail-order courses, so I really had to figure it out myself, and that took a long time. When I was fifteen, I wrote Paul Winchell a letter and I guess he found it interesting enough that he wrote back. One thing led to another and he gave me his phone number. He ended up being an inspiration and tremendous help to me with his advice and guidance. Paul was an unusual guy in every respect, from his massive talent to his personality and generosity. He was the first to tell me,

"'You have to have your basics down, and one of the basics is being able to have lip control, so that when the puppet talks or sings, nobody sees your mouth move.' So I practiced every day to get that down just right."

As talented a ventriloquist as Gary was, his show business debut wasn't as a puppeteer but as a jazz and big band singer with the Tommy Dorsey Orchestra and Sammy Kaye.

"They are as far apart as you can get, the music and comedy worlds," he told us. "I loved them both." But it was the puppets that pulled hardest at Gary's heart. He had always done impressions of famous singers and gradually moved from hand-held puppets to life-size models that resembled celebrities. Audience favorites were Frank Sinatra, Nat King Cole, and Elvis Presley.

"That's what put me on the map and got me on *The Tonight Show*. It was 1992 and Jay Leno had taken over from Johnny. He was looking for something different to put on the show. My agents submitted a video of my act and it was completely different from what he usually saw." From the exposure Gary received on that single show, he landed a two-year contract at a Trump Casino in Atlantic City. "I started the show with the smaller, hand-held puppets and closed with the life-size ones. Of course the larger models are harder to schlep around, but the payoff is so much greater."

Gary opened for most of the big names of the day, including Joan Rivers. "One of the items in Joan's contract, when I worked with her, was that she wanted palm trees on either side of the stage and a big band to play her on and off. She came on stage and exited to 'Anchors Aweigh.' The first time we worked together, I hadn't actually been formally introduced to her yet. I was downstairs in my dressing room getting ready and there was a knock on my door.

"It was Joan and she said, 'Are you ready?'

"I said, 'Almost.' Now remember, I had never met her, and you never know what the headliners are really like. So I introduced myself and finished tying my tie.

"And she seemed genuinely interested in me, asking, 'Where are you from? Da-da-da-da.' She couldn't have been nicer. Sweet like you wouldn't believe. There was a long hall to go down to the elevator to take us up to the showroom level. As we walked she took my hand and started skipping—we were skipping down the hallway!

"She told me, 'You never want to keep the audience waiting.'

"As an opening act, you are told *exactly* how long to be on stage—it's usually twenty-five minutes. As I came off, Joan's stage manager, Dorothy, told me,

"'You were terrific, but you only did twenty-three minutes. Tomorrow, you're going to give me the extra two minutes, right?'

"I worked with Joan many times after that, and it was always a pleasure. She was unusual in that she was always nice and very down to earth."

Gary worked many of the great joints around the country but Great Gorge was one he really made an effort to break into. He was a New York guy, after all, so it was close to home—and of course there were other attractions as well, such as the Bunnies!

"It took me a long time to get in there. Great Gorge had its own head of entertainment, and because I lived close, I'd go there periodically and try to sell myself to this guy, Steve. It took me a long time just to get a meeting with him. At that time, he was dealing mainly with agents he knew and putting their acts into the club. I'd get there, only to be told, 'He's busy, come back next week.'

"I was on the road, opening for a lot of great people, so I couldn't always be on his doorstep, but I persevered. After going back and forth for months, I finally got some face time with Steve, and at first he said, 'I'll think about it.' Finally, it was, 'Okay, I'll give you a date.'

"I did a fabulous job and just killed the audience, so he started to use me on a more regular basis. But it had been harder than getting a job with Joan Rivers, Don Rickles, Debbie Reynolds, or Joel Gray! It was worth it though, because the club was new and gorgeous. The food was fantastic and the girls were stunning—which was a little distracting. I had worked in revues with half naked girls, and after awhile you don't even notice it. *Who am I kidding!!* Of course I noticed, and it was wonderful. Top notch all the way!"

In a quirk of fate, sometime later—in 1982, to be exact—Gary was doing a sound check at Kushner's Hotel in the Catskills when someone approached him. "The guy looked familiar, but I couldn't put my finger on exactly who he was. I never forget a face but I'm bad with names.

"And when he said, 'Hi, I'm Steve, I'm your sound manager,' I asked him where I knew him from. He said, 'You used to work for me at the Playboy Club.' I remembered how many hoops he'd made me jump through and it gave me a small bit of satisfaction that he was now working lights and sound for me—because he'd really made my life miserable."

* * *

In our previous book, *Playboy Swings*, long-time Playboy staffer Jerry Pawlak waltzed us through the escapades of many of the musical entertainers. Now, he's back with a few choice tales of the comedians he encountered during his tenure at the Lake Geneva Club. As Victor Lownes described him, 'Jerry was a grace-under-pressure kind of guy.' Having worked his way through the ranks, he experienced and saw a lot. In his eight years at the resort, Jerry did a number of jobs, finally snagging a sought-after appointment as

Jerry Pawlak pouring wine and trying to coax a smile from Bob Hope: Courtesy of Jerry Pawlak

maître d' in the blue-velvet-draped VIP dining room.

"It was quite an opportunity to get a job there," Jerry pointed out, "and a chance to work my way up from the ground floor. I started as a bartender and it was my good fortune to have been working the night that the maître d' of the VIP room fired a captain. He looked around and asked the rest of us,

"'Who wants to be captain?' I couldn't say yes fast enough! That was my first promotion. Many people have asked me how to get a job like mine, and I tell them that the trick isn't to get it but to *keep* it.

"As I gained experience, I was eventually put in charge of arranging the entertainment and reservations for all the big names. We constantly had great entertainers coming through. You've heard me talk about Ann-Margret, Vic Damone, Jack Jones, and many, many others, and the comedians were some of the best. I worked with George Kirby, Corbett Monica, Norm Crosby, Joan Rivers, George Carlin, Woody Woodbury, and Freddie Prinze—and that's just off the top of my head."

Jerry Pawlak and Frank Gorshin look like they're planning some mischief: Courtesy Jerry Pawlak

Jerry realized that because of his short stature, he needed to come up with his own way of projecting a sense of authority. .

"I had to walk through the showroom, check the reservations, make sure the tables were laid out correctly, and guide the staff in the prescribed Playboy fashion. I started copying the strut of people who I thought had a macho, no-nonsense walk. I tried John Wayne's, but couldn't carry that one off. Then came Cagney and Bogart, but I just looked like a B-movie gangster. Finally, we had the great Bob Hope out to Lake Geneva to perform, and it just came together. He possessed straight posture, controlled arm movement, and had a very purposeful gait. And I could carry it off! Walking like Hope gave me confidence."

Others have told us that the comedians were not funny off stage. Julie Budd called them "peculiar." But Jerry forged close friendships with many of them. Frank Gorshin, for example, enjoyed goofing around with Jerry whenever he visited the Wisconsin club.

"Frank was probably the best act I ever saw," Jerry said. "He sang, he danced, and he did this crazy thing where he played around with the lights. They'd go dark and then come up and hit him and he'd twist his face—you'd swear you were seeing James Dean. A minute later, he was Edward G. Robinson. He was a remarkably talented guy and we became great friends; we had the same sense of humor and liked many of the same activities. One year, Frank was performing at the Academy Awards and since his wife didn't want to make the trip from Pennsylvania, he asked me if I wanted to go. I didn't go! You always think these opportunities will come around again, but we lose so many of them. I told Frank I'd go the following year, just assuming that he might go again and invite me. Or that somebody else would. But no one ever did!"

We're going to take a little detour here, for a Frank Gorshin story we can't wait to tell. Researcher Richard Halke grew up listening to stories about the antics of working at the Playboy Club from both his father and his grandmother Bea. Bea was on the kitchen staff, and used to reminisce about Frank Gorshin a lot. One incident in particular is embedded in Rich's memory.

"Frank walked into the kitchen after they closed one night, walked up to Bea, and asked, 'Can I get a little coffee?'

"Bea told him, 'The kitchen's closed.'

"He said, 'Aw, please?' and made such a pitiful face that she couldn't refuse.

"'Okay, I'll get it for ya,' she said.

"He pushed even more and asked, 'Can you add some cake or donuts with that?'

"'I'll see what I can do,' she said. She went off and got the stuff, came back and set him up, and as he was drinking his coffee and eating his cake, she said,

"'I understand you're on that Batman show. My grandkids *love* that show! They love the Batman'—that's what she called him, *the Batman.* She said, 'Would you please give me an autograph so I can bring it home for the kids?' And Frank had the gall to say,

"'Oh, I don't do autographs,' all grumpy. 'I know, but we're alone here, and it's for the little kids!' she said.

"'I told you I don't do autographs!'

"She couldn't help herself. 'Well, I don't give coffee and cake either,' she shouted into his face, and she swiped them back.' But here's the really funny part—and you have to visualize Frank with my Brooklyn-born grandmother. He looked at her in surprise, *thumbed his nose,* and said, 'Well, this is for your mother!' So she gave him the thumb back, 'Yeah? This is for your grandmother!' And they went back and forth like that for a short time, just having a ball. He ended up with his cake (maybe even a second piece) and she got her autographs—one of which was for me."

Back to Jerry, and his adventures booking and managing the comics, one of whom was Corbett Monica. "Really, there was no pattern," he pointed out. "The comedians were very different from one another and all just amazing. Anyway, at the end of Corbett's show, he'd tell the crowd, 'I'm traveling with my young daughter. She's so cute and so concerned about me that the first thing she asks when I get back to the room is going to be, "Did you get a standing ovation, Daddy?" 'And I hate to disappoint her.' So of course, the audience gets up and starts clapping so he can leave and get back to his little girl with good news. It was a clever bit."

Not all the comedians liked and befriended Jerry. George Carlin was just hitting his stride and pushing the boundaries of standup when he was booked to perform for the conservative Wisconsin crowd at the Playboy resort.

"He was almost thrown out of town, not just the Resort," Jerry told us. "I admit, I wasn't paying that much attention to his act, but I did catch a few remarks about the Vietnam War that didn't go over well with the patrons. I turned around just in time to see him flip off the audience and leave the stage. I had to comp the entire room for their dinner and lack of a show—forty people! I did tell them that I felt confident he would never play another Playboy stage, and Hef agreed. He was all for free speech but he was a savvy businessman, and he knew that if he wanted to attract families to the Resort—which was his goal—that type of behavior couldn't be tolerated.

Professor Irwin Corey was unorthodox and unpredictable in his own way, but he managed to stay just inside the lines.

"One night, Irwin came to me, wearing his tuxedo and goofy sneakers," Jerry remembered, "and asked if he could work the door. I said, 'Well, Professor, this is my bread and butter.'

"He replied, 'No, no, no, I insist. I'll work the door.' So what could I do, but let him work the darn door? It wasn't long before he was in full character, and I heard him say to one man, 'Five dollars? What do you think five dollars will get you?' Soon, I saw a few of my good, regular customers heading in, and thought, 'It's time for me to take over. Just as I got there, I heard Irwin say to them, 'So, what's with Florida? Why does it have to stick out so far? They should cut it off and shove it up the Mississippi!' He was a smart, clever, adroit man, who enjoyed seeing just how far he could push his limits—but I got there just in time!

"I liked Freddie Prinze a lot, and we'd hang out together after the shows. He did what is referred to now as *observational comedy*. Whenever he talked about everyday situations, I couldn't stop laughing, and I'm talking about off stage. I never knew he had any problems. We lost him way too early.

"It's a lot of stress running a showroom. Many of the entertainers had particular needs in their contracts that I had to make sure were carried out. Some stated, 'No serving during their performance.' Vic Damone only wanted pretty girls seated ringside because he said he couldn't sing love songs to fat guys smoking cigars. So everyone was always on edge, and on opening nights I'd have a staff meeting to go over everything. I'd go on stage—using my best Bob Hope stride—and hold a meeting with the Bunnies, which was about twenty girls; ten would serve food and ten cocktails. And I'd say, 'Does anyone want to see my banana?' They'd all boo and laugh, but it was my traditional ice-breaker. Today I'd probably be taken to court, after they fired me, but then it was just a method to release everyone's fears about the new headliner. For my fortieth birthday, the Bunnies gave me a bushel of forty bananas, just for fun.

"Whenever Jerry Van Dyke did a show here—he was great—we'd hang out. One time I took him into downtown Lake Geneva, to a bar, to play gin rummy. Well, it so happens, that I play rummy a lot and just the day before, the owner of the bar had beaten me at the game pretty nicely. As Jerry and I pulled up, he looked at the marquee and it said, 'Jerry's Number Two!' This was referring to me—because I had come in second—but Jerry thought I had the sign put up to slight *him.* As we walked up the stairs, he kept saying, 'That's not very funny.' It wasn't until we were inside and the bar owner told him the same thing that he believed me."

When Hef purchased the Playboy jet, which he christened the Big Bunny, Jerry was picked to work on it. "I was so excited," he told us. "They picked me of *all* the people, in *all* the clubs. It was an honor—a big deal." Jerry would finally have the opportunity to travel all over the world! He was crushed when he was called into Chicago headquarters and told that he wasn't getting the job after all. One person on the team had vetoed him. "I asked who turned me down, and was told Hef did. He'd decided he only wanted two men on the plane, himself and the pilot. I'm sure if he could've found a female pilot, there'd just be *one* man—him!

"Billy Falbo was a comic from Chicago and an excellent opening act. I had stanchion ropes as a guide for where people were supposed to line up for the show. About halfway through his show, Billy would always yell out to me from the stage,

"'Hey Jerry, why do you have those ropes across the front of the door? How do you expect people to get in?'

"And I'd shout back, 'You have it wrong, Billy, I put them up so your audience can't escape until the end of the show.' We did that back-and-forth, plus other gags, and the audience got a kick out of it. Simple things like that were funny in the sixties and seventies—it was a less complicated time. Billy used to bring hot goods from Chicago with him and the Bunnies couldn't wait for him to come. He'd bring TVs and mink coats with the labels cut out. He'd price them really cheap and the girls would load up. One night, about ten-thirty, I received a call from one of the girls saying,

"'Jerry, I just bought a mink from Billy and I'd like to show it to you.'

"'Well, come on over, I'd like to see it,' I told her. As soon as I hung up, it hit me—uh-oh—mink coat and high heels. I'm in trouble! Those years were a lot of fun."

Minsky's Follies was an old-time burlesque revue replete with statuesque beauties. When Irvin Arthur booked it into the Miami Playboy Club, it was an unprecedented success and ran for a record-breaking eighty weeks. Hoping to replicate the phenomenon, he took the show on a tour that was to end up at the Hollywood Palladium. One of the stops along the route was at the Lake Geneva Playboy Club. Not surprisingly, one of the showgirls caught Jerry's eye.

"I was dating one of the girls—I know, I know, I wasn't supposed to, but nevertheless—and one morning, she said to me,

"'Jerry, I've never caught a fish.'

"I said, 'It's Lake Geneva, I'll take you fishing, and can guarantee you'll catch a fish. I took her to a spot called Rushing Waters Trout Farms—a likely place to rope a fish, right? I knew that would make her happy. It wasn't long before she was catching one trout after another. After a while, I was getting concerned about the amount of money this was costing me, because you had to pay per fish. Granted, they also cleaned them for you, but it adds up. She caught ten fish! It was an expensive date, but she was so excited, and we took them back to the Playboy kitchen and the VIP chef created what he named Trout Bouile, and we fed the entire Minsky's crew."

Top: Jerry Pawlak with Woody Woodbury: Courtesy of Jerry Pawlak

Middle: Freddie Prinze and Jerry Pawlak: Courtesy Jerry Pawlak

Bottom: Henny Youngman and Jerry Pawlak: Courtesy Jerry Pawlak

The Hollywood Palladium would prove an unfortunate choice for *Minsky's Follies.* Burlesque depends on being able to see the gags, and it was cavernous. Anyone unfortunate enough to be seated at the back of the house needed binoculars to differentiate between luscious strippers and barrel-wearing clowns. It was an expensive miscalculation that resulted in Irvin's departure from the company, and a setback for Playboy's live-entertainment division.

* * *

Leo Anthony Gallagher, best known as Gallagher, was one of the most popular American comedians during the eighties. He made several appearances at the Playboy Clubs but the one at the beautiful Lake Geneva resort is especially memorable to him. It was New Year's Eve in 1979, and he was scheduled to go on before the always impeccably attired singer, Vic Damone. If you are familiar with Gallagher's act, perhaps you already see where this is going. The comedian was best known for his "Sledge-O-Matic" routine, in which he took a large mallet and bashed a smorgasbord of food items, climaxing with the demolition of a large watermelon. The audience was advised about the peril of sitting in the first few rows!

German dancer and actress Laye Raki and actress Viviane Ventura cause quite a stir when they visit the Playboy Club on a girls night out: The Curtiss Family Archives

On that night, Gallagher wanted the audience to have "a midnight smash to remember." As Mr. Damone was waiting in the wings to go on,

Gallagher swung his hammer with predictable results. Watermelon flew everywhere, including all over Vic's custom-made, Savile Row suit.

"The audience had to wait while Vic went back to his room to change, and that took awhile," Gallagher told us. "He was fuming! I believe a comedian is supposed to shake things up, present the unexpected and violate the traditional. Just as the Marx Brothers did with Margaret Dumont, you have to find some conceited, self-important person to smack in the butt, and Vic Damone turned out to be a great foil for that."

Vic may have smoldered at having to change his attire that night, but he told us that he, too, really enjoyed playing the clubs.

"The musicians were great," he said, "and Hugh Hefner was a super guy."

One of Prince Merid Beyene's first stops, on his visit from Ethiopia, was the Playboy Club: The Curtiss Family Collection

Best dressed Lee Radziwill and Russian dancer Rudolf Nureyev hit the Playboy Club on a night on the town: The Curtiss Family Collection

* * *

While attending Marion High School in Chicago, Ken Sevara would hang around the bleachers before gym class, mugging for his friends and doing impressions of distinctive celebrities.

"It was mainly just to pass the time and amuse myself," Ken told us, "but soon kids were coming early to see my 'show.'"

It wasn't long before his classmate, Jim O'Brian, followed his lead and began entertaining the gang as well. The two wise guys developed a friendly competition and the inevitable occurred: They teamed up.

"An older kid saw our shenanigans, and liked what he saw," said Ken. That kid—Tom Dreesen—would eventually become a highly successful comic and work with Frank Sinatra, as you already know.

"Tom ended up mentoring and managing us," Ken continued. "He told us we had guts. He took us over and taught us everything he knew about the business."

As Tom recalled it, "I managed Obie (O'Brian) and Kenny, and they would come to my house and do impressions of everybody. They were insanely on target. The first time I got them a job at a Playboy Club, they were nineteen. Playboy didn't pay anybody a lot of money. If you were good, it was steady work, but you had to be smart with money. I grew up very differently from these guys and definitely more street smart. When they were getting ready to hit the road for the first time, Ken called me to ask how much underwear he should pack. I kid you not! I had to remember that this was probably the first time his mother didn't pack his suitcase for him.

"They were both very young and inexperienced, but they were going to work the Playboy Club, which, at that time, was very glamorous and hip. In each town, there was a hotel where the entertainers got a good rate, and I told the guys this. So they got there and called me from the hotel:

"'Tom, we might have made a mistake here.' What did they do? They found the *best* hotel and checked into a *suite*. That's how naïve they were. The suite cost more for one day than they were getting paid for the week!

"'Kenny, what the hell is wrong with you guys?' I yelled into the phone.

"'Tom, hold on a second,' he said. 'Room service is here!'"

The Playboy circuit was great for honing one's craft, but it also offered some genuine life lessons. While many of the entertainers were veterans, some, like Kenny and Obie, were kids, and they did a lot of growing up out there. The Bunnies were a big help, and we don't mean that the way you think. They were genuinely helpful and ready with…sisterly (?)...advice about how to behave.

Ken and Jim were working the college circuit when Tom introduced them to Playboy. "Sam DiStefano was the entertainment director when we were there and a really good guy," Ken told us.

"We were so young that we'd be in one of the Playboy Club kitchens, or another place in the club, and more than one Bunny would come up to us, saying,

"'You can't be in here without your parents.'

"We'd say, 'You don't understand, we're your headliners this evening!'"

Many comedians told us that they'd been attracted to comedy as a means of escape—a way to get out of troubled situations or a life of pain. Ken was an exception. He had a warm, supportive family and a happy childhood. He planned on being a musician, and the day he informed his parents that he was quitting music, he could see a "Thank God" look in his father's eyes, which quickly turned to panic when it was followed by, "I'm going into comedy."

"I think he wanted to put a gun in his mouth," Ken said, "but in the end, he was very supportive. The first time we did Las Vegas, my dad was grabbing people in the lobby saying, 'That's my kid's name up there!' He was awesome. He'd knock on my door at seven in the morning, 'You've got to come out here. Your name is on the marquee. The letters are two feet high!' He was so proud. It gave me extra pleasure that I could do that for my mom and dad."

When Ken worked the Chicago Playboy Club, his parents would come to watch the show and enjoy the food. "They were so proud that we made our mark in our home town. Speaking of food reminds me of a funny story. When you worked the Clubs you were entitled to dinner. I love lobster, so every night I ordered it. One evening the manager came up to me and said,

"'Even I don't order the lobster!'

"I said, 'You ought to, it's delicious!' I'm surprised we lasted. We were just little kids. We were the second-youngest act ever to play Playboy at that point. Alan Bursky was the youngest."

Ken and Jim were booked to play the Atlanta Playboy Club when it caught fire—twice—delaying their engagement. It seemed a bit suspicious to them, actually, but the third time, it was the performers who were on fire, not the premises.

The duo eventually became consummate professionals, and they admit that Playboy had a lot to do with it. "That was one of the great things about working the circuit. They worked you to death—so many shows a day—that you learned. Once, when we worked the Baltimore Club, the room manager called us and before he even said *hello*, he said, 'I took a chance on you kids, and you better be funny.' It was the kind of cartoon conversation where you put the phone down but it keeps moving. So that night we walked out and there was an older singer on stage, doing her closing song to an all black audience. This threw us a little, because we had never worked a completely black crowd, but that was it. The singer was closing with "Bye, Bye Blackbird," and encouraging audience participation. Now, we had to keep that crowd and I was nervous. I told Jim, 'Just walk on stage shaking your head in disgust.'

"So, we were introduced and we both took the stage shaking our heads as if we couldn't believe what we had just heard—which was great—but really, "Bye, bye Blackbird?" The crowd got the joke and they roared! We found out that they were a group from Chicago, which is where we were from, and by the time we were done they were treating us as friends. 'Man, you've got to come over to our house and visit when you get back.' Things like that, we had them in the palm of our hands. My God, they were a ridiculously awesome audience. And that is what you have to do if you want to be successful as a comic. You have to think on your feet and be flexible.

"The Playboy Clubs—and each one was the same—were run like clockwork. When you came to town, you were expected to do PR to advertise the show. As long as you were on time, it was great. We got chauffeured around to the appointments in a limousine, and basically treated like a million dollars. It was a wonderful place to entertain people, and you always felt that you were in the hippest place in town. The Bunnies were decked out beautifully, and everything ran perfectly."

To sum up what Playboy meant to the comedians, we called on Bill Marx for help.

"There are a few reasons," he said, "that ambitious comedians went after Playboy. Of course, it was great exposure, but the good ones flourished because they *were* good. The Playboy circuit was so large, you could work steadily without wiping out your material; the folks in the Denver club hadn't yet heard your act from Phoenix, and so on. TV was wonderful for exposing you to a large, large audience, but your material was dead after that one show because everyone had heard it.

"The club circuit also gave comedians a feel for what was funny in different parts of the country. Just like the vaudevillians, who knew that different locations called for different jokes, the comedians on the circuit got a feel for that. That tutelage was priceless for any performer. Yul Brynner summed it up perfectly: When someone asked him, 'How do you keep it fresh, having done more than 7,500 performances of *The King and I*?' he said, 'It's simple. The cast and crew go off during the day and do whatever they have to do, and when we come back, it's a different chemistry and a different vibe, even though the lines are the same. That, plus there's a new audience every night.'

Bill continued, "It's that fourth wall that creates a life to the material, and that's where I think the Playboy circuit was so helpful. I can guarantee you that the Playboy Club on Sunset Boulevard in Los Angeles was quite different from even the one in Chicago. And that was priceless experience for an entertainer."

Playboy continued to build on that diverse demographic, opening clubs and showcasing comedy in most major—and some minor—cities countrywide and across the globe.

5

LEADERS OF THE PACK

"I had this weird dream that I was in hell, and I was making love to the ugliest woman in the world. She was so ugly—she was even ugly from the back. I look over and there's the devil, so I say, 'What did I do to deserve this?' and he says, 'Jackie, you're on my shit list!' And then I look next to me, and there's Jackie Vernon making love to Bo Derek. And so I ask… 'Jackie Vernon with Bo Derek? What gives?' and the devil says, 'Yeah, she's on my shit list too!'" –JACKIE GAYLE

When Jackie Gayle (née Jack Potovsky) died in 2002 at age seventy-six, the *Los Angeles Times* described him as "the veteran second banana." That just proves that the number-one newspaper in the movie capital of the world doesn't know *bupkis* about show business. Jackie Gayle was anything but a "second banana"; in fact, he was the very definition of a headliner. Jackie performed standup in every major club you can think of and opened for Tony Bennett and Frank Sinatra, among many others.

As Jackie put it, "For two years I was lucky enough to work with Frank Sinatra—he actually took me to Hoboken to show me the manger where he was born." (Rim shot.)

Jackie also played two unforgettable roles in two unforgettable 1980s movies: *Tin Men* and Woody Allen's *Broadway Danny Rose*. By casting him in that classic showbiz comedy, Allen effectively anointed Jackie as the archetypal standup man. Good choice. If there's one comedian who epitomizes the entire Playboy Club experience, it's Jackie Gayle.

Pat Lacy, who started as a Bunny at the Los Angeles club and eventually became one of the supreme Bunny Mothers, remembered that Jackie was very well-liked by the Bunnies in general.

"Jackie would say that when one of us was finished with her Bunny years, Playboy would retire her and send her off to a 'Bunny Ranch.'" Pat took pains to explain that he didn't mean anything like the Best Little Chicken Ranch in Texas (or Nevada); he meant a lovely home for retired Bunnies, "where they would be treated in the evenings to slide shows of big tippers.

"I mean, that's funny!" Pat effused, laughing as she recalled it. "I remember one night, Jackie was working in the Penthouse. In the middle of the week, the late show was never as full as the earlier shows. Even so, we Bunnies weren't allowed to sit down. We'd 'perch.' So, that night, I kind of perched on the back of a chair and put my feet up on the lower part of another one. I was just sitting in the corner holding my tray, and Jackie was on stage. He started doing an impersonation of Jimmy Durante, who he said always reminded him of a windshield wiper. I thought that was so hysterical that I started laughing and my feet went up, my tray fell on the ground, and I made the biggest noise: *Clack clack clack thomp!*

"Jackie just said something like, 'Could somebody please make sure that Bunny pays her cover charge?' He never skipped a beat! We were always happy whenever we heard that Jackie was coming back."

Jackie was such a fixture on the Playboy Club circuit that he was allowed to weigh in on who his accompanying acts would be. Around 1969-70, Jackie grew partial to a young, still unknown singer named Al Jarreau, who was then working with guitarist Julio Martinez.

Al and Julio had played dozens of smaller clubs, mostly up and down the west coast, when they had the good fortune to land a gig in a spot called Dino's Lodge, right next door to the Los Angeles Playboy Club. One night, the twosome went over to the Playboy to see Jackie work, and were surprised to discover that he had already checked *them* out. He wanted them to come work with him that May, for four weeks.

Jackie was equally generous to his fellow comedians.

"Jackie Gayle was *the* star of the Playboy Club," said comic John Regis. "We were very close—we even shared a house for five years."

John knew Jackie through Sally Marr and Lenny Bruce, and had been trying to crack the Playboy circuit for years when Jackie intervened on his behalf.

As John remembered it, "Jackie called Billy Rizzo [the Playboy booker] and said, 'Give John Regis some work.'

"And Billy said, 'Who's John Regis?' A perfectly natural reaction.

"So Jackie said, 'Look, tell you what. Give him six weeks, two weeks each at three different clubs. And give him some decent money. If he doesn't cut it, I'll come in and finish the job for him at his money.' And he was making $1500 a week at the time! So it was a no-lose situation for Billy.

"He called me and said 'John, I hear you're doing well…' Like it was his idea. He didn't want to admit that Jackie had told him to hire me, so he hemmed and hawed around and said, 'Well, listen, I can give you six weeks as a tryout. You'll start in Baltimore and you'll go from there to Kansas City, and Kansas City to St. Louis.' And I said okay, of course. But Jackie? He was like a brother to me!"

More than one person remembered Jackie that way. Second banana indeed! For the entire length of his long career, Jackie Gayle was never anything less than top drawer.

Tommy Moore, a borscht belt-style comedian and Playboy

regular in his own right, shared his unique perspective on Jackie.

"I was a young comic, traveling from Philly to New York weekly on the train to work at the showcase rooms. One night, another comic and friend, Drinda LaLumia, said,

"'Jackie Gayle is working the Playboy Club. I know him, so after our show let's go over and maybe he can get us in for free.' We went, saw Jackie—who was wonderful—and then he sat with us after the show. When he left, I got stuck with the check—twelve-fifty for each of us. That was twenty-five dollars before the tip! I only had twenty-eight to my name. Luckily I had prepaid my return train ticket but I still needed two bucks for the subway once I got to Philly. So I left twenty-six and was ashamed of the one-dollar tip. I ran out of the club, and on the train ride home I looked at the check, which I'd kept for tax purposes, and saw Jackie's autograph. Why would he autograph it, I wondered? Then I realized... he had *signed* for it, and no one had told me. I had left a twenty-six-dollar tip! Years later, I met Jackie for lunch in the cafeteria of the Atlantis in Atlantic City—which was once supposed to be the Playboy Casino—and told him the story. When we were in line for the cashier, he said,

"'I'll get the check, you leave the tip!'"

* * *

"My father wanted me to be a sex maniac, but I couldn't pass the physical." –JOE E. LEWIS

The legendary entertainer Joe E. Lewis (1902-1971) made two of his only surviving television appearances on *Playboy's Penthouse,* first on October 31, 1959, and then, two weeks later, on November 14. He was a showman who played a key role in defining the modern notion of standup, but today, he's best remembered as the spiritual father of the Rat Pack. Not only did Frank Sinatra play him in the 1957 movie biography *The Joker Is Wild,* but his general style, his comic take on life, and many of his specific jokes provided the template for the trio of Sinatra, Dean Martin, and Sammy Davis Jr. Throughout the years, when the three giants worked together, they readily acknowledged that Joe E. was their inspiration and spiritual mentor. In fact, nearly all of the entertainers of the day were influenced by Joe E., who was also a longtime Abbot of the Friars Club.

You youngsters may not be familiar with his work and legacy (we're very happy to change that), but there was a time when Joe E. was easily the most famous nightclub headliner working. When the Rat Pack borrowed his jokes and tag lines—including, "It is now post time!"—they didn't have to give him credit. Everyone in the audience knew who they were quoting.

We had occasion to think about Joe E. Lewis during our final interview with the great cabaret diva Julie Wilson, shortly before her death in 2015. We had asked her about working at the Copacabana in 1946, when she was just twenty-one. She told us she was singing in the chorus at that point, with an occasional solo number, but that the headliner was a "great, great male singer." We racked our brains trying to come up with the name. Was it Perry Como? Dick Haymes? Billy Eckstine? Turns out Julie was referring to Joe E. Lewis.

Thanks to *The Joker is Wild,* we knew he'd started as a singer but had run afoul of some mobsters in Chicago and gotten his face, tongue, and vocal cords brutally slashed. It took Joe E. years to learn to speak again, and his singing voice was never the same. Music's loss was comedy's gain—but music continued to play a key part in his comedy. He specialized in humorous parodies of contemporary hit songs, with the help of his accompanist and lifelong best friend, pianist Austin Mack, played in the movie by Eddie Albert.

Born Joseph Klewan in New York City, Joe started out in vaudeville. One of his early partners was the song-and-dance man Johnny Black (author of the song "Paper Doll," which became a major hit in 1943, years after Johnny's death). As Prohibition gave rise to the modern-day nightclub, Joe E. adapted his musical act for smaller rooms such as Chicago's Green Mill. It was when he announced he was leaving there to work at the New Rendezvous that he got nailed by the mobsters who'd been ordered to kill him. Luckily, they botched the job.

In learning to speak and sing again, Joe E. refashioned himself into an entirely new kind of entertainer, one who communicated in a direct and intimate way with audiences, using songs and inimitable one-liners.

Although Sinatra portrayed the entertainer—who originally worked as Joe Lewis, later adding the "E" to distinguish himself from the heavyweight champion—as a moody loner, he rose steadily to prominence, playing all the major clubs in the country including the Playboy Clubs. He was a key attraction at New York's Copacabana for many years and even worked occasionally on Broadway, appearing in two notable flops, *Right This Way* (1938), and *The Lady Comes Across* (1942). He appeared in the 1942 Universal movie musical *Private Buckaroo*, and made regular appearances on *The Ed Sullivan Show*, but nightclubs remained his bread-and-butter.

While some comedians—Joan Rivers and Kathy Griffin come to mind—have made a specialty of ridiculing celebrities, the only target of Joe E's humor was himself. Essentially, he spent some forty years telling audiences what a lowlife he was and getting laughs at his own expense. Nearly every joke was underpinned by the notion that Joe E. was a lazy, drunken bum. "I drink my gin straight and my scotch horizontal," he quipped. "Whenever someone asks me if I want water with my Scotch, I say I'm thirsty, not dirty." Or, "I'm a degenerate gambler—and not only am I a gambler, I'm not a particularly successful one. I follow horses...and the horses I follow, follow horses." Then there's, "I'm still chasing girls. I don't remember what for, but I'm still chasing them." Although Jewish by birth, Joe E.'s whole act could be viewed as one long Catholic confession.

For forty years, Joe E. wrote most of his own material, but also employed a small stable of gag writers who could supply him with additional one-liners and topical song parodies. He changed up his material endlessly to keep it current, but a few bits became perennials, most famously the moment when he'd pick up a shot glass and toast the crowd by saying, "It is now post time"—a not-so-subtle reference to his twin penchants for drinking and gambling. In 1961, Joe E. recorded his only comedy album, for Sinatra's Reprise Records label, titled, appropriately, *It is Now Post Time*.

Joe E. was married only briefly, to an actress named Martha Stewart, portrayed faithfully in the 1957 film by Mitzi Gaynor. He was close to his brothers, and to their kids and eventual grandchildren, and he treated the members of the Friars Club as his family. Like Milton Berle, he donated time and money to helping the Friars procure the East 55th Street townhouse that became their central "monastery," and he served as their most famous Abbot, eventually succeeded by Sinatra. In 1958, the Friars honored him with one of their famous "roasts," an event that was, thankfully, recorded for posterity.

Art Cohn's 1955 biography, also called *The Joker Is Wild,* ends with Joe E. being told by his doctor that he has two options: He can either go on drinking or go on living. Having spent decades consuming almost a quart of the hard stuff a day, the comedian somehow managed to wean himself from alcohol. Believe it or not, in nearly all of the extant footage of him, including his two *Playboy's Penthouse* appearances, when we see him taking a drink on stage, it's really water.

"I can't see without glasses—but it's *these* glasses, I'm talking about," he'd say, holding the shot glass aloft.

As wonderful as Sinatra is in the movie about him, there's one aspect of Joe E.'s onstage persona that couldn't be replicated, and that is the comedian's inherent joy. He may have been a self-proclaimed "low-life," but that life was clearly precious to him, as were the audiences he made laugh every night.

Neither the mob nor the bottle would make a victim out of Joe E. Lewis. Thanks to his resolve and resilience, he managed to live to sixty-nine, which—considering that he was marked for death in 1927—was remarkable.

* * *

"I always say one thing about a man who drinks: You are never drunk as long as you can lie down on the floor without holding on." –NORM CROSBY

Like a lot of the comedians we spoke to, Boston-born Norm Crosby started life as a normal working Joe. After attending the Massachusetts School of Art, he landed a steady nine-to-five job as an advertising manager for a woman's shoe company. Not surprisingly, that didn't feed his soul; what he really liked was comedy. He started learning the craft by performing on weekends in small local venues, and it wasn't long before he moved up a rung, to entertaining at regional civic events.

Lou Walters, the owner of New York's Latin Quarter, observed Norm at one of those events and booked him to perform at his nightclub. It was there that he started toying with words and meanings—eventually earning the moniker "The Master of Malaprop."

The Latin Quarter was a colossal nightclub with lavishly produced shows that included comedians, showgirls, dancers, even circus acts. Each act was strictly timed, and unknown performers like Norm started out doing ten-minute filler segments. As Norm worked his way up the ladder, Lou and his management team recognized his talent and held him over many times after his original contract had expired. By the end of his eighteen-week engagement at the New York nightspot, he had secured both an agent—the William Morris Agency—and a manager.

William Morris booked Norm to play the Catskills with another rising star—Robert Goulet. Because the two worked well together and hit it off personally, Norm was asked to accompany Bob on his upcoming tour. He went on to work with him for three years,

Norm Crosby and Jerry Pawlak: Courtesy Jerry Pawlak

and by the time he went out on his own, he was firmly ensconced in Las Vegas and a regular on the popular television variety shows of the day.

When we caught up with Norm, he shared his experiences at Playboy with us.

"Let me tell you about the Mansion," he started. "It was fantastic. There was a multitude of gorgeous people and always fabulous food, but the best part of it was the camaraderie and the attitude. The feeling there was just fun. It was a joy to be there and a compliment to be invited. Hef invited me to see the movies and the fights. The place was physically lovely, and Hugh Hefner was the best host in the world! There's no one better. When you walked into that place you felt *wanted*. You were *home*. You could just relax. Hef was in his robe, so there was an immediate sense of comfort.

"I worked the Boston Club and had a good time. I'm from Boston, and the man who ran the club there was an old friend. He asked me to come and do a special holiday show for a few weeks, and we had a ball! That was really a great club. I also remember Great Gorge—wow! What's not to like about that place? It was beautiful. There were different rooms in the clubs—a main room where they put name acts and then the smaller rooms upstairs or downstairs where they had music or lesser-known performers—and it was nice, because everyone got a chance to meet and get to know each other. You had people who were already established hanging around with new young kids looking for the opportunity to be discovered and try new material."

* * *

"I started in Chicago," says veteran funnyman Jerry Van Dyke. "I worked at the Chicago Club until they began to open more clubs around the country, and then I traveled between the different cities. I opened Miami and New Orleans. I was the first act in there—but I entertained at the Chicago Club the most. I played the banjo and told jokes—did a few sketches where I portrayed different characters—but basically, I was your regular old standup comic. I had an act from high school, so I guess you could say that I'd been at it awhile.

"In my day, you had to have a perfected act and a recognizable name to get booked into a hotel showroom or one of the few big-bang nightclubs around. There weren't any places, other than the small little joints, for comics trying to break into the business—places where you could bomb and get away with it. In the beginning, there were only a few clubs, and Irwin Corey was also around, so I'd see him a lot, coming and going, and he was *hilarious*! He was one of the funniest—really offbeat. I'll never forget when we first saw him. We loved him.

"Playboy was fantastic for the entertainment industry. They had really nice, well-run places. They even had a sign that said, 'No talking during the show.' That was unheard of. It was a big break for me—really a miracle—and a big changing point in my career. I was appearing at the Miami Club, and Earl Wilson—who was a major, major, columnist for the *New York Times*—stopped by and did a little blurb on me, and it really helped.

"Earl's column brought me to another level. I was offered my first movie, *The Courtship of Eddie's Father* with Glenn Ford and Shirley Jones. It was while I was at the Chicago club for one of the last times that I was also studying lines for that film. In addition to all that, Carl Reiner saw the Earl Wilson article and asked my brother Dick about me: 'Your brother's a comic, too?' He didn't know that until he read it in the paper, and after that, he put me on the *Dick Van Dyke Show*. My brother didn't put me on the show—Carl did!

"Playboy saved my life. It gave me the opportunity to make a living until I was good enough to be presented with other choices."

Jerry continues to make audiences smile today, most recently on tour in *The Sunshine Boys* with his brother Dick and in a recurring role on the ABC program *The Middle*.

* * *

J.C. Curtiss isn't a household name—even among comedy fans—but we can't understand why. He's been entertaining since he was

Jackie Curtiss and Lana Cantrell clown around as Bill flirts with an attractive Bunny: The Curtiss Family Collection

a baby (in the circus with his parents), and as an adult he's worked in most of the major venues around the world.

Jackie Curtiss held a variety of jobs when he left the Navy, ultimately becoming a big-band singer with Jack Fina, Del Courtney, and Frankie Carle. Then came the fifties and the eclipse of the big bands, and he found himself hungry for work. One thing Jackie had noticed from working the nightclubs was that each club had comedians, "and if they were even close to good, they were working the same club four or five times a year. So right there I said, I'm going to be a comedian! I wrote a comedy act; got a partner—Marc Antone—and we named ourselves Antone and Curtiss. The idea was to learn by doing. With a background in the circus and show business, it probably wasn't as scary for me as maybe someone else."

Antone and Curtiss were an immediate hit. When they opened for the Broadway star Gretchen Wyler, Gretchen and Jackie quickly became good friends, and he helped her punch up the material for her act. (She wasn't the only one to derive the benefit of Jackie's comedic gifts. Over the course of his career, he was often asked by friends and colleagues for writing and editing help.)

The duo moved on with Gretchen to Jack Silverman's International Club in New York, where Ed Sullivan himself checked out the show. Afterwards, an invitation to join Ed and Gretchen for dinner was delivered to Jackie and Antone. Ed told them that he loved their act and wanted to "introduce them to America." That, and have them on his show the following week.

After that very well received show, during which the comedians irreverently parodied the show itself and its host, Ed came back to their dressing room and told them he wanted them back on the following month. He even suggested that Jackie write him into all of their future routines—pretty surprising coming from a man known to be rather prickly.

As a result Marc and Jackie toured the country as "Ed Sullivan's Comedy Discovery Stars," and continued to appear on the TV show often. They began to command fees of more than $100,000 and all was going swimmingly—until Marc suddenly pulled out of the act, citing "family problems." According to Jackie, his partner's wife gave him an ultimatum: *show biz or me.*

Without a partner or a desire to go solo—although the latter would come later—Jackie spent his time recording and writing in Los Angeles. It was while at Goldstar Recording Studio, working on a record for Herb Newman, that Jackie became reacquainted with Bill Tracy, a comic he had previously encountered on his rounds of the clubs. It took a little prodding, but ultimately Jackie saw the wisdom in teaming up with the singer and consummate straight man. They opened at the Tally Ho and, within a few weeks, they were a hit, selling out the club every night.

After working together for a year and a half, the partners signed Bell-Court Artists as their agents. The change in management propelled them up yet another rung on the show-biz ladder: They were now playing top lounges and stages and opening for top-drawer entertainers such as Sarah Vaughan, Bobby Darin, the Nicholas Brothers, and Vic Damone. It was while opening for Vic at the New Chez Paree in Chicago that opportunity knocked yet again. Playboy talent scout Shelly Kasten came by and loved the interplay of Curtiss's antics and Tracy's straight-man charm. He immediately placed them under contract at the top of the Playboy roster.

Shelly himself had a pretty sweet deal. As booking agent for all of the Playboy Clubs—and good friend of Hugh Hefner—he was paid by Playboy and also received a commission from the talent. Curtiss and Tracy had no problem with it, because he set their salary at the top of the scale. Along with Jackie Gayle, they were the highest paid acts on the circuit—though, in their case, the fee had to be split down the middle.

"No one complained about paying Shelly his ten percent because we all made so much more in the long run," Jackie told us. "And we got seen by a lot of people."

Because Hef and Shelly prized the team, Curtiss and Tracy were hired to inaugurate each new club.

"The most prestigious club we opened was the London Playboy Club and Casino—the jewel in the crown," Jackie said, "but all the others were great, too: Kansas City, San Francisco, Cincinnati, Denver, Los Angeles, Montreal, and on and on. Sometimes the circuit lasted forty weeks a year. We had the best set-up, just heavenly, all the Playboy engagements we wanted, and yet we still appeared on many television shows, at choice openings, and made other high-priced appearances."

The waters were not still for long. A long-standing rule for working in the clubs was never to refuse a drink. To do so would be an insult to a paying customer. On more than one occasion, Bill Tracy was bestowed such an honor and was barely able to remember his lines during the second show.

Jackie gave him a year's notice to mend his ways—but during that year, he decided he wanted to go solo in any case. He started practicing solo material while continuing to work with Tracy. By the time the year was up, he had enough material for an entire new one-man act. He officially ended his arrangement with Bill on a Saturday night in Los Angeles and opened at the Denver Club on Monday—at twice the pay, since he no longer had to split it.

Jackie Curtiss delivers Julie Christie to new heights as Bill Tracy cheers them on: The Curtiss Family Collection

Jackie had so many great Playboy Club stories to share that it's difficult to decide which to include.

"The Beatles had just made long hair cool, so all the guys in the business wore it that way, too," he told us. "I didn't go quite as long as they did but I did grow it out. One night at the Penthouse in the Chicago Club, I walked on stage and immediately noticed this bald guy, one table back from ringside. He was obviously drunk and I could tell he'd be a troublemaker. Hecklers are all different but you can deal with them once you access what they're doing. You have the professional hecklers, who are with their girlfriends or business associates or whoever and want to impress them. These, you can handle. But if you get a nutcase, someone who just repeats and repeats the same thing over and over, it's more difficult. Well, this guy started right in, saying, 'Why don't you get a haircut?' I threw back a couple of lines that were funny and people chuckled, but he kept at it. After about the sixteenth 'Why don't you get a haircut?' I had to do something. So I stopped and noticed he was wearing a crucifix, visible because his shirt was open.

"So I said, 'OK, Mr. Why-Don't-You-Get-a-Haircut, I notice you're wearing a cross. Can I ask you a question?' That cut through all his retorts because I was touching on something about him.

"He said, 'Hey, what's going on, what's it to you?'

"I said, 'Are you a Christian? You must be. I'll make a deal with you. You bring me a picture of a crew-cut Jesus, and I'll let you cut my hair until I'm bald.' Of course, everyone applauded me and booed him, and that was the end of it."

Many performers have told us that the great thing about Playboy was the fact that it was a circuit.

"Shelly Kasten was responsible for most of that structure. It was genius," said Jackie. "If you could prove yourself up to the management's standards, you moved from club to club and honed your material for ten or twelve weeks. You learned the nuances of *different* audiences. The crowds in the South had different expectations from

Bill Tracy fluffing Jackie's tail: The Curtiss Family Collection

those in the Midwest or New York or the West Coast. For example, in the South, it was important to take your time, while in New York audiences expected a high-energy, edgier, and faster show.

"The London Club was great. Victor Lownes ran it—and ran it well—but they got a little resistance from people who thought of it as an invasion of naked girls and the magazine. Some of the press gave them a hard time, but I like to think that Bill Tracy and I helped turn those assumptions around. We opened the club and the press covered it and wrote—and I'm paraphrasing here—'You know, it's worth going to the club to see the cabaret. There's an American comedy team well worth seeing.' That little blurb changed a lot of people's minds and

Lee Marvin and James Garner relax after a day of filming, as Bunny Dolly Madison, makes sure all is well: The Curtiss Family Collection

Ursula Andress tries her hand at cards while Jon-Paul Belmondo looks on: The Curtiss Family Collection

gave them the courage to check it out for themselves. It was a star-studded night. The whole cast from *The Dirty Dozen* came because they were in town filming."

"I guess by now you can tell I'm a little irreverent. Once, right before the show, someone from management came backstage and said, 'There's an Arab Sheik out front and we know that in some of your shows you mention that you're half Jewish and half American Indian, but maybe you should eliminate mentioning you're Jewish. Well...you don't go to a comic and tell him what NOT to say! So I went out and I was introducing the celebrities in the audience, and I got to the Sheik and said, 'From the Far East we have a wonderful neighbor, his Imperial Highness—and I gave his name—and everyone clapped. I said, 'Sir, would you mind taking a bow?' and he started to stand up and I shouted, 'Open fire!' Luckily, it went over well. The audience fell over laughing and the Sheik laughed and invited me to have a drink with him after the show. It was a different time. We hadn't yet had the international terror situations that were to come. Today, I probably wouldn't push that envelope."

"When I think of the party that night of the London opening, it still seems surreal. I was sitting on big pillows on the floor with Ringo Starr on my left and Sidney Poitier on my right. Sidney liked the tie I was wearing. It was just a clip-on thing so I took it off and gave it to him. It was an incredible party. Thank you, Victor!"

From the start, Jackie was a favorite with the Bunnies, and not just for his jokes. At one time, the Bunnies worked strictly for tips—they didn't get a salary. At the end of some evenings they'd bring home two hundred dollars, which was great money for the time, but other nights—when there were conventions or something—the girls didn't do so well. That's when Jackie really earned the love.

"It started in Chicago," he explained, "when I befriended a German Bunny named Heidi. She was the cutest thing in the world. Many people who came to the shows had no idea the Bunnies had to survive on tips. So I worked the situation into my routine. I'd say something like, 'Coincidentally, folks, you know the Bunnies here don't get a salary. All they get are your tips. So be very careful, especially with Bunny Heidi. If you don't tip her, she's liable to inquire whether you have relatives left in Germany. This went over well, and made it so the girls didn't have to beg for tips."

Irwin Corey may be a master of impressions, but only Jackie can nail Irwin. "One time, we were at the Kansas City club. I was closing and Irwin was coming in. Most of the clubs kept a VIP booth in the back, across from the room director, in case Hef came in, or a policeman, or someone really important. Irwin came in for my closing twenty minutes, waved, nodded, and sat in the VIP booth. So I led with, 'You know folks, Irwin Corey is following me in. He'll be here tomorrow. I think we can agree he's great and really funny but I'm the only person who can do an impression of him, perfectly. And not only can I impersonate him exactly, but I can throw my voice like a ventriloquist. Let me show you.' Of course, Irwin was in the back picking up on where I was heading. So I said, 'The trouble with the world is sex.' And bouncing back came, 'The trouble with the world is sex.' The audience looked at me, stunned. I said, 'Sex is marvelous.' Back came, 'Sex is marvelous.' All this was part of what he does in his routine. So I continued, 'And another thing…' and you heard, 'Yeah, another thing—is that you're full of shit!' Which is a no-no at Playboy, but no one said anything. Irwin then got up and came on stage and we both went on well into the morning. That was one of the great nights for both of us. We were inseparable in Chicago. We'd actually go out to restaurants and pretend to be father and son—with the same voice.

"I love Irwin and loved playing tricks on him. Once, at breakfast, I asked him 'What are you doing after breakfast?'

"'I have to go to the Playboy office and sign contracts,' he said.

"I said, 'OK, see you later.' Then I got up and rushed to the phone, called Billy Rizzo—the booking agent at the time—and when Nancy, his secretary, got on the line, I said, in Irwin's distinctive voice, 'I have to cancel all my dates.'

"So when Irwin showed up to sign his contracts, Nancy said, 'You just cancelled them!'

"He knew right away what I'd done and said, 'I'm going to kill that Jackie Curtiss!' We played jokes on each other all the time."

Bill Tracy was by all accounts a baseball nut. He loved to watch games and Jackie liked to keep him company, whether it was at home watching on TV or at the ballpark. Jackie told us that one day, he and Bill were in Detroit for a Playboy booking and were watching the Cardinals and Tigers on TV. At one point, the batter walked over to confer with the catcher, who then stopped and called "time." Out walked the pitcher and umpire, and it was obvious from their body language—a lot of pointing and waving—that they were discussing something important. We'll let Jackie tell the rest.

"Then the announcer weighed in, saying, 'Well, I don't know what it is but there's some kind of brouhaha going on. We'll have to try and find out later and let you know.' Then they stopped and the umpire walked back to his spot and they went on with the game. We all assumed that whatever the issue was, it got worked out.

"So, that night, four or five of the Cardinals and a few Tigers came in to the club to see the show. We walked over to say hi, and Bill couldn't wait to ask,

"'What the hell happened out on the field today that you had to stop the game?'

"They laughed and said, 'We were talking about you! One of the guys said you were in town at Playboy, so I went out and told the pitcher and the umpire to get a bunch of guys together and we'd come see you. And we were working out who was going and what time.'

"So…the world was watching what we all thought was some argument or rule infraction and they were talking about how to get to the club to see our show!"

We shared a laugh about that one, and then Jackie changed the subject to reveal another treasured memory.

"One thing I'm very proud of from those years is the time I helped persuade Al Jarreau to keep at it; to not give up singing. He was despondent because in the very beginning of his career, he was so unique that the audience didn't know what to make of him. About eight or nine days into this particular engagement, we were sitting together talking and Al said,

"'This isn't for me. I'm quitting.'

"We talked for a long time and I kept drilling into him that he needed to give it time. The audience needed time to get used to his style. They didn't understand a lot of the great stars at first. 'Look at Nat King Cole,' I told him. 'He was playing piano when a patron insisted he sing and from that point on Nat sang but people didn't immediately appreciate it. The same with Frankie Lane.' I went on, 'People evolve, and if you're good, at some point they say, wow, *that's different but good.* I think you have the makings of a unique personality and a star. Don't quit. Please.'

"Years later, Julio Martinez, who was Al's partner at the time, told me, 'You know, you saved Al's life. He was ready to quit but after talking to you, he had a renewed energy. You had faith in him and he respected you.' It's nice to know I helped someone."

Jackie performed in many mob-run venues and, for whatever reason, had the respect and friendship of many of the bosses. At one point, Jackie was struggling both financially and emotionally through a dreadful divorce. He was facing bankruptcy and the prospect of never seeing his children, when he was approached while having lunch at the famous Schwab's Drug Store in L.A.

"I felt a hand on my shoulder. When I turned, I saw it was a familiar face out of Chicago. 'I hear you're having problems, Jackie,' the guy said. 'Word is, your old lady is screwing you with your kids.' I told him he had heard right, that it was bad but that I could handle it. I was sure that I would be able to work it out. He looked me straight in the eyes and asked me, 'Do you want her snuffed?'

"I couldn't believe what I was hearing! I told him I could never do that to the mother of my children.

"'Okay, kid,' he said, 'but if you ever change your mind...' Every once in a while, when things were really bad, I'd succumb to that fantasy. It was nice to know I had options! Only kidding—kind of!"

If you're wondering whether Playboy was among the aforementioned "mob-run" clubs, here's the answer straight from the top. It's true that the mob was a distinct presence in the nightclub business during the peak Playboy years, and it was hard to find any club free of their influence. But we'd heard that Playboy was the exception and wondered how that was possible. When we asked Victor Lownes about it, he definitively explained that at one point Playboy was in fact approached by certain "family members" who hoped to merge their interests with those of Playboy. One meeting with Hef, however, put the kibosh on the whole idea.

"Hef explained to these...individuals...that it was simply not in their best interest to be associated with Playboy, because the clubs were under constant government scrutiny," Victor said. "On top of that, the Church was using every weapon in its arsenal to try and close the clubs down for 'moral reasons.'" It didn't take long for the gangsters to back off permanently.

Back to Jackie, who visited the L.A. Playboy Club every chance he got, even when he wasn't performing there. On one of these visits, during the last half of 1971, he heard they were thinking of closing the Playroom due to tepid attendance. While most of the clubs around the country were thriving, the one in L.A. was a tough nut to crack. There just wasn't as much cache to the Playboy experience in a town where you could spot a celebrity eating a burger at the local diner.

Jackie flew to Chicago and approached Arnie Morton—one of the original Playboy partners—with some ideas about running the Playroom himself. He came complete with a projected budget and the conditions under which he'd agree to take on the task.

"I wanted to run the room more like a nightclub, with the emphasis on the entertainment. I wanted to break out of the

Trini Lopez and Bunny Dolly Madison:
The Curtiss Family Collection

traditional Playboy Club blueprint."

Arnie agreed with his wisdom but only committed to half the budget Jackie requested, and gave him three scant months to exhibit some sort of success. Soon Jackie was booking the room.

"I'd invite stars into the club as guests, with the understanding that I'd introduce them and entice them to sing a song or two. I'd pick up their check and the audience was thrilled to have the experience. We had the Joe Parnello trio at the club, and one night Sammy Davis, Jr., Tony Bennett, Count Basie, and Redd Foxx all came up. Sometimes, I'd invite stars to the stage to talk for a few minutes, even if they weren't performers. Another idea I had was to have an old-fashioned telephone with a speaker on the piano. I'd use it to

The Bunnies line up to greet Lawrence Harvey:
The Curtiss Family Collection

call various performers—of course it was all arranged beforehand. One time, I called Vic Damone in his dressing room after a show in Reno. I told him I was on stage at the Playboy Club with Joe and a room full of people, and asked him if he would be so kind as to sing us a song. Joe, now with our house band, was his former pianist, and that went over big with the audience that night.

"I had opened for so many stars and remained friends with most of them, so I didn't have any problems keeping that going. One of my closest friends was Rosemary Clooney, and at that time her best friend was Bing Crosby. Now I also do great impressions, and I did a really good Bing. So I called Rosie up from the club, pretending to be Bing.

"She said, 'Where are you, Bing?'

"At that point, I had to confess my little trick and she said,

"'Jackie Curtiss, you son of a bitch!'

"I said, 'Rosemary, there's a whole room full of people listening to us! She said, 'I don't give a fuck!' It was all good-natured fun. The Playroom became the place to go because of all these wild things I did. Word got around that it was a happening place." Jackie had the room operating at a break-even point at two-and-a-half months—just weeks away from the three-month deadline—and in the black by the end of the year.

"Another thing I initiated there was a kind of an audition system. I'd set it up with talent agents to get their clients to the club in the afternoon, where they'd rehearse two numbers with Joe, so they'd have it down. That evening, they'd be in the house and I'd say, 'Sitting in our audience is a wonderful singer I met on the Playboy circuit, Ms. Bonnie Jacobs. Bonnie, stand up and take a bow. Hey Bonnie, I know it's an imposition, but would you sing a song for us? Folks, would you like to hear Bonnie?' Of course, she had already practiced so it was a win all around. The audience thought they were getting in on a new talent and the singer had a chance to be seen and get a booking or two.

Jackie was responsible for offering a hand to many entertainers, including Regis Philbin. Regis was working for a local San Diego television show when he met Jackie and Bill Tracy, who were in town working a club. "When we were moving on, I said to Regis, 'If you're ever up North, give me a call and I'll introduce you around.'

Regis soon won the position of sidekick on *The Joey Bishop Show* and he and Jackie renewed their friendship. "What he wanted in the worse way was to be a singer…and he was *in the worst way* a singer! But he was the nicest guy and really pushed me to let him have a shot at the Playboy Club. 'I have arrangements, and people know my name from the Joey Bishop show,' he pleaded. So I put him in for two weeks and, even though he wasn't that good a singer, we had a great time. Plus, he brought in a totally new crowd. Part of breaking the Playboy rules was letting in people who weren't members. You didn't have to have a key to get into my room.

"Redd Foxx was a great friend and entertained at the L.A. Playboy all the time. He'd always thrill the audience. I'll never forget, once he called me over and said he wanted to try out a joke. 'You know they proved Adam was a white man, right? Did you ever try to take a rib from a black man…?' He was so funny.

"I worked at the Thunderbird with the Nicholas Brothers and they became two of my closet friends. One day I got a call from Harold [Nicholas] and he said he'd heard I was opening a room at the Playboy Club and he wanted to come in and play there.

"'Are you kidding?' I said. 'Absolutely!' I put a small four-by-six wooden tap floor on the stage for him to tap on. He stayed for six weeks. You talk about stars and celebrities coming to see him. *Everyone* knew and loved him. Stars told other stars and it became the hangout. Really, because of Harold.

"One unusual stand I took was to only hire male comedians and singers for the club. I figured women had nothing to go to a Playboy Club for. It was obvious why the guys went, but I wanted male entertainment to seduce the gals. I only used two girl singers:

One was a friend and the other was when some guys from the mob came to me and said,

"'You're going to put this girl in for two weeks.'

"I said, 'Absolutely.'"

Jackie completely revamped the Playroom, both financially and in terms of the quality and diversity of the acts. Although his stint at the helm lasted only a year and change—he remembers each of his fifty-five weeks in charge distinctly—his attention to every detail began paying off immediately. Sadly—for Playboy—the room quickly fell back into disrepair when Jackie departed to pursue other challenges. The headline of a local newspaper story printed just two months after he left trumpeted, "Where Is Jackie Curtiss When We Need Him?"

The Playroom would struggle on for years until, in 1977, another business-minded entertainer—Lainie Kazan—took over and again turned things around for Playboy. We discuss the swinging jazz hotspot known as Lainie's Room in detail in *Playboy Swings.*

* * *

How many comedians can follow Groucho Marx and hold their own? Not many, but Shecky Greene is one of them. Where other comics tend to hone and perform their acts in a very deliberate way, Shecky belongs more to the tradition of the late Jonathan Winters and Robin Williams. His work is a high-wire act with an improvisational feel—as if he's making up everything as he goes along and is willing to take any risk for a laugh. In his prime, he was almost like an honorary Marx Brother—perhaps "Shecko Marx."

The first time we saw him live was when he put in an unscheduled appearance at Feinstein's at the Regency in New York City. Keely Smith was performing when Shecky grabbed the mic and started riffing on the singer's Native American heritage.

"I remember that whenever you used to sing, it would rain like a son-of-a-bitch!" he quipped.

Shecky Greene tells us that with all tis ladies he didn't have a date. Hummm, somehow we doubt that: Courtesy Shecky Greene

Shecky began working at Playboy in the early 1970s, and his first stop was the newly opened Great Gorge resort. As we noted earlier, this particular enterprise was predicated on the hope that gambling would soon become legal throughout New Jersey, and Shecky was known for attracting the vast and free-spending gaming crowd. When that happy ending did not materialize (gaming was made legal in Atlantic City only), even the comedic stylings of Shecky Greene couldn't keep Great Gorge from hemorrhaging cash.

Although he ended up playing just about every major venue in the course of his long career, Shecky's home base was Las Vegas. While many performers considered the Vegas casinos a stepping stone to other kinds of work—in movies, TV, on Broadway—Shecky saw it as an end in itself. He liked the spontaneity of working in front of live audiences, in an unstructured setting. And, although others tended to succumb to the many temptations of the desert oasis, Shecky didn't chase girls or abuse his body with dangerous substances. (Perhaps that's why he's in such good shape at age ninety.) He did, however, have one vice: gambling, especially on the horses. So much so that at one point a thoroughbred was named in his honor.

Shecky liked Vegas so much that it was difficult to get him to leave and accept other kinds of work. His most famous acting job was as a semi-regular on the hit dramatic series *Combat.* His character, Private Braddock—no first name that we know of—was easily the most memorable on the show, but Shecky disliked the whole Hollywood scene, and whenever the cameras stopped rolling, all he could think about was getting back to his beloved horses. Clearly, Shecky's most indelible character was himself, and as such, he appeared on a wide range of variety and talk shows over a fifty-year period, most notably *The Ed Sullivan Show* on CBS and Sullivan's chief rival, *The Hollywood Palace,* on ABC.

When we asked Shecky about the rise and rapid fall of Great Gorge, he had a no-nonsense response for us. "People who wanted to go to a Playboy Club went to a Playboy Club," he said. "They didn't want to drive hours out of the city to go to a resort. I think that was a shock to Hef. He was also very surprised that they voted down New Jersey gambling. There were nights when we had probably seventy Bunnies and no customers. It was sad, because it was a gorgeous place, but people just didn't take to it. If New Jersey had legalized gambling throughout the state, that club would have done amazing business. But—they didn't."

The talented songwriter John A. Meyers told of traveling to the Great Gorge Club with the singer Margaret Whiting, with the sole objective of catching Shecky's act. "He was outrageous. He used to wrestle his accompanist to the floor. He always took off-the-wall chances. He was just great. You never knew what to expect. It was well worth the drive to wherever Shecky was appearing. Hugh Hefner had some great taste in entertainment, that's for sure."

Researcher Rich Halke had some wonderful stories of his own to share about the comedians, mostly told to him by his father and grandmother, who worked at the clubs.

"My grandmother Bea *loved* Shecky. She worked as part of the Great Gorge kitchen staff and would deal with a lot of the comics, mainly because they didn't have anywhere to go. Great Gorge was a beautiful resort, away from everything, so when they weren't working, many of them hung around the kitchen. One night, Shecky played a little trick on her. She was trying to move a cart loaded with drinks and coffee and, unbeknownst to her, Shecky started pulling the cart from the other side. She struggled with it, not understanding why she couldn't get it going. Some of the guests saw both sides of it and they were dying with laughter. The cart finally tipped over from her pulling and tugging so hard. Even though Bea claimed he got her into trouble, she loved telling that story. Her hero had played a trick on her!

Today, Shecky says that his show-business days are over—not because he's too old but because the clubs that are still around refuse to pay his requisite fee! Clearly, Hef and Playboy spoiled him. He does love to travel around the country and catch his old buddies' performances. And, once in awhile, he allows himself to be lured up on stage for a few saucy quips. We recently heard that he and his wife Marie left the California desert for a new home in Vegas—and we can't help hoping for a comeback.

* * *

One of comedian Rip Taylor's trademarks is his distinctive voice, which has helped him get numerous gigs doing voices for cartoons. We have fond childhood memories of him as the titular character in *Here Comes the Grump.* His signature rapid-fire delivery of gags, gags, and more gags—along with his use of zany props, costumes, and confetti—has made him a popular staple of variety and talk shows from *Ed Sullivan* to *David Letterman*, as well as game shows including *Hollywood Squares* and *The Dating Game.* It's difficult to imagine how the quintessentially American Rip might have affected audiences at the London Playboy Club, but he quickly filled us in on that.

As he told it, Rip "went native" even before the plane landed; as soon as he set foot on British soil, he almost unconsciously found himself talking with a British accent "so thick that you could eat it." He was liberally peppering his speech with Englishisms such as "teatime" and "cheerio"—phrases that no self-respecting yank would dream of uttering. Apparently, without even intending it, the Washington D.C. boy had turned into Terry Thomas! Fortunately, he had the mustache for it.

"I went nuts!" he told us. "I went to Moss Brothers costume shop and got the morning suit, pinstriped pants, the monocle, the bowler, the whole thing, and I *was* English!"

Rip was scheduled to play the London club for a month and he had never witnessed such a swinging scene in his life. It wasn't just Playboy that was hopping like a bunny; after Rip finished his last show of the night, he'd head back to his hotel and find the streets crowded with revelers. "It was as if the English had finally gotten around to celebrating the Allied Victory in World War II," he told us.

Rip recalled only one moment during his London run when he felt conspicuously alien. In the middle of one of his late sets, a very rowdy, well-lubricated group of "ugly Americans" began heckling him. He realized that the only way he could shut them up was to literally shock them into submission, so he addressed the crowd in his English accent: "Thank yew so much—anyone here from the jolly old colonies?" Of course, the yanks yelled loudly in response. At that point, he shifted back into an American accent, and shouted, "Big *fucking* deal," and then went British again, "Thank*yew*somuch for coming!" At the time, it was still relatively rare for a mainstream comic to drop the "F-bomb"—especially in London. The Americans howled with laughter, nearly falling over in their seats, and they stopped heckling him.

Did Rip have any final memories of his London experience? "Yeah," he said, "it took me forever to lose that accent."

* * *

Impressionist, singer, and comedian Rich Little began his career in his hometown of Ottawa, Canada, and was first inspired to mimic others as he sat in the Elgin Movie Theater as a boy. Completely captivated by the stories that unfolded on the screen, he'd go home and act out entire movies for his parents, complete with distinctive voices for each character.

As he related it, "My mother finally said to her friends, 'We never go to the movies. My son does them for us.' I could imitate most of the stars that were making movies back then."

After winning a local amateur acting contest, Rich went to work as a disc jockey, often incorporating his impressions of politicians and Hollywood stars into his show. One April Fool's Day, he was hired by radio station CFRB in Toronto to do a series of shows, each as a different personality. "I did the news as David Brinkley, a talk show like John Wayne, another as Elvis Presley, women's commentary as Walter Winchell—and it went on for the whole day. I thought it was quite obvious that it was me impersonating them, but just like with Orson Welles's *War of the Worlds*, people believed the real stars were there! They came from all over to the studio exit to try to meet their favorite celebrities! When I came out of the stage door and the station manager made an announcement that it had been me all the time, the crowd was not happy at all. They booed and threw things at me!"

In 1963, Mel Tormé invited Rich to audition for *The Judy Garland Show* and he easily won the gig, paving the way for his debut on American TV. After that, he was off and running, performing on the top TV shows and in clubs around the world—including the Playboy Clubs.

"Miami was my favorite club of them all," Rich said. "The

weather was sunny and that audience was particularly receptive to new material." That was his perception, anyway, until a friend set him straight.

"Oh, I was there last night," the friend told him.

"Did you see my act?" asked Rich.

The friend shook his head and said, "No, I was too busy watching the girls."

By now you are well aware that the Bunnies weren't supposed to date the entertainers. But…it seems that everyone we talked to was an exception to the rule—and Rich was no exception to the exception!

"There were all these Bunnies walking around in tight outfits and little tails, and there was one gorgeous girl who kind of showed an interest in me," he told us. "When you were a celebrity and headlining the show, you got a few perks. But if they found out you were dating a Bunny, you'd never work there again."

Known for being shy, Rich approached the girl slowly, but soon they were talking every night and eventually they did go out. The couple tried to keep their "special friendship" under wraps, even going so far as to insist on separate checks in restaurants—but Rich couldn't resist talking out of turn just a little bit.

"She was terrific," he recalled. "I told my folks and people back home about her, and my dad and uncles must have told people, and pretty soon the whole town was saying, 'Rich is going with a Playboy Bunny'—which I guess was the equivalent of dating a movie star. They were all jealous."

The next thing Rich knew, his girlfriend had staples in her navel: She was a Playboy centerfold! "My dad walked into the barbershop one day and on the mirror was taped her picture.

"The guys were all giggling and laughing, saying, 'Your son must be having a good ol' time at the Playboy Club.' My dad was so bloody embarrassed, it was unbelievable. He told them to take the picture down.

"My mother was worse, calling and saying, 'What the hell is going on?'

"I just kept saying, 'She's a sweet girl!' I didn't know that she'd posed for the magazine. I liked her a lot and didn't give a damn what the barber back home thought. I still have her picture. So... yes, Miami was my favorite club!"

Most of the comedy icons of the last century graced a Playboy Club stage, cracked us up on one of Hef's TV variety shows, or both. Unlike the up-and-comers, these giants didn't need a job or a paycheck (though they certainly enjoyed the latter). They genuinely enjoyed working for Playboy—and why not? It must be clear by now from the stories they told us that at the clubs, they had fun with one another, with the audiences, and, yes, with the Bunnies.

The TV shows offered their own enticements. It took just a day to film an episode; the booze in the glasses was real; it seemed that everyone who was anyone dropped by, and the surroundings (and again, the ladies) were lavish in their appointments.

The roster of high-level talent that passed through Playboy is such that it would be easier to name someone who *didn't* play there (though we can't think who that would be). Whether they were trying out new material, performing their favorite tried-and-true bits, or just riffing with their friends, the stars came out for Hef on a nightly basis.

David Frost and Bunny Dolly Madison:
The Curtiss Family Collection

6

THE PARTY COMES HOME

Comedian Don Adams and friends visit on Playboy After Dark

By 1959, Playboy magazine was a huge success. Having just come off of the triumph of the Playboy Jazz Festival, and in the hope of attracting yet more new subscribers and taking the bold step of branding himself as the face behind the Playboy name, Hef unveiled the TV variety show *Playboy's Penthouse.* As host, Hef first welcomed home viewers to "his pad" on October 24, 1959.

In an article by Bill Ingram, Hef said of his foray into television, "If we did the thing ourselves, and the viewers could meet me as a human being every week, then hopefully they would begin to discover, those people who did not read *Playboy*, well, son of gun, this guy isn't a dirty old man."

Variety shows of the time tended to follow an unwavering format: The host kicked off the proceedings and introduced a succession of guests who sang, told jokes, and perhaps sat on the couch for a few minutes to chat before it was time for the next act. But, as usual, Hef had his own spin on things. He decided to stage his show as a party-in-progress. Although he lived in his Chicago Mansion at the time, he sensed that hip, swinging, and upwardly mobile young bachelors aspired more toward sophisticated urban living. Thus, Hef's "penthouse" was born, and the guests at his weekly parties—including some of the most swinging entertainers around—couldn't wait to perform for Hef and his friends.

Each week, viewers rode the elevator to the thirtieth floor while listening to the jazzy theme song written by composer and songwriter Cy Coleman. When the doors opened, the party—supposedly on the top floor of the Playboy building but in fact on a soundstage in Chicago—was in full swing.

The setting wasn't by any means the most groundbreaking aspect of the show. Hef's provocative practice of mingling the races set off a bombshell in the industry, and is the primary reason the show ran for only two seasons. It may seem astonishing now, but American sponsors, networks, and audiences just weren't prepared, in 1959, to watch Nat King Cole share a sofa and discuss literature with Rona Jaffe.

Hef was similarly bold about broaching touchy political issues and inviting controversial entertainers to visit. To wit, the inaugural show featured the raucous "sick comedian," Lenny Bruce whose outspoken commentary on everything from race relations to religion made him a pariah on TV until Hef invited him to the party.

Words can be a kind of bomb, an explosive device that can hurt more than just your feelings; they can tear you apart. No one knew that better than Lenny Bruce—who would become the most unlikely guest on the most unconventional television show of its day.

The best example of Lenny using words as weapons was related to us by two very sharp cultural observers: Bay Area music critic and commentator Grover Sales, who knew Lenny well; and comedian and social activist Dick Gregory, who'd not yet encountered him at the time of the story they told. According to the two friends, once, around 1960 in San Francisco, they were talking about Lenny, who was in town doing a show. Gregory told Grover that he'd heard of Lenny Bruce, of course—Lenny was becoming a true social phenomenon at the time—but that he had yet to see him. So Sales spontaneously took him to Lenny's show. The set had already started, but even in San Francisco, which was far from the Deep South, the sight of a black man and a white man walking into a nightclub together was bound to attract attention.

Grover said, "Lenny spotted Greg and he stopped the routine and started looking around with that ferret-like, weasel kind of look that he had, kind of darting his eyes back and forth over the audience. Finally, he broke the silence by saying, 'Are there any *niggers* here tonight?'"

We dislike using the word, but Lenny clearly had no such compunction. The audience collectively gasped; no one had ever heard anything like that in a club before. As for Dick, he "stiffened like a retriever," according to Grover.

Lenny continued, "I think I see a nigger over there at the bar, talking to the two guinea owners, and next to them, I see a couple of lace-curtain micks, and there's a couple of spicks over there, and there's a squarehead talking to them and two grease-balls over in the corner... and two sheenies and one jigaboo." He went on like that for a few minutes, cataloging the entire audience using the most offensive racial and ethnic slurs imaginable. Whether from nerves or genuine amusement, the audience began laughing hysterically and didn't stop.

"It was the laughter of liberation," Grover explained.

And then Lenny topped himself. For his finale, he took on the persona of a slave auctioneer from some Civil War movie. Continuing to toss the n-bomb around liberally, he said, "Bid 'em up—two dykes, four kikes, and six niggers!"

When the audience was helpless with laughter, Lenny addressed them directly. "Why have I done this?" he asked. "For shock value? In reality, it was for precisely the opposite reason: to deprive the n-word of its shock value. If black people were to call themselves *niggers*, even when they're in the company of white people, or if President Kennedy were to announce that he was appointing two *nigger's* to his cabinet, then the word would lose all of its meaning and, consequently, all of its power to hurt us. And when that beautiful day comes, you'll never find some kid coming home from school crying because some *ofay* motherfucker called him a nigger."

As Grover told it, "Dick turned to me and said, 'This man is the eighth wonder of the world! You have to go back to Mark Twain before you can find anything remotely like him. If they don't kill him or put him in jail, he's liable to shake up this whole fucking country.'" (As a side note, a recording of this routine does exist—not on one of Lenny's famous albums, but on one of the many bootleg recordings that appeared after his death. Listening to it knowing that Dick Gregory was in the house makes it even more enthralling.)

To experience Lenny Bruce in the context of the comedy of the day must have been rather like hearing a solo by John Coltrane or Jimi Hendrix in the middle of a Guy Lombardo concert—he was that groundbreaking. Don't get us wrong; there were plenty of racists out there slinging the n-word, but never in "polite company." Racism was in the closet—at least among the cultural elite. It was those very hypocrites that Lenny had his sights set on—much more than the overt segregationists of the Deep South. He reasoned that avoiding certain "offensive" words gave them power, while bringing them out into the open defused them like the bombs they were.

Lenny was not exactly the perfect comedian for Playboy, home of the "tired businessman" seeking light entertainment. But Hefner had a genuine affinity for him, perhaps because they believed in the same principles. They were both iconoclasts, endeavoring to blast holes in the buttoned-down society surrounding them. Sex and race were hot-button topics, left all but untouched by mainstream entertainment. Depending on how old you are, you might recall that even married couples didn't sleep in the same bed on the sitcoms of the sixties. Comedians—even the ones who appeared on *Playboy's Penthouse*—joked about innocuous things such as TV dinners and their mothers-in-law. Neither Hef nor Lenny believed in shocking audiences just for the sake of shocking them; what they hoped to do was push against the limits of what was acceptable, break barriers, liberate people's minds. The revolution they started rages on to this day, carried forward by everyone from Amy Schumer and Sarah Silverman to Dave Chappelle and Bill Maher.

It's not surprising that Hef would recognize a kindred spirit in Lenny, and the kind of talent that he wanted to support.

"Lenny was a truth-teller," observed Grover, "and when you're commenting on the follies and foibles of our time, that could be perceived in some quarters as sick. But he wasn't a sick comedian, he was commenting on a sick society."

Lenny's breakthrough moment—when he evolved instantly from an emerging talent into a cultural icon—came in 1959, when he appeared on national television for the first time. Steve Allen was the brave soul who put Lenny on his show, a short-lived Sunday night variety hour meant to compete with the unstoppable *Ed Sullivan Show.* Just a few months later, Lenny appeared on the very first episode of *Playboy's Penthouse.*

The set-up on *Penthouse* would become typical of the format. Two recent Playmates (fully clothed for television), Joyce Nizzari and Eleanor Bradley, are going through a stack of new albums when they come upon Lenny's latest, *The Sick Humor of Lenny Bruce*. Its now-famous cover, showing Lenny relaxing over a picnic lunch in a cemetery, seemed extreme at the time but looks pretty mild by today's standards—and even by his own later standards. The Playmates confess to being big fans, and that's Lenny's cue to pop in for a conversation with Hef.

The informal nature of their chat seems a kind of a harbinger of Lenny's later period—including his legendary 1961 Carnegie Hall concert—where he didn't perform so much as talk extemporaneously. At one point, Hef asks him about his particular brand of comedy.

"You work areas of humor that are pretty controversial," Hef points out. "According to some people, pretty sick. Do you consider yourself a sick comic?"

At first Lenny denies this: "There's no such thing as sick comedy," his insists. "There's no such thing as beatniks...it's a writer's device." This may seem a bit disingenuous, coming from someone who titled his own album *Sick Humor,* but whatever. Bear in mind that the comics on the *Time* and *Life* list of "sickies" of the day included Bob Newhart, Shelley Berman, Jonathan Winters, Mort Sahl, Tom Lehrer, and Mike Nichols and Elaine May.

Surprisingly, the ever-edgy Irwin Corey was left off the list and, knowing the Professor, he was probably a little hurt by the omission. When we asked him about Lenny, he said,

"Lenny was a very good friend of mine. Since we had a similar style, we recommended each other for jobs when we couldn't do them ourselves. I even invited him to my daughter's wedding."

Lenny never did "shtick", but he did incorporate jokes into his rants. In his on-air conversation with Hef, he elaborates on his respect for Steve Allen, but also mentions that the producers of *The Steve Allen Show* refused to let him tell one of his most famous jokes. And then, of course, he tells it—and we can't resist repeating it. While in the Navy during World War II—in Malta, to be specific—he got a tattoo. The sight of it on his arm later on led to a hysterical fit by his aunt, a devoutly Orthodox Jew. Tattoos are strictly forbidden in the faith, and nobody who has one can be buried in a Jewish cemetery. ("You have to leave the world as you came into it," Lenny explains.) So, he was at his aunt's house in Jamaica, Queens, and she spotted the tattoo and started shrieking at him.

"What's the big deal?" he asked her. "When I'm dead, they'll cut off my arm and bury it in a gentile cemetery!"

Apparently, the *Steve Allen Show* producer decided that the joke was offensive to Jews and Christians alike. "What you're saying, in essence, is that the *gentiles* don't care what they bury!" the guy told Lenny—and both he and Hef have a big laugh over that. It was precisely that kind of thinking they both wanted to change.

As Hef tells Lenny, "Well, we hope that we're going to have no such problems with our show here...I sense a change in the times, an ability to discuss things more openly in TV and movies."

The struggle to forge a more open and equitable society would not be an easy one—and it continues to this day. By the mid-1960s, Lenny was getting arrested regularly for obscene speech in public. As other historians have noted, so-called "dirty" jokes were nothing new, but Lenny and his cohort were onto something much more threatening. Their humor held up a mirror to society, and not everyone wanted to look into it. Lenny wasn't just humoring us, he wanted to change the world; and if that meant getting arrested, so be it.

Hef supported Lenny as best he could, putting him on his television shows and booking him into the clubs—starting with the original Chicago venue. That took guts as well as generosity, since Hef was risking his own legal standing. If Lenny were arrested at a Playboy Club, Hef could be prosecuted as well—and he had plenty of problems of his own without taking that on. But Lenny appreciated what his friend was doing for him and behaved himself during his Playboy appearances, and at Carnegie Hall in 1961 as well. Never let it be said that the comedian couldn't control himself when he wanted to.

As Lenny's career progressed, his act did become unsuitable for Playboy's stages—but his friend Hef helped him in other ways, including encouraging him to write his autobiography. The result, *How to Talk Dirty and Influence People,* was serialized in Hef's magazine and came out in book form from Playboy Press, edited by Paul Krassner, the founder of the satirical magazine *The Realist* and a central influence on the counterculture movement of the sixties. Hef somehow knew that Paul would be uniquely suited to keep Lenny on track and on point.

Paul told us, "I had previously met Lenny in New York, when he was set to perform at Town Hall. He was staying at some funky hotel in Times Square and I had an issue of *The Realist* with me, in which was an interview with the psychologist, Dr. Albert Ellis, where he talked about language. Lenny was fascinated and asked how we got away with printing some of the things we did. At that time, most publications used dashes and asterisks, and readers had to guess what was really being conveyed. I explained that the Supreme Court had ruled that something was considered obscene only if it aroused prurient interest.

"'Prurient?' said Lenny, and he opened his suitcase and pulled out this mammoth dictionary! I found out he carried it everywhere with him—that, and eventually law books. At that point he was already paranoid—it would get worse—but as we were about to leave his room, he turned to me and asked, 'Did you steal anything?' Instead of pleading my innocence, I took my own watch out of my pocket and put in on his bureau. He didn't realize it wasn't his and he shouted, 'Ha!' and kissed me on the forehead!"

When it was set that Paul and Lenny would work together on the autobiography, they met up again in Atlantic City.

"We argued over something, which couldn't have had any importance because, in the years since, I can't remember what it was. But he said, 'I want to give you a lie-detector test.' By this time, Lenny was completely over-the-top paranoid and, frankly, so was I.

"I said, 'If you don't trust me, there's no point in our working together,' and I left. Not too long afterward, he sent me a telegram—you're probably too young to remember telegrams but that's what I received. It sounded like we were divorcing—'Why can't it be the way it used to be?' Really. It was a *please daddy, give me another chance* letter. So we agreed to try to get this book done. I flew to Chicago and met him at the Gate of Horn, where he was performing, and heard him telling the whole audience that he wanted them to take a lie-detector test!"

As it happens, Lenny was arrested for obscenity that night—as was George Carlin, who was in the audience and refused to produce an ID.

"The charge was obscenity," said Paul, "even though his stuff wasn't arousing prurient interest. The real reason was his irreverence about politicians and hypocritical religious leaders. That's what really got him arrested. There were no blasphemy laws then, so they used obscenity as an excuse for arresting him. Chicago had the largest Catholic Diocese and one of the largest Catholic populations. The head of the vice squad actually went around to the clubs and told them, 'I'm telling you as a Catholic that if you have that Lenny Bruce perform here and he makes fun of our Pope or religion, we're going to take away your liquor license.' Of course, the clubs couldn't afford that, so that was the start of him getting fewer and fewer bookings.

"Once, when Lenny was on trial in Chicago, it was Ash Wednesday and all the jurors had ashes on their foreheads; the judge had them, the bailiff, the prosecutor, spectators, everyone had ashes. It was bizarre. It seemed like a Lenny Bruce hallucination, but it was real life."

Playboy had its own run-in with the Catholic Church in 1959, when the organization contracted to hold the first Playboy Jazz Festival at the city stadium. The church protested and the city revoked the contract.

"Chicago, for all of its corruption—forget about it being run by the mob—it was run by the Church," Paul observed.

Over the next two years, Lenny would be arrested another fifteen times. Hef helped with his legal expenses and, as several comedy historians have noted, a number of old-school, "establishment" comedians and entertainers supported Lenny as well—among them Milton Berle, Buddy Hackett, and Sammy Davis, Jr. It was all a bit ironic, since Lenny had savaged them as thoroughly as any other cultural or political institution. In fact, in one of his most famous routines, he skewered Sammy Davis by having a judge address him as "Mr. Junior."

Even Jackie Gayle, whose style of humor was as far from Lenny's as one could imagine, rallied to his support. At a certain point, nearly all of Lenny's money—and plenty from his friends—was going to pay his court and legal fees. And, by the early 1960s, his raging drug habit was consuming the rest. Ultimately, and not surprisingly, Lenny imploded early. He died in 1966 of a drug overdose, at the age of 40.

Dick Gregory was right: "*They* put Lenny Bruce in jail and you could even say that *they* killed him, but *they* couldn't stop him from shaking up this whole fucking country."

Encouraged by Lenny's example, Paul Krassner embarked on his own career in standup, premiering his act in 1961 at New York's Village Gate. In 1971, Groucho Marx said, "I predict that in time Paul Krassner will wind up as the only live Lenny Bruce."

As the result of a grant from the Hugh M. Hefner foundation in 2014, Brandeis University acquired Lenny Bruce's personal papers and recordings. The Lenny Bruce Collection officially opened to the public in 2016, the fiftieth anniversary of his death. Also in that year, a new edition of *How to Talk Dirty and Influence People,* with a preface by the cranky comedian Lewis Black, was published by Da Capo Press.

* * *

Jackie Gayle, who keeps rearing his hilarious head in these pages, was, by all accounts, Hef's favorite comedian. Perhaps that's why he could get away with saying to Hef,

"By the way, Madame Tussaud called and she wants you back at the museum." He certainly holds the record for most performances at the clubs. Born in Brooklyn in 1926 as Jack Potovsky, he was also the same age as Hefner, and was the only comic to appear three times on the short-lived *Playboy After Dark*, in 1969-1970.

Jackie was a natural for the show, which debuted at the height of the "generation gap." He had a knack for appealing to both sides of that divide. On the October 23, 1968, episode, he starts out talking about Mayor Richard J. Daley, notorious for his attempts to maintain order in the Windy City in that tumultuous year. Jackie suggests that the TV news might be improved somewhat by giving the short, pugnacious mayor the voice of Edward G. Robinson.

"I don't want to pick on him too much, though," Jackie jokes, "because I still have relatives living in Chicago."

Nodding to another generation of viewers, Jackie then switches from current events to jokes about World War II, opining that the German army was so effective because its soldiers had the most efficient music to march to—as opposed to the Italians, who were trying to march to Louis Prima or "Come Back to Sorrento."

"You can't march to that," he insists. "That's for serving minestrone!... Meanwhile, the Japanese had guns, grenades, and Sony televisions that turned into cigarette lighters."

As Jackie's comedy toggles between eras, he spies Hef with two twenty-something models and says to him,

"I'm very impressed by your nieces. Remind me to give you a map to the nearest schoolyard." Next turning to a girl sitting on the floor, he asks, "Your mommy dressed you like that?" Jackie winds up his moment in the spotlight with a funny riff on the legendary entertainer Eddie Cantor—an icon to his older viewers but possibly unknown to the girl he's just finished teasing.

In Jackie Gayle's most notable *Playboy After Dark* appearance, on October 23, 1968, he shows off his drum technique by playing "Big Noise from Winnetka" as a duet with his bassist, Jerry Friedman—but there's no drum kit in sight. Instead, Jackie employs his sticks against the bass itself and, ultimately, the bass strings. As you'll recall, Jackie had started his career as a drummer, but thanks to his friend Lenny Bruce and Lenny's mom, Sally Marr, Jackie turned his talents from rim-shots to one-liners. The rest, as they say, is history—but it's fun to get a taste of the talent he left behind.

Most of the veteran entertainers who cut their teeth at the Playboy Clubs and are still working today were gracious enough to talk to us—and they all paid tribute to Playboy's vital role in encouraging young talent as well as showcasing the greats. The February 5, 1961, episode of *Playboy's Penthouse,* for example, features the national TV debut of Jack Burns and George Carlin. After hitting it big as a team, the two would become even more successful individually, with George making a solo appearance on *Playboy After Dark* on March 1970. Two other rising comedy stars, Larry Storch and Bob Newhart, had their budding young careers nudged along by their exposure on *Playboy's Penthouse* in November 1959. The stellar line-up of both shows is evidence that Hef held comedians in the same esteem that he held jazz singers and musicians, showcasing an average of three of funnymen per week.

Every once in awhile a skit doesn't quite seem to land—or maybe you had to be there. The December 19, 1959, episode of *Playboy's Penthouse* included a poker game populated by Henny Youngman, Professor Irwin Corey, Gary Morton, Don Adams, and Joey Adams. There was no script, of course—and watching these nutty guys improvise in TV time—which they weren't very good at—makes for a unique segment, to say the least.

* * *

Thank heavens for YouTube and DVDs, because the old Playboy TV shows serve a purpose today beyond simple nostalgia. They form a living record (albeit a low-def one) of some of the best work of entertainers who were already legendary by the time Hefner published his first magazine., we talked about Joe E. Lewis and his impact on Frank Sinatra and the Rat Pack—the Vagabonds, who can be seen on *Playboy's Penthouse* Season 1, Episode 25, exerted a similar influence upon Louis Prima and other high-energy entertainers whose shows combined comedy and music.

The careers of the Vagabonds and Louis Prima, in fact, ran somewhat parallel, and the influences went back and forth. The main difference between the Vagabonds and Louis Prima was that, while the trumpeter was also a master comedian, he occasionally played a song "straight," and was certainly gifted enough to pull it off. The Vagabonds, on the other hand, never played anything straight. Even when they started what sounded like a romantic or sentimental song, they ended up going for laughs by the end.

Their act might seem strange today, when genres and categories are more fixed. The Vagabonds were often described as a "vocal-instrumental group," but they were considerably more than that. Among them, they played two guitars, an accordion, and a bass; all four members sang, but they also danced, told jokes, and cavorted around the stage nonstop. Louis Prima, on the other hand, was always *prima* on stage: Everything revolved around him. His long-time singing partner, the adorably deadpan Keely Smith, played straight woman to his antics, though, in all fairness, she did end up stealing the show more often than not. The rest of the band, from Sam Butera on down, were all foils for Prima's antics.

The Vagabonds were like four Louis Primas performing at the same time—a set of musical Marx Brothers with no straight men. Where Prima was a major recording star, with numerous hit singles and many albums to his credit, the Vagabonds were more of a live act that had to be seen to be fully appreciated. They made only a handful records, none wildly successful. They also made a few forays into radio and took a few turns on film, but, like Joe E. Lewis, their true home for decades was on the supper club circuit.

That might have been the end of the story for the Vags, but television provided them with a revival. They became omnipresent in the early days of the small screen, thanks to the two most influential talent presenters of the era, Arthur Godfrey and Ed Sullivan. The two impresarios competed for the services of the multi-talented quartet.

In their appearance on *Playboy After Dark* in 1960, Hefner brings them out by saying—without the slightest touch of irony or exaggeration—"I'd like to introduce you to a group that certainly needs no introduction on television, ever since the old Arthur Godfrey days. I'm sure you remember the Vagabonds!"

The Vags were all Italian-Americans, with the exception of their famously Swedish bass player—a running joke with the group. As we said, they were a collective and shared the stage democratically, but their acknowledged leader and founder was guitarist Dominic Germano who, like his three partners, had been born in San Francisco. Around 1931, Germano formed a trio with two friends from North Beach, accordionist Atilio Rizzo, and Tony Servidio, who sang and blew on a jug—yes, these were the days of the jug bands. They called themselves The Italian Vagabonds and played on the streets and local ferries. Servidio left fairly early, and the others were joined by a second guitarist, Al Torrieri, and eventually Pete Peterson on bass.

Now known simply as the Vagabonds, the quartet attracted the attention of Hollywood fairly early and appeared in nine movies between 1937 and 1946, including *Saratoga,* with Clark Gable and Gene Harlow; and *Something to Sing About,* produced by James Cagney. The best known of their films today is *It Ain't Hay* (1943), with Bud Abbott and Lou Costello. You can't miss the group backing up leading lady Grace McDonald as she leads a large parade down the street, singing the patriotic number "Glory Be." Even Peterson is marching, mammoth upright bass and all.

By 1939, the Vagabonds were successful enough to open their own club. Financed by friends and family, The Vagabonds Club opened on Geary Street in San Francisco and was an immediate success, although it lasted only three years before the four partners enlisted to go fight World War II.

At the end of the war, the Vags inaugurated their return to performing with their scene-stealing appearance in the film *People Are Funny*, in which they get considerably more numbers than star Jack Haley. Around the same time, they also made a radio appearance alongside the most famous Italian-American in the world, Frank Sinatra (on Sinatra's *Old Gold* show of December 19, 1945). Their zaniness is apparent even without visuals in this four-minute spot, in which they make mincemeat of the country music standard "You Are My Sunshine." But there's no doubt that the group's true métier was television, a format that had the power to elevate nightclub performers into superstars and—for a decade or so during the heyday of variety shows—bring back vaudeville. The Vags were regulars on *Arthur Godfrey and Friends*, which is how most of their fans, including Hugh Hefner, remember them to this day. Sadly, no kinescopes of the Vagabonds on *Godfrey* appear to be in circulation, but there is an excellent clip of the group on the *Colgate Comedy Hour* of September 19, 1954, performing their "Vaudeville Medley" and Hawaiian Hula routine. (Variations of both bits can be found on their Unique LP.) Broadcast from the Hollywood Bowl, the show was hosted by Eddie Fisher and featured Louis Armstrong and Peggy Lee. That fact alone reveals caliber of the company they kept.

Around the same time, the group opened its second Vagabonds Club, this one in Miami Beach, in conjunction with their manager and conductor, Frank Linale. Miami in those days rivaled Las Vegas as an entertainment destination (the illegal gambling didn't hurt), and was promoted heavily on TV by Arthur Godfrey and Jackie

Gleason. The place quickly became a hotspot, not least among Italian-American celebrities including Sinatra and Dean Martin, pre-Rat Pack.

"A lot of people from showbiz, like Jackie Gleason, came in there," said Ann Carlton, an accordionist who also performed at the club. Her reminiscences were part of an interview in the *Biscayne Times* published in 2012, when she was ninety-five. "Frank Sinatra, Victor Borge…they'd sometimes come in and perform free for the Vagabonds because they wanted them to be successful. It was really a wonderful place."

During these happy years, the zany Vagabonds were at the center of musical and cultural life in Miami. Tony Bennett and his family were frequently in the club, and Tony's sister Mary told us how she loved Dom and Tilio like family. The Vags also enjoyed a mutually beneficial relationship with a relatively subdued musician, the legendary singer-accordionist-organist-songwriter Joe Mooney. Blind from birth, Mooney became famous on 52nd Street in the 1940s, but spent much of the following decade working at the Vagabonds Club, often in the company of the quartet. Everyone we asked about it—including Tony himself—remembered that Tony Bennett was the last headliner to play the club, in September 1957.

By the late 1950s, both the club and the Godfrey show were behind them, but the Vags continued to appear frequently on *Ed Sullivan*. By a generous quirk of fate, their first appearance on the show coincided with that of the rising superstar Elvis Presley, on September 9, 1956. They sang their classic take on "Up a Lazy River." Curiously, it was a rare show not hosted by Sullivan himself, who was out of commission due to a car accident. The emcee duties were taken over by the esteemed dramatic actor, Charles Laughton.

The Vags made six appearances on Sullivan between 1956 and 1964, and for the last one they shared the bill with Sammy Davis, Jr., as well as the rising husband-and-wife comedy team of Jerry Stiller and Anne Meara. By this time, the group's first bassist, the comically dour Swede Pete Peterson, had died and been replaced by a jovial Italian. Even his name—Eddie Peddy—was both funny and rhythmic.

The group's best surviving video appearance is the *Playboy's Penthouse* show of April 2, 1960, both for its video quality (Hef has always been a stickler about the preservation of the old two-inch videotapes) and its documentation of the Vags at full throttle. They start in on a contemporary pop song, "Primrose Lane," and within about thirty seconds, Dom and the gang are gagging it up, their comedy, camaraderie, harmony, and ad libs anticipating the Rat Pack—albeit with four Dean Martins.

Their next number, if that's the right word, is an international segment, framed by Victor Young's classic waltz, "Around the World." The bit includes a south sea island "witch doctor" routine followed by an ethnic air that sounds like a mash-up of Japanese and Hebrew. There is a unison performance that includes a patriotic rendition of the "Mickey Mouse Club March." Dom then starts to deliver a high-speed impersonation of Louis Prima singing "When You're Smiling," at which point Eddie comes on wearing something akin to a Beatles wig—in actuality, a Keely Smith wig—and trains a deadpan gaze on Dom. They start a Neapolitan love song in the Louis-and-Keely tradition, but are tripped up when Eddie somehow gets his fingers stuck in his bass frets, his pantomime resembling something Harpo Marx might do.

The segment climaxes in their signature number, Hoagy Carmichael's "Up a Lazy River," but again, Eddie hijacks it. He starts tuning his bass in the middle of the song and leaps spontaneously into the "Dragnet" theme, then the "Big Noise from Winnetka," and briefly into an operetta quote—appropriately, Rudolf Friml's "Song of the Vagabonds." They somehow bring it back to "Lazy River" while bouncing as if on pogo sticks—one of their trademark bits. It's amazing enough to see Dom and Al playing in perfect unison while pogo-ing—but Eddie is right in step with them as well, bouncing like a bunny rabbit while holding his bass horizontally as if it were a giant guitar. This entire routine was an extravagant departure from classic Playboy TV, which tended to resemble an urbane (if high-octane) cocktail party. Audiences tuned in each week to see who might be on the invite list—and certainly got an eyeful that night.

The group's last hurrah on television arrived courtesy of Lucille Ball, who featured them in two consecutive episodes of *The Lucy Show* in 1966. By this point, Ball was using her show liberally as a vehicle for other talent. On other episodes that same season, Paul Winchell, George Burns, and Phil Silvers made guest appearances.

"Lucy Gets a Roommate," the first episode that featured the Vags, also starred the emerging comedian Carol Burnett. She played a shy librarian who gets toasted on "Italian water" (i.e., *vino*) and starts belting out "Hard-Hearted Hannah" with the Vags (which now featured drummer Roger Pearsall).

In the following episode, "Lucy and Carol in Palm Springs," the Vagabonds (announced by name this time) do two of their signature numbers: a Hawaiian medley with vocals by Burnett and lots of jumping up and down; and "Up a Lazy River," this time with both Lucy and Carol interjecting themselves into the band and the spirit. Lucy gets the last word by reciting a goofy little poem that caps the show, concluding with the lines, "This lazy river does nothing from dusk to dawn. / Why, it's so lazy that the fishes would rather yawn than spawn."

That same year, the quartet played the Red Dolphin Room in a club called Tony's Fish Market in Miami, where they famously received a visit from Jackie Gleason. There are photos of the Great One rocking out on guitar with the gang. But soon, Al Torrieri would retire and Tilio Rizzo would pass on. Germano and bassist Dino Natali continued working as the Vagabonds into the 1970s, with various replacement Vags, until they, too, retired. Germano died of cancer in Carson City, Nevada in 1996, at the age of 83.

In January 1968, Dom Germano made a remarkable record with another partner: Tony Bennett. The two had been friends for many years when Bennett brought Germano into Columbia's 30th-Street studio in New York, where they planned to make an entire album together called *Friends*. They recorded eight songs but only one of them has ever been released: "The Glory of Love," credited "by Tony Bennett and his San Francisco Buddy, Dominic Germano." Judging by the vitality, energy, and congeniality of the two, it would be great to hear the other seven tracks. For this brief, glorious moment, Tony and Dom became a two-man edition of the Vagabonds and you can almost hear the smiles on their faces as they sing. In what has now been ninety years of making people smile, this is one of the most joyful recorded moments of Tony's entire career.

With the Vagabonds, even tempo was funny. Sometimes they'd go so fast they left the audience breathless; other times, they'd drag out a song at such a snail's pace that listeners would sweat with suspense. It was as if they were comic masters, always carefully calibrating their punch lines. And of course, that is exactly what they were.

* * *

Hef's invitees to the Penthouse weren't exclusively singers and comedians. Reflecting his great admiration for the art of illustration, he also brought on the occasional cartoonist.

To wit, on October 31, 1959, on the show's second episode, a burly, bearded figure strolls in wearing a trench coat and a slouch hat. He might be mistaken for a foreign correspondent if not for the artist's portfolio he carries in place of a reporter's notebook. Hef introduces the newcomer as follows:

"Kids, I'd like you to meet Shel Silverstein, cartoonist for *Playboy*. Shel has just returned from a trip all around the world for the last two years, for the magazine." To commemorate the Halloweeniness of the occasion, Hef introduces Shel to Vampira, the performance artist and TV host, who has made a surprise appearance.

Thanks in large part to his fortuitous launch in the pages of *Playboy,* Sheldon Allan Silverstein enjoyed one of the most remarkable careers in American culture—as you'll discover later in the book.

Shel would make one more TV appearance with Hef, on *Playboy After Dark* on August 8, 1968, but it is his works on paper (and record) for which he'll be remembered. He died in 1999 at the age of sixty-eight, having left us enough books to uplift us, cartoons to amuse us, and songs to please us for many lifetimes.

* * *

In early 1958, when Phyllis Diller appeared on *You Bet Your Life* with Groucho Marx, she'd already honed one of her best early routines, an extended riff about air travel, and she reprised portions of it in her 1960 *Playboy* TV appearance as well as on her 1962 Verve album:

> *I adore the champagne flights—I like to be higher than the plane! But the worst are those "thrift flights," with none of the costly extras—like landing gear. And boy, these flights I'm on, these paste jobs, they're not allowed to land at an airport because it would ruin morale. They don't really land, they just lose altitude. And I'm not nutty about old planes. They just paint these old planes over and over, and I'm against it, because paint is heavy. And they never quite paint over "Spirit of... something or other.*

By the time Phyllis stepped out of the elevator into *Playboy's Penthouse* on February 13, 1960, she was a bit more heavily made up and styled than she'd been on Groucho's show, but not yet the caricature she would ultimately become. If you were seeing her for the first time, you might not be entirely sure whether she was trying to look funny. It isn't her best TV outing; she spends a little too much time dumping on stewardesses ("fresh out of idiot school") and making other assorted wisecracks that come off—at least to today's ears—as more mean-spirited than funny.

As Phyllis's comedy evolved, she became more comfortable and confident and most, if not all, of her barbs were aimed at herself and her fictional family.

* * *

It's not over-the-top to call *Playboy's Penthouse* America's first reality show—but it was too controversial and too far ahead of its time to survive. With boundless optimism, Hef believed he could follow his principles and present the top players in entertainment regardless of race or gender. Networks and sponsors begged to differ, and after warning him more than once about his policy of "equal rights on the couch," they cancelled the show.

Playboy After Dark premiered in a slightly more enlightened decade and lasted just a little bit longer: from 1969 through 1970. Ten years after *Playboy's Penthouse*'s first episode, the updated show was broadcast in full psychedelic color, complete with flamboyant orange shag carpeting, red walls, and black tile flooring. Again it pretended to take place at Hef's swinging pad and featured the stars of the day—including some rock-and-rollers who seemed a bit ill-at-ease among the usual swells. This time, there were microphones on view. The party, it seemed, was becoming a performance.

Hef trying his own hand at comedy on SNL:
NBC Universal/Getty Images

7

LAUGHABLE LADIES

"I was actually the world's ugliest baby. When I was born, the doctor slapped everybody! My father asked the doctor, 'Is it a boy or a girl? He said, 'No.' He said that it was the first full-term miscarriage that he had ever witnessed. I was thirty years old, my mother was still trying to get an abortion." –PHYLLIS DILLER

Speaking about her fellow female comedians, Joan Rivers once said, "Nobody ever came up to any of us—when we were little girls especially—and said, 'You know what? You're beautiful!'"

Well before Joan built a career around her self-proclaimed unsightliness, Phyllis Diller was the queen of comically exaggerated self-deprecation. ("I don't know how to describe the way I'm built. All I can say is that if I was put together by Mother Nature, then God is a litter bug!") Phyllis's peak years were the 1960s, and she helped to christen the decade with an appearance on *Playboy's Penthouse* on February 2, 1960. One of her key bits, as recorded on her 1962 comedy album, *Are You Ready for Phyllis Diller?*, was introducing the frock she was wearing as coming "from the Jackie collection." After a pause, she would add, "... Gleason!"

In an age when women wore bright, colorful outfits, especially on television—as if to test the capabilities of the new color technology—Phyllis's clothing went beyond psychedelic. In the late sixties, especially, when hair became a social statement, Phyllis wore fright wigs with a touch of reality, only slightly more outrageous than you might see on older women attempting to look contemporary. Phyllis always wore gloves, but it was never quite clear whether she was emulating the well-heeled, upper-crust ladies of the day or the great clowns who had inspired her, from Emmett Kelly to W. C. Fields.

Phyllis Diller and Bunnies: Ron Galella Collection/ Getty Images

Female standup comedians were so rare before Phyllis that when she made her first TV appearance, she didn't even describe herself as a comic, but as an "entertainer." That was on Groucho Marx's *You Bet Your Life*, on January 30, 1958, and her interview started like that of a thousand others on the show. She told Groucho that she had five kids but that she had "beat the rap," i.e., she was no longer a full-time housewife. She was forty years old at the time, which, as she continued to tell people for decades to come, was hardly prime time for breaking into show business.

Phyllis was born in Lima, Ohio, in 1917. "You know you're old when your birth certificate is on a scroll," she famously quipped. She married Sherwood Diller in 1939 and they set up housekeeping in Ypsilanti, Michigan, where her six kids were born. (One of them died in infancy.)

"In our playpen, it was standing room only," she said. "It looked like a bus stop for midgets."

By the time their youngest, Perry, arrived, Phyllis was no longer just a stay-at-home mom; she'd taken a job as a copywriter for a local advertising agency. After a few years of assorted jobs in local radio and TV, Phyllis began working as a standup comedian in 1955. Her initial breakthrough was at the Purple Onion—a club closely associated with the Beatnik movement. She later said that the first set was easy because the house was filled with her friends and relatives; it was the second set, performed in front of strangers, that was the hard one. She got through it, kept working on her act, and ended up playing the Purple Onion for nearly two years straight.

Watching her appearances on the *Ed Sullivan Show* and *Merv Griffin Show* in the mid-sixties, it's clear that she had honed her voice and persona to a T by that point. Her tone, attitude, outfit, and delivery were unique and somehow seamless.

"Dreamer that I am, I still go to the beauty parlor. They've got a special entrance for me marked 'emergency!' Today I overheard them discussing mercy killing." You can tell that she'd been influenced by Bob Hope, the greatest mentor of her career.

From the mid-1960s onward, she became Hope's number-one foil, delivering her jokes almost passively, in a way that seems reminiscent of Hope's own understated attitude. *I know this line is funny...I'm just waiting for you to catch up to me,* she seemed to say. Addressing the audience, she'd angle her head slightly downward, making them work just a little bit to hear and comprehend her remarks—drawing them into her world rather than spewing her jokes at them freely.

There's one additional element that set Phyllis apart from her peers: the invention of her husband, "Fang." While Joan Rivers spoke often (if not always completely honestly) about her real-life husband Edgar and daughter Melissa, Phyllis was unfettered by the reality of her domestic life. Fang was a larger-than-life creation of the comedian's fertile imagination—a composite, she said, of her two husbands and every other dumb guy she'd ever encountered. She called him Fang because, "he has only one tooth, about two inches long. At first I thought it was a cigarette."

Creating a fictional husband freed Diller to insult him with alacrity, without risk of losing the audience's sympathy. And once in a while, she'd allow Fang a zinger of his own.

"Today I was practicing the Australian crawl, it's a beautiful stroke. My husband comes over and says, 'You idiot, get in the pool!' I got news for you, I can't do it in the pool, I do it in the grass, that's where I always do it. Who do you think taught me to do it in the grass? Fang, the idiot! He knows I can't do it in the pool, I tried to do it in the pool once and I darn near drowned."

With the help of Fang, Phyllis became a true female equivalent of Hope and Milton Berle, comics who could put everybody else down because they'd already put themselves down. They weren't in the business of throwing people under the bus so much as dragging a few folks down there with them.

At one point during the mid-sixties, *Playboy* magazine thought it might be fun to have female comedians pose nude—just for laughs, of course. Phyllis was all too game but, sadly, her photos never made the cut. Too unsightly, you say? Quite the contrary. Underneath her frumpy housecoat and fright wigs, Phyllis was quite the babe! The editors decided she was just too sexy to be a part of the gag. We have to wonder how she felt about that.

Because of her late start in comedy, Phyllis didn't relish many of the rituals involved with coming up through the ranks—and that included traveling the country on the Playboy circuit. Luckily for her, the variety shows of the day—including *Playboy's Penthouse*—were a great vehicle for her antics and her appearances on them fast-tracked her rise to stardom.

Although she appeared in her fair share of movies and TV shows, Phyllis's real bread-and-butter was performing live, which she did year in and year out for forty-seven years, by her own count. She simply stepped on stage in front of several thousand people and started talking. Seventy minutes later, her viewers emerged, having forgotten their own troubles for a while and feeling a little better about themselves.

Phyllis finally retired from the road in 2004, but continued to accept acting roles. She enjoyed a late-in-life resurgence as a recurring character on the animated series, *The Family Guy*, thus winning over a whole new generation of fans. In 2012, Phyllis died at the glorious age of 95. You can't tell us that Phyllis Diller wasn't beautiful.

Bea Halke—who, as you'll recall, worked in the kitchen at Great Gorge and met everyone who was anyone—told her grandson Rich that she'd once been tempted to hit the road with Phyllis. As he recalled it, "Phyllis Diller was another comic who had little to do before and after her Great Gorge appearances. She didn't have anyone to hang out with. My grandmother was older than most of the other waitresses there, so they gravitated toward each other. Bea was from New York and they related to each other on many topics and shared life experiences. By the time Phyllis was set to move on, they had forged a growing friendship—so much so that Phyllis offered her one of the famously coveted jobs, as her traveling secretary. This was a huge deal; later there was even a documentary on Phyllis's 'traveling secretaries' and their adventures. Unfortunately, my grandfather had cancer, and Bea had to turn down the offer, but whenever she talked about it she said, 'Oh, I so wanted to take it.'

"Maybe it's a little off topic but, speaking about my grandfather and his battle with cancer, I have to mention that somehow the insurance company wasn't going to cover all the costs for the operation he needed. Someone told Bea, 'Submit the bill to Hef. He always liked you, and you never know. Bea refused to ask him for help, but unbeknownst to her, one of her co-workers did it on her behalf, and Hugh Hefner signed off on it. He paid for my grandfather's throat cancer operation. After that, Bea always said, 'Anyone who says anything bad about Hugh Hefner, I'll stab them in the eye!'"

* * *

"Why should a woman cook? So her husband can say, 'My wife makes a delicious cake' to some hooker?!" –JOAN RIVERS

Circling back to where we started—with Joan Rivers—she was probably the biggest comedy superstar to launch her career at the Playboy Clubs. She started performing at roughly the same time that the clubs were opening and worked at most of the early ones, most frequently Miami, as part of a trio billed as, "Jim, Jake, and Joan." As her frequent television appearances began to raise her profile, her stature at the clubs rose commensurately. The trio broke up and Joan continued working the circuit on her own—one of the few women standups to do so. Ultimately, she headlined at the resorts, putting her in a league with Bob Hope and Milton Berle.

Joan always pushed the envelope of what was acceptable, with her material as well as her presence in a male-dominated industry. As a young woman appearing on *The Tonight Show* and *The Ed Sullivan Show*, she joked about her marital and domestic woes, going so far as to appear on the air visibly pregnant. This just wasn't done in the 1960s. In the 1970s, she made us laugh about the plight of unwed mothers and the future of women's reproductive rights; in her own sixties and seventies, she was always the first to make a joke about the aging process, and found an almost unending source of humor in the obsession with plastic surgery—mainly her own.

Joan made fun of her difficult relationship with her own mother and was the first to admit that she was never able to be the parent she wanted to be to her own daughter. As pointed as her barbs could be—including endless "fat jokes" about Elizabeth Taylor and, more recently, Adele—we always felt compassion for her. No other comic more skillfully employed humor as a coping mechanism to contend with the difficult losses she experienced when her trusted friend Johnny Carson turned on her and her beloved husband Edgar committed suicide. It was almost as if Joan had earned the right to make fun of others by making herself her own biggest target. She refused to take herself seriously, and expected others to do the same.

One anecdote will serve as evidence of how much the world has changed since the 1960s, when both Joan's career and the Playboy Clubs were new. In 1965, when she was still holding down a day job, Joan was contacted by an agent who'd managed to get her a brief spot on *The Jack Paar Show*. As always, she made herself the butt of the jokes. In addition to jokes about her own unsightliness as a child ("My father was a doctor…His first words when he saw me were, 'Does that look right to you, nurse?'"), she talked about working in an office. As she told it, she was in the habit of stealing stamps from somebody else's desk and selling them for half price. In an interview many years later, she insisted that was a true story.

The office she referred to on *Paar* was that of agent Irvin Arthur, who, as you know, eventually became the key talent coordinator for the Playboy Clubs. He remembered the stamp kerfuffle well. But something about the story offended the very proper Mr. Paar. "A doctor's daughter wouldn't steal stamps," he pronounced to his producers afterward. Joan was barred from ever appearing on the program again. If this mild intimation of wrongdoing was too controversial for Paar, who lived until 2005, one can only imagine what he must have felt about the topical humor of the ensuing decades. (If he were alive today, surely a few minutes of Chris Rock or Amy Schumer would kill him!)

Irwin Corey recalled meeting Joan at Irvin's office in 1955, and following her meteoric rise through the comedy ranks.

"She was a brilliant woman, her nightclub material absolutely hilarious." Irvin told us that he would overhear Joan on the office phone, talking to club and venue owners who wanted to book talent. "I'd hear her telling them how funny *she* was, trying to persuade them to give *her* a chance, and imparting as many jokes as quickly as she could. I finally told her I thought she needed to audition full time. And I became her agent."

In the overall arc of her career, Joan had a lot in common with the singer-pianist-composer Nina Simone, who also became a symbol of female empowerment. (Coincidentally, they were both born in 1933). Simone's early ambition was to become a classical pianist and she started playing jazz and standards as a means of supporting herself through music school. Although Simone became a huge star in the jazz world, she always felt under-appreciated and even rejected because she had never become a classical pianist. Likewise, Joan yearned to be taken seriously as an actress and felt she'd failed to achieve that. The 2010 documentary portrait of Joan, *Piece of Work*, is peppered with her rants about never having received the respect she felt she was entitled to.

Anyone who has seen one of her routines knows that Joan grew up in Brooklyn (where she costarred in a play with Barbra Streisand long before anyone had heard of either of them) and then the suburb of Larchmont, New York. She held a variety of jobs in stores and offices before going to work for Irvin, who told us, "I eventually had to let her go, because when a good booking for a comic would come in, she'd always try to snag it for herself."

She formed Jim, Jake, and Joan with Jim Connell and Jake Holmes. "We'd play all these dives in Greenwich Village for bupkis," she told us. "We'd pass the hat and sometimes the hat wouldn't come back at all! Or—worse—it would come back with a severed head in it."

This was the age of the folk music boom, but what tends to be forgotten is that a number of the folk groups incorporated a healthy dose of comedy into their acts. The Limelighters, for example, did comedy bits between songs; and, of course, the Smothers Brothers were comedians who happened to be credible folk musicians as well. Jim, Jake, and Joan, with their deft use of song and guitar, were equal parts Peter, Paul, and Mary, and Mike Nichols and Elaine May.

When we interviewed Joan in 2014, a few weeks before her death at age eighty-one, she told us about the group. "The guys sang some folk songs and I was the comic. Offstage, they were always arguing, so I was the glue that kept us together for as long as we were. We didn't last long, but we played at quite a few of the Playboy Clubs." According to Joan, they made their biggest impression at the Miami Playboy, and went on to appear in a very low-budget theatrical film, *Hootenanny a Go-Go,* a.k.a., *Once Upon a Coffee House,* filmed down there.

Watching that film, it's clear that the division of labor wasn't quite as distinct as Joan implied: She joined in on the music in places and the boys took part in the comic bits, at various points spoofing a toothpaste commercial, a weather report, and former Nazi rocket scientists working at Cape Canaveral.

By 1965, when the time the film was made, it was clear that the trio's days were numbered. Despite Paar's ban, Joan would soon work in television again, first as a writer and occasional ensemble performer on *Candid Camera* and then as a regular on Johnny Carson. In her early appearances on his show, he introduced her as a comedy writer who occasionally performed. Carson may have been her first champion, but Ed Sullivan was her next one, introducing her on his show as, "my daffy little friend." In her early years, she'd make endless fun of her inadequacies as a housewife and her own lack of sex appeal.

By the late sixties, Joan was working the clubs regularly. "To be a woman comic," she told us, "especially back then, you had to be very strong, stand up for yourself, and be a lion tamer. My idea of heaven is to be on stage with an audience laughing at me while their stomachs are full." On another occasion, she added, "If I hear one more young female comic talk about how I 'opened the door' for her, I'm going to bust her in the chops!"

Joan, who was so organized that she kept an intricate filing system of every joke she had ever written, spoke with high praise of the efficiency of the Playboy organization. "They ran a tight ship, with a rule for everything. But I think that's probably what made it run so well. Nothing was left to chance."

When we asked about her favorite memories of the Playboy years, her response surprised us.

"The Bunnies weren't sluts!" she stated emphatically. "They were pretty, wholesome young women. I thought they'd all be a 'certain type,' but they weren't. That surprised me. They were actually very good company. I liked to hang out with them more than anyone else between shows."

Joan had one very special memory of the Playboy resorts, involving her daughter Melissa, who was born in 1968. "A couple of years after I had Melissa, she occasionally traveled with me. One time, I took her to Lake Geneva and the girls there made a tiny Bunny outfit for her. I thought it was so sweet of them and I had to peel it off her. She was only two and she loved it."

It was a treat to experience the tender side of Joan Rivers, the woman who reduced so many public figures to masses of jelly with the power of her words. She was actually moved nearly to tears by the thought of her baby daughter in a Bunny outfit.

Her other treasured memory of Playboy was a little more offbeat.

"It was the corn!" she cried. "Don't ask me why, but Lake Geneva had the best fucking corn I've ever tasted in my life!"

In the final years of her career, Joan included a comedy bit about how *Playboy* magazine offered Melissa, who was around forty at the time, a staggering $400,000 to pose nude from the waist up.

"I brought her up all wrong," Joan said. "I brought her up

to have morals! She called me and said, 'Mother, I turned down *Playboy*. What do you think?' What do I think? What do I think!!! You stupid [expletive deleted]! I think you should ask for $200,000 more to show your [expletive deleted], that's what I think!"

Lou Alexander—who keeps popping up in these pages—shared his escapades with the novice comedian and window dresser Joan Molinsky, a.k.a., Rivers. After Lou was discharged from the Marines, he worked nights at a nightclub and his wife, Beth Hamilton, worked as a model for Bond's Department Store. One of Beth's colleagues—you know who—was a window dresser who constantly lamented her plight. What she dreamed of, she said, was a career in comedy. Beth finally admitted to her friend that she was married to a comedian.

"He's not doing that well, though, because he just came out of the service. He's working at the Golden Slipper on Long Island."

"Could I meet him?" Joan asked.

"So she came out that night with her boyfriend," Lou recalled, "and I could see she was scraping by, because I noticed her bra strap was held together by a safety pin. We laughed about it years later, but that night, I told her, "Watch what I'm doing on stage. Of course, you can't do the same material, because I'm male and you're not, but you can tailor it to work for you. All comedians do that—take a little bit of material from here, a little bit from there. Everybody starts that way. All through my show, I see that she's writing and writing and writing. She's getting it all down."

After Lou finished, he went over to her table, bought her dinner, and they talked. Joan wanted to know what she should do next.

"You go to Greenwich Village and find any place where they'll let you up on stage. You're going to stink for a long time, so you might as well get used to the idea now. You have to stink in front of people! You can't do it in front of a mirror at home. You have to find your way—get feedback from a real-live audience on what works and what doesn't. Get your timing down and learn how to move. They're going to throw quarters, and if you're lucky, you'll get a dollar here and there. Just find a stage."

A few weeks later, Lou got an invitation from Joan to come to her show and critique her performance.

"Joan's a fast talker nowadays, but that night, she was going a million miles an hour. After the show, she ran over and sat down, and I suggested she slow down—talk a little slower. 'What are you talking about?' she asked.

"I said, 'Do yourself a favor and take your time. When you get to the punchline, say to yourself, 'One, two, three...punch line.' So the next time I saw her show—a week or so later—this is what happened.

"She told her story and said, 'One, two, three'—*Out loud*!! I fell on the floor.

"I said later, 'You're supposed to say that to yourself, not to the audience!' Look, she had never done this before, and I'm sure she was nervous as hell, but she got the hang of it—And how!!"

Another great admirer of Joan is the "ventro-impressionist" you met earlier, Gary Willner. He often opened for her, and offered us a window into yet another side of her personality. "She knew exactly what items she wanted...clothes, jewelry, paintings, furniture...and each job she did, the money was slotted for a particular item. I'd meet her backstage and she'd say, 'Tonight's show is for the new breakfront!' There was no one like her."

* * *

The legendary singer Mimi Hines told us that the opening of Lake Geneva was almost stalled because, "They were still putting in plants and trees on opening day—but overnight it all blossomed into this wonderful landscape that looked as if it had been nurtured for years. It was really cool. Everybody gussied up to come and see the shows there. The guys were in suits—there were even a few tuxedos—and the ladies had on beautiful cocktail dresses. The resort atmosphere was all old-time glamour—plus the clubs were run so smoothly. At least that's how it appeared to us as entertainers.

"Phil [Ford] and I loved the Wisconsin Club. We were married as well as partners, and during the day, we played golf, got a facial or massage in the afternoon, and then hit the deck for the show at eight. I miss Phil and the fun of our act so much; I can't tell you. We always opened with a rousing song, then did a second kind of swing number, and from there, we'd go right into the 'Sayonara' sketch. Phil and I coined the phrase 'rots a ruck'; everyone loved it, so we always did a variation of that. After the show was over, we'd stay up late, giggle and laugh, and write down the ad libs that we had come up with that night."

Because of their brilliant shows, Mimi and Phil came to be called "the spoilers" because other entertainers weren't keen on following them.

* * *

Most everyone we've talked to sang Playboy's praises and reminisced about how much they'd enjoyed performing at the clubs. Kaye Ballard, on the other hand, has never been known for following the pack. "I did not like playing at the Playboy Clubs," she said, the minute we asked her about it, "with the exception of the one in Lake Geneva. That was a wonderful place—but no one paid any attention to me at the other clubs. They were more interested in ogling the Bunnies. They were really the nicest girls, though, and they always had my back. I'd be on stage about to go crazy because the audience was talking, and the Bunnies would try to calm me down by whispering, 'Oh, Kaye, don't trip out, don't trip out!' Of course, the male comics loved it at the clubs, because they were all making out with the Bunnies!

"I was so-called 'hot' during those years and headlined the clubs. I didn't have an opening act. It was just me and my sweet Arthur Siegel, my pianist and a great composer. He made me laugh. Back then, you rarely heard profanity in the acts, and at Playboy, it wasn't allowed. Totie Fields and Phyllis Diller were wonderful performers who didn't have to resort to that, and they were phenomenally successful.

"Today, I like Ellen DeGeneres and I love Lily Tomlin and loved Joan Rivers. They go all the way back to the Playboy days, and Ellen and Lily are busier than ever. Joan could get filthy, but there was always an element of truth in everything she said. I saw her on stage near the end of her life and thought, my God, she's so wonderful because she's discussing honest ideas."

* * *

Just prior to landing her first engagement at the New York Playboy Club, Lily Tomlin was performing at a club called Upstairs at the Downstairs, in a chic cabaret revue directed and choreographed by Sandra Devlin. The show portrayed the company as a tiny band of counterculture people who had broken into the showroom and taken over. The room was the size of a postage stamp, seating fewer than a hundred people.

As Lily explained, "The audience consisted of midtown New Yorkers who were used to going to this cabaret and seeing shows with songs that rhymed words with Oedipus Rex and the like, and instead, we'd come in and take over like guerillas. As part of the act, one of the guys in the revue set fire to his arm, and we swarmed him to put it out."

Apparently, nothing was off-limits or sacred with this bunch. Robert Kennedy had just been assassinated, and even he was worked into a skit.

"I would never have played the Playboy Club in those days," Lily went on. "I was too much of a feminist. But Sandy Devlin said, 'I got us a job. We're going to take our show to the Playboy Club.'

"I said, 'What? *This* show?'

"And she said, 'No, I'm putting together something new and

it's going to be great.'"

There were no blazing arms in the Playboy revue, and although Lily had been reluctant to perform there, she went along out of her legendary sense of loyalty. And that's how Lily got her start at Playboy.

The show started with Lily out front, playing an all-around goofy hostess seating people as they came into the room. She'd clean tables, empty ashtrays, and engage in all manner of zaniness before the other performers hit the stage.

"There were four or five of us," Lily said, "and we did monologues, sang songs, and carried on. Lyrics to certain songs were changed. There were a few songs where we altered the chorus. There was a litany of verses about *muff diving* and *beat your meat* that, in the songs, really wasn't as overt as it sounds. They were more puns and innuendos: a song about a pig farmer that had a twist—that sort of thing. We had to play to what we conceived the club was, right? I'm not saying everything was like that, but a good part of it was. And, of course, I threw my lot in with the rest. Once I go, I go all the way!

"I did a couple of monologues on my own, and as a result, got a big review from the TV critic Chauncey Howell. I did have fun. I lived in Yonkers at the time and had to catch the last train, so I would under dress for the final number and leave right off the front of the stage and run for the exit to catch the train."

Marcia Donen Roma, known back in the day as Bunny Marcia, remembered a part of Lily's act she thought was so side-splitting that forty years later, she still cracks up talking about it. "I truly can't remember the whole spiel but it involved a coffin with a character—Fred—laying in it. It was hysterical but another Bunny recently told me she only performed it a few times because the club thought it was too morbid."

Lily continued, "What I loved most of all was eating in the kitchen with the Bunnies and the cook. The woman that cooked was sort of like everyone's mom, and all the Bunnies were there in their wrappers. We'd all sit around a huge table with oilcloth on it—it was a regular down-home kitchen and the exact opposite of what was going on in the showroom. I was hooking a rug at the time, and I'd be at the table eating and hooking my rug and having a great time! Oh my God, I have very heavy memories of it—it was the antithesis of what I would have done, politically."

Like Playboy top executive Victor Lownes and others, Lily loved the music of jazz legend Mabel Mercer. Using almost the same words to describe her feelings as Victor had (you can read all about that in *Playboy Swings*), she told us,

"I was *mad* for her and such a huge fan that we'd go to listen to her at the Bon Soir every chance we got. We went as a group and never had any money, but we'd scrounge up a quarter for the coat check because we could go without eating or drinking, but whatever boys we were with would have to check their coats. We'd just stand there and listen to Mabel. Joanie [Rivers] was getting famous and she had the room on weekends, and Mabel played there Monday, Tuesday, and Wednesday. When I was asked to open for Mabel, I was in seventh heaven! I'd drive down from Yonkers, pick her up in Harlem, and we'd drive down to the club together. Heaven."

Lily was soon faced with choosing between two TV offers in Los Angeles—*Laugh-In* and *Music Scene*. "I chose *Music Scene*, because I was foolish enough to think that it was hipper, and—of course—we were canceled mid-season," said Lily. "Luckily, the offer for *Laugh-In* was still on the table. I went on in the third year, and as soon as Ernestine was aired, I exploded. *She*, I should say, *she* exploded!"

* * *

Singer, comedian, and actress Dana Lorge told us that by the time she'd started playing the Playboy Clubs, she already knew what she was doing.

"Before that," she said, "I did all of these horrible jobs to learn how to work an audience with snappy comebacks. That's the way you learn. People talk to you from the audience, and they're not always complimenting you, so you become quick with the zingers.

"I played the Boston Playboy Club and they had an open mic set up later in the evening for comic wannabes, after the main shows were done. Well, I have to say, the audiences on those nights were tough. I'm a singing comedian, and I'd be on stage and doing well with the regular audience—but the kids in the back waiting for the show to end so they could go on? They had their arms crossed. They were criticizing every move I made, saying things like, 'Oh my God, I can do so much better,' 'That's a horrible joke,' and on and on. I'd stay to watch them, and each one was worse than the next! One of them got up on stage and said, 'Good evening, ladies and gentlemen...' looked at the audience, said, 'Thank you,' and left the stage. I think he realized it wasn't as easy as it looks from the audience. That's the difference between amateurs and professionals. We all know what it takes to get up on a stage and deliver a show that's worth what the audience paid—and we *support* each other.

"Well, *mostly* we support each other. Once, I opened for Henny Youngman—this was just before I worked my first Playboy Club, but it illustrates how I segued from straight singing to comedy. I had a seven-piece band that didn't read music. We'd talk over everything in rehearsal, and it seemed as if it was all in order, but when I introduced a song, they'd play something else completely. I wouldn't know the song they were playing, plus, it would be in the wrong key. So I started joking around about the situation and telling funny stories because I was determined that I wasn't going to mess up Henny's opening. Oops. It turned into a disaster, because Henny was furious. He called the agent and said never to hire me again. He was jealous that I was being funny when he was the comedian.

"The New York Playboy Club was wonderful. Art Weiss played piano and I wore a gown that gave the illusion of being see-through, and the guys in the audience went crazy! I got a standing ovation just for walking onto the stage—before I said a word! Can you imagine? I thought, wow, they like me, and I didn't do anything yet!

"Great Gorge was a beautiful club—just dazzling. I played there shortly after it opened. I was rehearsing when Myron Cohen walked in with his wife. God was he great, and so gracious. He walked over to me and introduced himself and his wife and said,

"'I'll be working with you and I'm looking forward to it.'

"You don't hear that much, and I thought, 'Wow, what a gentleman.' He was also an elegant dresser. I worked with so many great people but some really stand out in my mind, and he was one of them."

After Playboy, Dana continued to entertain and amuse crowds around the world, and produced a variety show presented in New York nightclubs. On April 23, 2015, she succumbed to complications from lung cancer.

* * *

Hef has often been accused of chauvinism but we don't believe that's a fair characterization, and we don't feel the artists and staff we talked to would either.

For starters, as Dick Gregory so elegantly expressed it, "Hef doesn't care if you're black, white, or purple; only if you can sing a song or tell a joke."We'd add that he doesn't care if you're male or female. He and his clubs have been responsible for launching the careers of many entertainment icons of both genders, and his magazine has moved the causes of feminism forward. (Yes, it has. Hef has been campaigning for the rights of women to control their own bodies for decades.)

Need further proof? Talk to Lainie Kazan. When Lainie presented Hef with some ideas for breathing new life into the clubs, he granted her complete autonomy over one of his rooms in L.A.—the same one that Jackie Curtiss had run for a while until 1972. She christened it Lainie's Room and quickly filled it with great acts. Music was the main event at Lainie's (and you can read more about it in *Playboy Swings*), but a number of comedians hit the stage as well, including Norm Crosby, Don Rickles, and Totie Fields.

Thrilled with Lainie's success as an impresario, Hef asked her to duplicate it in New York and Lainie's Room East was born. She might have kept at it longer, but Francis Ford Coppola lured Lainie into films. What became a loss to live entertainment was definitely a gain for comedy on screen.

* * *

Marilyn Grabowski, photo editor of *Playboy* magazine, spent forty years reviewing centerfolds and shaping the image of the world's sexiest magazine. It was Marilyn who first brought Pamela Anderson to Hef's attention, and over the course of twenty years, Pamela would appear in the magazine more than any other model. Marilyn is also credited with enticing celebrities and movie stars to pose for its pictorials, thus setting it apart—at least for a time—from any other "men's publication."

In addition to Lainie and Marilyn, a healthy number of women have served in top management positions in the Playboy hierarchy. Trust us that *Playboy* has actually empowered and emancipated women, in part by giving them the opportunity to put their creative and business talents to work, earn a great living—and have some fun in the process.

8

"A GREAT PARTY, INDEED!"

The King of Jingles, Steve Karman, is most famous for his sharp melodic taglines, including, "Nationwide is on your side," "When you say Budweiser, you've said it all," "Aren't you glad you use Dial?" and "Wrigley's Spearmint Gum carries the big fresh flavor." But he's most proud of the jingle he created in 1977 for the New York State Tourism Board: "I Love New York." In 1980, Governor Hugh Carey declared that little ditty the state anthem. Steve responded by giving the song rights to the state as a gift!

Steve was one of the first—possibly *the* first—to copyright his commercial jingles, thereby providing himself with a royalty every time one of them aired. But before Steve developed into the savvy scribe of singable slogans, he did the rounds of the Playboy Clubs.

"I was a contestant on the Arthur Godfrey talent show and lost," he told us, "but that was when I thought I had a chance to make a good living from singing. I started working different small clubs all around the country. I remember the Purple Onion in Indianapolis, the Metropolitan Windsor in Ontario, The Lotus Club in Washington D.C., and even a club called The Gay Haven in

Detroit. Then, one day, I was booked to play the Chicago Playboy Club. It was a lot of work—they needed three acts for each of two showrooms so they hired six acts. You did your act in the first room, had a break, and you moved on to the second room, and finally you came back to the first one. You usually did four shows a night, sometimes five on weekends.

"The women I worked with were all okay singers. No one I worked with became a star, but the comics were great! Billy Falbo was wonderful to work with and I loved Jackie Gayle. As a performer, I watched everyone's act every night—I didn't just go hang out in the dressing room. Jackie had some great lines. He'd get up on stage and say, 'At the Playboy Clubs everything is a buck and a half.' Then he'd look at a Bunny and say, 'Well, almost everything.' He was great and very sharp.

"Playboy was one of the great employers, and you didn't have to have a hit record, you didn't have to be a star. I was primarily a folk singer during that time—working with a guitar, doing Harry Belafonte sort of songs. I had a genius for *not* being in sync with the trends. Everyone wanted to hear songs similar to what Pat Boone and Bobby Darin had on the radio, so I worked up an act where I wore ties and jackets, and by the time I had it together, the trends had changed to folk singers.

"Every Friday night, all the entertainers in town—not only at the Playboy Club, but all over Chicago—were invited to the Playboy Mansion, and that was a thrill. You had to take off your shoes because the carpet was completely white all over—wall-to-wall—everywhere! The place had a swimming pool where you could sit around outside if you wanted, but if you went down a level, you could sit on couches and watch people swim from the inside. They also had these unbelievable things called 'headphones.' I mean, who knew from headphones then? And you could plug these things in and listen to great music and watch people swim. I never saw anyone nude, but I know that's what the big attraction was.

"On those Friday nights, Hef would lay out this huge buffet dinner for what must have been forty or fifty people. I recall Tony Bennett was there one of the times I was. He was working some joint in Chicago and came over to hang out. Hef was wonderfully hospitable. He had a small jazz trio playing and we could tour his bedroom. He had a gigantic round bed and again, everything was white—plush, white carpet; white, white, white, everywhere. You couldn't actually enter the bedroom but you could look in—like you do in museums.

"I was a very happily married man, but, I must tell you, I worked with a lot of guys who professed to be very happily married and managed not to be alone at night. But I became the guy the Bunnies would look to for advice. They always had questions: 'Do you think he's telling me the truth, that he was using his body to warm her up because she had a chill?' Those kind of questions—that's a true story! I'm not kidding! I remember her face. She was an absolute knockout, and if I had been a single guy, I would have made a move on her too, but it was different. I was the big-brother type....

"I had a great time working with Sam DiStefano. [Sam fronted the house jazz trio in Chicago before rising through the ranks to entertainment director for the whole circuit.] He was a superb musician, to be able to go in there and 'cut the show.' He had a tight band and a *wonderful* attitude, so much fun on stage.

"Billy Falbo did a joke about a musical saw and he had an actual saw. He would take out a bow and, using his mouth, go 'Mhhmmmm'—as if he was playing the saw. I would watch Sam—he'd end up on the floor laughing! You know someone is a good comic when you've heard his act and you want to hear it again. Guys like Buddy Hackett can tell the same story fifty times and it's funny every time. I would watch Sam and he'd fall off his piano when Billy Falbo played his musical saw. It was great.

"No one made a killing working there, but the idea that there was a place like the circuit to work was groundbreaking. Hef's genius was tapping into the times. His folly was not knowing when the times had changed, but for as long as they lasted, it was a great party. A great party, indeed!"

As Steve mentioned, he was married and had three small children, whom he used to, in his words, schlep around with him when he could, sometimes piling everyone into the car to drive to Florida or wherever, for the next engagement. He told us he would write letters home and eventually got to the point where he could afford to phone instead. But, of course, it wasn't the same as being home. Eventually, he gave up the circuit—and judging from his trail of writing and business successes, it was a smart move!

* * *

Southern-born Lonnie Shorr's comedic style has often been compared to Will Rodgers, with his easy wit, conversational satire, and social observations. Like many other performers, Lonnie credits Playboy for helping him to find his niche while he worked the circuit for two continuous years, at an average of thirty-five weeks each year.

"The first club I worked at was New Orleans. It was a tryout that my manager in Chicago arranged for me. To be hired at any of the Playboys, you had to have a working act and be fairly well established, but every now and then, they would try new up-and-comers. It was a great learning experience for me because I actually learned and perfected—well, you never perfect it—but it helped shape my delivery.

"I found my rhythm and technique at the clubs, mainly because we did so many shows. Typically, you did two or three shows a night. That could easily increase if you had attendance of fifteen percent of the room capacity. In other words, if the room sat a hundred and you had fifteen, you did another show. So you were doing a minimum of sixteen or seventeen shows a week. And you quickly figured out what worked and what didn't. One thing that set Playboy apart from the other clubs, and how things are today, is that you had to have a clean act, no four-letter words and no cursing. There were guys who were a little suggestive but nothing overt—I mean, it was like church compared to today. The room manager actually wrote reports to send to the head office after every show. If you received a negative mention in a report, it wasn't a good thing."

"I remember once, during Mardi Gras in New Orleans, I did six shows in one night. I went from one room to another, back and forth. It was great for me to do so many shows because it taught me to concentrate and keep my head in the game. I'd follow the girl singer, finish my show, and pass her in the hall as I was going to the room she'd just left. About four-thirty in the morning, the guy in charge of operations happened to be in town visiting and checking us out from Chicago, and he asked me,

"'If we can get ten people, will you do one more show?'

"'I can't talk,' I told him, I just really can't talk anymore!'"

This "guy in charge" was clearly Matt Metzger, who comedian Stewie Stone called "the corporate ice man," sent to fire people. Whenever he was due at a Club, everyone said, "The iceman cometh."

Lonnie has had the opportunity to work with many very talented people, including the singer Marlena Shaw, whom he tells us held the hearts of the musicians. "They were all in love with her. Linda Hopkins and Nancy Paine were two other singers I crossed paths with. If you stayed on the circuit, everyone became your friend. The first time I played a club, I was kind of standoffish because I was in a new city and didn't know anyone, but when I came back, they were like family. During the day and after work, we'd go and do things in small groups. I did a lot of walking around and exploring each new city. I probably walked every street and alley in San Francisco. It just so happened that I was in Los Angeles the day after Sharon Tate was murdered, and the city was so tight, you could feel the tension. In New York, we'd walk around all day and go to the museums. It was terrific. I made a lot of good friends. It wasn't only the people who worked the clubs who remembered me.

I had familiar faces in the audience. If people knew you were coming back, they'd show up to support you."

After two years of performing at the Playboy Clubs, Lonnie went on to do 350 television appearances, including 126 on *The Merv Griffin Show.* "Everyone asks me about the breaks I've had. I have to answer that I worked hard but was also lucky and Playboy was a huge stepping-stone for me. Johnny Johnston opened for me once in New York. He had a popular cover of Joni Mitchell's song 'Both Sides Now.' The William Morris agent Harry Kalcheim was scheduled to come and listen to his show. What happened was that he was running late and missed most of Johnny's show, catching only the last few minutes, and he decided to relax a little and watch a small bit of my act. He liked it and stayed for the whole thing. Afterwards, he came over and gave me his card and asked if I had a manager. I knew that William Morris was the top. I signed with him immediately and the next night, he brought everyone from the agency to my show.

"Harry was responsible for the careers of many of the really big stars, not the least of which was Elvis Presley. He kind of took me under his wing, and I left Playboy because he put me into bigger things. But if I hadn't had those two years working at Playboy under my belt, I never would have impressed him enough to sign me, and I wouldn't have achieved anywhere near what I have. I signed on Wednesday and on Thursday I did *The Merv Griffin Show,* on Friday *The David Frost Show*, and then Vegas and the Copacabana and many other television shows. It just didn't stop."

* * *

Howard Beder spent the first nine years of his Playboy career as a singer, before segueing into comedy for his final year in the trenches. "I never thought I knew it all," he told us. "I took advice whenever it presented itself. The entertainment community is tremendously encouraging to young talent—you just have to be smart enough to listen. I was the lead singer in a group called the Mello Mates—two guys and a girl. We were performing down in Greenwich Village when Sammy Davis, Jr. came in. He liked us and took us on the road with him. Frank Sinatra was another supporter in those days, attending his shows and complimenting him on his technical gifts. He once walked onstage during one of Howard's performances and told the crowd,

"'If my kid could sing like this guy, I'd be the happiest guy in the world.' Now *that's* encouragement.

"During the mid-sixties," Howard told us, "I had a hit record called *Tumbling Tumbleweeds.* It had originally been recorded by the Sons of the Pioneers, but I had a great arranger put a rock beat behind it. It hit the *Billboard* charts in 1965 and I went around promoting it, which was a little tough because the payola scandal had made everyone afraid to push a new artist.

"After that, I was working in Winnipeg and I wanted to get on the Playboy circuit. My agent did a lot of the booking for the Chicago Club so he got me a date there. I took a Greyhound bus from Winnipeg to New York, and then on to Chicago.

"The first night, I was waiting my turn to go on after another singer and a comedian. That was the typical lineup in those days. They were not doing well with the audience. A bunch of wise guys were yelling things. So when I was introduced, I came from the back of the showroom and shook hands with people and talked a little to them as I walked toward the stage. I felt I had put them at ease, so I told them to calm down, quiet down—which they did. I got up on stage and my act went great. That's how they started to use me. That was how I got onto the circuit.

"When I was starting out, Larry Storch, the great comedian, told me, 'If you're on stage and your material isn't going like you want—if you're not getting the reaction you expect—*do not* let the audience know it's bothering you. They're like sharks smelling blood in the water, and they will deliberately climb up on you just to see you sweat!'"

Howard was booked as a singer but he was also a good writer and very funny. At the Playboy Clubs, he was paired with a comedian and, as was typical, they hung out together—sometimes for breakfast, lunch, and dinner. Howard would write down snippets of their chit-chat and other things that came to mind during the day, and in the evening, he'd hand his notes to the comedian.

"It was just stuff we'd said at the table, but it was amusing and the comics sometimes put it in their acts. They all told me the same thing: 'What the hell are you doing singing? *Do you have any idea how funny you are?*'"

Eventually, Howard did add comedy writing to his résumé, providing material for many of the recording comedians in addition to writing a television script for Walter Matthau.

"I used to open for Flip Wilson at the Playboy Clubs," he told us, "before he was famous. And we became very good friends. In fact, he would stay up late working on material and I'd keep him company. Flip told me, 'Oh my God, you have such a comic mind that you've given me a million good ideas without even trying.' I remember saying, 'Thanks, but what are you talking about?'

"Playboy was my life for ten years, so I made many close friends there—including Pat Morita. We were on the road together a lot. I have to digress a minute here and explain that, when I was very young, I used to play cards really well; I had an incredibly good memory. Sometimes, I'd even be set up by backers, who'd stake me and then we'd split the money. One day, Pat Morita told me that he was a gin rummy player and suggested we play for a quarter a point. After the first night, I realized that he didn't have a clue. He couldn't even shuffle—he was showing me the bottom card every time!

"So, the next night, I came in and gave him a letter, and I said to him, 'Do me a favor. Don't open this until the end of our engagement.' So he put it in his room and forgot about it. By the end of the run, he owed me hundreds and hundreds of dollars. *He was really bad at cards*!

"He said to me, 'I'll have to pay you over time... my wife... I have two kids....'

"I said, 'Remember, I gave you a letter? Read the letter.' So he went and got it and opened it, and in the letter, I said, 'Pat, you are the worst gin rummy player I have ever run into. I would not take your money. It would be stealing. You are terrible.' It's the truth!

"I met George Carlin down in New Orleans. The first time he opened for me, he was still part of Burns and Carlin. All the acts stayed in the same hotel and we'd eat our meals together, so we all became very friendly. George's wife even became good friends with my wife. George could do voices well, and once, he called me, got my answering machine, and pretended to be Victor Lownes: 'Hey, Howard, this is Victor. We have a new policy now. We're going to do at least four shows a day, maybe five. And you'll have to work Sundays, and you're going to work all the lounges....' He went on for a while, and then, in his own voice, he said, 'Hey, this is George Carlin, how ya doing?' I still have that recording. I'll play it for you sometime. He was a very nice man.

"New Orleans was the best and the worst Playboy Club—remember, this was segregated America in the early 1960's. The club was above a famous restaurant, Moran's, and a few doors down from Felix's Oyster Bar. Across the street was the Acme Bar, which supposedly had the best oysters in New Orleans. I'm a big oyster guy, so I was in heaven. They had the best seafood down there.

"As I said, I worked at Playboy for ten years—nine as a singer. We all hung around the Mansion, and every comic used to tell Hefner how I'd helped him with his material. I was really a comic all along, masquerading as a singer. So one day, I was at the airport and I got a page. It was the director of entertainment at Playboy and he said, 'Look, you have to go to Cincinnati right away. Their comic got sick and he can't go on.' And I said, 'This is Howard Beder. I'm the singer.' He said, 'Listen to me. Hefner says every comic you ever worked with tells him how you could be a comedian. He said to give you one year as a comedian with a free pass—no matter what the room manager's report says, you're okay. So go be a comedian, but go to Cincinnati now!'

"Hef did that for me. I had a guaranteed job at Playboy for a year to work on comedic timing and audience reaction and important things like that. It was a gift—but once in a while, it didn't go so well. One time, I was on stage and a man with a portable iron lung decided to sit ringside. They ran his electrical cord in between my legs, across the stage, to the outlet at the far end. The lung was going 'whoosh, whoosh, whoosh,' and no one was laughing at the jokes because they were so disturbed by it. So I stopped and said, 'Sir, one of us is going to die here. It better not be me.' And I reached down and acted as if I was going to put the plug out... and the place went nuts! They started screaming with laughter. The nurse had to hold the poor guy down because she thought he might have an attack—he was laughing harder than anyone else!

"Another time, I did a show where everyone was deaf and mute—I'm not kidding! So they put a lady on stage to sign my act for them. No one was laughing, so after five minutes, I stopped the show, walked over to her, and said, 'Please sign exactly what I say. Please tell them I don't think your fingers are funny!' She signed that to the audience and they roared with laughter."

Over time, Howard worked at all the Playboy Clubs, including the ones in London and Jamaica. "Hefner was fantastic," Howard said. "Every year, he would tell them to book me for a month at the Jamaica Club during my children's Easter break. My family would come down for a good portion of the time and we'd have two suites on the ocean! I was one of the highest-ranking acts during all those years, both as a singer and a comedian, and I'm very appreciative for all they did for me. It was a great job."

* * *

Kelly Monteith's first job as a solo comic was at the 183rd Street Art

Theater in North Miami Beach. He described it to us as, "a strip club that also showed dirty movies. These same movies would be shown on prime-time television today, but back then, they were very risqué. There was a matinee and two or three showings a night and we'd do a show in between the movies. I was the comedian emcee and I'd go on stage after the movie and do five minutes, then I'd introduce the first girl, and after her I'd do another five minutes and introduce the second stripper. The best thing I can say about strip clubs is that you learned how to survive. It was a way most of us started out back then, but I knew I had to get out.

"I got to know Billy Rizzo who, at that time, was a booker for the Playboy Clubs, through other comedians. After paying my dues at the burlesque houses, I decided that I was ready to move on and called Billy, who arranged a weekend audition for me at the Chicago Club. I worked the Playroom—the smaller room with a bar—on a Friday and Saturday, and Billy didn't come to see me until the last show on Saturday. I was really nervous because, up to that point, the audiences had liked me and everything was great, but any comedian will tell you that you rarely hit a home run in all five consecutive shows. Somehow, it went well and Billy gave me some circuit work in the same room, starting at the Cincinnati Club about three months later.

"Playboy had a great circuit and they gave me the first steady income I ever had in show business. Jamaica was the most amazing job because you only had to work one show a week! Ocho Rios was just this little-bitty town. Jamaica back then was still very tropical and unspoiled—it was great. The people were nice, the club was wonderful… I mean you had the Bunnies, the pool, the beach, all the food and liquor anyone could want, and you could chill out for the entire week. How can you beat that? I always thought the Jamaicans were very sweet people.

"One of Jamaica's great products was *ganja*—the powerful marijuana that grew there. You would give one of the kids five bucks and he'd run into the jungle and come back with a *bale* of the stuff—it looked like a tumbleweed of pot. Of course, you'd have to clean it and weed out all the sand and twigs.

"Once when I was working at the New York Club, there was some kind of FBI investigation into the Mafia and they were calling the employees in for interviews. I never got called in, but I was nervous because I was sort of friendly with a guy who hung out at the bar a lot. He was an ex-boxer and I think he was a low-level enforcer—a strong-arm guy who retrieved money that was owed to *certain people*.

"I used to do a couple of jokes about the Mafia in my act, and the boxer guy told me once, 'Yeah, they're pretty funny but I don't think the guys downtown would appreciate those jokes too much.'

"I remember thinking, 'Whoa, maybe I better leave them out of the next show.' Nothing ever came of the investigation and I was sure glad I wasn't interviewed because I recall saying to myself, 'Jeez, if they ever call me in, I'm not going to squeal on *that* guy!'

"I worked the Los Angeles Club before I was really ready for it. I wasn't very good, to be honest with you. I worked with Arlene Golonka [best known for playing Millie Swanson on *The Andy Griffith Show*]. She had all her friends and family there on opening night and I followed her, but everyone just wanted Arlene back. To top it off I asked her if that was her real name. She got pissed off and said, sarcastically, 'No, I *changed* it!'

"Aside from that one time in L.A., I had great experiences at the clubs. The Bunnies were very nice girls. It was a good opportunity for them to make a lot of money—much better than if they worked as a secretary or clerk somewhere—and they were protected. No one was allowed to make rude remarks or touch them. Plus, there was a certain cachet about being a Bunny—a kind of status—and that costume made every one of them look amazing. We weren't supposed to ask them out, but we never paid attention to that. We had to be selective, though, because if you asked one on a date and she rejected you—well, you just blew your chances. The other girls would know immediately they you had hit on her and none of them wanted to be your second choice. I guess I picked well because my first wife was a Bunny from the Denver Club—Bunny Diane."

The clubs provided Kelly with the first steady income he ever had in show business and he told us it was, "a way to develop, in a lot of ways anonymously, since they didn't get much press because they were private clubs. It gave me the opportunity to evolve as a performer and a writer, and not to mention that it gave me a regular income to count on. I could actually buy clothes! "

Kelly got his break on *The Mike Douglas Show*. He was working at the New York Playboy Club when he got a letter suggesting that he take the train from New York to Philadelphia to audition for it. He aced the audition and landed his first television appearance. From there, he appeared on *The Jack Paar Show* and was singled out in a review in *Time* magazine. Throughout this period, he continued to work at the Playboy Clubs, right up until he began appearing regularly on *The Tonight Show* and *Merv Griffin*. Kelly eventually landed his own show on CBS—*The Kelly Monteith Show*—and after an appearance on the English talk show *Des O'Connor*, he was offered his own series on the BBC, which ran for six years.

While living in London, Kelly renewed his friendship with Victor Lownes and he and his wife were invited to Victor's country home, Stocks, for the wedding of Victor and Marilyn.

During his BBC series run, he toured the United Kingdom, selling out concerts in England, Wales, Scotland, and Ireland and putting in a Command Performance for Queen Elizabeth II. He also performed at a "Night of a Hundred Stars" in the presence of Princess Margaret.

Kelly currently resides in Los Angeles, where he writes and produces independent films.

* * *

Often called a comic's comic, Stewie Stone has opened for such notables as Sonny and Cher, Frankie Valli and the Four Seasons, Natalie Cole, and Aretha Franklin—in addition to being a headliner in his own right. When we asked him how he came to work for Playboy, Stewie took us back to his days as the social director for the Concord Hotel in the Catskill Mountains.

"I was emceeing a bathing-beauty contest," he said. "We had about 3,000 people there and I was doing a Rickles and Schmitz bit when this gentleman sauntered over to me and said,

"'You're very funny. Could you talk for twenty minutes on stage?'

"I said, 'How much?' To which he replied, 'Five hundred dollars.'

"'I'll do thirty,' I said.

"Turns out, the guy owned the Boston Playboy Club, which was a franchise at the time. They had extra shows on weekends and they needed comics to fill the slots. He hired me three or four different times and I got good marks on my reports, so he called the Playboy booker, who put me on the circuit around the world. I played thirty to forty weeks a year for Playboy for a good four years."

Joining Stewie for our chat was Bruce Charet, who, for many years, worked closely with Alan King as his assistant. Bruce has given a lot of thought to the Playboy organization and the reasons behind its success.

"The Playboy Clubs," he said, "were around before the comedy clubs. Before there was anything, there were the Playboy Clubs. They filled a niche. It's interesting, historically, that the Playboy Clubs came into being just as the traditional nightclub circuit was dying. They were really the last vestiges of nightclub life in America before the comedy-club explosion. The nightclub era ended in the late sixties, and that's when Playboy was going the strongest. Thanks to them, all of us guys who had played the nightclubs could still work and get paid. Once the comedy clubs revved up, nobody got paid.

"Playboy was the last gasp of the old culture, the pre-Vietnam culture. The clubs were the last place anyone saw a comic work in a tuxedo. The club scene is a very important part of American popular culture, and because they had the Playboy brand on them, they seemed hip. So the whole scene was able to chug along for a while, beyond when the rest of that culture died. Playboy employed so much talent and was so important to the development of comedy because comedians had places they could constantly work."

Stewie interjected with a description of the clubs' talent-evaluation process. "The room directors would grade you. You'd do three or four shows a night and get an A, B, C, or D on your report card for each one. If you got failing grades, you didn't stay on the circuit. In New York, you did three shows, unless a lot of people showed up, in which case, you had to do a fourth. After the third show was over, the entertainers and musicians would mix with the crowd and mumble, 'That was the worst show I've ever seen; I'd never go see a show like that again,' trying to talk them into *not* hanging around for another set! Oh my God, it worked every time.

"I'd have to say, the Denver club was my least favorite. It was so dead. The joke was that when a customer walked in, the manager would call up a Bunny and say, 'Put on your outfit and come to work.'"

Bruce theorized, "The thing about Playboy was that it presented a curious political conundrum. On one side, the company published a salacious, under-the-counter, taboo men's magazine; on the other, they were great defenders of the First Amendment and women's rights. No question, it was a liberal place to work.

"Hefner came up with a great gimmick when he decided to hire pretty girls, dress them up, and call them something other than waitresses. Combine that with the concept of selling 'keys,' which made every guy feel like he owned a part of the place, and you had gold. Hef made blue-collar workers earning eighteen thousand dollars a year feel like James Bond for an hour-and-a-half.

"Another great idea was that everything at the clubs was priced the same, a dollar-fifty. A drink was a dollar-fifty—a steak, coffee, cigarettes—everything was a dollar and a half. That changed when the powers that be decided they should upscale the place—offering fine dining and all that stuff—which was the kiss of death.

"Victor Lownes and Shelly Kasten were hip, while Hef was far more analytical. That's his journalistic thing. He was constantly analyzing the Playboy lifestyle from an intellectual perspective, figuring out what the public wanted from the fantasy. And he was brilliant at it—more than brilliant.

"The New Orleans club had the most beautiful Bunnies because they were from all over the South," Stewie told us. "Once, I was down there opening for Al Frazier, a handsome black singer. He started his act and you could hear some rumbling in the room. I had just come offstage, and at one point, I had said something about being Jewish.

"Suddenly, I could hear some guy yelling, 'I have to pay money to see some black singer and some Jew comic?'

"I shot back, 'You're not paying for this show. I'm paying for it!'

"I turned to the room director and said, 'I'll pay for his show if he doesn't like it.' Well, he couldn't shut up.

"He starts in, 'You're not buying me . . .'

"We went back and forth for a while, until I tried to make light of it by saying, 'Oh, the world is about brotherhood. We should all get along.' He got up and ran out of the theater! That was the worst thing that ever happened to me at a Playboy Club, and when you think about it, that's not too bad."

Stewie worked the Playboy circuit until other major venues caught on and started to call him. His next gig was touring with Frankie Valli and the Four Seasons, and he's been going ever since. Bruce lives in New York—he's a regular at the Friars Club—and for the last few years his main projects have been producing Broadway-bound musicals, including a stage version of *Robin & The Seven Hoods,* in addition to a Broadway biography of Connie Frances.

* * *

Dick Capri—whose comedic style is anchored distinctly in the Borscht Belt—was married to a June Taylor dancer. It so happened that her best girlfriend was married to Don Adams, the star of the popular TV show *Get Smart*. "We became friends," said Dick, "and Don was very friendly with the guy who booked the Playboy Clubs. So I have Don to thank for getting me work there. I worked the clubs for years, off and on. I also took other jobs, opening for a lot of singers who had hit records at the time. I was always the opening act."

As he explained it, Playboy had a hierarchy of sorts. Headliners naturally commanded more money than up-and-comers, and they got more perks. While the big names had their transportation, lodging, and meals covered, most of the openers had to fend for themselves.

"In those days," Dick said, "we had to pay our own way to the job. They didn't pay for anything. Sometimes, they had a kitchen with food for the entertainers, but not always. At Playboy, we were always booked for two weeks, not one, like at some other clubs, but the first week just paid for our expenses. It wasn't until the second week that we broke even or maybe made a few bucks to put away. Not a lot—but a few. I was making five hundred a week there, and I was happy to get it.

"I worked all the Playboy Clubs they had during the late sixties and early seventies, even the one in England. There, I had to tailor my act a little, because even though they spoke English, certain American expressions didn't translate.

"They let me stay at the hotel they had over the club there—well, I should say, they rented me a room. The truth is, I was glad to get a room that was only a few steps to the club. The English food was awful in the sixties. They took leftovers and mixed them all together and called it 'bubble and squeak.' I could never eat it. Bangers and mash?—Yuck!

"The Playboy Clubs all seemed the same to me, which was

the idea, I guess. They were all run the same, and we all made the rounds, so the acts were the same. Most of the comedy rooms were small—so small that the Bunnies were taught to serve from the rear of the tables, never from the front, so as not to the block the view of the performer. I thought that was smart.

"Show business is funny. You're in a club for two weeks and you get friendly with the people you're working with—then it's over. This one time, I was at the Great Gorge club with Carmen McRae, the jazz singer, and we became very, very close. We had a lot of laughs together—she was a pal, a good pal. When we finished the job, she slipped a note under my door that said, 'When you get to California, give me a call'—all very nice. I still have the letter. A little while later, she was working at the Living Room in New York and I decided to go check her out and catch up. When I got there, she looked at me as if she'd never seen me before!

"'Hi, Carmen, Dick Capri,' I said. She gave me a look, turned and went on stage, and that was that. That happens a lot. You're friends out of town, but when you get back to reality, forget it—you're done. Brushed off!

"The girls, the Bunnies, all had a great look, with their long legs and pushed-up boobs, perfect makeup, and cute ears—they were cute as could be!

"I worked with some nice people during my Playboy years, all over the country: Miami, Boston, New York, Chicago, everywhere. Most of those folks are dead now, of course. Everyone I know is dead." (We may have lost some of our favorite entertainers, but they're not *all* dead, Dick!)

Dick told us that he'd gotten into the comedy business when he was in high school, as a way to meet girls. After graduation, he went to New York and entered some of the amateur contests that were so abundant and trendy in those days. He often won. It was during this period that someone offered him his first paying job.

"The first time you get paid to stand up in front of an audience, you're hooked," he told us. "So I hung around, worked on a routine—starved—worked the Playboy Clubs . . . and I joined the Friars Club, a famous show-business gathering place in New York.

"My first manager, Martin Goodman, was a very big-time guy—he managed Carol Burnett and Jonathan Winters. He only took me on because he got drunk. The way it came about was that I was working in Bermuda and he was there vacationing with Jonathan Winters. While I was performing, they were in the audience having an argument about something. Apparently, Martin said to Jonathan, 'I could make a star out of anybody! I could make a star out of that guy!'—meaning me. After the show, he came over and gave me his card and said, 'I think you're destined for great things. Call me.' But he was so drunk that he gave me the wrong telephone number.

"I looked him up and went to his office and, of course, by then he was sober, but he signed me anyway and sent me on a few auditions—not many. But the auditions went well—maybe because they were impressed that Goodman was handling me. Next thing you know, I was on *The Ed Sullivan Show*.

"Back to the Friars... One night, I got up on stage there, and the guy who managed Engelbert Humperdinck and Tom Jones was in the house. He liked me and asked me to open for them on the road. I got six weeks each with these fellas, starting in 1973, and I stayed with Engelbert for twelve more years. We got along well.

"When you're a comedian working with a singer, you're his constant companion. You hang out with him after the show, in the dressing room, at dinner, just keeping him company and amusing him. The big job isn't entertaining the audiences; it's entertaining the star."

In 1991, Dick made his Broadway debut in *Catskills on Broadway*, co-starring Freddie Roman, Louise DuArt, and Mal Z. Lawrence. He can still be found hanging out and making people laugh at the Friars Club.

* * *

Jeremy Vernon's first shot working for Playboy was a disaster. "It was at the Chicago club," he told us. "I was the new guy and they put me in the Library, which was more or less a waiting room for people who couldn't get in to see the main show. The headliners in the two other showrooms were Jackie Vernon—no relation—and George Carlin. At that point, George was still doing a very traditional act, wearing a three-button suit and doing parodies of television commercials and so on.

"The Library was a really tiny room, holding just forty or fifty people. I first followed a woman who sang songs from operettas, which was not the right material for the Playboy Club, and then another woman who sang folk songs—also not great for that audience. That was my setup and I bombed. The Bunnies hated me, because if the audience isn't having a good time, they don't order drinks. Everyone hated me, so I thought…that's it for me and Playboy. They'll never ask me back."

If Jeremy had been right about that, he probably wouldn't be in these pages. As it happens, fate took a different turn.

"I was working in New York, at the Bon Soir, and my agent, Lee Salomon from the William Morris office, brought in Shelly Kasten, the Playboy booker. Shelly watched my set and said, 'You have a job'—just like the flop in Chicago never happened—and he booked me in Miami. I was a big hit there, so they sent me to Jamaica—Ocho Rios. Miami and Jamaica were usually a package deal.

"Jamaica was a lot of fun and you didn't have to do as many performances as you did in the States. Plus, I made friends with one of the Bunnies."

But Jeremy, we queried, isn't it against the rules to date the Bunnies?

"Oh, that's nonsense," he told us. "Sure you can. We actually kept score. One of my good friends—Lou Alexander, another comedian—came back from working the Chicago club, and the first thing I asked was, 'How many Bunnies did you date?' 'Eleven,' he told me, but he exaggerates, so I bet it was only seven or eight.

"The Bunnies had their own games, too," Jeremy explained. "They would come over to me and stroke my arm and say, 'Oh, what a lovely suit. What's the material?' They'd flirt and flirt: 'What's that cologne you're wearing? It's so nice.' But as soon as I'd ask one of them for a date, she'd say, 'Oh, we're not allowed to date!' I knew it was BS!

"Jack Carter later told me that Vegas showgirls amused themselves in the same manner. Once, when he was performing out there, the girls had a contest to see how many of them could get Jack to ask them out. Of course, they had no intention of fooling around with him. The Bunnies were even worse—they wouldn't even accept the date.

"There was a Bunny in New Orleans who had a reputation as a live wire—well, that's a polite word for it. She was very bubbly and upbeat and was the girlfriend of all the comedians. Whoever was in town, she'd date him for that week. She wasn't my type, being a little stocky, though well within Bunny standards. One day, she cornered me and said, 'You're the only comedian who hasn't hit on me. Why?' Not to embarrass her, I said, 'Oh, it's because I'm gay.' I had heard girls using that as an excuse, so I figured it might work. After that, she invited me up to her place, and all the other Bunnies were running around in their underwear and some were even braless. I guess they figured I was no threat, more like a girlfriend—which was fine with me!"

As much as we loved all the comedians we met—and we did adore every one of them—it became clear that, as a group, even more than the singers or other performers, they behaved like a bunch of over-age frat boys when they were around the Bunnies. And we reached this conclusion just from the stories they told us. Imagine what they *didn't* say!

"After a rocky start in Chicago," continued Jeremy, "I did pretty well with the Playboy audiences—except for the time I decided to move from New York to California. I packed everything, sold my furniture, and put what was left into my big Oldsmobile. I thought I was lucky because I was able to pick up a gig on the way out, at the Playboy Club in Detroit. Again, I ended up following a very strange act: Phyllis Branch. She was an African American singer who performed some kind of voodoo song in an eerie, weird voice. She ended it crying—with big tears rolling down her cheeks!

"I said to her, 'Please don't leave them like that; I have to follow you,' but she said,

"'You take care of yourself and don't bother me.'

"When you have a stiff audience, you do stock lines like, 'What is this, an audience or a jury?' Or, 'Let's all hold hands and contact the living.' Even that stuff didn't get them to smile.

"As I left the stage, a Texan says to me, 'You've got the wrong attitude, boy!' Well, I didn't do well there, and the boss wrote a report that I happened to see, that said, 'Not very good.'

"Once I got to California, they wanted to send me to Chicago. It was winter and it was beautiful on the Coast, but Chicago? *Oh my God.* I told my agent, 'I don't want to go to Chicago in the winter.'

"He shot back, 'You have to! Playboy wants you there. I won't take my commission. Just go and do it.' So I did, and that's when I started to get booked in all the other clubs. That's when I went on the circuit. I'd work twenty weeks in a row, take a few weeks off, and then start the rounds again. It was the first time in my career that I was able to put away any money.

"The image that Playboy was trying to project was that the clubs were for players, wealthy guys, *bons vivants*. But in some of the out-of-the-way places, it was really just a bunch of seed salesmen in brown suits and black shoes. Rednecks. In one of those clubs, I was coming toward the stage from the back and a guy said to me,

"'This steak is *raw*.'

"I said, 'Yeah—so?'

"He said, 'Do you hear me? This steak is raw! You work here, don't you?'

"And I said, 'Yes, but I'm not in charge of steak. I have nothing to do with your steak.'

"Everything was a buck fifty—that schmuck's steak was a buck fifty! Coffee, drinks, cigarettes, everything—a dollar and a half. They used to say that was so the Bunnies didn't have to do any addition or subtraction.

"I met Hugh Hefner once—there was a party going on at the Mansion. I wasn't invited but Nick Caesar, the singer, was. He said, 'C'mon, we're going to the Playboy Mansion.' He knew from working the circuit that all of the entertainers could get in. We got there and Dick Richards was manning the door, checking off who could and couldn't enter, and he said, belligerently,

"'Who invited you?'

"I said, 'Check the list.' What do you know? We were on it! He just didn't want us to be there because we were competition for the girls.

"Eventually, I started getting offers for Vegas, and I did a lot of television shows, so I stopped doing the circuit—*Stop the circuit, I want to get off!* Please, no more, I can't do this anymore. But I loved it while it lasted. I met great people, made a living, worked on my career, and got a little recognition."

* * *

Fast forward to John Regis's life after vaudeville. John found himself in the Air Force as a drill sergeant, trying through humor to get the recruits to *want* to do what he wanted them to do without "having to beat them over the head with it." This was during the Korean War. At that time, there was a huge problem with soldiers going AWOL. They were drafted but had nothing to do stateside, so they'd go into town on passes and never come back. The commanding general needed to fix the situation. Eventually, a certain

Sergeant Gavin turned to John for help.

"Sergeant Gavin was a terrific guy," John said. "He was a master sergeant and had been with me since the day I got out of basic training. So when he told me that he wanted me to take over Special Services, because the commanding general was upset about the AWOL rate, I said, 'What do you suppose I can do about it?'

"He said, 'That's up to you—just do it!'

"Before you know it, I was the director of entertainment, and we started having talent shows. For the finals, we borrowed a local schoolhouse auditorium, because a lot of civilians wanted to come. The contestants could rack up points—twenty-five for this, twenty-five for that—in four different areas: material, costume, presentation, and cleanliness.

"I really pulled off a coup when I got Dan Dailey to act as one of the judges. Frank Gorshin was in the service at the time, and he was one of the contenders. That's where his great career as an impressionist started. Dan gave Frank a one-hundred-percent ranking. No one else had ever gotten a perfect score.

"On the scorecard he wrote, 'I'd love to have ten percent of this guy.' When I told Dan that Frank was being discharged in two weeks, he agreed to help him get started in Hollywood. He gave me his card with his agency number on the back, and I gave it to Frank, and he was on his way.

"Jerry Van Dyke was also at Lowes with me, and he was a pain in the ass, but a friend. So that's how I met Jerry and Frank. Sadly, we've lost Frank, but I see Jerry all the time, and we *all* entertained at the Playboy Clubs!

"Sally Marr, Lenny Bruce, Frankie Raye, and Jackie Gayle were all real tight friends of mine. Jackie was the star of the Playboy Clubs and like a brother to me. We even shared a house for five years. I was performing at the Body Shop, a high-class strip joint in Los Angeles, and Jackie heard me, and we connected and became very close. (As mentioned earlier, Jackie was instrumental in snagging a spot on the circuit for John).

John was slotted to work the clubs in Baltimore, Kansas City, and finally Boston. He made them laugh in Baltimore and got good reports—but Kansas City was a disaster:

"Al Frazier, a very gifted black singer, opened for me there," remembered John. "The night started out badly, with only six people in the audience, because Dwight Eisenhower was being buried and the funeral procession was going right through Kansas City. Then, while Al was singing, a woman pulled out a cigarette. He went in his pocket, came out with a lighter, and leaned over to light it for her—and she slapped it out of his hand!

"'Okay,' he said, 'All right. That's it. Good night.' And he walked off the stage... And then came, 'Here's the comedy star of our show, John Regis!'

"Of course, I *bombed.* It was a nightmare—one that probably wouldn't have mattered if the manager hadn't been there to see it. Al Frazier was an old timer, been around a long time with Playboy, but I hadn't. The manager wrote a scathing letter to Billy Rizzo and all the other managers on the circuit saying,

"'This is the worst act I've ever seen. Don't book him.'

"After the show, I went down to Al's dressing room and said, 'Al, I can't follow that. You can't do that to me.'

"He apologized, saying, 'You're right, man, I was wrong, but you saw what happened... We have to deal with these things sometimes.'

"I killed in the second show but the manager wasn't there to see it. Later, I get a call from Billy Rizzo. I explained what had happened but he said, 'Man, you really got the wrong manager. He sent a letter to everyone on the circuit. I'll try to get you some other dates, but as of now, after you do Boston, it's over.'

"In Boston, I was supposed to open for this Spanish guitar player and singer that they were really hot for, but at the last minute, they couldn't get the visas for him. Instead, they brought in an act from New York and decided I should close the show. Either way was fine with me. After the first show, which went very well, the manager came and asked me about Kansas City. I told him the story, and he showed me the famous letter. It said, 'Don't ever book this guy. He's the worst.' So the Boston manager wrote his own letter that said,

"'Not only is he not the worst guy I've ever seen, he's one of the best, and he can work for me anytime.' He was a very nice man—and I liked that club, though it was supposedly owned by the mob.

"Sally Marr was one of the funniest human beings I ever knew. She was incredibly comical, just off the top of her head. She did some standup under her real name, Sadie Kitchenberg. She didn't know how to handle an audience, but she was funny—at least to Lenny, Jackie, and me. Sally had carte blanche at the Playboy Mansion and she was my favorite date. She knew everyone in the business. We had an arrangement that if I 'got lucky,' she'd take a cab home.

"After that crazy trial by fire, I worked the circuit forty weeks a year for seven and a half years. It was like going to college for comedy!"

* * *

When Lou Alexander was eighteen, he began to follow in his father's footsteps—along with best buddy, Howard Storm. As we mentioned earlier, Howard was the son of a vaudeville comic; so was Lou. When the two teens teamed up, they billed themselves as Storm and Gale—and they were the youngest comedy team in show business at the time.

Lou recalled, "Howard and I were best friends and are to this day. One day, when we were fourteen, Howard said, 'Let's put an act together!' I'm pretty impulsive and spontaneous, but luckily, I had the sense to say, 'Don't you think we should finish high school first?' In due course, we did come up with an act and appeared in all the strip houses until I was drafted."

Lou was drafted into the Marines, which was highly unusual, but with the war raging in Korea, the War Department was determined to beef up all the armed forces. From August 1951 to October 1952, every fifth man drafted was the property of the US Marines—lucky Lou.

"The Playboy Clubs were very important to me. I tried and tried to get that first booking, and I just couldn't get in. They didn't want to take a chance on me because they were only about a year old. They were taking the hot guys at the time, names like Irwin Corey, Jeremy Vernon, Jerry Van Dyke, and Jackie Gayle. Jackie was a star at Playboy. Everyone loved Jackie, and he was very close to Hefner. Luckily for me, Jackie saw me perform somewhere and put a good word in with the powers that be: 'I saw this guy, Lou Alexander. Why aren't you using him? Use him. Put him to work.'

"So they hired me, and after I worked the first club, they sent me on the circuit and that was my employment for two years. It was my start. It was steady employment and a great place to break in new material and get ready for talk shows, which we all fantasized were just around the corner. At the start, you had great people going to the clubs, because they were new. They were *the* hip place. Not like later on, when every schmuck was going to the club because they had one in every little small town in the country. At the beginning, it was really special—all the high-line people would brag, 'I've got a key and a private club to go to!'"

Lou's excitement ebbed a little when the reality of working at the Chicago club set in.

"That club," Lou told us, "had three or four different rooms, with different entertainers in each, and the customers would go from one room to the next to see each performer. There was a hierarchy, and you'd be assigned a room depending on your popularity. There were great, experienced, talented entertainers like Jerry Van Dyke and Jackie Vernon and many other big-name folks. I was the new guy and at the bottom of the totem pole, so I was consigned to the Library. The Library was the *pits* for any comedian. They all wanted the main room, or at least the second room, because the Library was the *bottle breaking room*!"

From the repeal of Prohibition in 1933 up until 1964, all liquor and spirit bottles manufactured and sold in the United States were required by law to carry an embossed marking clearly stating that the bottle could not be reused—and had to be broken when it was empty. This was to discourage the reuse of the bottles for home-made, unregulated liquor, and also as a means to protect the new alcohol-tax revenue.

I'm sure you see what's coming.

"Because of the law," Lou explained, "when they finished a bottle, the bartenders had to break it. And my room—the Library—was the room where all the bottles from the club were sent to be destroyed. Now, you have to picture me as a standup comic—all the other rooms held a hundred or more people, and my room supported sixty. I'm in the schmuck room! But—again, I say—comics are great, because we hang together. All the other comedians would say, 'We've got to go see Lou tonight, because they're going to break the bottles on all of his punch lines. It's funnier than any movie just to see Lou's face when he gets to the big moment and—crack!' So, all the comedians would come and see me and roll on the floor. The management knew everyone was going to die a terrible death in that room, and I actually died a better death than most. Ultimately, they booked me at all the clubs they were opening, and I worked the better rooms. But that Library—it was the *death* room!

"I had a lot of fun in Chicago—besides the dating perks. We just had so much fun, all the comedians hanging out together; we stayed in the same hotels, went to the same after-hours joints, and chased the Bunnies. The interesting thing about that rule of non-fraternization between the Bunnies and the performers was that they couldn't stop it! That never really took hold. You can't stop a comedian, or any entertainer, from looking at a good-looking girl—and that same girl will always look back at you.

"I have to say, I was wild at that time. I was a young guy, not married, and I worked at the Playboy Club with all these beautiful Bunnies. One night, as I closed and was getting ready to move on to another club, a Bunny came over to me and presented me with a cup—similar to a trophy cup—with a plaque on it that said, 'You broke the house record by dating twelve Bunnies.'"

We want to know who kept score!

The Chicago Club was fun for Lou but the Los Angeles Club was the most important and beneficial to moving him to the next level in the entertainment hierarchy. L.A. was the place to be seen for television variety shows and casting agents were always looking for untapped talent. It was also the cool, hip spot for celebrities to unwind with drinks, dinner, and maybe a show. It was there that Joey Bishop saw Lou and put him on his show. Steve Allen did the same.

In turn, the great TV exposure led to a gig at another club—The Interlude—where Lou opened for his then-girlfriend, the hip hypnotist Pat Collins. It was at the Interlude that he met one of his longtime idols, Milton Berle.

"This is a great story about comedians in general," he told us. "For the most part, we are a very warm-hearted group. Milton and I still talked about this years and years later. He came into the Interlude one night and saw me, and after my show, he walked up and said, 'I like your style. I'm going to help you.' Here was my idol wanting to help me! Pinch me!

"I said, 'Great!' I was thinking he wanted to put me in a movie or on a television show. But here's what he did. He said, 'I'm going to come to your show once a week and I'm going to heckle you, but before the show I'll go to your dressing room and tell you what I'm going to say. This way you can think of things to say back to top me.' That's what this great man did for me. He came in once a week and heckled me, and I'd have all the toppers—the comebacks—and I'd kill him.

"He'd put on this act: 'Look at this kid, he's got me again.' And after a while, maybe two months, it was all over town that there's some schmucky kid killing Milton Berle at the Interlude. I loved him. I loved Berle. We became very good friends. He was a great guy, a very kind, sweet man.

"Victor Lownes didn't like me, not because I didn't do well at the club—I was doing as well as anyone could with the bottles breaking and all. He didn't like me because one of those twelve girls I dated was his girlfriend—though I didn't know that at the time. If I had known that—I'm not a jerk. You don't go out with the girlfriend of the guy who runs the club! He came over to me one day and said, 'Look, you know you're not supposed to date the Bunnies, but we know the comedians do. Stay away from that one!' Yes, sure, OK..."

Lou's friend John Regis told us what it was like working with Lou at the Chicago Playboy Club. "One time, there were three of us walking down the street and there were beautiful girls all over the place—airline stewardesses and Bunnies and office girls—and Lou would stop each one of them and say, 'Hi, I'm Lou Alexander, star of the Playboy Club. How would you like to see the show tonight? Have you ever been to the Playboy Club? Oh, you haven't? I'll meet you in front of the door...' And the other guy said to me, 'Doesn't it bother you that he tells them he's the star of the Playboy Club?'

"'No, it doesn't,'" I told him, "'because if there are any left-overs . . .'"

John was on a roll. "Another day, we were out walking and along came this girl. She was gorgeous and, true to form, Lou said, 'Hi there, I'm Lou Alexander, and I'm the star of the Playboy Club.

"While he was talking, she took out a piece of paper and a pen and wrote, 'I'm deaf, would you please write your message?' *Hi there, I'm Lou Alexander, star of the Playboy Club...* He didn't miss a beat; he just wrote it down. Both of us other guys were standing back, not believing it was happening. Sure enough, she showed up that night—with her mother, who was also a knockout. After the show, he came out with one on each arm and I said,

"'Lou, what if you introduce me to her mother?' I'm older than

Lou and thought that was fair.

"'No,' he said. 'I need her to translate!' I love Lou."

Lou eventually said goodbye to the Playboy Clubs, moving up to more elite nightclubs including the Copacabana, but he kept in touch with his friends there and visited the Playboy Mansion whenever he got the chance.

* * *

In summing up his feelings about the Playboy circuit, comic Dick Lord told us, "Playboy was fantastic for us guys in the trenches—the good, hard-working comedians—and there were many, many of us. Sometimes, two comedians played a club at the same time, one in the Playroom and one in the Penthouse. When your show wasn't on, you'd go watch the other guy work. We could hang out together and learn from one another, which was great. We'd talk about the business and see what other comedians were doing. Even the traveling was great. I saw places I probably never would have seen. I'd never been to New Orleans before I played the club there and don't know if I'd have stopped in Detroit on my own. I learned a lot about people and saw a lot of the country. It was good."

We owe a huge debt of gratitude to Dick Lord, Lou Alexander, and all of the other comedians we talked to for opening our eyes to the large cadre of talented performers who worked—really *worked*—the Playboy Club circuit. These guys truly were in the trenches, some for many years. But to hear them tell it, it wasn't such a bad tour of duty!

PART TWO

THE SCRIBBLERS

9

FUNNY ON PAPER

Playboy wouldn't be Playboy without cartoons. Great gutsy quantities of full-color, full-page cartoons fill the magazine every month, to say nothing of frequent, multipage cartoon spreads and the less flamboyant but no less funny black-and-white chucklers that pepper the back pages. These cartoons are created by the most gifted coterie of dotty draftsmen ever assembled under one aegis. High time, then, to spotlight such vitally important chaps on this Playboy *page."* —PLAYBOY EDITORIAL PAGE, MARCH 1959

More than any other category of artist, cartoonists are *born*, most knowing what they want to pursue from their earliest buds of consciousness.

"I can't remember when I didn't want to be a cartoonist," announced Arnold Roth. His grandmother owned a candy store in a working-class neighborhood of Philadelphia during the Depression, and as a child of four or five, he would make drawings for people. "By five, I could draw Popeye and Mickey Mouse, so I stuck with it and I loved it."

The Depression spanned an entire decade, of course, beginning with the stock market crash in October 1929. At its nadir, fourteen to fifteen million Americans were unemployed, and it wasn't until massive manufacturing for World War II began in earnest, providing work for anyone who wanted it, that the American economy could be considered healthy again. But perhaps there was a bright side to the sense of hopelessness people felt in that dark time: It gave rise to a generation of daydreamers.

Jerry Siegel and Joe Shuster's comic-book hero Superman burst onto the scene in 1933, with epic strength and an unwavering mission of saving those in trouble. He and his fellow cartoon creations—from Popeye and Mickey Mouse to Dick Tracy, the Lone Ranger, and the Green Hornet—provided a much-needed escape from the harsh realities of the day for little boys and girls everywhere.

The cadre of renowned artists, illustrators, and cartoonists of the time used their work not only as a means to escape poverty but as a way to express their fantasies of a brighter future.

When Hugh Hefner first began to conceive the magazine that eventually became *Playboy*, it was a foregone conclusion that artwork would play a major part. He'd always been a fan of comics and panel cartoons, and had spent many years drawing his own as a young man; in high school he created a comic-book autobiography, *School Daze*, and his college publications are full of his creations. As late as the mid-1950s, in fact, Hef was still considering cartooning as a career, and many examples of his efforts appeared in early issues of *Playboy*.

Photo spreads may have put *Playboy* on the map, but cartoons were just as important to its blossoming identity. Saucy, irreverent, and joyful, they could convey things that no pictorial ever could: ideas. Upscale magazines of the day, including *The New Yorker* and *Esquire,* had already established that they could be intellectual and humorous at the same time, and had made the inclusion of cartoons a staple of their editorial plans. Hef (as he always did) took the whole concept one step further, understanding that cartoons could be naughtier and more cutting-edge than words and photos as well.

As far as he was concerned, the cartoons in *Playboy* completed the package. He was determined to have the best illustrators available on his staff, and he was prepared to pay for the privilege.

The definitive *Playboy* artist of the first few years was Jack Cole (1914-1958), who died under mysterious circumstances at the height of his success. At the time of his death, Jack had recently moved to Chicago as a means of strengthening his connection with *Playboy* and Hefner. His cartoons never disappointed his exacting boss.

The short but remarkably prolific life of Jack Cole was marked by endless transformations and mysteries. In the same way that his greatest character, Plastic Man, could shape-shift from a parachute in one panel to a garbage truck in the next, Jack himself made the almost unheard-of transformation from a creator of children's comic strips into an innovator of the super-hero genre, and eventually into one of the pioneers of adult pin-up art. Ironically, Jack spent many of his professional years spinning crime stories for *Police Comics*, yet the tragic circumstances of his death have yet to be unraveled some sixty years later.

Jack's career may have been brief, but he enjoyed two golden ages: the years 1941 to roughly 1950, when he masterminded the adventures of his own creation, Plastic Man; and again from 1954 to his death in 1958, when he drew panel cartoons for *Playboy*. Throughout both of these stages, Jack's specialty was manipulating the tactile sensations of human flesh. When Plastic Man stopped a crook from shooting him by stretching his fingers right through the barrel of the gun, or shot his tongue about ten feet outward to lick a lollipop on the other side of the street, Jack's superior draftsmanship and storytelling made the fantastic gestures believable.

Likewise, when two gorgeous girls sashayed across a page of *Playboy* and one commented, "Let's walk past the YMCA and listen to the windows break!" there was no doubt that's actually what would happen. Jack drew girl after girl with a breathtakingly beautiful face, wasp waist, and what can only be described as "national endowments." Like Plastic Man, Jack's *Playboy* girls still seem at once fantastic yet completely credible, with figures that stretch human imagining to the limit.

Born in New Castle, Pennsylvania, Jack grew up enamored of both silent films and newspaper cartoons, and both would keenly influence his work. He learned the basics of cartooning from a correspondence course, married his childhood sweetheart, and headed for New York City, where he was determined to become a famous artist and illustrator. His original goal was to draw for the syndicated comic strips but, in just the first example of remarkable timing in his life, he arrived just as a new medium for artists was taking off: the four-color comic book. In about 1936, Jack went to work for Harry Chesler, one of the first "packagers" in the emerging industry, and became part of a studio that produced finished comic-book stories that Chesler then sold to various publishers.

Jack had gotten in on the ground floor—the basement, even—of what would quickly become a huge industry. Over the next five years or so, he created mostly comedy characters, including a fair share of wisecracking midgets and hillbillies. Then, thanks to Superman and Batman, superheroes became the craze and Jack switched to creating costumed action figures such as the Comet and Daredevil. It only remained for him to combine the two genres and come up with the first superhero to be as dynamic as the best crime-fighter and side-splittingly funny.

Enter Plastic Man, who made his debut in 1941 in *Police Comics* #1. The character was an immediate hit and it's not hard to see why. His stories were packed with both adventure and slapstick comedy. Plastic Man was the alter ego of Eel O'Brien, a former small-time crook. When a vat of acid fell on him, he became empowered to stretch his body at will. After recovering from the accident in a monastery, Eel set himself on a righteous path—not as a vigilante but as a duly appointed agent of the FBI (complete with sunglasses that predated the Men in Black by fifty years). Plastic Man caught crooks by assuming all sorts of wacky shapes. And, if the man of rubber wasn't enough for readers, his sidekick was a middle-aged goofball named Woozy Winks, a burlesque-show-style stooge who was forever getting into scrapes that "Plas" had to rescue him from. Plastic Man's adventures were well-plotted, brilliantly characterized good guy/bad guy stories that could stand on a shelf with Captain Marvel—but they were considerably funnier.

Plastic Man was a favorite with kids, and one of those was surely the fifteen-year-old Hugh Hefner, then saving up his dimes for the monthly issues of his favorite comics. *Police Comics* and *Plastic Man* were also widely read by young servicemen, and thrived both during and after the war. Perhaps that's because, even then, Jack had an eye for the ladies. In *Police* #49 (1945) both Plas and Woozy fell under "The Spell of Thelma Twittle," a statuesque blonde with ample proportions, a ditzy attitude, high heels and a tight, shiny skirt. She could easily have appeared in a *Playboy* cartoon ten years later.

Throughout the years 1941-53, Plastic Man was appearing in two monthly magazines at once—that's two sixty-page books written, penciled, and inked by one man. Jack's propensity for extravagant detail put him continually behind the eight ball—and he was doing other work as well, for his friend Will Eisner at Smash Comics on *The Spirit* and a *Spirit* clone called *Midnight.* The workload was tremendous. When, at the end of the 1940s, the original superhero vogue began to subside, it must have been something of a relief for the artist-writer. Having wanted to draw for newspapers and magazines all his life, Jack finally got his shot in 1954, when one of his cartoons was accepted by a brand-new magazine out of Chicago.

It's easy to see what Jack and Hefner saw in each other. Hef was as devoted to the comic arts as he was to jazz and the other finer things, and Jack was thrilled to be graduating to the kind of adult platform *Playboy* represented. Hef and Jack instantly bonded—so much so that within a short while, the editor-publisher persuaded his new friend to uproot himself from the East Coast and move to Illinois.

"Hef offered me a staff job but I prefer to work at home," Jack wrote to a friend. Mr. and Mrs. Cole bought a house in Cary, Illinois, about seventy minutes outside of Chicago. "That's as close as I want to be to the joint," Jack explained.

Comic book historian Ron Goulart interviewed Ray Russell, who had been on the magazine's editorial staff at the time, about Jack.

"I hardly knew him, said Ray. "None of us, except Hef, really knew him. Hefner handled all the cartoon stuff at the time... The only conversation I had with him was at a Playboy party, about a month before he died. He made a cryptic remark which, broadly paraphrased by my battered brain over a quarter-century or so, was something to the effect that if he ever relaxed his self-discipline, 'I could become an alcoholic.'"

Art Spiegelman, the contemporary artist behind *Maus* and other groundbreaking works, observed, "Cole's goddesses were estrogen soufflés who mesmerized the ineffectual saps who lusted after them." Jack arguably reached his apogee with the magazine in July 1955. In the contributors section up front known as Playbill, his bespectacled picture was published over the caption, "Like all the best cartoonists, he is, of course, mad. Not dangerously so, just enough to make life interesting for himself and for more mundane souls like us."

The same issue featured extravagant praise for "Females by Cole" in the letters section. A reader in Hollywood wrote, "This series is in a class of its own and one of the most interesting features I've ever seen in a magazine."

Another reader seconded the emotion by asking, "Will you ever publish 'Females by Cole' in book form or perhaps all in one issue? They're great!"

Finally, that issue featured a Cole pièce de résistance, called "Man at the Beach," five pages of pretty young things reclining in the surf and sand. Like most of his *Playboy* artwork, it was lovingly rendered in watercolors, with so much sensitivity and even love that most of the girls appeared to have their bikinis literally painted on.

Just as Plastic Man vanquished his enemies with his ever-shifting shape, even today, these voluptuous creatures capture the hearts and imaginations of anyone lucky enough to gaze upon them. Ever the prankster, Jack clearly loved to play with these forms: One bathing beauty stands in front of a hairy muscleman in such a way that it looks at first as if she has hirsute, beefy arms; another topless temptress looks like the rear end of a male fisherman positioned in the background.

We'll never really know what inner demons Jack was battling. All seemed right on the professional front: Hefner was delighted with his work and, responding to requests from readers, did indeed publish a collection of *Playboy's Females by Cole*. In 1958, Jack realized another long-held dream when he started his own syndicated daily comic strip, *Betsy and Me,* rendered in a cartoony style very different from that of either Plastic Man or his *Playboy* work. And yet, just two months after the strip began publication, on August 13, 1958, Jack purchased a gun and shot himself in his car.

Earlier that day, he had mailed a suicide note to Hefner, in which he stated that he didn't blame anyone for anything that went wrong (never elaborating on what that might have been). He mailed a second letter to his wife of twenty-four years; she kept the contents of that note a secret and avoided Cole's friends, coworkers, and family from that moment on. In *More About Betsy and Me,* a 2007 compilation of the strips, editor R. C. Harvey spoke of Cole's death as "one of the most baffling events in the history of cartooning."

Jack Cole's boundary-breaking work is still loved and appreciated sixty years after he drew his final panel. In addition to providing the template for many other heroes, such as Elongated Man and Mr. Fantastic, Plastic Man himself has been regularly revived by DC comics over the years, and made the centerpiece of several animated TV series. Like Victor Lownes, A. C. Spectorsky, LeRoy Neiman, Shel Silverstein, and many other people employed by Hefner, he helped forge *Playboy's* identity and make it the cultural giant that it was.

Jack's cartoons were everything that Hefner wanted in his pages and more. They were sexy, funny, and beautifully rendered, and—to use a term that hadn't really come into its own at the time—empowered. Today, it's easy to describe the early *Playboy* cartoonists as sexist, and by contemporary standards they may seem to be, but in the mid-1950s, Jack and his colleagues were taking matters a radical leap forward. Compared to the way women were generally portrayed then, Cole's ladies—and those of many of the other artists—were remarkably liberated. And they were the center of their universe: Everything in Cole's cartoons revolves around the women, and everything that happens is in relation to them.

* * *

Doug Sneyd, who had more than 450 cartoons published in *Playboy* starting with the September 1964 issue, was its definitive cartoonist of the sixties and seventies—the magazine's heyday. Doug had an eye for the minuscule details of current fashion and mores, and chronicled the sexual revolution via his exquisitely vivacious women. A lifelong Ontarian, Doug was born in Guelph in 1931, one of seven children. Not surprisingly, his family didn't have the spare funds to send Doug to art school. "I took the correspondence path of study with the *Famous Artists Course*," he told us. "It was more or less the Rockwellian school of illustration, and was quite helpful to me. I got about two thirds of the way through—to about lesson eighteen of twenty-four—when I came to a chapter titled, 'Earn While You Learn.' So I forgot the course and went on the road painting murals."

His first commission brought a tidy sum, with which he bought a Vauxhall (a characteristically offbeat British automobile) and traveled the country doing murals. His travels ultimately landed him in Montreal, where he was hired by a design and advertising firm as a junior illustrator. Rapid, Grip and Batten was the largest studio of its kind in North America, employing more than fifty artists.

"For the year and a half I was there, I painted portraits on the side," he recalled. "One interesting assignment was at the Latin Quarter Nightclub, where the woman who owned it wanted portraits of her orchestra."

Doug was next offered assignments by W.J. Gage and Company, doing textbook illustrations, and it was then that he started to freelance full-time. Soon, he found himself heading to Chicago on business, and, knowing it was the land of *Playboy,* he decided to bring samples of his illustrations in hopes of getting some work for the magazine.

"This was in the days where you could just pop in," he said. "You didn't need an appointment.

"So the art director looked at my stuff and said, 'Well, it's great for illustrations, but we'd rather use you as a cartoonist.' That wasn't really my bag, I hadn't done any cartooning and I didn't consider myself a cartoonist, so I said to him that it wasn't my cup of tea.

"And then he told me what they paid and I said, 'I like that kind of tea!'

"At the start I told them, 'I don't think I can come up with the captions.' But that wasn't a problem because they easily supplied them. And eventually I started submitting and getting my own accepted. We'd collaborate. They'd come up with the gag and sometimes I'd sweeten it or change it, or call Michelle Urry [his cartoon editor and fellow Canadian] and say, 'This doesn't work. How about *this*?' I'm sure you've been told how Hef looked at everything, and had to approve it. I'd send gags to Michelle in New York, from there they went to Chicago for approvals, then they were returned to me."

In 1969, Doug settled with his wife and young family further north in Orillia, where the third floor of their home was his studio overlooking Lake Couchiching. He continued working on hard-news cartoons for newspapers throughout North America, thanks in large part to his exposure as a Playboy cartoonist.

"I was in *Playboy* magazine extensively when Martin Goodman, the managing editor of Canada's largest newspaper, *the Toronto Star*, phoned me and asked if I'd do a hard-news cartoon five days a week on the World News page. It was a two-column-wide cartoon called 'Doug Sneyd.' So *Playboy* indirectly got me into that field and I did an awful lot of editorial and hard-news cartoons."

Later, Doug also came up with a cartoon strip he called "Scoops," and traveled to ninety cities in Canada and the States over the course of sixty days to sell it into syndicated markets.

Two things about Doug's *Playboy* cartoons are worth noting. First, he took the craft of what comic-art buffs refer to as "good-girl art" to its apogee: The women in his drawings were so sexy and so realistic that his work probably should have been categorized as *pictorials* rather than *cartoons.* In fact, in all our years of ooh-ing and ah-ing over the beautiful girls drawn by Sneyd, we've never paid much attention to the captions. It's not the humor that's important in Sneyd's work, it's the glamour.

Second, Doug represents a generational shift from Jack Cole and the earlier *Playboy* cartoonists, particularly in the depiction of males. Men in the 1950s issues tended to look like close relatives of "Mr. Esquire"—a character created by E. Simms Campbell—or the Monopoly Man. Except for a few hunks drawn by Chuck Miller, the men chasing the girls in the earlier cartoons were usually walrus-mustached sugar-daddies with big pot bellies and even bigger sacks of jewels and furs. Sneyd's men, by contrast, looked like male models or soap-opera stars. Although they never got center stage, they somehow belonged in the same company as his amazing females. In the 1950s, the women were depicted as showgirls and gold-diggers and their primary interest in the men was financial; by the 1970s, the girls were working at all kinds of professions and were interested in boys for the same reason that boys were interested in them.

As beloved as Jack Cole's work was, we surmise that most of *Playboy*'s male readers would rather have been depicted by Doug. This makes sense to Doug. "If you're going to make the girl pretty, like the girl-next-door, or what some refer to as the 'Sneyd Girl,' then the guys should be like that, too," he told us, "although I did also draw a lot of character-type faces: you know—the guys with big noses and so on."

Just because Doug, now a youthful 84, is devoted to his lovely girlfriend and super-efficient Girl Friday Heidi Hutson doesn't mean he's stopped looking at beautiful ladies. In fact, he's found a new talent for matchmaking—for Hef! We thought you'd appreciate this story:

At a comic arts festival in 2011, Doug spied a perfect 11. "I was at the Toronto Reference Library selling books, and it was my practice that when someone purchased one, I'd sketch a portrait of his wife or girlfriend along with my signature. Well, there was one girl who was just beautiful—Hollywood perfect." Doug found out her name was Shera Bechard and that she was French-Canadian—from Kapuskasing. Later, her boyfriend stopped by and promised he'd email Doug some photos of her—which he promptly did. Doug passed along the photos and information about this very special lady to Playboy. Not long after, he got a call from his "discovery", informing him that she was going to be Miss November!

"Around the holidays, we received a Christmas card from the Mansion," he continued. "On the card was Hef—who had recently been jilted by Crystal Harris [Miss June 2011]—surrounded by his two new girlfriends, one being Ms. Bechard." Prior to Crystal's return in late 2012 and their eventual marriage, Hef was quoted as saying about Shera, "She's my number-one girlfriend."

You'd think that having worked for Hef for over fifty years, Doug would have met with him on a semi-regular basis—but it was only recently that Doug and Heidi had the free time to visit Hef at home in Los Angeles. "We were told to call whenever we were in L.A., and a few years ago, in 2012, we were doing a convention and thought it would be a great time to call Shera. We had become friends with retired bandleader and Hef's good friend, Ray Anthony, and had previously asked him to sign a CD for us, so it was a special surprise to meet him and congratulate him on his ninetieth birthday. The evening included dinner and a movie—*Bridesmaids 2.*"

Nowadays, Doug and Heidi spend the warmer months in Ontario and winter on the Alabama Gulf Coast in Orange Beach. Before we'd even asked, Doug volunteered that he doesn't understand the reasoning behind the recent reorganization of the magazine and the elimination of both nudes and cartoons.

"After pretty girls, *Playboy* is the cartoons and the joke page. I always loved the joke page; it was one of the first things I read when I got the magazine. Besides meeting fans of my work while exhibiting at cartoon conventions, it's a plus visiting with some of the cartoonists from *Playboy.* That's wonderful."

* * *

One of the most popular satirical cartoonists in the country—and perhaps worldwide—Jules Feiffer grew up during the Depression with no other aspiration but to draw. He recalls his puerile drawings at the age of three, asserting that they weren't all that different from the crayon doodles of other toddlers, except for his attitude. "I think all kids are basically talented and gifted," he told us. "My contention is that they don't lose their talent as they get older; they just start to get educated. They start being told by the experienced grownups how to really *do it well,* and they begin listening to others instead of themselves. And slowly, whatever made them passionate about doing the work is overcome by the will of the authorities. That is, the authorities do what authorities do, which is to take the fun out of it.

"I never listened to the authorities so I kept the fun, and I have as much fun today, at 87, as I did when I was five. What was clear to me at an early age was that when I followed the rules, disaster followed. It was one bad break after another, one rejection after the next. If I did what my instincts told me, which was often against the rules, things started to happen that I liked. And so, I basically stopped following the rules because they were destructive."

Jules grew up in the Jewish section of the Bronx during the thirties and forties, and everyone was poor.

"One took that for granted, it wasn't a special state," he explained. "It was, however, a rowdy, noisy, contentious, and very competitive neighborhood. If you had sports skills, you excelled and became a big shot. I had no athletic talent at all. I had lousy coordination. I couldn't catch or throw a ball. I had to survive some other way. So I started drawing on the sidewalk. None of them could draw Dick Tracy. I could. None of them could draw Popeye. I could. Suddenly, I found that drawing cartoons was a way of, not just establishing my presence, but a means of survival, and of being admired. It looked like a good way to get through childhood and, perhaps, adulthood."

Jules was a zealous fan of comics, first the newspaper variety and then comic books and books *about* comics and cartooning. In reading the biographies of his idols, he determined that they had glamorous lives, even rubbed elbows with show-business personalities.

"They made over $150,000 a year—which today would be the equivalent of a million or more," Jules said, "and I thought, Jesus, this is what I want to do. I want to do what I love and be accepted for it, and hang out with movie stars. What's better?"

Jules's mother Rhoda always encouraged him to draw.

"She started life as a fashion designer, before it was acceptable for women to have careers, and was doing very well as a single woman," he said, but went on to explain that in those days, for women, having a career was considered just a place-holder for the "real" job of being a wife and mother. "She was an unhappy woman," he continued. "My assumption is that her family basically pressured her into back-shelving what she loved to do in order to get married. My father was a very sweet, gentle man, but I believe she surrendered to her mother, and the cultural wishes of that generation and time, and gave up her dreams and was never really happy after that. So when I showed talent as a cartoonist, I think I became a substitute for her frustration. She invested a lot of hope in me, in terms of becoming a success, to make up for what she had been deprived of.

"At the same time, my mother became the family breadwinner during the Depression, because my father couldn't keep a job for more than a brief period. She'd work at home and go door to door, trying to sell fashion sketches down at the garment district on Seventh Avenue, and keeping us all alive. None of this was appreciated by our neighbors, because she was supposed to be home—she was considered too lofty, too stuck up, and—huge crime—she didn't sound Jewish. She was raised in Richmond, Virginia, and didn't have an accent. She looked and sounded like a WASP."

Observing these childhood contradictions may have been why Jules shied from rules and regulations himself, pulling more toward the activism, cynicism, and irony that would saturate his cartoons and comics. Not quite ready to leave the subject of his mother, Jules said, "She always followed the rules and the rules were like a pie that kept, repeatedly, hitting her in the face. Once she wiped the pie off her face, she would go back to following the rules. In most families, there is very little learning curve. People tend to repeat the same mistakes over and over. The more they make mistakes, the more they defend them. And that's what I realized I had to get out of that cycle."

As Jules came of age, comic books were flourishing and an entire generation of adolescent young men was becoming obsessed with sex—or the idea of sex, anyway.

"You know, before my generation there was no sex. I was fortunate to come on stage at a very unfortunate time, in terms of politics. It was right after the years of the Great Depression, which were years of rabid and acceptable anti-Semitism in the United States, the coming Holocaust in Europe, and the acceptance of that by a vast number of Americans. In *The Great Comic Book Heroes*, I brought up my theory about Superman. Jerry Siegel and Joe Shuster were two Jewish boys from Cleveland at the height of American anti-Semitism and the rise of Hitler in Europe, and they, like all nice Jewish boys, wanted to assimilate—they just didn't want to be Jewish but *American.* What they saw as *American* was the America they saw in movies—which was actually an America invented by Jewish producers—and that dream state didn't exist. That's what they wanted to belong to. They'd go to high school and see all the good-looking jocks getting all the girls—all the *Lois Lanes*—and they didn't. So Superman became a fantasy of assimilation; that is, if only Lois Lane knew my *true identity*. If I rip off my clothes, I reveal I'm not really this *schmuck* Clark Kent, with glasses and a bad complexion; I'm really—zoom—Superman, stronger than those other jocks. That was this great and irresistible fantasy that fueled many generations of young men, who felt, whether Jewish or not, like little schmucks who weren't good enough athletes and weren't big enough or strong enough to make it, so you made it in your fantasy."

Jules told us that the Hungarian-born writer and cartoonist Will Eisner came onto his radar when he was around eleven or twelve. Born and reared in the same Brooklyn neighbor that Jules would later occupy, he was also steered toward art by a parent, but in his case, it was his father.

According to Jules, "Will was doing comic-book work that didn't look like anyone else's. It didn't read like anyone else's. It was so striking and fresh and, although I didn't have the name for it then, *primitive.* He was inventing the field and, as he progressed, it looked less and less primitive; he was the one who sophisticated it. I was in love with him and his work. When I was sixteen, I went down to his office just to show him my work, and we talked and talked and talked and talked. He didn't think I had any talent at all but he hired me, essentially as a groupie, to have someone to converse with at work. I spent most of the time cleaning up.

"I idolized him, but at the same time, I was a still a snotty, wise guy, Jewish kid. Once, in great innocence, I said to him, 'You know, it's funny, but in *The Spirit*, the drawing is better than it has ever been. The storytelling is better, but the stories aren't as good as they were in the 1940s. Why don't you write as well as you did then?' It never occurred to me that I could have, and maybe should have, been fired for that. He said, 'Well, if you think you can do better, why don't you write one?' So I wrote one. And I did do better, and he liked it. He did some editing and then published it, and then he had me work on another. Within a very short time, I found myself working on *The Spirit* and learning as I went."

Jules worked for Will Eisner until he entered Pratt Institute in 1946-47, and again upon graduation a year later. "I came back and worked with him until I was drafted, at the end of 1950. I went into the Army in January of '51, but even then I continued writing some of the *Spirit* scripts for that month."

Jules reports that one highlight of working for Eisner was the office atmosphere. "Of course, he was the final word on what went on at the studio. But in the comic business, this was the place where other young cartoonists wanted to migrate. They all wanted my job. Eisner was the one that you wanted to show your work to. So kids like Harvey Kurtzman—before he was Harvey Kurtzman and created *Mad* magazine—came, and I met him, and we became friends. All the young wannabes would gravitate to that studio because it was where you felt your future might be. Eisner didn't insist your work look like everyone else's. He was quite happy to see individual talents flourish and did everything he could to encourage young cartoonists. There was a movement going on and stuff was happening. *All* that was the highlight—I was on a road I now understood was going to be my entire life.

"It was an exciting time. The last great period of excitement had been the 1920s Jazz Age, the Flapper Age, the Algonquin Round Table, jazzy Broadway, and the birth of screwball comedies and movies—that time was explosive and absolutely wonderful. Then it went dead and culture froze. The early movies of the thirties showed women who were strong and opinionated. They had jobs. There was Barbara Stanwyck, Carole Lombard, Rosalind Russell—they didn't take shit and were fighters. They didn't have to be nice. And then in the post-war years, women became the moms and girlfriends, essentially the support systems for the struggling guys. They became boring and uninteresting and they had no role to play on their own.

"We were the most notorious of all of the allies in the war. We lost the least, and yet we saw noir movies about betrayal and fear and we were told we couldn't trust anyone. Science fiction developed a huge following: Foreign creatures were invading us –which was a metaphor for Communists—on TV and in comic strips and books. Everyone was looking under the bed for enemy and we were making them up. We were also enjoying the first sizable middle class in history. Everything was getting better. Families who, a generation before, had been poor and had no history of ever making money, were now owning their own homes. They had washers and dryers and their kids were going to good schools.

"This had never happened before and the response was paranoia. The response was fervent anti-Communism and red hunts. Also, air drills in schools, where kids had to hide under their desks, because we were sure the Russians were going to bomb us. There were ludicrous contradictions at that time, and I and other members of my generation began responding. Mort Sahl began performing at the Hungry I, doing the first of the brilliant social commentaries ever seen in nightclubs and cabarets. Then came Second City in Chicago, and out of that came Mike Nichols and Elaine May. Suddenly, political satire was being used for entertainment—and in my *Village Voice* comic strip, I was saying things that you would never find in magazines. Addressing issues like how do men and women relate to each other; what happens before, during, and after sex; what actually happens *in life.* Entirely new ground was being explored and voiced. What made it resonate so successfully was that my readers, and those cabaret audiences, approached it with a collective *woof* of relief. They thought, 'Finally, here's something that sounds and looks like what's going on in my life!' Eisenhower's era was repressive in all areas, including sex, and now sex was exploding all over the place.

"Hefner was notable among those putting it out there. He forced the conversation and he was shocking. First, *Playboy* was viewed simply as a "girly magazine" and then the writing became interesting and Hef started collecting the best cartoonists that ever existed outside of *The New Yorker*. He helped invent Shel Silverstein, for one. No one had ever seen anything like Shel before. *Shel* had never seen anybody like Shel before, and he was a great influence on me. There were other truly first-rate cartoonists: Jack Cole, Gahan Wilson, John Dempsey, and a bunch of others. I was happy to be a part of it all.

"My only dream, when I went into the Army, was to be a newspaper strip artist. I had found, with Eisner, that I could write in his style but I couldn't draw in the realistic adventure mode. When I tried that stuff, it looked awful. So I switched to humor and thought I'd do a traditional, vaguely satiric daily humor strip.

"Suddenly, politics came to the floor. It was the Korean War. It was McCarthyism. All at once, I became obsessed with something other than a career; I became obsessed with what was happening to the country, and my own political, sociological response to that. I didn't want to be a newspaper cartoonist anymore. I wanted to do works of tough, hard-hitting satire in magazines and books, or wherever—more in line with the work that William Steig was doing with his books of introspection and psychology; also Steinberg and the French Romanian cartoonist Andre Francois. I began looking at different countries and working in different styles. While in the Army, I wrote a book called *Munro,* about a four-year-old boy who was drafted by mistake, and how he tried to convince the authorities that he was only four. But the Army didn't listen to anyone but itself, and they convinced *him* that he wasn't four, because *they* didn't draft men of four. That was my first satire." (In 1961, a film adaptation of *Munroe* won the Academy Award for animated short.)

In case you are feeling impatient, we're fast approaching Jules's intersection with *Playboy*. "I loved *The New Yorker* cartoonists at that time," he told us about his post-military period. "They had a brilliant crew of cartoonists. But outside of Steinberg and sometimes Steig, it was seen as pure entertainment, pure humor, with no editorial content. My work, whether it was about politics or family or sex, was *all* editorial content. I was making points and *The New Yorker* had no interest in that, and I had no interest in redefining myself to meet the market. So, basically, I was staggering around, working for the *Voice* every week, which didn't pay me. They had no money but I was getting an audience. And then Mr. Hefner came into view."

Hef had apparently seen and liked a collection of Jules's cartoons called *Sick, Sick, Sick* and had been following his work. It was the late fifties, and a prominent literary newspaper, the *Observer*, was rerunning the cartoons Jules produced for the *Village Voice*. The *Observer*'s vast distribution included Western Europe, thus broadening Jules's exposure exponentially.

"It made me a rock star in Europe!" he enthused.

"Hef wrote me a letter saying that he thought I would fit brilliantly into the *Playboy* mold. Plus, he'd pay me $500 a month for monthly submissions, which was more money than I'd ever seen. We're talking about the late fifties—1958-59. My agent Ted Riley, Hef, and I worked out some guidelines and I started submitting. I was very suspicious—ambitious but also paranoid about being usurped. I didn't know Hefner, and I had mixed feeling about the magazine. They had some wonderful cartoonists, but its attitude about sex was not mine. I was worried that he wanted me to do cartoons that would fit the *Playboy* model, just as *The New Yorker* wanted me to fit theirs. The charm and beauty of the *Voice* was that they let you be anybody you wanted to be—but other papers didn't, and I didn't want Hefner to remodel me or turn me into somebody

I didn't want to be. So we had a conversation. He assured me that was not going to be the case.

"Hefner was the cartoon editor—no matter who else might have had the title, he personally edited everything himself. I quickly started submitting work and he'd send back notes, and I discovered that he wasn't trying to turn me into a *Playboy* cartoonist. He was editing from the standpoint of my own view and attempting to make my view stronger. Nine times out of ten he was right and I learned to trust him. I learned that this guy wasn't trying to seduce me, but was trying to make me famous—and why should I object to that?"

"The monthly process was relatively straightforward, I'd submit a rough one- or two-page draft for a cartoon and get back maybe three or four pages of panel-by-panel breakdown of where he thought it was right and where he thought it wasn't right. He'd send all these mild suggestions, and after a few months, I thought, laughingly, 'Oh my God, I'm being edited by Edmund Wilson!' His attention to detail was extraordinary, and he was usually right. More important to me than anything else was that he was attempting to strengthen the individuality of my own personal approach, and to make the work better from my own point of view. He taught me a lot that way."

According to Jules and other contributors, edits had to be carried out quickly and efficiently in order to accommodate the magazine's relentless deadlines. Today, it seems almost inconceivable, but the interactions between far-flung artists and Hef—who rarely left his Mansion in Chicago—were carried out entirely by mail.

"Hef would write this thing called a letter," Jules joked, "put it in an envelope, write my address, stamp it, and send it out. Three or four days later I'd receive it, and would make notes in the corners, and send it back to him. And so it went. Even considering this antiquated procedure, he created an atmosphere where I knew he was on my side. He didn't try to obliterate me with criticism, as so many people who give you good advice end up doing.

"From my post-Army days, I instinctively knew what to draw.

Much like an improv artist, I didn't need much direction. After I figure out my opening line, I see where it is going to take me, follow it along, and, maybe six panels later, it develops into something real. Or I trash it and start all over. But I let my characters and situations take over; I basically quiet my head down and let my gut take over and the characters speak. Occasionally back then, I'd do longer narrative series, which I like very much. They'd run four to six pages with little story lines—very much like my earlier work on *Munroe* or *Passionella* [a graphic narrative twist on Cinderella that Jules created in 1957]."

Hef may have had the final word on every aspect of the magazine—and really all that happened within his organization—but he did employ cartoon editors, and one of the prominent ones was Michelle Urry.

"I knew Michelle when she was first hired as an office girl," Jules told us. "There were two women in Chicago I was crazy about. One was Bobbie Arnstein, Hef's personal assistant, who became a good friend, and Michelle. Both were smart, sexy, women whom I had an enormous amount of fun with. And they were not, by anybody's description, *Playboy* types. They were too quick, quirky, and funny for that, and in their own ways, rebellious. Michelle never edited me; I dealt with Hef directly. But we were good friends and cared for each other. She was a support system for a couple of generations of cartoonists—the young ones breaking in. She would embrace them and buoy them. She'd cajole them and open her home to them. She'd have parties where they would meet everyone they were enamored of. She created a culture where cartoonists could meet and hang out and learn from one another, and she did it because she loved the form. She loved young cartoonists and she loved helping people. She had a wonderful heart.

"Hef and I would also talk on the phone but that wasn't the norm. He came to New York infrequently. This was prior to when he started wearing pajamas, but he still didn't like to travel. He preferred to refashion the environment into his own, even going so far as to control day and night by keeping the shades of the Mansion drawn. He began inviting me to the Mansion on North State Street when I would make trips to Chicago on various book tours for my cartoon collections, and we had lots of conversations and developed a real affection for each other, a real friendship.

"One time, he took me to a bar and asked me, 'What do you think of this place?' 'Looks nice,' I said.

"'This is going to be the Playboy Club,' he told me. Being in on the birth was very exciting.

"We had a very open friendship. I could get drunk and say offensive things to him, or disagree with him, and later, I'd feel awful and think I was going to get fired. He always brushed everything off. Those were not the years I necessarily behaved well, and it never bothered him. Once he moved to Los Angeles, I visited less. I never liked staying there, although I *loved* staying with him in Chicago. I had a ball there, and as a matter of fact, got many of my ideas for writing *Carnal Knowledge* from my stay at the Playboy Mansion in Chicago."

10

ARTISTS EXTRAORDINAIRE

In *Playboy Swings*, Cynthia Maddox unpacked the juicy details of the invention and evolution of the Bunny outfit—and no one was more qualified to do so. Cynthia was a blond-haired, blue eyed, all-American Venus, the kind of girl that *Playboy* magazine built its reputation on. Fresh out of high school, she began working at Playboy headquarters as a receptionist and quickly attracted the attention of both Victor Lownes and Hef (as well as most of the male employees). In a race between the two executives for her affections, Hef won out. But don't feel too sorry for Victor; he ended up with the London Bunny, Centerfold and Playmate of the Year Marilyn Cole. The two remain married to this day, and enjoy life in England.

Back to Cynthia. In addition to her clerical duties, she gave office tours, and occasionally served as Playboy's goodwill ambassador. She would appear a remarkable five times as a *Playboy* cover girl between 1962 and '66. When off the clock, she lived with Hef at the Mansion and traveled with him to a variety of events around the country.

Once, while accompanying him to the Jazz Awards in New York, she met and hung out with many of Hef's favorite jazz performers, including Ella Fitzgerald, Benny Goodman, and Duke Ellington. After traveling with Hef to Los Angeles for a visit with the pin-up artist Alberto Vargas, she became the subject of one of his illustrations, which was featured as a full-page in their April 1966 issue.

"It was like being with a movie star," Cynthia said, quickly clarifying that at home, Hef was not the "man about town", portrayed in *Playboy*. The couple valued the time they spent just relaxing and cuddling while watching old Charlie Chaplin movies and eating comfort food.

Yearning for a more prestigious position within the Playboy organization, Cynthia worked her way through the ranks at the magazine until she was appointed cartoon editor, reporting directly to Hef.

"Hef had drawn comics and cartoons as far back as he could remember," Cynthia reminded us. "I think the real meat of *Playboy* was the intellectual content—including the cartoons. The centerfolds were the addendum. The cartoons not only entertained but advanced the social messages that we believed in. They were a new kind of cartoon, the kinds that were also being done in *Esquire* and *The New Yorker*.

"I would get submissions from various artists around the country, many of whom I knew, which gave them an edge. I'd have the arduous task of going through them all, including all the ones from readers. The hardest part was to find a joke without a visual. Hef and I and many others would think up jokes and send them out to our regulars, and make decisions based on what they drew to accompany the joke. A majority of them were tits-and-ass—we were *Playboy*, after all—but many were smart, sophisticated, and ironic.

"Leroy Neiman was a friend of Hef's and always brought his artwork around. Hef bought many of his pieces, along with those of Shel Silverstein and Jules Feiffer. They were friends, all sharing the same sense of humor and friendship, and were in the office all the time. LeRoy and Shel ended up with permanent positions in the company. Then there was Harvey Kurtzman and Will Elder, with *Little Annie Fanny*—a parody of Little Orphan Annie. This was yet another type of humor, which included a lot of nudity. Phil Interlandi and Mort Gerberg were two of my favorites, and whenever I got a submission from them I'd pick something out. I felt the biggest sense of accomplishment when I could convince Hef to run one of my choices or get him to change his mind about using a certain cartoon. He always controlled the final content in every single area.

"It was an amazing time at *Playboy.* I'd be sitting at my desk and all of a sudden Lenny Bruce would walk in, sit down, and chat with me—although, it was difficult to have a dialogue with him because his mind was on another level entirely. Danny Kaye would come dancing through the offices, then, 'Oh look, Duke Ellington! That's nice.' This was just the way it was. The office had a homey feel, almost like a club atmosphere, and whenever musicians or actors, or personalities were in town, they'd swing by and hang with everyone. It was all very intellectually stimulating and the mood was relaxed and casual, although there was a massive amount of work being done, always.

"For me, coming right from school, to be working with these bright, interesting, and respectful people was completely intoxicating. Looking back, it was an era of simplicity, honesty, newness, and awakening for the whole country and it was a good time. It was a fun time."

* * *

Within a few years, many of the *Playboy* cartoonists had developed little specialties. E. Simms Campbell (1906-1971), for example, had a recurring fascination with harems and the overweight sultans who ruled there. A long-time veteran of *Esquire,* Campbell is also known to history as the first African-American cartoonist to achieve prominence in national, mainstream magazines. He was also a close friend of Cab Calloway and a part of the Harlem music and cultural scene.

Chuck Miller was like the Norman Rockwell of *Playboy*, his work was remarkably vivid and on a par with the best illustrators of the era. On the other end of the style spectrum from Shel Silverstein and Gahan Wilson, whose work was more cartoony, Miller's pieces were like fully realized paintings with humorous captions. Chuck was once described in the magazine as "a Chicago illustrator-turned-cartoonist especially for this magazine, whose full-color pages are always brightened by one or more beautiful, bountifully proportioned females." Chuck's scenarios always involved some sort of sexual or exhibitionistic situation: nearly naked girls bounding out on stage for a burlesque show or being led out of a patrol wagon; a couple in bed together or making out with abandon in the back seat of a Buick; you get the idea.

One of Chuck's most famous drawings depicts a startled couple walking in late to an office party where a good time has clearly been had by all. Pooped partygoers are passed out in collective pile, many with glasses still in hand and one with a lampshade on his head. It is the surprised newcomer—the woman—who holds center stage, drawing our attention as the Madonna might do in a Renaissance painting. More times than not, the gag or punch line was a completely separate enterprise, often written by someone else.

"Austria-born Erich Sokol is the creator of those delightfully provocative no-nosed cuties who resemble Brigitte Bardot." The uncredited editorial writer (quite possibly Hef himself) was right about that: Erich drew blond women, brunette women, red-haired women, Caucasian women, African-American women, Native American women, Polynesian women, Asian women, and, in one memorable instance, alien women in a spaceship with blue hair and green skin, wearing space helmets and stiletto-heeled go-go boots (presumably the height of fashion on the Planet Venus) but nothing else. And none of them have noses. In Erich's drawings, the nose was simply implied, taken for granted but never rendered explicitly. Breasts and bottoms, on the other hand, were lovingly rendered in exquisite detail.

In a squib discussing their cartoonists, *Playboy*'s editors write, "Sokol was arguably the most gifted artist who ever worked for *Playboy*, with a keen eye for all of the elements of good drawing—composition, clear silhouettes, original color harmonies, interesting staging, and a keen sense of light and shade." To us, the most remarkable thing about Erich's work is the balance between the cartoonish and the realistic. The women, while possessing an almost otherworldly beauty, seem three-dimensional (and how!), with a palpable physicality. The men, conversely, are much more cartoon-like, with exaggerated noses and dopey grins. And yet, the two genders seem to exist quite naturally together. This artist's view is male-centric, to say the least—depicting 3-D ladies in a 2-D world.

Our favorite Sokol panel is set in the South Seas and depicts two grumpy white dudes surrounded by staggeringly beautiful island women. *Muumuus* cover only the ladies' lower halves and their breasts stand high and proud; naturally, viewers barely notice the men. The caption reads, "I'll tell you why I hate this island—I'm a leg man." It's completely absurd, yet somehow relatable (if you're a man, anyway).

"We're in paradise," the guy is saying, "but I can still find something to complain about." That, Erich is telling us, is the sort of man who reads *Playboy*.

* * *

Shel Silverstein was born in Chicago in 1930 and studied English at the University of Illinois, before a stint in the Army. Like several of the artists we've profiled, Shel first published his cartoons in a military newspaper—in his case, *Pacific Stars and Stripes*. Back in Chicago, he began submitting his work to various publications and was soon a regular in *Look, Sports Illustrated*, and other magazines. Shel began drawing for *Playboy* in 1957 and his work continued to grace its pages off and on through the mid-1970s, even as he was becoming known as an author, playwright, and popular songwriter.

He never did the kind of pen-and-ink panels we tend to associate with the magazine, however. Shel's drawings were more like witticisms, one-liners in visual form.

At one point, *Playboy* devised an assignment for Shel that must have made him the envy of his fellow scribblers: He was tasked with traveling to glamorous and offbeat spots around the world and sending back an illustrated travel journal capturing his adventures. Over the course of eleven years, Shel sent dispatches from a host of world capitals, as well as more "specialized" locales such as a nudist colony and the Chicago White Sox training camp. In 2007, the monthly features were collected in a book called *Playboy's Silverstein Around the World.* Just as most "traditional" *Playboy* cartoonists simultaneously illuminated the beauty of women and the single-mindedness of the obsessive males who lusted after them, the cartoons in Shel's travel series made fun of Americans abroad while remaining overwhelmingly respectful of foreign traditions.

"Silverstein Among the Arabs," was a typical entry, published in the August 1959 issue. One drawing shows Shel confronting a Muslim balancing a huge pack on his head. Confounding our expectations, it is the Arab who is astonished at the American's manual dexterity:

"I always wondered how you in the West could carry so many things with your hands," he says. Unlike many artists and writers of the time, Shel preferred to make himself the butt of the humor rather than the "other." Another panel shows him standing in front of what looks like the palace of an Arabian sheik, gesticulating dramatically while a local woman tells him,

"For Heaven's sake, cut out that 'Open Sesame' stuff and ring the doorbell!" Perhaps the funniest panel shows Shel being harassed by a local merchant, who threatens him that by refusing to buy his souvenirs, Americans are "driving us into the arms of the communists!" This was the kind of humor that poked the West where it smarted.

In light of Shel's subsequent career, his early success at an elevated form of cartooning seems a fitting point of origin. Shel elevated every art form he touched, most notably children's books, but also music. Shel's books spoke to more than just children (and remain classics) and his country-and-western songs? Well, we're not even sure what those were, but "A Boy Named Sue" is unforgettable.

The Giving Tree, Shel's most beloved and enduring children's book, was published in 1964 and has remained in print continuously ever since. It has been called dark and pessimistic, but millions of readers have been moved enough to share it with their children the minute they are old enough to understand it.

By the time that book came out, Shel had already published the hilarious *Uncle Shelby's ABZ Book,* a kind of parody of children's literature. In one passage, Uncle Shelby tells his young readers that there is no magical Land of Oz, but that maybe someday they can go to Detroit. His instructions to kids to drink ink and throw eggs at the ceiling may not sit well with today's protective parents, but we guarantee you that nine- and ten-year-olds have always found it funny. (We know this from personal experience.)

Shel was unceasingly prolific: He published two-dozen books of writings and drawings, many of them difficult to categorize because they are simply unique. He also released eighteen albums of original songs, mostly in a country and folk vein. Our personal favorite is his first album, the 1959 *Hairy Jazz,* a boisterous collection of songs from the Roaring Twenties accompanied by the Red Onion Jazz Band. The record includes "Broken Down Mama," probably the first Silverstein song ever recorded.

As a songwriter, Shel was overwhelmingly successful. He was the primary writer for the highly popular folk-rock band Dr. Hook & the Medicine Show, as well as the country singer Bobby Bare. Both Bare and Dr. Hook recorded hit versions of Shel's ballad, "Sylvia's Mother." Since his death, Bare and the Nashville singer Bob Gibson have separately recorded tribute albums to Shel: *Makin' a Mess: The Songs of Shel Silverstein* (1995), and *Twistable, Turnable Man: A*

Musical Tribute to the Songs of Shel Silverstein (2010), respectively.

Shel wrote folksongs about the beatnik experience in the late 1950s, including "Bury Me in my Shades"; and rather diabolical children's songs, such as the child-pleaser about being eaten by a boa constrictor. But, without a doubt his best-known songs are his two all-time Nashville standards, Johnny Cash's "A Boy Named Sue" and Loretta Lynn's "One's on the Way."

In a way, it's not surprising that the composer of these two classics started his career at *Playboy*, a magazine that constantly questioned existing notions of gender roles and sexuality. These songs are all about masculinity and femininity. "A Boy Named Sue" tackles what it means to defend one's manhood in the most extreme conditions imaginable. On the other side of the coin, "One's on the Way" explores the sometimes-unreasonable expectations that society confers on women. Later in his life, Shel parodied his own creation with "The Father of a Boy Named Sue," which deals with homosexuality and incest in a comically creepy way.

* * *

One of the most beloved cartoon characters of the twenty-first century has to be green-eyed, red-bow-pigtailed Mandy—hatched from the fertile, ribald mind of Dean Yeagle and debuted in *Playboy* in 2002.

We find it interesting that many of the cartoonists and illustrators we spoke to seem to have followed similar paths, regardless of the era into which they were born. Dean was born in 1950 and grew up in Philadelphia drawing Disney characters from the time he could hold a crayon.

"I just loved Disney movies, and from fairly early on, decided that animation was what I wanted to do," he told us. "I aimed for it for the rest of my life."

Ultimately, he enrolled in the Hussian College School of Art in his hometown, which he called "a minor little school. I very quickly understood that they didn't approve of cartoons there, so after my first formal year, I started working during the summer at a local animation studio. It was so small that they needed me to do whatever I could handle, and I started really learning animation. They'd have me do design, layouts, storyboards, and some actual animation. I did ink and paint for backgrounds and a little of everything. It was a very valuable thing, almost like being an apprentice, and I did it until I had to go into the service. The Vietnam War was on so I joined the Navy."

Dean was stationed on two different small destroyers, the William R. Rush and the Basilone. Before shipping out, he'd met his future wife Barbara—an artist herself— and in order to stay close to him, she enrolled at the Mozarteum School in Salzburg. This allowed her to follow Dean's ships and after his first six-month cruise, they were married. A woman of many talents, Barbara went on to illustrate children's books and *Jack and Jill* magazine, and was also accomplished on the viola and piano.

After Dean's discharge from the Navy, the Yeagles landed in New York, where Dean worked freelance while he made the rounds of the studios in search of a permanent position. He ended up at Zander's Animation Parlour. Jack Zander, known as the "Matisse of Mice," was the animator of the *Tom and Jerry* cartoon series. His career spanned animation's golden age and the studio was known as the Disney of the East for the high-quality work it produced. Dean worked with and learned from Zander for seven years before moving on to form his own studio with Daryl Cagle and a colleague from Zander's, Nancy Beiman.

"We mixed our last names together and came up with the company name Caged Beagle. Daryl dropped out early, and Nancy and I were partners for a few years before she left to work at Disney. So, ultimately, it was solely my company. I still did work for Jack Zander when he needed me and I made a lot of animated cereal commercials, including Cookie Crisp and the anthropomorphic bee for Honey Nut Cheerios.

"Then *Playboy* came up. The Playboy Corporation sent around a flyer to all the animation companies, announcing that they were holding an animation contest with a $20,000 prize! I soon realized that, in order to win, I'd have to spend close to that amount to produce something prize-worthy. So instead, I sent them drawings to show what I might do, and I got a call from Michelle Urry, the cartoon editor, saying 'Where have you been?' I've worked for them ever since."

Michelle had already worked for *Playboy* for thirty-five years when she discovered Dean in 2000.

"They have been so *very* easy for me to work with," Dean said. "I would do five or six sketches and send them in to Michelle. Hefner then looked and made his choices and then I finished those he selected. And they paid immediately! The *Playboy* cartoons I did were done in Photoshop. I'd do them in pencil first, scan them in and do the finish in Photoshop. This is a great way to work because not only can I do it but I can *undo* it.

"Michelle and I corresponded by mail, always by letter. Both Hef and Michelle hated computers, and she wouldn't tell him I did my stuff on the computer. At first I'd tell Michelle, 'Well, I'll send you a CD,' and she'd say, 'Oh, no, no, no. Don't do that. I've got to see it. I have to have it in print. I realize you do it on the computer, but print it out for me.'

"There was a little bit of an acclimation curve because, at the start, she'd send me back prints and say, 'The color isn't right.'

"I'd try to explain, 'Well, that's because you're taking a photograph of a print. I'll send you the CD and you can give it to the printers and the color will come out fine.' That's how we ended up doing it, but she really didn't want Hef to know that I did the work on a computer. It was kind of funny.

"Michelle was quite an interesting character. She'd say, 'Stop writing me on the damn email. I don't do email! Call me on the phone.' If she liked you, she never stopped fighting for you. A few times she sent things back with a note, 'I don't know why Hef didn't like this. I tried and tried and tried to get him to but he said no.' Timing had something to do with it, also. A couple of times, I'd send stuff he'd rejected back to them a few years later and they'd buy it.

"I was lucky as far as having my stuff edited. In the beginning, Hef kept saying that my heads were too big. 'Reduce the head,' came the note. It was probably true, since I'd come from animation, where you do a lot of characters with heads about a third the size of their bodies. Mandy was about five-and-a-half heads tall, and people are supposed to be about seven heads tall. I recently tried scaling her up against a photograph of a woman standing straight, to see if the proportions worked. Of course, Mandy was *not* your averagely proportioned gal!"

After her—literal—unveiling in *Playboy*, Mandy became a well-known and much appreciated figure around the world. At the opening of a gallery show featuring Dean's cartoons, he was approached by a woman who ran a well-known Paris comic shop.

"My father would love to meet you," she said. "He's a huge fan of Mandy."

Dean continued, "I went outside and she introduced us and I found out he was the President of the Natural History Museum in Paris. He took us on a personal three-hour, behind the scenes tour. This was an important, serious man, and he took us around and had lunch with us. Not only that but he invited us to the Lido the following night for what turned out to be a extravagant Parisian experience: the wonderful fanfare of the historic and fantastically expensive Lido with gourmet dinner and more fine Champagne than anyone should have—and all because of Mandy."

* * *

No one uses a quill in the twenty-first century—right? Wrong. Englishman Mike Williams does, and you may have seen his quirky "reverse joke" cartoons in *Punch, Private Eye, The Times, Sun* or (most likely) *Playboy*.

Mike was born in Liverpool-on-Sea and trained as an illustrator in commercial art studios. He started his career at Henry Pybus and Littlewoods in Liverpool.

"Catalogues were illustrated then," he explained, "and they were all done by artists—no photographs. By sketching the products, we made them look much better than they actually were."

So what about this quill? We had heard (we thought we misheard) that Mike actually used such a thing.

"Yeah, not only do I draw using a quill but I go find my own pens on the beach, usually from seagulls. It's comical; I forget how young people don't know about such a thing. It goes back to the fourteenth century, when people used big goose-feather quills. So I gather my own and sharpen them. They're really the same as a pen, but more flexible—and more unpredictable."

Mike's use of the pen and Dutch alkaline watercolors produces wonderfully vivid cartoons, fresh and contemporary in spite of the means used to create them.

"The alkaline is unusual and very forgiving," he told us. "When you make mistakes you can easily correct them with alkaline."

For ten years, Mike happily trod a career path from catalogues to advertising, ultimately working on campaigns for large corporate clients such as BMW, Guinness, and the international bank Julius Baer, At Baer, he was responsible for creating their corporate polar bear logo. You're probably thinking that bank advertising is a far cry from cartooning, but Mike's sense of humor was irrepressible, and led him to the burgeoning world of comic art.

"Right about 1965, cartooning was becoming very popular with artists, an 'in' thing to do. It rode in on the back of the Beatles. They made a big success of animation and there was a lot of it around; it was really the forerunner of the demand for cartoons. So I started submitting my funny drawings, and *Punch* was the first to buy one.

"My parents were avid readers of *The New Yorker* and other American literature, so I experienced a kind of Anglo-American humor. It's different from English humor but I understand it and am a big fan of it. So I sent off some cartoons to *Playboy.* It was like sending stuff into outer space, sending it to America."

At that particular time, *Playboy* was looking for artists with a working mastery of color—and Mike completely fit the bill. His unusual technique produced hues that subliminally drew viewers into the scenes. "Michelle Urry was the editor at the time and she was brilliant. Even though we fought a little, she was the best cartoonist I've ever come across, always encouraging. Later, when I became cartoon editor for *Punch,* I suddenly had perspective and realized what her problems must have been."

As we've said (and said), Hef had strong ideas about every cartoon and liked to impose them on the artists. But, just as Arnold Roth did, Mike sent only completed work to Chicago.

"I couldn't have dealt with too much editing. I'd have committed suicide. Either that or I'd have sat up high somewhere and picked people off with a gun. I'm far too much of a prima donna to have tolerated that. I suspect that maybe Michelle threw her body between Hef and myself, but seriously, he was always good with me. *Playboy* was a good, steady source of income. Their new policy [of no longer accepting cartoon submissions] is madness! If they think *Playboy* sells for the articles, they're dreaming. *The New Yorker* did the same thing and sales dropped until they reinstated the drawings. Magazines should be a collection of elements, with something for everyone; pretty girls, cartoons, articles, everything."

During the time he contributed to *Playboy,* Mike visited New York often and always spent time with Michelle Urry—sometimes as her personal houseguest. It seems that was a common practice of hers: She offered shelter, food, advice, and encouragement to numerous budding and established artists during her almost thirty years at *Playboy.* By all accounts, Michelle was a "take no prisoners" kind of gal, and when she faced a cancer battle, very few of her friends knew about it.

"She didn't give me a clue," Mike told us. "I was still arguing with her right up to the end. I felt really bad about that. And they never allowed me near the Mansion. I was kept away from it. I don't think my wife would have been too pleased with me going anyway. I'm surprise anyone came out alive, to be honest, from what I've heard!

"I went to school with John Lennon and he had a strange history, but Hugh Hefner, good god! He's defied everything and broken all of the rules, hasn't he? Living off Pepsi and spending the day in his dressing gown...if that doesn't sound like a recipe for living to ninety, I don't know what is!"

* * *

Clive Collins, another of the Brits who found his way into *Playboy*'s pages, studied graphic design at Kingston School of Art and worked in marine insurance before starting his life on the funny pages. His early life had a lot in common with many of his American contemporaries. "I've drawn ever since I was a child. It was my favorite hobby and I used to paste the drawings on the walls of the bedroom I shared with my brother, though I never made any attempt to sell any of my work early on. It wasn't until I got a very boring job at an insurance company—the same one where my Dad worked—that I thought life might be more pleasurable if I had some sort of money-making sideline to ease the tedium. I guess it was seeing cartoons in newspapers and magazines that gave me the idea I might make some money with them. I managed to get a job in a small artwork studio in the early sixties and started selling a decent number of cartoons to various publications."

Clive's work began appearing regularly in *Punch* in 1964, and he ended up getting a job as a political and editorial cartoonist at Rupert Murdoch's *Sun* when it debuted in 1969. Just a year later, Clive moved to *The People*—one of Britain's oldest newspapers—as their first-ever political cartoonist. At the suggestion of one of the publishers, he submitted under the pseudonym "Collie."

"It didn't really bother me, not having my name on the work, as I was still beavering away doing spot cartoons under my own name elsewhere," he admitted. During the Falklands War, Clive worked at Murdoch's *Sun* as a political cartoonist, and at the same time was asked to fill in for JAK, the regular cartoonist on the *London Evening Standard.* Working for both enterprises, he obviously couldn't use his real name, so he decided to sign his work for *Standard,* "Ollie." Imagine his amusement when his editor at the *Sun* complained that his work wasn't as funny as that of his rival, Ollie!

"*The People* was short-lived," he said, "but I managed to make a living selling gags until one day Michelle Urry came to London, contacted my agent, and said she wanted to meet some English cartoonists. It was arranged that I'd meet her, along with Mike Williams, Ken Taylor, and Bill Asprey. The lunch was held on board a boat moored alongside the embankment in London."

At this point (1972), Hefner had purchased the magazine *Oui,* in an attempt to compete with the more explicit *Penthouse* without compromising its own standards. The *Oui* experiment was not a complete success and *Playboy* would end up unloading it in 1982—but it did bring some new European talent into the *Playboy* fold.

"Hef planned for *Oui* to act as a sort of European *Playboy,* so there were a number of French and Belgian cartoonists on board too," Clive continued, "and we were all given contracts. The magazine didn't guarantee they'd give us work but agreed to pay us generously if they did. I barely sold anything to them and eventually *Oui* folded, but I continued to send things to Michelle and she bought one or two, but nothing of note. When I look back to the muddy colors I was using—this was all pre-computer days—I can understand why. In fact, it wasn't until about twenty years ago, when I began to use an Apple Mac to color my artwork, that I started to make any headway with her. I'd had a lot of success at *Punch* at that time, and to sell to *Playboy* was the icing on the cake.

"Then Michelle died and I thought that was it. No more *Playboy*. But the reverse happened. Amanda Warren, who became Hef's Cartoon Deputy, liked my work and started to buy on a regular basis. *Playboy* paid extremely well, and I loved the fact that I was finally getting gags into a great magazine. *Punch* folded in 1996, so *Playboy* became the premier market for me. I never met Hef nor went to the Mansion, but when I was in New York I met Michelle and she would take me to dinner and look at any work that I had brought with me."

We asked Amanda what it was about Clive's humor she was drawn to. "Without a doubt, his work encompasses that biting, wicked British sense of humor, and Americans can't get enough of it. I just can't resist."

"I was shocked and saddened when I heard about *Playboy's* demise," Clive commented. He knew very well that *Playboy* continues on, but he wasn't the first to express his dismay at the magazine's current "no cartoons" policy in this mordant fashion. "I had a bunch of work in consideration for quite a while—much longer than normal—and wondered why it was taking so long to look at it. Various rumors reached us here in England about a change in format, but nothing specific until Amanda wrote and told me. I was paid well for all the work I had published in *Playboy* and I miss it terribly. Over here now is a satire magazine—*Private Eye*—to whom I've sold a few gags, but there's no big player any more."

What's a cartoonist to do? Clive is enjoying semi-retirement, and in 2011 was appointed the honor of MBE for "service to art," as part of the Queen's Birthday Honors at Buckingham Palace.

* * *

In what seems to be the trend with cartoonists, Don Orehek has memories of drawing from the age of three. He hadn't perfected the art of satire at that point, but was experimenting with faces and replicating the subjects his father delighted in sketching. "My father

Don Orehek and Hugh Hefner sharing some laughs: Courtesy Don and Suzy Orehek

was in the Austrian Army and, long afterwards, he was still illustrating Austrian soldiers. Like any kid, I liked soldiers but instead of playing with toy ones, I drew them. The kids in school were forever asking me to draw them their own."

As Don's tastes and techniques matured, he leaned toward more traditional representational art: seascapes, lighthouses, and the like. But he soon discovered that sarcasm sold better and began drawing cartoons of everyone's favorite scapegoat: lawyers. He threw in doctors, just for fun. Don sold this work to small Greenwich Village shops.

"I could draw something once and just keep copying myself," he said. "There was one image I sold forty-five times: 'Kill the Lawyers.' People loved those things."

Don did a stretch in the Navy, on the destroyer Escort, where he spent most of his time on duty drawing cartoons. Even that didn't make the time pass fast enough, though, and Don wanted out of the engine room.

"I went to my commanding officer and asked to be transferred to the laundry. He said, 'Forget it, I showed your *shit'*—that's what they called cartons then—'to a couple of guys I met on the beach, and they want to meet you.'"

It turned out that the two guys had a fledgling Navy newspaper and their cartoonist was being discharged.

"'Draw something for us,'" they asked me. So I quickly drew a fire hydrant with a dog taking a leak on it, with a goofy caption. They laughed like anything and I got the job. I spent the remaining two years of my time in Public Information, doing a comic strip named 'Cyphers,' about an old bum who drank a lot but still got the girls. That went over big with the sailors."

After his discharge, Don attended New York's School of Visual Arts on the GI Bill. He meet a lot of cartoonists, who all seemed to be submitting and selling their cartoons—including some lewd ones—to various magazines. "I started selling to little joke books and yes, to the raunchier places, also. For those I'd use pseudonyms: Kobasa, DiBenvenuto, Sam de Sade, and a few others. I worked steadily for four years selling gags.

"One day, I went up to *The Saturday Evening Post* and the cartoon editor said, 'Mail me your stuff and if I buy one you can see me in person.' I wanted to get her attention. There was a poem by Joyce Kilmer, *Trees,* and I hated it, so I drew a very irreverent cartoon about it. It turned out that the editor also disliked that poem and she bought the cartoon. And that was the beginning of a very nice relationship with *The Saturday Evening Post.* All this time, I really wanted to sell to *Playboy* and I'd send stuff to them, but I never had any luck. Then, in 1967, I sold a cartoon to them and got 120 bucks for it—good money! The next year I sold another, this time for $130. So I was bold and sent Hefner twenty of what I considered my most *Playboy*-esque cartoons. Michelle Urry bought *nine* of them at $300 a piece."

Don's *Playboy* career was up and running. Between 1968 and

2015, the magazine featured 245 of his cartoons. "Every month or so, I'd send Michelle submissions, she would pick those she liked, and then she'd fly out to California to show Hef. He usually agreed with her choices but not always. Then I'd receive the roughs back and I'd do the finishes and add the colors. The first go-round was in black-and-white with a wash, and then watercolor. The OKs from Hef were actually handwritten and Hef personally signed off on all the art so there was never a misunderstanding.

"I liked Michelle—she was a good gal. When one of my cartoons appeared in the magazine, she'd send me the copy with a handwritten note saying something nice about the cartoon."

Don's ace record-keeper and wife, Suzy, estimates that from December 1966 through December 1994, Don sold more than 12,000 single cartoons—and that figure doesn't include books or all of the work he sold before and since. In 1966, he traveled to Vietnam with a group of artists under the auspices of the National Cartoon Society and U.S. Department of Defense. Upon his return, he and his fellow cartoonists were invited to the White House and personally thanked by President Lyndon Johnson for entertaining American and Vietnamese troops.

* * *

Mort Gerberg's intellectual and expressive satire and cartoons have appeared in a multitude of media, including film and television, magazines, books, and newspapers. His on-the-scene reportage sketches continue to amaze long after the events they depict have passed into history. Mort commented and drew on the spot during both the 1972 election and Richard Nixon's second inauguration on NBC, with Robin Cook and Edwin Newman. To help promote this new form of election coverage, the network executives scheduled an appearance for him on Election Day, November 7, 1972, on *The Today Show*, where he penned a political cartoon while being interviewed by Barbara Walters.

"Barbara Walters had a reputation as a barracuda, and I was nervous about appearing with her. The head honchos said not to worry, that Frank McGee would host my segment. The morning I showed up to do the show, they told me that Frank was sick and Barbara was doing it after all."

In the course of the segment, as Barbara displayed and discussed one of Mort's books, she tried to set it down on Mort's tilted drawing board, but it slid down toward him. She grabbed it and tried it again a couple of times, and finally, very annoyed, snapped, "Oh, what am I to do with this book! To which Mort replied, "Buy it, Barbara."

That got a big laugh from everyone on the set, including Barbara. The two proceeded to chat on the air for a nearly unprecedented twenty minutes.

We're always curious as to the genesis of a cartoonist's interest in the genre. "I was a kid from New York growing up," explained Mort. "I was small. I wore glasses, I got beaten up. What I did was draw. It didn't really start to take, except maybe as an expression of self, until junior high school, when I drew for the school magazine. I liked the idea of cartoons and finally, in high school, I drew a comic strip. There wasn't any thought about me going to art school because there wasn't any money for any of that."

Following an uncle's advice to get a basic college education, Mort majored in advertising at tuition-free Baruch College of the City College of New York. The Army came next; he was sent to Anchorage, Alaska, where he first put his talents with words on display as an editor of the post newspaper published by the Public Information Office. "I did a lot of writing in the Army and thought, 'This is what I'm going to do—I'm going to be a writer.'"

Soon after returning to civilian life, Mort was hired as a reporter for the Park Row Service in New York, which provided hometown news to subscribing newspapers around the country. When Park Row went out of business, a friend who knew of Mort's drawing and writing abilities advised him to check out *Cosmopolitan* magazine. It seemed that they were retooling the entire operation and had an opening for an advertising sales promotion manager. With only a vague notion about what "sales promotion was," Mort decided to go for it.

"So, I put together some samples I had done in school and the Army, along with other odd bits, and went to see the publisher. 'Terrific,' he said, and so I was with the company for two years before a headhunter got me a bigger job at Ziff-Davis Publishing Company, where I was the advertising copy chief for seventeen of its magazines.

Mort was happy to be writing and drawing but not passionate about the subject material. He continued doing gag cartoons every chance he got, mainly for his own amusement.

"I was just not happy, and actually got so angry on one occasion when a piece of my copy was changed that I smashed my hand through a glass door in my office, badly cutting a finger. 'This is stupid,' I thought, and I quit."

Mort had a car and a few hundred dollars, so he took off to Mexico for a sabbatical of sorts, living on the side of a hill, practicing writing and drawing the life he saw around him. After a little over a year, "I finally had the courage to mail some of my drawings to *Esquire*, and to my great surprise and joy, they bought a nine-panel cartoon sequence. 'Wow, maybe I can really do this,' I realized, and I came back to New York. I gave myself six months to see if I could make it as a freelance cartoonist. I didn't know a lot of people, but I had a friend—Jerry Yulsman, a staff photographer at *Playboy*—who knew many people in publishing."

One of them was the editor of one of the lesser-known men's magazines and gave Mort the opportunity to read "slush" —unsolicited manuscripts—for him. "I'd go in a couple of days a week and read, and while there, I'd look at the cartoons in the magazines. 'These are not funny cartoons,' I said, 'they're terrible!'

"'Okay,' the editor shot back, 'if you're so smart, you're now the

Cartoon Editor.' I began calling cartoonists whose work I admired and asking them to come and submit work. Slowly, I began to learn the cartoon world. I met all the people just starting out at that point."

By 1962, Mort's cartoons were being sold to a battalion of small men's magazines that proliferated during that time, with names such as *Gent, Dude, Swank,* and *Cavalier*. "These were basically the forerunners of the tits-and-ass magazines," he explained. 'You worked your way up through those until you got to *Playboy*."

Finally, he made a sale to the prestigious *Saturday Evening Post* and Mort finally began to feel he could make a living doing what he loved.

One day, Jerry Yulsman called Mort and told him that Hugh Hefner was coming to New York.

"I'm not even sure I even really knew who Hugh Hefner was," Mort admitted, "but I was interested in new magazines. Jerry explained that Hef was the owner of *Playboy* and was starting a new publication, *Show Business Illustrated*. 'I think you should come meet him,' Jerry said. 'Maybe you can sell some cartoons.' So I went down to their office in midtown Manhattan, and Hefner was with this knock-out blonde—Cynthia Maddox. I couldn't believe anyone could be so gorgeous."

While Jerry, his wife Anita, and Hef were deep in conversation, Mort started talking to Cynthia, whose title was Cartoon Editor. She encouraged Mort to submit work for the new publication.

"It was an interesting situation, so I began sending in rough ideas for *Show Business Illustrated*." The magazine didn't catch on, but Cynthia persisted in encouraging an unconfident Mort—this time on behalf of *Playboy*. Desperately trying to establish herself as more than Hef's girlfriend, she promoted Mort to Hef while at the same time encouraging him not to give up.

On perhaps his third submission, *Playboy* bit, but not completely. They wanted Mort's ideas but intended to assign someone else the task of illustrating them.

"They gave two of my ideas to Dedini and one of the other established cartoonists, maybe Sokol. My third idea was given to Dink Siegel, a wonderful illustrator with a realistic style who was, maybe, a fourth cousin of mine on my father's side. That took me back to when I was a teenager with this blooming interest in cartooning, which of course the family was very much against. Cartooning was hardly any kind of job for a Jewish boy. But someone sent me to see Dink, and I was very impressed. He had a wonderful office in a classic French building on Fifth Avenue, just a beautiful place. Dink was an extremely gentle, soft-spoken man from Atlanta. He used gorgeous color, just marvelous. So *Playboy* bought these three ideas from me to give to others to illustrate, and I got a note from Dink. He said he couldn't imagine why they had asked him to do the finish drawing of my rough, which was so wonderfully drawn already that I should have been able to do it myself. Such a gracious man. Of course, when I saw Dink's version in the magazine, I thanked him for doing such a beautiful job.

"After that, the second and third batch I sent them, they said I could draw the finishes myself, and from that point on, I started selling them with some regularity, still working with Cynthia, who would always be delightful and encouraging."

"I think the development of the *Playboy* cartoon really bloomed when Michelle Urry came in. I received a notice that this new person was coming in to work the cartoons. I spoke to her on the phone and said, 'Oh, are you from Canada? You have a Canadian accent,' and she fast-mouthed back some Jewish comment, because she was a *Jewish* Canadian. She could be a pistol. I went to see her at her office at the Chicago Mansion, and Shelly—Shel Silverstein—was there and I remember him taking me around. Michelle really took over that job and was really very clear, very specific. She had her own aesthetic. She was not Hef's girlfriend who was also the Cartoon Editor.

"I have notes from Michelle that are priceless. I also have handwritten notes from Hef on how particular cartoons should be done—

how they *should* be done. He would always write on the roughs or the 'okays.' Most of the instruction would come through Michelle, though, in very clear letters that she sent. For the first number of years, what Hef wanted from me was mostly black and white. I was politically oriented and socially conscious of contemporary events that were going on, and that's what I did cartoons on. For Hef, that kind of material belonged in black and white, in the back of the magazine. At the same time, I realized that color paid more and I thought, 'I can do tits and ass as well as everybody else,' so I'd submit a bunch of sexy ideas in color also.

"I happen to have the first 'okay' on a color finish that Michelle was allowing me to do, and it was very specific. It was not just her interest in the work, but her ability to communicate both Hef's and her desires that made her good—and she did so in a way that was crystal clear." With that, Mort shared with us a portion of a letter from Michelle:

> *On this black and white, I am perfectly willing to do it in this nice blue wash, but I would like you to tone down the yellow from the announcer and make him monochromatic as well. I don't think the cartoon will suffer and in effect I want to make it two-color. It's a very nice wash, in the manner you have it done here. I think it's a little gaudy with the yellow and brown on the guy. It's going to be blue and white. The man and woman are just about perfect as far as positioning and expressions…'*

"This is very specific stuff. She's writing here again, including a note from Hef:

> *I'm really glad to get this in color because I think it nudges Hef along when you do it in such a painstaking fashion. However, we can't nudge him about anything right now.*

PLAYBOY
MICHELLE URRY
CARTOON EDITOR

June 25, 2002

Mort Gerberg
189 Waverly Place #6
New York, NY 10014

Dear Mort:

Ok for two-column color on:

"I've lost my desire to draw any distinction between naughty and nice."

For the following, please see Hef's note.

"If you think sitting on Santa's lap is fun, Miss Drew, you might also like to try Santa's face."

Looking forward to the finishes which we'd like to have in as close to July 18th as possible.

Sorry to hear you are losing your studio. Please let us know where we should send your material and you may want to change where you receive the returned artwork where you'll be more regularly. I presume you are going to try to work from home?

Very best-

jt
Enclosures

Mort's letter illustrates Hef's attention to detail: Archival material from Playboy magazine.

"I had one with Santa on the couch, talking to a psychiatrist, saying, 'I lost my desire to draw any distinction between naughty and nice.' This was fine, but Hef sent a handwritten note about another holiday cartoon in the same batch, where the punch line was, 'If you think sitting on Santa's lap is fun, Miss Drew, you might try Santa's face.'

Hef wrote:

Mort, Let's put this in a store with a regular Santa and a pretty, young, naïve woman with a smile on her face. The art should be very sweet and innocent, à la Norman Rockwell—Hef.

from HUGH M. HEFNER

Mort- Let's put this in a store with a regular Santa + a pretty young, naive woman with a smile on her face. To make the gag funny, the art should be very sweet + innocent, a la Norman Rockwell.

—Hef

Hef is known to include hand written thoughts on each cartoon correspondence: Archival material from Playboy magazine. Reprinted with permission. All rights reserved.

"I think that kind of attention was what really elevated the level and quality of the cartoons to a greater height. Michelle was a wonderful woman, and always tried to let everyone know where they stood. Here's a letter from 2002: '…It's great. I told you over and over we couldn't do this package without you. You continue to play a large and vital part in the magazine. Thank you for all your efforts. Enclosed bonus check.'

"It was nice. She was a mensch. Here is probably one of the last notes she wrote me, from May of 2006. She died in October. 'I'm not having lunches, coffee, or anything anymore, unless it's corporate high command or Hefner.' This was a reference to her practice of taking "her" cartoonists to lunch. Every once in a while, she'd call up and say, 'C'mon, let's go to lunch.' She kept her illness from everyone. I never knew why she wore the eye patch and sunglasses until later. She was a challenging person, but quite loved. Hundreds and hundreds of people squeezed into her loft for her memorial service."

Mort remembered that it was as far back as 2009 that things started to wind down. Amanda Warren had taken over as Cartoon Editor and Mort noticed that fewer and fewer of his submissions were being selected. Amanda would write, "Thank you, but Hef didn't make any purchases from this. While he didn't find anything this time, he enjoys your humor and wants to continue to see more of it." When asked his thoughts on the announcement in 2016 that *Playboy* is no longer taking cartoon submissions, he offered his typically unbridled thoughts.

"What do you think my opinion would be? I think it's terrible. First, they're putting clothes on the girls, which again seems counterintuitive to what the magazine is about. There was no real, good reason for that, except that, yes, you can get porn on the Internet now. But this seems like a weak excuse, because there is still pleasure in looking. There's a certain parallel existence, in that *The New Yorker* is sort of changing in its own way, in that same area.

"Both *Playboy* and *The New Yorker* have been defined largely by their cartoons, and I think, over the years, as will always be the case, there will be a change in aesthetics. That was more apt to happen at *The New Yorker* because the editors changed. In the case of *Playboy*, the editors didn't change—it's been Hefner all along, although Michelle's activism helped develop new talent—but Playboy was clearly defined by its humor —its many great, great artists. You know the joke, 'I only read it for the fiction'—but it was largely for the cartoons.

"The 'new' *Playboy* that I saw has a feature in the back of the magazine, 'Cartoonist in Residence.' I'm sure whoever it is, is a nice person, but it does not follow the long tradition of many different cartooning voices. The announcement about 'no more cartoons' was a particularly strange one, because Hef identified himself as having a real love of cartoons, and was a cartoonist himself. And that was always clear in his ideas and the attention he paid to all matters. He was really paying attention.

"Michelle once wrote me a note about a sex cartoon I had done, 'Mort, you did a wonderful job on this, but you made the girl's tits too pointy.' I laughed out loud.

"I phoned her and said, 'Michelle, give me a break. I made the tits too *pointy*?' Yes, I had to go back and fix them. With that kind of attention, how did this happen? It seems like some takeover by a foreign body or alien creature. All of my friends and colleagues, people like Gahan Wilson and Sidney Harris—long-time contributors like myself—we just don't understand it. Change is a challenge."

* * *

Several of the cartoonists have reminded us of the fact that, before Hef ever dreamed of conquering the publishing world—and, in the process, creating a worldwide brand—he harbored aspirations of making his mark as a cartoonist. From the time he was a young boy, he doodled about the happenings of his eventful life, communicating in images his own particular view of the world around him. His artwork also allowed him to portray himself as the hip, suave, and confident ladies man he aspired to be. Over the years, Hef bound his autobiographical cartoons into volumes and, by 1953, when he launched *Playboy*, he was already up to volume 52!

His efforts did not go unpublished. In 1951, just two years before the launch of *Playboy*, Hef published a seventy-four-page comic book called, *This Toddlin Town: A Rowdy Burlesque of Chicago Manners and Morals.* It showed promise—but Hef faced stiff competition from the many graphic masters—including the ones we talked to—who emerged during the heyday of comic books and newspaper funny pages. It's our good fortune that Hef's talent as an artist went largely unsung. Otherwise, the Playboy empire might never have been born!

11

THE MAD MEN

"All cartoonists are geniuses, but Arnold Roth is especially so." –JOHN UPDIKE

The talking picture made its debut just two years before Arnold Roth was born in 1929, and it was but one in a vortex of influences over his career path. The popular arts were being showcased everywhere. People were unemployed and many, having given up on finding work, sought to express themselves and their situations in various media in an effort to stay busy and distracted from their pitiful circumstances. Workmen put their skills on display by whittling wood into toys and household goods; women fashioned toys from scraps of fabric; and aspiring artists propped themselves against gritty tenements with paper and crayons and drew superheroes to save the day.

"Everyone felt and saw these expressions, and influences; they were in the air to grab," Arnold Roth told us about his early years. When he was eight, Arnold attended free art classes on Saturdays and Sundays, sponsored by the Works Progress Administration. "Because of the Depression," he explained, "we had the best teachers in Philadelphia teaching us. There were a lot of excellent artists giving little kids lessons.

"I was in an exemplary boys high school—Central High School—throughout the whole World War, and I was drawing and painting all the time. The first job I remember was producing a comic book for a local guy who owned companies in Philly that was manufacturing stuff for the war. I did a couple of eight-page books in black and white, showing what a great guy he was. Of course, he was making a fortune off the war, but that wasn't what the book was about.

"I was the resident cartoonist for all the high school publications, too, and was called the 'class artist.' I was drawing all the time. After graduation, I was given a scholarship to the Museum of Philadelphia and School of Industrial Arts. This in itself was pretty amazing, because all the GIs were coming home and going to school on Uncle Sam, and here I was with a scholarship."

Arnold attended art school for two years while playing saxophone in a band at night to make money, jazz being his second passion. There was pressure on Arnold to perform well at school—in fact, more than he realized. He wouldn't find out until quite a while later, but prior to his first day of class, the faculty was told he was a genius. Things went well—until they didn't.

"I was expelled. Someone had destroyed some property and the administration blamed it on me. Growing up in my neighborhood, where property was defaced and destroyed for no reason, I abhorred that kind of thing, but it was blamed on me although I was completely innocent. Of course, I wasn't so innocent about being chronically tardy. I was playing in bands at night to bring home money—during those days, everyone was expected to contribute to the household income—and I'd show up late for class. On top of that, I'd show up in a cheap tux because it was easier to go directly to school from whatever club I was playing at. The suit was a sort of greenish because it had sat in Sporty Morty's Clothing window for too many sunny days. One drawing teacher led the 'charge of the light brigade' to kick me out. She was a good woman and a wonderful teacher but she found me incorrigible. If I had known what a tough school it was, I wouldn't have gone there in the first place."

Television was beginning to have a huge impact on the culture, and Arnold and a few friends seized the opportunity to become a part of the burgeoning industry. They formed a small company to develop ideas for TV shows. Arnold was the artist and his partners handled the writing and business sides. Bond Bread, a national chain, took an interest in the fledgling troupe, but they were slightly ahead of their time, it seemed, and not enough households yet owned TVs to make their work lucrative.

Then came a setback for Arnold of mammoth proportions. "I got tuberculosis and had to spend over a year recovering in a sanatorium," he told us. "After I came out, I went back to art school and started freelancing, selling a few drawings here and there. I put together a portfolio and went up to New York on a regular basis to hustle it—as we used to say."

In 1953, *TV Guide* started publishing and Arnold was just the man to illustrate it. "I did at few drawings for them at first, but eventually I did *tons* of work for them through the years."

Things were beginning to fall into place. Curtis Publishing was based in Philadelphia, so, in addition to his work for *TV Guide*, Arnold started selling his illustrations to the prestigious and *Holiday* magazine. "They had Ronald Searle for the big stuff—for good reason—but I gradually began to make my mark there as well." Other publications soon began seeking out his sometimes outlandish and always hilarious cartoons, including the cream of the crop, *Esquire* and *The New Yorker*.

Typically, an art department would tell an artist what they were looking for in a cartoon, the artist would then do and redo a sketch until the final work was agreed upon, and only at that point would the cartoonist produce the final drawing. While Arnold was recuperating at the sanatorium, he gave a lot of thought to how he wanted to work, and what artistic interference he would accept.

"The *New Yorker* took a deep interest in my work but I knew what their system was. Even though I was starving, I didn't want to do work and then be told by an editor how to make it different or better. Throughout my career, I didn't do sketches. I would take a job, do a drawing, and tell them, 'If you don't like it, I'll do another.' That's the way I've worked my whole career. I wanted to do it the way I wanted to do it. And, of course, one I delivered a finished product, they never wanted any changes. So I got very lucky my whole life.

"This is where *Playboy*—or at least Hugh Hefner—came into my life. Hefner was starting a magazine called *Trump* [in 1956], and it had all the same guys who had done *Mad*. *Mad* had been a huge, huge success the moment it broke onto the scene and Harvey Kurtzman was the genius behind it. So Hefner got Harvey, and Harvey got all 'the usual gang of idiots' who had been working at *Mad* together: Al Jaffee, Will Elder, Jack Davis, and so on. And they all moved over and to work on this new magazine, which was a polished, full-color, quality-paper publication.

"Two different people were responsible for introducing this new comic magazine to me. I was in New York hustling my portfolio and an excellent cartoonist named Ed Fisher told me about it." Arnold went on to tell us that the other person he heard about it from—indirectly—was the saxophonist and composer Paul Desmond. Arnie and Paul had met around 1957, when the musician had come into a little studio Arnie shared with ten other guys. One of them had a used Leica camera for sale. Paul, along with Dave Brubeck, was beginning to make waves in the jazz world, but he wasn't "smothering in money"—as Arnie put it—so the group had chipped in for him to buy the camera. Arnie happened to be working at the studio on the Sunday Paul answered the ad for the Leica, and it was the beginning of a lifelong friendship.

"Paul and the guys were traveling all the time, and Paul told me about this really funny magazine, a comic book that he'd first seen at a train station. He brought me back a copy of *Mad* and naturally I went crazy over it because Harvey Kurtzman and Al Jaffee reflected exactly the same outlook I had. I got to know everything about Harvey, even though at that time I had never met him.

"Ed knew all the *Mad* guys so I went over to meet them—and Harvey knew my work. He hired me immediately. My stuff was appearing in a few magazines by this time—we're talking about the mid-fifties. As a matter of fact, Harvey put me on retainer not only to draw but to write graphic ideas that he would take a step further, or give to one of the other guys to work on. Jack Davis and Willie Elder would do those drawings because they weren't writers at all, but illustrators. Everyone there was likeable and very talented. That's how I wandered into that world. I didn't write text but would do ideas. Jack Davis didn't do ideas but was an illustrator. That's the way it usually went then, we each had our own particular strength and niche."

Unfortunately, *Trump* didn't last long. Hefner had financed it with a bank loan just at the time when television was gaining traction and attracting advertising while magazine sales and profits were suffering. Seemingly invincible weekly institutions such as *Colliers* folded. The day the bank called in its loan was a particularly trying one. "I was in the *Trump* office on that particularly calamitous day," Arnold told us. "Harvey told me the news about *Colliers* and said that all of the artists had been in looking for work. We hadn't even hit the stands with our first issue when Hefner pulled out. We eventually printed two issues from the material already completed, and we had half the third complete. That material ran in the pages of *Playboy* a few years later.

"Hefner was so contrite about the entire situation. He *really* wanted us to do a magazine for him. So he gave us space in his New York office for free. There were five or six of us and we pooled our funds and went into business for ourselves. We started a magazine called *Humbug* and struggled with it for about a year, until we were all broke. We were all doing other work, of course. I was getting more and more assignments from magazines, so I wasn't under financial duress. *Hallelujah*! But the other fellows had families and some were scrambling.

"Our big hurdle came in trying to find a distributor. The biggest one in the business—American News— had closed overnight. They owned all the newsstands in train stations and every desirable corner in every large city. So we were in trouble and Harvey said, 'It isn't just us. *The New Yorker* also doesn't have a distributor.' So we put out eleven issues and went out of business."

"That was when Hefner became very interested in my work; I sent a few things to *Playboy* and they liked them and used them. It got to the point where they would say, 'Would you do a full-page piece?' which I did. I would send it and they would paint it, and over the years, I illustrated a lot of articles for them, too. Harvey Kurtzman was producing *Little Annie Fanny* on a monthly basis and was always running late."

Each episode of that iconic comic strip—one of the most famous (or infamous) features in *Playboy* history—was imagined, drawn, and written by Harvey. It was then rendered in oil, tempera, and watercolor by Willy Elder. *Annie Fanny* irreverently and hysterically chronicled our shifting culture and morality, and was unique in its scope. Each of its ultimately 107 episodes—some running as long as seven pages—were complete works of painted art. But, as brilliant as he was, Harvey's inability to meet deadlines proved extremely costly and disruptive to the magazine. Finally, reinforcements were approved.

According to Arnold, "Jack Davis, Willy Elder, Al Jaffee, me, and a few others were hired to help him out and keep everything on schedule. Of course this worked, but it also got to be expensive. It got to the point where I'd come up from Philadelphia, and Al Jaffee, Willie, and I would stay at the Algonquin Hotel hacking away on

Little Annie Fanny. We had a suite with two bedrooms that we'd use to work in. They each had beds and a fold-down desk, but no artist equipment—no drawing boards or anything, and just two lamps on the nightstands. Al and I worked together and we agreed there wasn't enough light to work in, so we took the shades off and still needed more light. So we called down to room service: 'Can you send up two more lamps'? The guys came up with two more forty-watt lights and we still had to call for more. Once we hit ten lamps, we had enough light to work in, but it had gotten tremendously warm, so we stripped down to our shorts and undershirts.

"The pages were cut into separate panels and passed around so we could each do our individual contribution. One of us would do the background, etc, but *only* Willy Elder was allowed to touch Annie Fanny. We did everything we could to help Harvey get it out in time. At some point, Al and I both realized we seemed to be repeating the same panels. We knew they weren't sequential but couldn't figure out the story line. Finally, I went into the adjoining room and asked Willy, 'You know, it's not sequential, but we don't understand what's going on. Maybe it's like a dream story, where the same thing keeps happening?' It turned out that Willy didn't like the background colors we had done—even though we had followed his explicit instructions—so he had soaked out what we had done and kept sending them back to us to redo!

"This went on for about four days, but we were being well paid. Eventually, Hefner found it cheaper to fly us out to the Mansion in Chicago to work than keep us at a suite in the Algonquin."

Working in New York was clearly fun while it lasted. During one trip, Caroline Roth, Arnie's wife, decided to dress up and take her husband out to dinner, to give him a break from work. Remember, the only thing the hotel knew about these guys was that they were from *Playboy*, that they kept ordering lamps, and that they ate breakfast at any hour of the day or night. When beautiful Caroline arrived, Arnie promptly informed her that he couldn't possibly take time to go out, but that she should order whatever she wanted from the room-service menu. Feeling a bit miffed, Caroline ordered the most expensive thing she could find—Chateaubriand!

Imagine the scene when the chef himself showed up to carve the beef—while two artists sat drawing in their underwear surrounded by ten lamps and one lovely lady tapped her foot impatiently. That might have made a good cartoon, though we have no idea what the caption would have been!

Some accountant in Chicago must have noticed the charge because, before you could say, "Please pass the sautéed julienned vegetables," the guys received a call to pack up and return to Chicago.

"I don't think it was the most fiscally sound decision to move us from New York to Chicago to finish that one edition," said Arnold, "but nevertheless...we were chauffeured from our hotel to JFK and the four of us placed in our first-class seats. I had done a good deal of traveling for *Sports Illustrated* but this was the first time I had seen a phone on a plane, and Willy just couldn't get over it. Right after we took off, he called his wife:

"'Hi, Jean, guess where I am? No...no...we're on an airplane!' He hung up and a little while later he was at it again: 'Hello, Jean, guess where we are now...No...no...no we're flying over Cleveland!' Finally, we landed in Chicago and Hefner's limousine picked us up to take us to the Mansion. When we got into the car—there was a phone there, too! So it was, "Hi Jean, guess where I am now?'

"Harvey and Al were saying, 'I'm going to kill him if we don't get to the Mansion fast.'

"The good news was that Art Paul, the art director of *Playboy*, had everything we needed already set up for us: supplies, drawing boards, pencils, everything, so we could work twenty-four hours straight, which is exactly what we did—although...it was the Playboy Mansion so there were distractions.

"We were told to feel free to go anywhere we wanted. All of us read the magazine and had heard about the bar that looked into the swimming pool. So we said, 'We have to see this.' There were swimming trunks available, so we made ourselves a drink and took turns watching each other swim underwater. At last, I said, 'I don't think it's supposed to work this way. I'm not supposed to be having a drink in this beautiful setting looking into the water as Harvey Kurtzman paddles by.'

"Willy shared a room with Harvey and I bunked in with Al. Harvey and Will shared a connecting bathroom with some of the Bunnies, or they could have been Centerfolds. Willy wasn't happy and eventually told us, 'I'm going to tell you something about those Bunnies. They're filthy!'

"I said, 'They're so beautiful, so well appointed in every way, I can't believe it. What happened?'

"He said, 'Well, we're sharing a bathroom with them'—and I thought, 'Oh, no, is this going to be disgusting? Do I really want to hear this'?

"He goes on, 'They wash out their lingerie and hang it up to dry in the shower!' I couldn't control myself! 'America is full of men who would pay you to have a chance to look at those bras and panties worn by the Bunnies, and you're complaining?!'"

Arnold wanted to share one more Mansion story before moving on. "It was really early one morning and we'd been up all night working. We wanted to have some breakfast before going to work again, and down the staircase came one of the most beautiful girls I'd ever seen, just lovely in every way. We all sat straighter and said, 'Good Morning! Good Morning!'

"'Where you all from?' she asked in this heavy Southern accent.

"We said, 'New York, where are *you* from?'

"She said, 'Mississippi.' I'm telling you, this girl was perfect.

"'Wow,' one of us said, 'you're up early.'

"'Well, I'm just getting in. I've been out all night. I just got in a few days ago and they were showing me all the Chicago clubs.'

"'How'd you like them?'

"'Oh, they were great. But there's a funny thing. Everyone I've met is a Jew.' Hmm. So one of the guys said, 'a *Jew*?'

"'Yeah, everyone I met! They were all Jewish! They were nice but...all Jewish!'

"I said, 'I know how you feel. You know, my whole life, everyday, like you, I'd come to breakfast, and all I would meet were Jews. My mother, my sister, my father, my brothers...'

"And she said, 'Yes, that's exactly what I mean...' And all four of us cracked up!

"'She's mine.'

"'No, she's mine!'..."

In case you were wondering, they did finish the strip—pretty much on deadline, though considerably over budget.

So there would be no misunderstanding, Arnold had made it clear to Hef from the start what he considered to be "acceptable editing." As he told us earlier, he didn't do sketches but would redo a drawing if requested.

"I wanted to enjoy life, so that's the way I worked," he explained. "Although, we did have some interesting discussions. I produced '*History of Sex*,' a cartoon series for *Playboy* in the seventies. It was a comic history of famous ancient Greeks, Romans, and whoever else popped into my mind, on collectible postcards that you could cut out and save if you wanted. Well, one month featured King Midas sitting on a chair with a huge penis that he has obviously just touched—because it's about three feet long, at attention, and *gold*—and he's thrilled. So I got this long letter from Hefner in Chicago, saying, 'I know you don't like to do things over....We love the drawing, we love the page, the only problem is that you didn't draw the penis right!' This was delivered via a six-page, single-spaced letter. 'I know you don't like to change things, but can you just change the penis—see sketch.' He had attached a page where he drew what he wanted: It showed two parallel lines going up—bottom to top—with an inverted V on the end, and he wrote, 'That's the way to draw a penis. So please make it look like my sketch.'

"I was working on a deadline for either a *Sports Illustrated* spread or a *Times* cover when that letter arrived, and my wife read it to me so I could keep working, and she went into hysterics! I wrote back and said, 'You're right. Your drawing is probably the best way to draw a penis, but that's the way I draw noses, so, for clarity's sake, I drew the penis the way I did.' And that was the end of it.

"The *History of Sex* feature was very popular, but one day, Michelle Urry called me up and asked how long this history was going to go on. I think I was on *History of Sex and the Future* by that time, and I said, 'As long as I'm paying double tuition."

Arnold and Caroline ultimately moved from Philly to Princeton, a lovely town known for its very well-heeled, often snobby businessmen, many of whom owned nearby factories or held prestigious positions at the college. It was at one of the first parties the Roths attended there that Arnold was approached by a gentleman who ventured, "Someone told me you draw cartoons for *Playboy*."

"He said this in an artificially shocked manner," said Arnold. "I could tell he was very wealthy and used to telling people what to do.

"'Yes, I have for years,' I told him.

"'Aren't you ashamed,' he shot back, and all I could say was,

"'What?'

"Well, he went on and on about the vices of the magazine, making it pretty clear that he was well acquainted with it. So finally, he gets done pontificating and says, '...and people say they buy it for the articles.'

"I shouldn't have encouraged him but I couldn't help it. 'Well, you oughta read the articles,' I told him. 'They're very good and have a social conscience.' He just kept blubbering, 'Oh, yeah, give me an example.'

"I said, 'They were the first magazine to come out against nuclear testing.'

"He thought a minute and finally blurted, 'Sure. They would! If anybody wants to live it would be *those* guys.' And I thought, 'Why am I talking to this man?'

"There were plenty of sneaks and psychos in publishing, but Hefner's a real *mensch*, as we say in the trade. He always keeps his word, is reliable, truthful, and always fair. Harvey, Hefner, and I had lunch one time when he was in New York, and Harvey had to leave for an appointment. I was doing a lot of work for *Esquire* at the time and Hefner didn't have to do anything for awhile, so I suggested, 'We're right near *Esquire*.' Now, they were bitter rivals. 'Would you like to come up and meet the art director?' I asked.

"So Hefner said, 'Sure.'

"It was the strangest thing because we went to the office, which is right by St. Patrick's, and I said, 'I always go in the back door.' So we did, but there was nobody there—no receptionist, no one. So we just wandered over to Robert Benton's office, whom I thought he'd enjoy meeting. He was a very nice guy but this was really an outrageous thing to do, to just walk into his office unannounced. Well, he wasn't there and the forthcoming issue layout was pinned up on the walls. This was not something he was anxious to have his competition see, I'm sure! We waited a few minutes to see if he'd come back. Hefner was smoking his pipe when this other guy came in with three or four other people, obviously giving a tour of the building: '...and this is our art director's office' etc. And he kept staring at Hefner, like, trying to place this familiar face and pipe.

"After the group moved on, I asked Hef if he knew who that was, and he said, 'Oh, of course I do. That was Arnold Gingrich!' Arnold had given Hef a job and had run *Esquire* forever.

"'Do you think he recognized you?' I asked him.

"And Hefner said, 'Well, I don't know, but I do know that if the situation was reversed, and I came to Art Paul's office at *Playboy* and saw someone who looked exactly like Arnold Gingrich, I wouldn't have moved on and left him alone so quickly.'"

Among his many other projects, Arnold drew the comic strip

Poor Arnold's Almanac—and the proceeds helped him pack up his wife and two small children and move to England. "The dollar was so strong and we wanted to travel before the boys had to attend school. We only spoke English, so London was our obvious choice."

During the year that they were there, Arnie was a frequent contributor to *Punch*, and naturally fell in with the cartoonists there. He ended up sending a lot of them to *Playboy*. "The Brits all said, 'Oh, *Playboy*? You mean the one with the naked girls?'

"So I would say, 'Well, are you against naked girls?'

"Of course the right answer would have been, 'Not frequently enough'—but they all said, 'Well, of course not.'

"'So, what's your objection?' I'd ask, and they really didn't have one, once they got used to the idea. The clincher was when they asked, 'What do they pay?' Of course, they paid very well."

* * *

"I've been privileged to know many brilliant cartoonists, but the incredibly creative, supremely talented Al Jaffee is right up there at the top of the list"—Stan Lee

When sitting down with Al Jaffee, it's hard to know where to start. With his creation of the iconic "Fold-In" that's still a favorite feature of *Mad* magazine? "Snappy Answers to Stupid Questions?" The trials of starting *Trump* magazine? Humbug? His memories of working for Stan Lee? Drawing for Timely Comics? Or maybe—since he's ninety-five and going strong—we'll just ask about his secret to longevity.

"Wake up every morning."

Next topic.

"My childhood was somewhat peculiar," Al admits. He was born in Savannah, Georgia to immigrant parents from Zarasai, Lithuania. When he was six, his perennially homesick mother moved her four sons to her rural hometown village in the old country. A year later, Al's father took time off from work to travel over and bring the entire family back to the States. Another year passed and Mildred once again moved the troop to her Lithuanian shtetl in Eastern Europe, but this time, it was four years before Morris could save enough money to retrieve his kids. He came back with the three oldest ones, and it took another few years before Al's youngest brother would join them. Al never saw his mother again, and believes she was a victim of the Nazi invasion.

"So that was an unusual start," he comments. "I didn't understand the local language [in Lithuania] and no one there spoke English. My cousin Daniel spoke reasonably good English and was my unofficial interpreter. My experience was that of any kid moving into a new community. You're tested. So I used cartooning to ingratiate myself with the local kids. You'd always get a big laugh if you could caricature somebody. What I did was pick out one outstanding feature, like curly hair or pants that were too long, and made a drawing of it. The kids loved it. They had never seen anything like it before."

Al reports that his childhood was happy in many ways, but some things were hard to grasp. "If someone gave you a coin in the United States, you could go to any number of local stores and buy things. You couldn't do that over there. They didn't have toy stores and the kinds of products that children like—like ice-cream cones. The winters were brutal, and we didn't have electricity or indoor plumbing. There were more than a few times we went hungry and had to steal fruit or bread. It was strictly business there, very primitive, and everyone was scratching for a living."

As an attempt to bridge his kids' two worlds, Al's father would send a huge roll of American cartoons every month. "My brothers and I just loved those things, and we managed to keep up with what was going on in the States through the Sunday funnies," he told us. "It also helped us retain and improve our English. We were constantly asking our mother 'What does this word mean?... What does that word mean?' And the words would become part of our vocabulary. The comics and Sunday funnies were a good connection to the America we loved and left."

Al came back to the States for good in 1933. "I was in the first class of the High School of Music and Art in New York City, which was created by then-mayor Fiorello La Guardia. He loved the arts and realized that all kinds of trade schools had been created during the Depression to give a head-start to kids who would be graduating and looking for work—things like Needle Arts, Printing and Engraving, Tanning—but nothing existed to teach the arts. So he created the High School of Music and Art. I was fortunate to win one of the coveted spots in the very first class, along with Will Elder and, later, Harvey Kurtzman, Al Feldstein, and many, many talented guys. For a variety of reasons, we respected and admired one another—each one of us could do things that were amazing to the others. At that time, I think I impressed some of them with my woodcarvings, which were very elaborate and also humorous. Harvey had a unique style and sense of humor. Willie was *wild*, and very, very funny—and he put that into his drawings. So we had a sort of friendly competition over who could impress the others more.

"Many of the students were training to become fine artists or, at the least, fine illustrators working for the *Saturday Evening Post*, *Collier's*, or *Liberty*. But Will, Harvey, and I, and several others—we fell in love with satire and the comic business.

"Music and Art was a serious school for serious students and cartoons were not serious! Willie Elder was so captivated by *Snow White and the Seven Dwarfs* that he drew a wonderful series, in full color, and proudly brought it to school—but when the art teacher laid eyes on it, he said, 'Don't bring that kind of garbage in here. This is a school of fine art.' Painting, etching, pastels, sculpting, all this was acceptable. It was a wonderful school, and I did all those things, and I think I would have been happy as an illustrator or even a fine artist, but I had to make a living. So I got into the cartoon business.

"The Great Depression was on, and jobs of any kind were extremely challenging to find. I had no idea what I would do for a living, but no one was picky. If you heard a rumor that you could make some money pushing a cart in the garment district, you thought that had possibilities as a career choice."

As luck would have it, Al graduated at a particularly opportune time to work in cartooning; innovative comic books were proliferating. "At the start, many comic books were just reprints of the Sunday Funnies. But then entrepreneurs like Max Gaines and Vin Sullivan decided, 'Why wait just to reprint old comic-strip stuff? Why not write and illustrate *new* comics?' That's how Will Eisner's *Spirit* was born, and *Superman* and *Batman*. The burgeoning comic-book business opened up huge opportunities for any of us who could lift a pencil and scratch paper.

"I created *Inferior Man*, an innocent bit of satire of *Superman*. This was in the 1940s and very early in the business. Satire hadn't caught on to the extent that it would. This little nobody fancied himself a superhero but of course he was totally inept. I was having fun doing it just for my own amusement, when someone said to me, 'Will Eisner is hiring. Why don't you take your portfolio down there?' So I went to see Will and he bought *Inferior Man*, and had me sitting in his big studio filled with lots of other cartoonists."

Eventually, *Inferior Man*'s story line ebbed and Al was at a loss. Mr. Eisner terminated Al, but was kind enough to try and help him find some work with colleagues at other studios. Al got a tip from fellow cartoonist Alex Kotsky that Chad Grothkopf needed pencilers and he went right over.

Chad was an excellent artist and illustrator, and had created a craze in the industry for his mastery of the thick-and-thin brush stroke. He could brush stroke from a hairline to one-eighth of an inch in one fluid motion, a style that everyone was attempting to copy. But penciling wasn't his thing, so Al was hired on the spot to pencil a feature written by a kid named Stan Lee.

"I'd work on it and then Chad would put his master strokes on to finish it," Al told us. "I was doing a lot of work for little money and soon decided to strike out on my own. I made a portfolio and included some of Alex's work also—he needed the money and had helped me get the job working with Stan Lee. The first place I decided to go was to Will Eisner.

"He took one look at Alex's work and said, 'I want to hire *that* guy.' Well, I decided my only resort was to see this fellow Stan Lee. So I went to see him at Timely Comics, where he'd become editor, and he showed me some of his work.

"And I said, 'Yep, that's my penciling.'" Stan was dubious, so he reached over and picked up a script from a pile of submissions, handed it to me, and said,

"'If you can do this properly, you'll have a job.' The script was *Squat Car Squad,* about the antics of two bumbling policemen, and I proved I really had worked on his ideas before. We clicked and he gave me other things to create on my own, such as, *Silly Seal* and *Ziggy Piggy*, both of which made big money for Timely Comics. Animal features were very popular because of all those Disney cartoons that featured rabbits and birds and who-knows-what-all-else."

We were eager to fast-forward to *Mad* magazine, and Al was ready to talk about it. "Harvey Kurtzman talked me into writing a script for *Mad* when he was editor, and I wrote a story about boxing, which was given to Jack Davis to draw. After that, Harvey kept pressuring me for more, and at the time there was a big, big story in the sports pages about the superb golfer Ben Hogan and his magic touch. So Harvey suggested I do something on Ben and I did, and he said,

"'OK, this one you can illustrate.' After having created so many comic strips and books, something new—like the early *Mad* magazine— was enticing to me. This was my first job for *Mad* as a writer and artist."

We've already talked about how Harvey was seduced away from *Mad* to work for Hefner on *Trump*—and that he took the "usual gang of idiots" with him. Al and the rest were enticed by not only the chance to try something brand new, but also to work for the boy publisher of *Playboy*. In those early days, *Mad* was printed in black-and-white on newsprint, almost like a daily newspaper, which limited what the artists could do. *Trump*, on the other hand, was endowed with an "unlimited budget" from Hugh Hefner as well as a staff of the foremost talent in cartooning. The magazine would also be printed in full color on heavy, glossy paper. The possibilities seemed endless.

"Harvey had asked Hef for money to hire the absolute best talent available. It was just terrific. We all jumped at it," Al said. Sadly, as we noted, the dream was short-lived. People were accustomed to buying comic books for a few cents and really didn't care about the paper quality as much as the cover price. In fact, the high gloss might have worked against *Trump*. Apparently, comic books just weren't supposed to look elegant.

"When *Trump* quickly went out of business and a year later *Humbug* folded, I needed work and went back to *Mad*, not knowing if they'd shoot me on sight or what. But I took a chance because *Mad*, like all magazines, was yearning for writers more than artists. The attitude in the editorial offices was that there were many cartoonists floating around—they were in the waiting room with their portfolios by the dozens—but that what they desperately needed was content.

"I knew Bill Gaines and Al Feldstein were *very* angry at Harvey for taking away Wally Wood, Jack Davis, Will Elder, John Saverio, and myself—so I approached Al very cautiously and said, 'Al, I know I was with the enemy, maybe I'm a *persona non grata,* but I have six scripts that we didn't use when *Humbug* folded. . . .'

"He didn't even let me finish before he said, 'C'mon down.' So I went down and handed him the six scripts, and all were immediately handed out to various artists. They were all used and I had a steady job as a writer."

Al was still working as a regular at the magazine on the day we sat down to talk—nearly sixty years later. In fact, we found him puzzling over his latest Fold-In—but that's getting a little ahead of the story. *Mad* was blazing a new trail in satire, and good satire is a lot more complicated and difficult to render properly than, say, cavorting seals and pigs.

Al made many submissions and contributions to *Playboy* throughout the *Mad* years—and Hef eagerly published them. Many have told us they can pick out an Al Jaffee cartoon without a glance at the signature.

"I'm sure Arnold Roth did a wonderful job of explaining the whole *Little Annie Fanny* adventure to you, and I don't want to bore you by repeating any of it, other than to say, that it was a strange way of working. Really? All these talented artists working on an assembly line to get this one story out? Can you picture fourteen painters working on the Sistine Chapel? Hefner wanted that cartoon in every issue and Harvey and Willie were incapable of that kind of heavy production, so they needed help. In theory, it might have worked; Willie would do all the Annies and we'd work on the other figures and background. But with all the back-and-forth and redo's, it became very awkward and complicated. Arnie and I used to laugh hysterically, because Arnie would do his bit, someone else would do his, I would do mine, and then it would get to Willie and he would change it all back to what he had done originally! It was crazy. It was piecework—just to make a buck and help friends. Harvey and Willie were all good personal friends. I also submitted, on my own, many cartoons to *Playboy* that weren't as intricate as *Annie Fanny* and didn't require as much attention.

"I liked Hef's attitude. The bunch of us would relax and talk with him casually about all kinds of topics. He was a self-made man. He knew what he wanted and pretty much how to get it, and he was very nice to us. He didn't impose his will. He was always very nice and polite and made suggestions rather than demands. I found him very pleasant to work with."

Playboy was influential in another monumental development in Al's legacy. The *Mad* Fold-In for which he is best known was inspired by *Playboy*'s most famous feature. "I was always looking for something new to create and sell. I remember clearly that one Monday morning—after a weekend of partying—I sat down and threw as many magazines as I could gather on the floor, and said, 'I have to come up with an idea that is different.' I opened all the magazines and—of course—*Playboy* had the centerfold. Next came an issue of *National Geographic* with a big fold-out in full color. Even *Sports Illustrated* had a fold-out of a new stadium idea. I thought, 'Gee, they're all doing these fancy, full-color fold-outs. Why doesn't *Mad* do a cheap, black-and-white fold-*in*?'

"I though of it as a one-shot gag. I came up with a very simple idea, where a drawing is folded vertically and surreptitiously inward to reveal a new secret picture. I brought it to Feldstein, and said, 'You're not going to buy this idea, because it will mutilate the magazine.'

"He loved it! He ran to Bill Gaines's office and came right out saying, 'Bill loves it also, and if it mutilates the magazine, they'll buy another.'

"The first one was Elizabeth Taylor—who was in the news for her husband- switching—on the left side, and over toward the right side was Richard Burton and Eddie Fisher. And the question was, 'Who's going to be Elizabeth Taylor's *next* big passion?' You thought it was going to be Richard Burton but when you folded it over, it turned out to be a kid standing in the right-hand crowd. Burton disappeared and this kid wound up in an embrace with Elizabeth Taylor. And the answer to the question was, 'Someone in the Crowd'—to infer that she'd take anybody.

"A month or so later, Feldstein came to me and said, 'Where's the next Fold-In?'

"I said, 'That was a one-shot gag.'

"He said, jokingly—I think—'You'll do another Fold-In or you can't work for me.'" Since then, there have been 600 Fold-Ins, give or take a dozen. Guess who still has a job?"

Current generations of artists and writers are awestruck when it comes to Al and what he's accomplished. A few years ago, he did a bit of work for the whippersnappers at *The Daily Show*. They'd requested a Fold-In to accompany their book, *America*.

"I finished the Fold-In and called the station, asking how to deliver it to them.

"'Do you want me to send it by messenger?' I asked.

"'Oh no, Mr. Jaffe, would you mind delivering it personally?'

"This meant I had to go all the way across town, but okay. When I got there, I tried to leave it with the receptionist but once she'd called upstairs, she said, 'They're all coming down to get it.' The whole crew came down: Jon Stewart, Stephen Colbert, and all the others. They had been fans since they were kids. Naturally, getting into their kind of business, they'd have been fans of magazines like *Mad*!"

In 2006, the show celebrated Al's eighty-fifth birthday on the air, with a Fold-In cake. As he described it, "There was this big rectangular cake that said something on top, and Colbert pulled out the middle of the cake and pushed the two sides together, and where it had said something nice about me, it now said, 'Al, you're old!' It was a total surprise to me and the folks at *Mad*. I wonder what they would say about me now, ten years later!"

Sixty-one years later, Al continues to create the Fold-Ins by hand. On March 2016, Guinness World Records recognized him as having the longest career of a comic artist—seventy-three years and three months. And counting.

12

THE VARGAS PLAYGIRLS

"Show me something more beautiful than a beautiful girl, and I'll go paint it."–ALBERTO VARGAS

While Alberto Vargas (1894-1978) was more of an illustrator than a cartoonist—and his work was not terribly comical—I would be remiss to omit this seminal artist from our story.

If Alberto is to be remembered for one thing, it should be that he elevated the pin-up painting from the low end of popular culture to a high art form. In that respect, his career resembles that of another American icon, his almost-exact contemporary Norman Rockwell (1894-1978). What Rockwell did for perky school boys and other archetypes of Americana, Alberto did for well-scrubbed, fresh-faced—and nearly naked—women. In fact, "Vargas Girls," as they came to be known, seemed every bit as wholesome as Rockwell's soda jerks and gossipy spinsters. They may have been posing in the altogether, but they radiated a sense of delight about it—as if they wanted nothing more than to show off their abundant assets for a legion of appreciative viewers.

Alberto Vargas with wife and lifelong muse Anna Mae:

Alberto's work has set the standard for the glamorous pin-up for decades, inspiring and influencing illustrators worldwide. Yet, his start was a typical one. The son of a well regarded Peruvian photographer, Max Vargas I, Alberto gravitated toward art at an early age. At thirteen, his father recognized his emerging talent and taught him the relatively new and infrequently used technique of airbrushing.

Sam Shapiro, who today represents the Vargas family, explained further. "Alberto worked in watercolor and eventually, he incorporated airbrushing. His father would shoot portraits and Alberto would touch up the negatives with this airbrush technique that he was becoming extremely proficient at."

In 1911, Alberto and his brother Max traveled to Europe, where a Continental education and apprenticeships as a photographer with the Julien Studios in Switzerland and Sarony Court Photographers in London had been arranged for him. On a visit to Paris, Alberto became enamored of the erotic work of the Viennese artist Raphael Kirchner, especially his watercolor illustrations of women. These would exert a demonstrable influence on his later work.

A young and dashing Alberto Vargas:

The international unrest and imminent approach of the Great War compelled Alberto to leave Europe after only a year. His plan was to sail to Peru, after a quick stop to explore New York. But (as often happens with artists and aesthetes), he found himself immediately captivated by New York's vibrancy and sophistication—and particularly by the beautiful and self-confident American women he encountered. His previous exposure to the fair sex had primarily been confined to the more conservative Victorian ideal; Charles Gibson's iconic illustrations of vivacious, upper-class "Gibson Girls" were a revelation. Although fully clothed—overclothed by later standards—Gibson's ladies hinted at a sexual awareness that bewitched young Alberto. Much to his father's disappointment, he resolved to stay in New York and make his way as a freelance artist.

Alberto's first significant position was illustrating fashions for the Adelson Hat Company. It was while executing a piece for a store window that he was spotted and asked to present his portfolio to Florenz Ziegfeld. In less than a day, he was commissioned to paint twelve watercolor portraits of the Ziegfeld Follies' leading ladies. His friendship with "Ziggy"—a nickname Ziegfeld tolerated from only his closest friends—lasted until Ziegfeld's death in 1932. Vargas credits Ziegfeld with teaching him the difference between "nudes and lewds." Alberto worked for Ziegfeld for twelve years, until the Great Depression took its toll on the Follies.

In 1934, Alberto and his bride, Anna Mae Clift, a redheaded showgirl who had been one of his initial models and became his lifelong muse, decided to follow some other Follies alumni—including W.C. Fields, Eddie Cantor, Barbara Stanwyck, and Will Rogers—to Hollywood, where he was hired to paint pastel portraits for Twentieth-Century Fox. Work for the other major studios followed. Among the Hollywood beauties he painted were Ava Gardner, Anne Sheridan, Marlene Dietrich, Hedy Lamarr, and Jane Russell.

In 1939, Alberto joined in a studio union walkout in support of higher wages. This honorable act spelled the end of his Hollywood career—Alberto found himself blackballed and unable to support himself on the West Coast. He and Anna Mae traveled back to New York, hoping to reconnect with some of his previous employers. As luck would have it, *Esquire* was looking for a replacement for the ever-popular George Petty, and Alberto assumed the position. In 1940, the first of the notorious Vargas Girl calendars was introduced.

Thanks to the international exposure he received in *Esquire*, Alberto's distinctive work rapidly became known worldwide. However, bitter business disagreements caused a permanent rift with *Esquire* in 1946. The following decade, leading up to Alberto's partnership with *Playboy*, was financially challenging; he'd take just about any assignment he could get in order to survive and pay the legal bills his falling-out with the national magazine had necessitated.

Reid Austin, *Playboy*'s art director, had been drawn to the seductive innocence of the Vargas Girl when he was thirteen, and his esteem had only grown by the time he became an assistant art director in 1956. As Sam explained it, "Reid revered Alberto's work to the point where he photocopied one of his most stunning images and taped it to the outside of his cubical, and every time Hef walked by, he'd take notice and make some kind of approving comment."

We don't know for sure what influence that had on Hef, but it must have sunk in on some level. At the time, *Playboy* was still relatively new on the scene, expanding rapidly but on a marginal budget. Hef set up a meeting with Alberto and Anna Mae—offering no guarantee that he'd hire the artist. The couple traveled to Chicago and showed him a collection of Alberto's previously unpublished nudes, drawn over the previous decade. Despite his financial strictures, Hef quickly purchased six paintings for the magazine. A few months later, *Playboy* ran a five-page feature on the evolution of the Vargas nude.

"It was only a few years later, that Austin was promoted to art director," Sam recalled. "It was then that *Playboy* actually engaged Alberto to paint something specifically for the magazine." It's interesting to note, that in an era of contracts running to hundreds of pages, the relationship between Alberto and *Playboy* was a gentlemen's agreement, completed on a handshake between Alberto and Hef—or "El Jefe," as Alberto referred to him.

The first *Playboy* Vargas Girl appeared in the September 1960 issue. Over the next few decades, Alberto would contribute 152 paintings, including two front covers.

"Alberto's use of watercolor and airbrush produced his signature, exceedingly delicate look," Sam noted, "and he was *extremely* secretive about both the process and his materials. He only ever let a handful of people watch him paint and he never shared his technique with anyone. When he'd finish a painting, Anna Mae would pack up all the paints, sketches, and finishes and throw them out. Not only that, to protect his secrets further, she'd go to many separate trash cans, in obscure locations away from the house, to dispose of them. Alberto painted with a very specific red-hued paint combination that he felt was his, and he didn't want competitors to even know what brands he mixed. "

The public rivalry between *Playboy* and *Penthouse* in the late 1960s pushed the bounds of acceptability, and also tested Alberto's Spanish sensibilities. His mantra, after all, was "erotic but never vulgar."

"Alberto was thrilled to be making reliable money after such a long financially unpredictable stretch following the debacle with *Esquire*," Sam said. "At the start, Playboy paid him $500 per page and it soon rose to $1,000, with double that for a gatefold. But Hef's continuing demand that he be more sexually explicit and add anatomical details to his pictorials was a very hard and controversial issue for him to wrestle with. He'd always used a hint of suggestion with the girls he painted, but Hef wanted more."

The Vargas family lived in a suburban house in Westwood California that they had purchased in 1936, and Alberto would remain there until his death in 1982. It had a separate bungalow in the rear that Alberto used as his studio.

"Every morning Anna Mae would make him a giant cup of coffee," recalled Sam, "and he'd take that plus his cigarettes—which he claimed he never inhaled— and head to his studio. On some of the preserved sketches that we have, you can see big, brown rings from where he put this gigantic cup of coffee down. He had a rigid schedule that always began at eight sharp and ended at four. Anna—who was his guard dog— was always so loving and caring of him, and didn't allow anyone to disturb him during work hours. They had an intercom and he would often check in with her and talk about whatever was going on."

Sadly, Anna Mae took a fall from which she never fully recovered, and passed away in 1974. This was an immeasurable loss to Alberto, who had never considered the possibility that she might pre-decease him. Through the years, Alberto had painted portraits and tucked them away, unpublished and rarely viewed, as an insurance policy so that Anna Mae could live comfortably upon *his* death. He continued to work after this heartbreak, but his soul was never again fully in his efforts.

"Reid Austin was the *Playboy* middleman with Alberto," said Sam. "He'd come West at least once a year and the Vargases would always insist he stay with them. They'd discuss the following year's art direction. Most times, Alberto would have sketches that Reid would take back for Hef's approval, and they'd go back and forth that way.

"Alberto was world-renowned by then and people who visited would be ecstatic at the opportunity to see unpublished Vargas work on the walls of their house. Alberto *loved* being an American. That was a big deal for him, and when he received his citizenship he did a lot of free work for the military, via *Esquire*. He never expected payment; he just wanted to support the American war effort. He watched football and followed politics better than anyone.

"Toward the end of his career, his eyes were faltering but he never admitted to anyone that anything was wrong. He discontinued applying the airbrush, a technique he had employed for almost sixty years, and his use of color became deficient. The *Playboy* art department was sensitive to this and managed his decline by having Dennis Magdich retouch his images. They knew about his eyes but respected him so much they didn't want to say anything to offend him. They just let him keep working. 'Just keep doing what you're doing,' they told him."

Alberto's personal journals don't provide an answer as to why he kept working as his sight failed him, but we wonder if it was because he didn't want to let down his fans and friends at *Playboy*. For his part, Hef didn't want to take away Alberto's purpose. That's how genuine friendship works.

Like Rockwell, Vargas enjoyed a long career, painting consistently from the 1920 through the '70s. While he's best known for his pin-ups girls, his work as a whole can be seen as a history of our standards of beauty—from the Clara Bow types of the 1920s, with their bee-stung lips and rolled down stockings; through the more erotic "island" girls of the 1930s (think Dorothy Lamour in a sarong); to the more liberated types of the 1960s, in go-go boots but little else. His final great and truly iconic image was of an amazing redhead (model Candy Moore) lying prostrate in a body stocking atop a Ferrari. It graces the cover of Candy-O, a 1979 album by the rock band The Cars, and projects that classic feeling of sheer pleasure that was the hallmark of every Vargas girl.

13

QUEEN OF THE PIN-UP ARTISTS

"I don't believe that talent is defined by gender." - HUGH HEFNER

There's a lot to see in the art of Olivia De Berardinis. There are beautiful women of every shape and size, playing every possible role: sexy female sailors, football players, witches, cops, and cowgirls; voluptuous nurses, mermaids, and teachers; enticing aliens, angels, devils, and sea creatures. But what you don't see is every bit as important as what you do: In all of the thousands of lush pin-ups painted by Olivia—known to generations of fans simply by her first name—you will not a see a woman experiencing pain, being dominated, or being coerced into doing anything she doesn't want to.

The term *empowered* may be a tad overused today, but in the early seventies, when Olivia began creating her work, it wasn't in the air at all—at least not in reference to women. Yet, it's the first word that comes to mind when you look at her bevy of beauties. They are always in control and doing their thing (to use a phrase that *was* in the air back then). They follow no one's orders and adhere to no moral compass but their own.

It's no surprise that when Olivia makes a public appearance—which she still does, frequently, at gallery shows, book signings, and comic "cons"—more than half of her eager audience is women. There's a reason for this beyond the obvious one. Unlike her male role models, Alberto Vargas and George Petty, Olivia cares as much about women's fashion as she does about the female forms filling it out. Her images are filled with detail that even a non-fashionista can appreciate. Silk or cotton, leather or vinyl—you can always tell exactly what these ladies are feeling against their skin as they move through their world. You can sense the pinch of a stiletto, the grip of a garter, and the tug of a corset. Each garment seems carefully chosen and lovingly rendered, in a very special fashion twist on what comic art devotees used to call "good-girl art": Olivia's "good girls" are endowed with an in-your-face sexuality.

Pin-up art, or "cheesecake," to use the term Olivia herself prefers, is supposedly about the female body, but in her hands, it is also about the face. The key to what her women are thinking is in their eyes, which gaze back at us even as we gaze longingly at them. Olivia's women are more than bodies with faces attached; the faces are the center of everything and the bodies are there to deliver what those faces promise.

That's Olivia's view of it, at least. She shared it with us—and much more—when we visited her and her dishy husband and partner Joel at their home and studio in the Zuma Beach area of Malibu.

"I don't want to paint the girl next door who just happens to be over there, which is Hef's idea of a pin-up," she explained. "I want to create a woman who *knows* what she is doing. Her come-hither look, her intentional gaze, is an invitation. She wants to be a part of whatever sexual activity is going on. She is taking part in the sexual attraction, the *game*. The game is, 'I'm dressed up like this. Let's play.'"

The fact that Olivia is a woman is not the only thing that sets her apart from most of the artists we talked to. She's perhaps better described as a "serious" illustrator, rather than a gag cartoonist, but that doesn't mean her artwork is devoid of humor and playfulness—not at all. In fact, humor is essential to it. There's inherent jokiness in the image of a pin-up girl sliding down a fire pole wearing nothing but a helmet, or a scantily clad angel with her halo in her hand. But the girls are clearly in on the jokes, not the object of them. Olivia's paintings draw on both uses of the word *burlesque*: art as satire and a showcase of the female form. These ladies don't exist because of the male gaze; they invite it and gaze right back.

Olivia De Berardinis was born in Long Beach, California, in November 1948, and her mother was clearly the first "empowered" woman she knew. The Second World War was over, but Olivia grew up knowing that her mother had played her part in it. A photo of Connie De Berardinis reproduced in one of Olivia's books shows her in uniform as a WAC. Her husband Sante was also in the service.

"My mother was a big influence on me," confirms Olivia, "because she was a really *sexy*-looking lady with an incredible figure."

The artist recalls that she drew her mother looking "sort of like a Barbie doll" even before Mattel introduced Barbie in 1959. And when Barbie did come along, around Olivia's tenth birthday, the doll certainly exerted an influence on her and her whole generation. Remember, Barbie was not only was the first "adult doll" for young girls, but the first to pursue a variety of careers, from secretary to stewardess. (Doctors and businesswomen would come a little later, but still—Barbie was never just a mom or a homemaker.) She easily qualified as "empowered."

Olivia was already drawing beautiful women when, as a young child, the family moved to New York, thus providing her with the double advantage of being a California girl with a New York upbringing. She attended the School of Visual Art, where she studied with the celebrated photorealist painter Chuck Close, but doesn't hesitate to tell us that she never graduated.

"I just f**ked off a lot during school, really. I was lost until the age of about twenty-five. I did what that generation did, these were the hippie days. During that time, I was living in Soho, painting minimalist paintings. I wound up waitressing for a while." Before Joel, there were a lot of abusive boyfriends and, Olivia says, "a lot of opportunities to make poor decisions. Around twenty-five, I got into a panic about where my life was going, and the men I was hanging around with. I was going down a real loser path, and then a lightning bolt hit me. I got serious and trained myself to become this outrageous workaholic."

Playboy and its culture had always been a part of her life. Her parents had read the magazine from the beginning, and when the New York club opened in 1962, when Olivia was thirteen, they became members. She told us that she still has a few of their old membership cards.

"Only when you've seen a show like *Mad Men* do you get an idea of what the climate was like back then. My father took me to the Playboy Club. I remember, as a young teenager, suffering through their drinking there. The lifestyle Hef was pushing appealed to my parents. It was young, bohemian, and dangerous. I'm watching the series *Masters of Sex*, right now and they mention Hef. When I asked him about it, he said it was accurate; he gave them funds to help with research. It's just so fascinating how much he had to do with the sexual revolution."

In many ways, Olivia's parents were the perfect Playboy couple. "At the Club, my mother would get defensive and my father would be winking and grabbing," she recalled. As Olivia describes her, Connie was a beautiful and uninhibited woman who had no qualms about posing nude for her daughter—and even walked around the house that way. The way Joel described it, Olivia's parents wanted to bring the Playboy Club home with them. "The first day I met them was at their house," he told us. "Olivia took me there. I'd heard about her parents' wet bar and I wanted to make sure I saw it. So I went downstairs in the basement and there it was.

When Olivia was twelve or thirteen, she'd painted Playboy Bunnies and Playmates on the side of that bar, and they were still visible."

As we mentioned, Olivia was profoundly influenced by the two major pin-up artists of the twentieth century, George Petty and Alberto Vargas—and especially the latter, because he drew extensively for *Playboy* and she got to know him personally. As she told it, "Reid Austin, the *Playboy* art director, set up a time for us to meet Alberto at his home, because he knew how much I admired him. This was in 1979, when Joel and I were just married and on our honeymoon. Alberto was more than I expected, starting with kissing my hand when I walked into his house. He was very gracious and generous with his time, truly an old world gentleman. We spent the entire day together and when he found out we were newlyweds he insisted on taking us to dinner at his favorite restaurant, Sizzlers Steakhouse! His wife had just passed, and there was a lingering sadness about him. She had been his whole life. He was just waiting to die and be with her again.

"Petty and Vargas came from generations where the women were more docile, they were baking cookies. My generation was into feminism, and the women who were the pin-ups of my time were like Ripley from *Aliens*—the girls that held guns. We went from girls with muffins to women with guns and scowls."

Olivia had already been drawing women for twenty years when she decided to tackle the men's magazines rather than continue suffering in a Soho garret for the pleasure of painting minimalist images that no one wanted. The idea seemed quite natural to her.

"I didn't have a portfolio. I had some drawings of women and I was thinking, 'Where am I going to go with these? Where am I going to get a job in illustration?' I looked in the sex magazines and men's magazines and I saw that the illustrations were *horrible* in most of them. I couldn't stand the way they drew the women—so crudely. It was just creepy and perverse; there was no elegance to sex there at all. There was no dignity."

Mind you, this was a world apart from Petty and Vargas; their pin-up girls may have been sex objects, but at least they were rendered with respect and dignity and were genuinely erotic. At that point, in the mid-to-late 1970s, *Playboy* was at the mountaintop of a huge industry of men's magazines, and set the standard to which others—such as *Penthouse* and *Club*—aspired. Others, such as *Hustler,* rebelled against the refinement of *Playboy*—but there's no doubt that every publication of its kind was profoundly influenced by it.

As a newcomer to the field, Olivia knew she couldn't go straight to the top, so she made the rounds of the other publications. "I'd go into the offices and—'Come on in!'—I was treated *very* well by most of them. Almost all of them invited me to illustrate for them, including *Club* and *Hustler*. At that time, I knew them all and they were all anxious to have me, because there was really so little talent in those places. Being insecure, I thought this was the place to learn my craft, and there was also something exciting about being a woman in a man's world. There was something about the feeling that I was not supposed to be there that excited me. I thought illustrating for sex magazines would be a fun but temporary job until I began my 'real' career, whatever that would be. I always thought I'd go back to fine art one day. I thought the pin-up work was just for fun—and money."

In 1977, Olivia and Joel launched a publishing company called O Card to distribute Olivia's images in the form of greeting cards.

"The cards were erotic," Joel told us, "but not filthy. Well...a couple of them were a little over the line." The two were married two years later. "We had a kosher wedding," he said. "My parents were very conservative Jews. They had no idea what Olivia did for a living. I didn't dare tell them. Just the fact that she wasn't Jewish was horrifying enough."

Olivia calls Joel "my partner in crime," but what she really means is that he's her collaborator in business, her photographer (since she prefers to paint from photos), and her all-around best friend. When we sat down together, he recounted the fact that when Olivia's magazine work and cards started attracting some attention, they were approached to do some gallery shows.

"These weren't A-list galleries at all," he explained. "They were hole-in-the-wall galleries that sold erotica and such. You had to get on a freight elevator and go to the fifth floor just to find these places. And we would always be shocked. *Huge* crowds would show up, and all of the art would sell."

Olivia worked for *Playboy*'s competitors for roughly ten years, and had stories about all of them. She fondly remembered the late Bob Guccione of *Penthouse*, not least because, like Hefner, he had been a cartoonist himself and had a special affection for artists.

Joel said, "Bob *loved* her work. He would sit on the floor with a Coke and flip through her sketchbooks." The two were less thrilled when *Penthouse* publicly announced that Olivia would be doing a regular feature every month—without having discussed it with them first. Or the time Guccione waved a finger and cautioned her, "not to work for the rabbit."

Larry Flynt of *Hustler* was an even more outsized character than any of them. Olivia recalled one of his infamous parties, at which he walked up to her and said, "Hmm. Nice piece of ass I haven't had yet."

"I thought, 'Am I imagining he said that?'" she told us, "but more recently, I found out that was something he said to everybody." She also discovered one memorable room in Flynt's mansion: "This party was downstairs in a room that was filled with hay and stuffed beavers—he called it, 'the beaver room.' Nothing but beavers! It was *memorable*—such an awesome visual. I couldn't have imagined that. Hay!" she repeats for emphasis. "The ceiling was hay!"

Olivia first began to work for *Playboy* around 1985, at the instigation of Marilyn Grabowski, who had been the magazine's West Coast photo editor for twenty years at that point. For five of *Playboy*'s six decades, it has been Grabowski who determines the basic look of all the pictorials and photo features. She has more to do with the way *Playboy* looks than anybody but Hefner himself. They had come up with the idea of taking some of Olivia's fantasy images—which were already well known—and recreating them with actual models and photographers.

"There were some really great paintings among them," Joel recalled, "and they said, 'We're going to recreate these.' A lot of them were really difficult, because Olivia can paint things that are fantasies—girls with wings flying in the air and floating...these are not easy to make in reality."

It was the model Lillian Müller who had come up with the idea and motivated Hef and Marilyn to go forward with it.

"Lillian told Marilyn about me and Marilyn found me," said Olivia. "Back then, *Playboy* really put so much money into everything. Insane amounts of money. So they sent her to come see me—she came from L.A. to New York, shipped Joel and me back, and put us up in the Sunset Marquis. This was our first introduction to L.A. and we were like, "Wow." Today, I would never have seen anybody. They would have just taken my stuff off the Internet!"

Olivia and Joel are both smart, urban, sophisticates, but their first visit to the Playboy Mansion was something they'll never forget. "We were just there for a impromptu visit with Carrie Leigh, (Hef's then-girlfriend and 1983 Playboy cover girl) no party or anything, just a casual get together. And, set up off the back patio was this amazing three-tiered ice table—about six feet high. On it was shrimp and caviar and lobster and just about every delectable you can name, and all of a sudden this ridiculous looking thing—an emu—saunters over like *la de da*, and starts pecking at it. Can you imagine? We were doing our best to act as if this was a normal, everyday occurrence—and we're New Yorkers, we're used to seeing a lot. I don't think I heard a word Carrie was saying, though, because I was so flipped out by this surreal setting."

That was over thirty years ago, and Olivia and Joel have been important members of the *Playboy* family ever since. In fact, to cement their relationship with the magazine and Hef, they moved to Malibu in 1987. The move also provided them the opportunity to show in larger, more prestigious galleries. Olivia noted that in the early days, "When I first came to Hef, you know, my women were a little too aggressive. So I had to make them smile and stuff like that. I wasn't doing that. They weren't soft enough. Vargas was the king of pinups for the entire planet, and Hef chose me to attempt to fill his slippers. There were people who told him they weren't sure I could do it, but Hef gave me the chance to prove myself. He allowed me to sit on that throne."

In Olivia's collection of her own work, *Malibu Cheesecake*, ,, Hef is quoted as saying, "Olivia is for me the next logical generation of the work that Petty and Vargas did—Vargas in particular... I just think she's the best." His decision to showcase her has been validated time and again, as she finds herself the leading legend of pin-up art alive today.

Olivia was pleased to report that one of the collateral benefits of her relationship with Hef was the opportunity to get to know one of her idols, perhaps the most legendary pin-up model of them all, the "notorious" Bettie Page. Hef counted Bettie as a friend, in addition to a fellow crusader in the sex wars. Well before the Bettie Page revival of the 1990s, Olivia discovered her astonishing images when collector–publisher Jeff Rund showed her some vintage 1950s girlie magazines.

In *Malibu Cheesecake*, she writes, "Bettie's photos formed a bridge from the 1950s image of pin-ups—smiling women holding muffins fresh from the oven. This passivity morphed into a dominating, whip-wielding icon." It wasn't until years later, after painting Bettie from iconic photos, that she met Bettie herself—newly emerged from seclusion—at the Playboy Mansion.

Olivia and Joel were regulars at the Mansion during its last golden era, in the 1980s, '90s, and 2000s. Just as Leroy Neiman,

Jack Cole, and Shel Silverstein set the visual style for *Playboy* in the age of Eisenhower and the beatniks, Olivia's paintings were its icons in the age of MTV: slick but soulful, passionate, and playful, they made sex into something fun and even frivolous without defusing its mysteries and magic.

For the last ten years or so, Olivia has created an original painting for every issue of *Playboy*. She was the "house artist" during the final flowering of Hef's celebrity, when the E Channel series *The Girls Next Door* made him a star of the new phenomenon known as "reality TV." The show, which ran from 2005-2010, introduced him to the grandchildren of the original *Playboy* readers of fifties. Much of Olivia's time during those years was spent painting the cast members, especially the power trio of Holly Madison, Bridget Marquardt, and Kendra Wilkinson. She also prepared special illustrations for Hef to use as invitations to his legendary parties and other gatherings at the Mansion.

The relationship between Olivia and Joel and Hef and *Playboy* remains solid, even as Hef slows down. In 2016, just as he turned ninety, the magazine was radically redesigned and Olivia was one of the few members of the "younger old guard" to survive the sea changes. It would take more than a switch from R to PG to keep her saucy vixens from the magazine's pages.

As Olivia and Joel approach their fortieth anniversary and Olivia's seventieth birthday, she is more popular than ever—having shown several generations of girls what it looks like to be a beautiful, sexy, smart, and—yes—empowered. To be honest, we did find one image in *Malibu Cheesecake* of a woman in a truly submissive pose, seemingly forced to consent to something against her will. Turn to page ninety and you'll find a rather amazing painting of Bettie Page in a cowboy outfit, holding onto a hobby horse, being forcibly held down and spanked by a voluptuous blonde in a Native American Indian outfit. Yes, we'll give Olivia a pass just this once. And yes, we memorized the page number.

THE GALLERY

WORKS BY:

Doug Sneyd
Don Orehek
Mort Gerberg
Dean Yeagle
Arnold Roth
Clive Collins
Al Jaffee
Vargas
Olivia

"Yeah, Mom, it's pretty hot here. But don't worry. I'm getting lots of water."

"Hank, as in hanky-panky."

"I've been here eight years, and I've never noticed any difference between Democrats and Republicans."

Doug Sneyd—Courtesy of Doug Sneyd. Archival material from Playboy magazine. Reprinted with permission.

"The good news is, you won't have to make the trip anymore. I'm setting up a website."

"My marriage counselor finally solved our problem. He ran off with my wife."

Don Orehek: Courtesy of Don Orehek. Archival material from Playboy magazine.

"I loved the little mutt, but he was wearing a wire!"

"Dammit, Leonardo! I hate when you bring work home with you!"

"Try thinking of me as part of your journey, Lisa, not as your final destination."

"I'VE HAD A REQUEST, BUT INSTEAD, I'M GOING TO SING ANOTHER SONG."

"I, on the other hand, am looking for a short-term relationship — like maybe forty-five minutes, an hour."

"Oh, it's stylish battle armor, certainly...but I wonder if it's really PRACTICAL battle armor..."

Dean Yeagle: Courtesy of Dean Yeagle. Archival material from Playboy magazine.

"Just a moment, while we decide who's going to conduct the exam..."

*"Giving your Champion your **glove** would have been sufficient."*

Clive Collins: Courtesy of Clive Collins.

"D'you suppose ***she's*** *the bundle he's making on Wall Street?"*

Clive Collins: Courtesy of Clive Collins.

"I hope you don't mind - I always enjoy a cigarette and a tweet afterwards."

Clive Collins: Courtesy of Clive Collins.

"Oh, you poor dear! Has that husband of hers come home early? Why don't you pop up here out of the cold?"

Clive Collins: Courtesy of Clive Collins.

Courtesy of Arnold Roth

Courtesy of Arnold Roth

Courtesy of Arnold Roth

how would america be different without hugh hefner
and his dream? our resident sage examines an empty and desolate
world in which pajamas are worn only for sleeping
Arnold Roth

Vargas
PLAYBOY

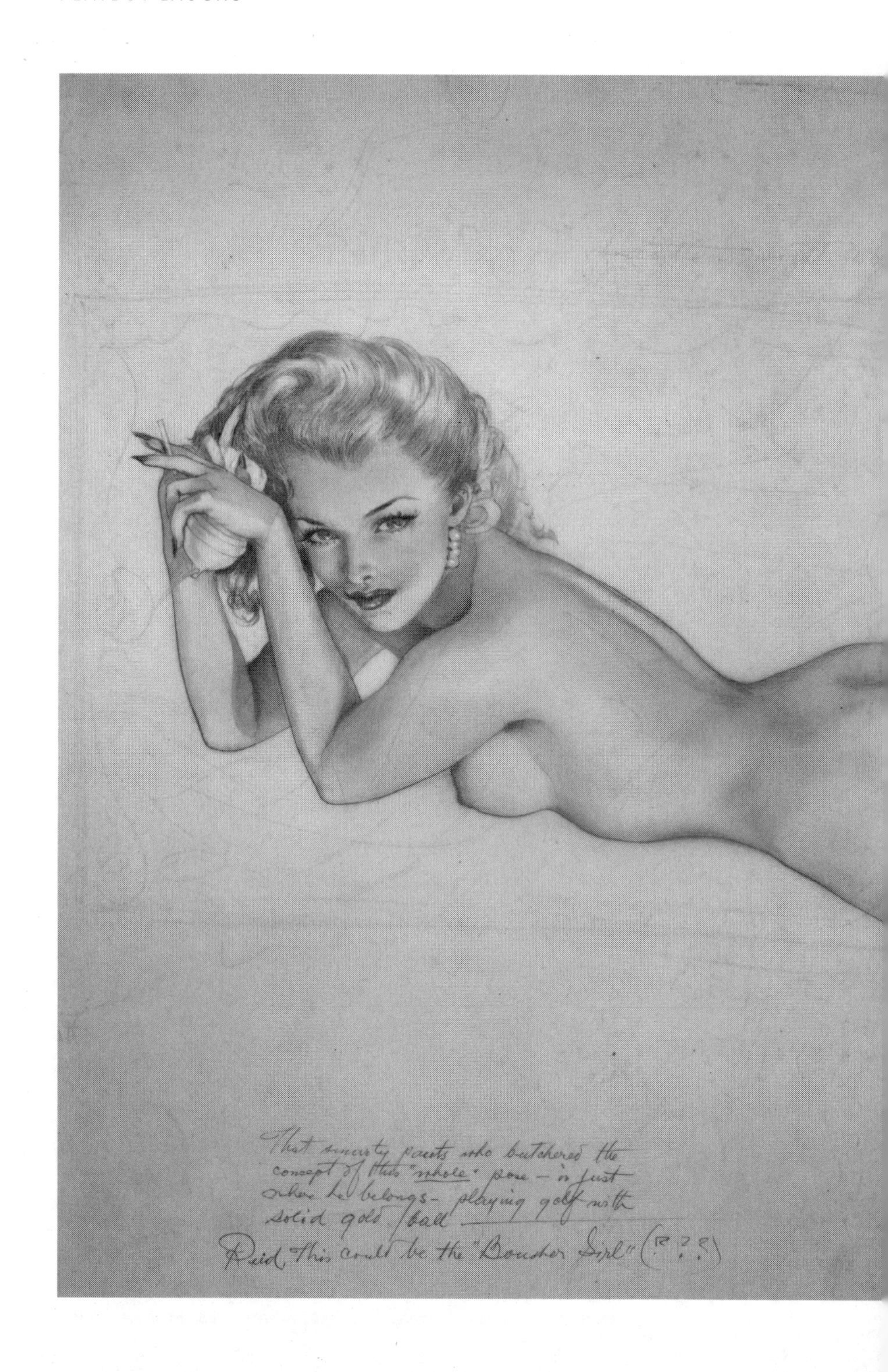
concept of this "whole" pose — is just
where he belongs — playing golf with
solid gold ball
Reid, This could be the "Boudoir Girl" (???)

Note Hef's hand written comments. Alberto Vargas—

CHECK NEC
SHOULDER
ANATOMY

Note Hef's hand written comments. Alberto Vargas—

Vargas

Jungle Red. Model: Mamie Van Doren. Olivia : Artwork Copyright © Olivia De Berardinis All Rights Reserved

Here's Looking at Me. Model: Bettie Page. Olivia :

"Are you the one who doesn't believe in the Easter Bunny?" Olivia : Artwork Copyright © Olivia De Berardinis All Rights Reserved

The day the funnies stopped

Al Jaffee: Courtesy of and with permission of Al Jaffee

14

THE HOUSE THAT HEF BUILT

Hef waits while Groucho Marx finishes bussing Playmate of the Year Elizabeth Martin: Ron Galella Collection/Getty Images

It's safe to say that this book wouldn't exist without the vision and drive of Hugh Hefner. But, more important than that, the landscape of our culture would be starkly different, as would the lives and careers of the many entertainers and artists profiled here. It is no exaggeration to call Hefner a pioneer, and it seems worthwhile at this juncture to celebrate his accomplishments.

Let's start with the magazine, since that's where Hef started. What seemed at first to some just a showcase for the prurient quickly proved itself to be much more: a repository of great literature, art, and topical humor; a platform for progressive ideas and styles of living; and a call-to-arms for sexual and social revolution. Within its pages, Hef and his staff pushed the boundaries of civil and gay rights when these causes were truly revolutionary. And, contrary to what some may believe (but validated by many of the women whose lives he changed), he fought steadfastly for women's rights, addressing such issues as abortion and the legalization of the birth-control pill, and employing hundreds of women in all aspects of his businesses.

There's a reason why *Playboy* has enjoyed such a long and successful run—even as many other magazines have come and gone—and it isn't just the profusion of female pulchritude. In addition to entertaining and titillating us, Hefner has continually challenged us to question our own assumptions and move beyond them.

Then, there is the rest of the Playboy empire, and its impact on popular culture. Through his groundbreaking clubs, TV shows, and jazz festivals, Hefner provided a vast network of venues where artists could develop and hone their craft and audiences could enjoy the latest and greatest in live entertainment. As we've noted—and it still comes as a surprise to many—at its peak, Playboy was the largest employer of entertainment talent in the country.

* * *

Hugh Marston Hefner was born in Chicago on April 9, 1926, to Grace Caroline and Glenn Lucius Hefner. Hef—although he wouldn't assume that nickname until many years later—was their first-born; Keith followed three years later. By all accounts, they were direct descendants of the English Separatist leader William Bradford, as well as Mayflower Compact signatory John Winthrop, leaders in the settlement of the Massachusetts Bay colony.

Hef grew up in a conservative Methodist household where he absorbed the traditional Midwestern values of hard work and fairness. By his own account, his family was never demonstrative; though he felt loved, he can't remember once being hugged or kissed by either parent. Rather, Hef's notions about love and romance came from the films he steeped himself in, depicting dashing virile men and beautiful starlets.

Throughout his years at Steinmetz High School, Hef never distinguished himself academically, but he did make his mark by founding a student publication that would showcase his own passions for drawing and writing. (Clearly, the child was father to the man!) At fifteen, he published an autobiographical comic book called *School Daze*, along with numerous editorials. He also began to speak out publicly on behalf of student rights and liberties.

Hef met Millie Williams at a school mixer, when he was a high school freshman, and they were soon inseparable. To placate their parents, and in a singular moment of grown-up clarity, they agreed to postpone any matrimonial plans until they were both older. After graduation in 1944, Millie went on to the University of Illinois and Hef enlisted in the Army, where he continued to exercise his talents by providing cartoons for various military newspapers.

Completing his military obligation after two lackluster years, Hef returned to Chicago and joined Millie at the University of Illinois, earning a Bachelors degree in arts and creative writing. Once again, he was drawn to the campus editorial office, and was soon editing and contributing to the college magazine, *Shaft.* In an obvious foreshadowing of big things to come, Hef inaugurated a new feature: "Co-ed of the Month." He and Millie married after graduation in 1949.

Hef believed he could make a living as a cartoonist, and began submitting to every publication in town. Undeterred by rejection slip after rejection slip, he proceeded to self-publish a racy comic book of his own, *That Toddlin Town: A Rowdy Burlesque of Chicago Manners and Morals.* This satirical view of Chicago life spanned a whopping seventy-four pages—the norm was thirty-two. The budding humorist would probably have continued drawing and submitting his work to recalcitrant publications far and wide, but he began to feel his obligations as a family man and took whatever "day jobs" he could find.

He worked in the office of the Chicago Carton Company and as an advertising copywriter for Carson Pirie Scott before landing a job that moved him closer to his calling—but alas, it was short-lived. He had barely settled into his duties as a promotional copywriter for *Esquire* when he was informed that the company was moving its editorial headquarters from Chicago to New York. Hef was invited to move with the team but declined when his request for a five-dollar raise was denied. With a wife and young daughter to support, Hef returned to yet another mundane job, as newsstand promotional director at the Publisher Development Company. Although he wasn't particularly happy in his new role, working with the newsstands inspired an epiphany. Hef came to see that there was a hole in the market for a sophisticated, high-quality men's magazine—one that would not only showcase nubile, unclad women, but would provide a forum for progressive ideas; *his* ideas. The seeds of the "Playboy philosophy" had been planted; they just needed room to grow.

Including a bank loan collateralized by his apartment furnishings and funds supplied by friends and family, Hef managed to amass the $8,000 he'd determined he would need to launch his dream. The new magazine began to take shape on a card table in his living room, and Hef was thinking big. Marilyn Monroe had always filled a particular space in his dreams and yearnings, and he was betting that his target audience felt the same. With a careful eye on his budget, he licensed a popular photo of Marilyn from a local calendar company—a cheaper option than photographing a model or purchasing a Marilyn picture from her studio archives.

In another canny business move, Hef delivered his finished magazine to newsstands in November of 1953 without a date on it—thus extending its shelf life through the holidays and beyond in case it didn't fly off shelves. He needn't have worried: The magazine ended up selling more than 50,000 copies and providing enough income to pay off his backers and finance the next issue.

The *Playboy* era had arrived. True to his vision, Hef surrounded his lovely centerfolds with provocative articles on a wide range of topics—with a special emphasis on jazz. The first issue included a feature on the Dorsey Brothers and it was followed over the years by profiles, reviews, and other coverage of every jazz artist of note, along with many film stars, sports figures, and politicians. When *Playboy* inaugurated the first of its iconic in-depth interviews, in September 1962, the subject was Miles Davis and the interlocutor was Alex Haley.

By the end of the 1950s, *Playboy* had more than a million monthly subscribers and Hef wanted to celebrate its five-year anniversary with a rapturous party—a jazz party, to be precise. Thus, the first Playboy Jazz Festival took place in 1959. To plan the program, Hef and Victor Lownes made a wish list of their favorite musicians and vocalists, including Ella Fitzgerald, Duke Ellington, Count Basie, Stan Kenton, Frank Sinatra, Oscar Patterson, Dizzy Gillespie, Dave Brubeck, Bobby Darin, Louis Armstrong, and more. Everyone replied with a resounding yes—with the exception of Frank Sinatra, who was filming in Hollywood and couldn't get away, and Nat King Cole, who was on one of his historic South American tours.

The festival attracted more than 68,000 attendees and inspired prominent music critic Leonard Feather to declare it "one of the greatest weekends in the history of jazz." But, as we mentioned earlier, the remarkable event almost didn't happen at all. Recalled Victor, "It was supposed to be at Soldier Field, a park owned by the city of Chicago. But when the Catholic Church found out the event was sponsored by *Playboy*, they complained and the city backed out of the deal."

Victor tried to make the powers that be see that it was in the best interest of the city to back such a prestigious event, but he was given a flat no—and later turned down by the Chicago Stockyards Arena as well. With little time to spare, he approached Arthur Wirtz, the owner of the indoor Chicago Stadium. "Arthur let me have it," he told us, "and it all ended very happily. The three-day event was a big sell-out."

In addition to the groundbreaking line-up of musicians, the festival represented a social milestone. It was one of the rare events of the era to be racially integrated both on stage and in the audience. The first day's proceeds were donated to the National Association for the Advancement of Colored People (NAACP) and the Chicago Urban League. With the festival, Playboy became firmly established as something beyond a magazine: It became a genuine brand.

After this immense triumph, promoters bombarded Hef, hoping to make the festival an annual event, but the next one wouldn't happen for twenty years.

"Playboy was growing extremely fast back then," explained Victor, "and remember, we produced the first festival all by ourselves. We didn't have the time and energy to do another one for quite a long time."

Over the course of roughly six months, from August 1959 to February 1960, Playboy launched three new ventures that firmly established the organization as a major presenter of entertainment. The first was the Jazz Festival; next, during the summer of 1959, the *Playboy Penthouse* TV show premiered, making Hef a household face as well as name, and offering a fresh new format for talent and talk; and finally, the first Playboy Club arrived.

It was leap year, February 1960, when the Chicago club opened its doors with much fanfare. It may have been members-only, but it was by no means exclusive: Anyone who filled out an application and paid his dues was rewarded with the coveted bunny-head key. Arthur Wirtz, with whom they had worked with on the Jazz Festival, offered up a vacant building that suited their needs perfectly.

Arnold Morton decided that the menu would be good-quality but inexpensive and uncomplicated fare, including steak and chicken dinners for $1.50. But the most groundbreaking aspect of the club was the Bunnies. It wasn't the first nightclub to employ pretty waitresses in skimpy outfits—but the Bunny uniform was something new altogether. Its satin corseted body suit, cuffs, collar, and bow tie were provocative to say the least; and the addition of a fluffy tail and bunny ears added a touch of fantasy. The Bunny became the avatar of the Playboy brand. Young women, excited at the prospect of making a good living in a glamorous setting, lined up down the block in snowstorms and heat waves to get a crack at becoming a Bunny.

Tides of opinion turn, of course. By the end of the sixties, radical feminists were denouncing the Bunny uniform as a symbol of chauvinist oppression; but in 1960, being a Bunny seemed to many the most liberating job a young woman could get. Ultimately, the historic importance of the uniform was recognized by the Smithsonian Institution in Washington D.C., which made it a part of the collection.

Whatever else they are remembered for, the Playboy Clubs will certainly go down in history as a premiere showcase for both emerging talent and established artists. The quality and quantity of comedians and musicians Playboy employed were beyond compare. On any given day, it was not unusual to see Mel Torme or Johnny Mathis hanging out at the Playboy offices kibitzing with Hef and Victor about life, pretty girls, and where to listen to jazz. Mabel Mercer—a personal favorite of both Hef and Victor—opened the Chicago club, and was soon followed by Bobby Short, Irwin Corey, Mae Barnes, and scores of others.

By the end of its first year of operation, the Chicago Playboy Club had 106,000 members and held the record for selling more food and drink than any other Chicago club. Embracing the innovative new business concept of franchising, Hef swiftly moved to open clubs around the country, and eventually the world. All too soon (though not soon enough), he realized that having franchise partners meant giving up his tight rein on standards, and the franchise clubs were hastily repurchased by the corporation at high prices. Well, nobody's perfect.

The London Playboy Club and Casino was wildly successful,

and soon made up for that misstep and a variety of others. Playboy's timing couldn't have been better when opening in London in 1966. England had recently passed the Betting and Gaming Act, meant primarily to legalize keno and bingo in churches and schools. But the legislation had a loophole and in marched gambling of all types, with little oversight. Sensing an opportunity, Victor scouted locations and soon Playboy had its first casino. The establishment was so profitable that it bankrolled others in the chain and—for better or worse—allowed them to remain open well past the point when they were profitable. At their peak, the clubs, casinos, and resorts numbered forty, and select cities had more than one.

In 1971, Playboy went public. Its initial stock price was considered a bargain at $23.50. (The stock certificates, featuring a nude beauty by the name of Willy Rey, are sought-after collectors' items today.) Playboy executives became millionaires overnight. Ultimately, however, the company paid the price for being managed at the whim of one shareholder for twenty years. That, coupled with the economic downturn of the 1970s and an inherent inability to stick to a budget, took its toll on the corporate bottom line. When the London club closed in 1981, the handwriting was on the wall; by 1988 the reign of the Playboy Clubs had come to an end.

In 2011, Hef took the company private, hoping to leave some sort of legacy to his sons. He was able to repurchase all outstanding Playboy shares at $6.15 each. While Playboy no longer has stages on which to present live entertainment, they have amassed a large Internet audience for the magazine, as well as the company's trove of soft-core pornographic films and images.

The world seemed to wobble a little on its axis last year, when Playboy announced that it had sold the legendary Playboy Mansion. (Don't worry, Hef has a lifetime tenancy.) Not only that, but after sixty-two years, *Playboy* magazine would cease to include depictions of fully nude women.* A third development, equally shocking to some, soon followed: *Playboy* would no longer accept cartoon submissions. The cartoons had been a mainstay of the publication since its first issue hit the stands in 1953.

Pulitzer Prize-winning cartoonist and author Jules Feiffer voiced an opinion shared by many when he said, "This makes no sense at all. We're in a time when more interesting work than ever is being done graphically. There's an explosion of brilliance, both male and female, out there. Young people—and middle-aged artists—are doing some extraordinary, innovative, inventive work and this is the time to be doing more. Perhaps what is called for is to redefine

Looks like Hef is getting some advice from George Burns: REX Images

what they think a cartoon is and let in some of the newer voices who are doing so much to change the scene."

As always, nobody tells Hugh Hefner what to do. And don't count the magazine out just yet. In spite of the changes, sales are up and there is new life in its editorial, literary, and feature pages. Even at ninety, Hef continues to surprise us and to contemplate the future.

We may not be able to look ahead, but we can look back. With his Playboy Club circuit, Hef exerted a huge impact on the history of comedy, successfully bridging the gap between the nightclubs of the fifties and the comedy clubs of the seventies. Without the support Hef provided, standup may well have dwindled away. It would certainly not have developed into the robust art form it is today, and who knows what would have happened to the fortunes of such talents as David Letterman, Billy Crystal, Jimmie Walker, Steve Martin, and many, many others.

Hef continues to surround himself with good friends from the comedy world. Perhaps that—as much as the ladies—is the secret to his vitality. At ninety, he carries on the tradition he started decades ago of hosting weekly dinners followed by movies. One night a week is set aside for a current film, another for a classic *film noir*, and sometimes a third is added for one of his favorite Chaplin movies. On an occasion when we attended "movie night," we thought we noticed Hef doodling cartoons on a pad of paper. Or perhaps we just imagined it.

* Note: On February 13, 2017, Cooper Hefner, Playboy's Chief creative Officer, announced that due to popular demand, nudes are returning to the pages of the magazine. Many agree that the twelve month experiment, omitting nudes, wasn't their most thought through.

Playboy Chronology

DECEMBER 1953

The first issue of *Playboy* magazine is published, featuring Marilyn Monroe on the cover.

JANUARY 1954

Playboy magazine's second issue introduces the "Playmate of the Month" feature.

NOVEMBER 1955

Victor Lownes joins *Playboy* as promotions director.

1959

Hugh Hefner purchases a house in Chicago that will become known as the Playboy Mansion.

AUGUST 7–9, 1959

The first Playboy Jazz Festival is held at Chicago Stadium, to celebrate the magazine's fifth birthday.

OCTOBER 24, 1959

The TV series *Playboy's Penthouse* premieres. It will run for two years.

FEBRUARY 29, 1960

The first Playboy Club opens in Chicago.

1961

Clubs open in Miami and New Orleans as franchises, but are repurchased by the organization the following year.

SEPTEMBER, 1962

Playboy publishes the first "Playboy Interview"—with jazz great Miles Davis.

OCTOBER 16, 1962

The first successful franchise club opens in St. Louis.

JANUARY 12, 1964

The first international franchise club opens in Manila, the Philippines.

JANUARY 12, 1964

The first Playboy resort opens in Ocho Rios, Jamaica.

MARCH 1965

Jennifer Jackson is the first African-American Playmate of the Month.

JUNE 28, 1966

The Playboy Club and Casino opens in London, the first Playboy establishment in the U.K.

JANUARY 18, 1969

The television show *Playboy After Dark* premieres. It will run for two years.

JULY 1970

The first Braille edition of *Playboy* is published.

1971

Hugh Hefner purchases the Playboy Mansion West in Los Angeles; it remains his home to this day.

NOVEMBER 3, 1971

Playboy Enterprises goes public.

JANUARY 1972

Marilyn Cole becomes the first playmate photographed fully nude. She'll go on to become Playmate of the Month in January 1972 and the 1973 Playmate of the Year.

SEPTEMBER 1976

Lainie's Room opens at the Los Angeles Playboy Club, making Lainie Kazan the first and only woman to run a Playboy Club location.

DECEMBER 12, 1976

The first Japanese Playboy Club opens in Tokyo.

JUNE 15–16, 1979

The annual Playboy Jazz Festival debuts at the Hollywood Bowl in Los Angeles.

APRIL 9, 1980

Hugh Hefner receives a star on the Hollywood Walk of Fame.

APRIL 14, 1981

A Playboy Club opens in Atlantic City, New Jersey, but fails to secure a gaming license.

APRIL 15, 1981

Victor Lownes is fired.

SEPTEMBER 1981

The London Playboy Club and Casino closes.

APRIL 1982

Christie Hefner, Hugh's daughter, is appointed President of Playboy Enterprises at age twenty-nine.

NOVEMBER 1, 1982

The Playboy Channel hits the airwaves and will later be re-launched, as Playboy TV, on November 1, 1989.

JUNE 30, 1986

Flagship Playboy Clubs close in New York, Los Angeles, and Chicago.

JULY 31, 1988

The last remaining U.S. Playboy Club closes in Lansing, Michigan.

AUGUST 1994

With Playboy.com, the organization expands its presence to the Internet.

OCTOBER 2006

The Las Vegas Playboy Club and Casino opens—the first of the twenty-first century.

DECEMBER 5, 2010

A 21st Century Playboy Club and Casino opens in Cancun, Mexico.

JUNE 2011

A 21st Century Playboy Club and Casino opens in London.

SEPTEMBER 19, 2011

The TV show *The Playboy Club* debuts on NBC, only to be canceled less than a month later.

JUNE 2014

For the first time since 1979, the Playboy organization doesn't produce the Playboy Jazz Festival.

OCTOBER 12, 2015

Playboy Enterprises announces that starting with the March 2016 issue, the magazine will no longer showcase completely nude women.

JANUARY 2016

Playboy Cartoon Editor Amanda Warren sends out letters to artists stating that the magazine will no longer be accepting cartoon submissions.

JULY 20, 2016

Hugh Hefner steps down as editor of *Playboy* and his son Cooper assumes the position of creative director.

AUGUST 17, 2016

The Playboy Mansion is sold for $100 million, on condition that Hef can remain in residence for life.

JANUARY 11, 2017

Victor Lownes dies in London at age 88.

FEBRUARY 13, 2017

Cooper Hefner announces that, due to popular demand, nude photos are returning to the magazine.

Playboy Club Opening Dates

CHICAGO	02/29/1960	DENVER	12/09/1967
MIAMI	05/10/1961	DENVER *	11/10/1977
NEW ORLEANS	10/05/1961	CLERMONT, UK	03/06/1972
ST. LOUIS [F]	10/16/1962	PORTSMOUTH, UK	12/1972
ST. LOUIS [F] *	12/01/1975	MANCHESTER, UK	12/13/1973
NEW YORK	12/08/1962	TOKYO, JAPAN [F]	12/09/1976
NEW YORK *	02/29/1976	BALTIMORE	07/11/1964
PHOENIX [F]	12/19/1962	BALTIMORE *	07/10/1977
PHOENIX [F] *	12/19/1973	DALLAS	07/27/1977
DETROIT	12/28/1963	OSAKA, JAPAN [F]	02/01/1978
DETROIT *	10/11/1973	NAGOYA, JAPAN [F]	07/16/1979
KANSAS CITY	06/13/1963	VICTORIA CASINO, UK	03/1980
MANILA	01/12/1964	SAPPORO, JAPAN [F]	04/25/1980
CINCINNATI	09/16/1964	BUFFALO [F]	04/24/1981
CINCINNATI *	11/07/1975	ST. PETERSBURG [F]	05/08/1981
LOS ANGELES	01/01/1965	SAN DIEGO [F]	12/17/1981
LOS ANGELES *	06/23/1973	LANSING [F]	09/17/1982
BOSTON	02/26/1965	COLUMBUS [F]	12/07/1982
ATLANTA	03/06/1965	OMAHA	05/18/1984
SAN FRANCISCO	11/13/1965	DES MOINES	12/03/1984
LONDON	07/01/1966		

RESORTS

JAMAICA	01/04/1965	MONTREAL	07/15/1967
LAKE GENEVA	05/06/1968	CHICAGO TOWERS	11/01/1970
MIAMI PLAZA	12/22/1970	GREAT GORGE	12/22/1971
BAHAMAS	04/11/1978	ATLANTIC CITY	04/14/1981

F=Franchise Clubs

*Clubs listed twice either relocated or closed and then reopened after renovations

Acknowledgments

My deepest thanks go to Hugh Hefner, who refused to live anyone else's dream and, in so doing, broke barriers too numerous to chronicle here. In the process, he gave countless artists the opportunity to hone their craft and provided the millions of patrons of the Playboy Clubs worldwide (as well as TV audiences and magazine readers) with top-notch entertainment of every variety.

To the incomparable Will Friedwald, who makes my world a much more interesting place, and who contributed significantly to the Playboy stories.

Thank you, Teri Thomerson and Dick Rosenzweig, for continuing to make time in your busy schedules to answer all my picky little questions and concerns, and to guide me through the magic maze of Playboy.

Bill Marx, you're an angel for so graciously taking the time—from what I know is a very full schedule—to write the Preface and introduce my readers to the world of comedy.

Thanks, also, to Laura Ross, my angel-with-a-whip editor, who held me to task at every turn, then dried my tears so I could get back to work and deliver the best book possible to my readers.

I am grateful to Mark Cantor, who gave me the idea for the Playboy Trilogy—yes, there's more to come. Thank you, Mark, for suggesting a way to keep the party going.

Julie Horne, your photographic and artistic skills make everyone look their best.

To all of the comedians, vent-impressionists, cartoonists, illustrators and artists, I can never show my gratitude sufficiently. It is your wonderful stories and musings about Playboy that bring this book to life. I thank you for entrusting me to tell your tales.

To my dear friend Kathy—who values her privacy—thank you for your constant encouragement and support, and the best launches a girl could ever dream of.

Bobbi Stamm (Curtiss), I send you hugs of appreciation for sorting through and sharing with me your elaborate archive of articles and photos.

Margie Barron, thank you, not only for taking the time to reminisce about your days at Great Gorge, but for sharing items from your voluminous photo and memorabilia collection with my readers.

Loving gratitude and appreciation go out to Stan Musick, and Jerry Pawlak for showing kind patience in sharing their Playboy adventures.

Jeff Abraham, my outstanding PR agent, your assistance in getting the word out about the work I do is invaluable.

Thank you all!

—PATTY

Index

Photographs are indicated by italics.

Tonight through Sunday, August 18
SID CAESAR
at the
playboy club-hotel
LAKE GENEVA-WISCONSIN
Reservations: 1-248-8811
WOODY WOODBURY, Sept. 24-Oct. 6
ATLANTA
3 SHOWS NIGHTLY 9:15-11:00-12:45.
MISTY MORN
Pretty and Curvy
Exotic Dancer
BILL FISH TRIO
Plays For The Three
And Dancing
Dinner Menu
SLAPPY
THE PLAYBOY CLUB
ST. LOUIS
JUNE 13 through JUNE 25
You raved about these acts on the Johnny Carson Show --don't miss them at the Saint Louis Playboy Club now!
BLUES-JAZZ PERFECTIONIST
LANA CANTRELL
MIRTHQUAKERS SUPREME
CURTISS & TRACY
OPENING JUNE 30TH IN THE
TWO ALL-NEW SWINGING
-MIAMI-
PEGGY LORD
Steam-heated Singer-Comedienne
THE WANDERERS THREE
Fabulous Folksingers
PATTI LEEDS
Beautiful Blues-Belter
JERRY VAN
Comedy and Pantomime
PLUS
JULIAN GOULD TRIO
TEDDY NAPOLEON
and swinging pianist
HERBIE BROCK
COMING ATTRACTIONS
OPENING JULY 22nd
MARTINE DALTON
PENIE PRYOR
MICKEY ONATE
MARK RUSSELL
JIMMY AMES
OPENING AUGUST 12th
MARK RUSSELL
THREE YOUNG MEN
FRED BARBER
VAN DORN SISTERS
LURLEAN HUNTER
CLUB OPEN 7 NIGHTS A WEEK
EARLIEST SHOW IN TOWN—PLAYBOY'S PENTHOUSE 8 P.M. DINNER SHOW
LATEST SHOW IN TOWN—2 A.M. IN THE PLAYBOY LIBRARY
TONIGHT through Sunday
More powerful
Able to leap frogs at
IT'S SUPER
He's back at the Playboy Club he opened:
Kansas City's Favorite Comedian
JACKIE CURTISS
Also
Songstress
PAM DE ORIAN
Backed up by
The John Elliott Trio
Now Appearing in The Penthouse
PROF. IRWIN COREY
FOREMOST AUTHORITY